CHARLOT /L ~/,~~/ ~/, /,/~/ ~ ~ ~ E

"A vividly detailed rendering of a real life caught in a maelstrom of 20th-century horror."

—*Kirkus Reviews*

* * *

"The story of Charlotte Salomon is perhaps the most dramatic Holocaust narrative we know. Based on decades of research and reflection, Pamela Reitman brings Charlotte's experience vividly alive in *Charlotte Salomon Paints Her Life*. Sad though it is, this wonderful novel will give you hope."

—Norman Fischer, Zen priest and poet, author of *Selected Poems, 1980-2013*

* * *

"Evocative and moving, this gorgeous novel is perfect for fans of historical and literary fiction. With a firm grasp of the relevant history, Reitman immerses us in the time period with perfectly-placed details and captivating drama. From page one I was swept along for the glorious ride, anxious to discover what destiny awaits Charlotte."

—Heather Bell Adams, author of *The Good Luck Stone*

* * *

"Inspired by artist Charlotte Salomon's extraordinary work and life, Pamela Reitman's novel is both deeply compassionate and unsparing. In her interweaving of fact and fiction, she honors Salomon's memory, while sustaining the urgency of historical and contemporary questions about daily life under threat of violence, about the sanctity of connection and about what sustains dignity in a state of emergency. In keeping with Salomon's legacy, Reitman's is a clarion reminder of why not turning away remains imperative under any and all circumstances."

—Darcy C. Buerkle, Professor of History, Smith College and author of *Nothing Happened: Charlotte Salomon and an Archive of Suicide*

"Reitman's re-creation of Salomon's life is composed of two opposing themes: art as a tool to interpret trauma, and the intractable tentacles of family secrets and shame that threaten to choke artistic expression. Blending fact with fiction, the novel is a touching synthesis that celebrates Charlotte's fearless belief that only in art can one defy 'the erasure of identity.'

Charlotte Salomon Paints Her Life is a powerful historical novel, at turns winsome and wrenching, about a gifted artist caught in the maelstrom of madness and war."

—Peggy Kurkowski, *Foreword Reviews*

* * *

"Pamela Reitman has created a gorgeous, haunting portrait of a willful young Jewish woman who paints to save her life, to remember everything in images and words, as Nazi jackboots approach."

—Parul Kapur, author of *Inside the Mirror*

* * *

"Pamela Reitman's vividly imagined novel dares to explore beneath the surface of Charlotte Salomon's remarkable paintings, a body of work that managed to survive the Nazis even though the artist herself did not. While Reitman's fictional account is supported by careful and extensive research, she acknowledges her own artistic choices to embellish and interpret. This haunting book should help to bring more well-deserved attention to Salomon's important archive, and to remind a contemporary audience of innumerable losses beyond the frame."

—Elizabeth Rosner, author of *Survivor Cafe: The Legacy of Trauma and the Labyrinth of Memory* and *Third Ear: Reflections on the Art and Science of Listening*

* * *

"The life of Charlotte Salomon, a gifted painter and writer, was cut short at Auschwitz when she was only 25. Miraculously her work survived and has been exhibited around the world, but she's still not as well-known as she could be. Pamela Reitman's wonderful novel will change that, I hope. I was moved and gripped by this story, which is a great read but also an important contribution to art and Holocaust history."

—Rita Goldberg, author of *Motherland: Growing Up with the Holocaust*

"Pam Reitman conveys a true story of unspeakable evil and of great creativity and love in a novel's vivid, sinewy prose. Reitman inhabits Charlotte Salomon's inner life and allows readers to experience how Charlotte conceives her art to save her soul. Pam Reitman brings to life this harrowing, inspiring tale of death and defiance with a deep understanding of what such desperate horror, fear, and hope entail. *Charlotte Salomon Paints Her Life* is a brilliant novel of compassion, resilience, and triumph in the face of evil."

—Hilton Obenzinger, author of *Running through Fire: How I Survived the Holocaust by Zosia Goldberg*

"Exceptional storytelling—an engrossing account of a young Jewish woman's struggle with art and a dysfunctional family while fleeing Nazi pursuit."

—Paul Jeschke, Retired Journalist and Broadcaster

* * *

"Reitman has drawn Charlotte Salomon's world, painted it actually, in all the vivid brushstrokes, colors, and intensity that one imagines Salomon brought to her own masterpieces. A beautiful tribute to a tremendous talent written by another gifted artist."

—Simi Monheit, Author of *The Goldie Standard*

* * *

"In gorgeous and at times breathtaking prose, the author takes us inside the mind and heart of a young German-Jewish painter coming of age during the Nazi era who used her talent to document her daily struggle to survive and evade capture."

—Laurie Barkin, RN, MS, author of *The Comfort Garden: Tales from the Trauma Unit*

* * *

"Charlotte Solomon couldn't have found a better person than Pamela Reitman to write her life. Despite her personal suffering as a Jew during the Second World War, Charlotte told the story of her life and imagination through her art. Ms. Reitman has done the same, this time through her eloquent words and the imagination of a writer gifted in portraying Charlotte's world as if through the eyes of a painter."

—Jane Anne Staw, author of *Small: The Little We Need for Happiness*

"Encounter an unforgettable woman in the most challenging circumstances imaginable. *Charlotte Salomon Paints Her Life* tells an engrossing story of an artist navigating family trauma and illness, political turmoil, love, and passionate, committed, skilled talent. Pamela Reitman's imagining of Charlotte's inner life inspired me to look into her art. Read this book....you'll love it and want more."

—Dorothy Richman, Rabbi, Makor Or: A Jewish Meditation Center, and Rabbi Emerita, Congregation Beth Sholom, San Francisco

*   *   *

"*Charlotte Salomon Paints Her Life*, a novel by Pamela Reitman, is a Holocaust story, both literally and universally--in the sense that, at any moment, any of us could be waylaid and prevented from completing our life's work.The story breaks off before it is finished, just as it will for each of us, but finally, life is affirmed in the care and respect Ms. Reitman brings to her subject and in the simple beauty of the prose. I was left with a frightened awareness of the beauty of my own life and a rededication to its purpose."

—Sherril Jaffe, prize-winning author of The Faces Reappear, Expiration Date, You Are Not Alone and Other Stories, and other works of fiction.

*   *   *

"Pamela Reitman's *Charlotte Salomon Paints Her Life* thoughtfully examines the intersection of personal loss and artistic expression. Through the lens of Charlotte Salomon's experience, marked deeply by her mother's suicide, the novel explores how grief and creativity intertwine. Reitman portrays Charlotte's journey with sensitivity, highlighting her efforts to navigate a world shaped by both personal and historical challenges. The novel offers a nuanced look at an artist striving to reconcile past traumas through her work."

—Roger Grunwald, Founder, The Mitzvah Project

*   *   *

"Intense and transporting ... Pamela Reitman paints a vivid chronicle of a passionate and talented young woman filled with hope and despair, caught in a maelstrom of epic proportions. Well-researched and riveting, Charlotte Salomon, like her hundreds of paintings, will not be easily forgotten."

—Sharon Bard, Ph.D., former NPR interviewer, author of *Steeped in the World of Tea* and *Reinventing the Wheel: Self-healing for Spinal Cord Injuries*

CHARLOTTE SALOMON PAINTS HER LIFE

A NOVEL

PAMELA REITMAN

Sibylline
PRESS

AN IMPRINT OF ALL THINGS BOOK

Sibylline Press
Copyright @ 2025 by Pamela Reitman
All Rights Reserved.

Published in the United States by Sibylline Press,
an imprint of All Things Book LLC, California.
Sibylline Press is dedicated to publishing the brilliant work of
women authors ages 50 and older.
www.sibyllinepress.com

Distributed to the trade by Publishers Group West
Sibylline Press Paperback
Paperback ISBN: 9781960573919
eBook ISBN: 9781960573209
Library of Congress Control Number: 2024941325

Book and Cover Design: Alicia Feltman

Credit for Charlotte Salomon's Self-portrait in oil (1940) on the cover
(and art in back of book) is courtesy of:
Collection Jewish Historical Museum, Amsterdam
© Charlotte Salomon Foundation

In memory of my father, Arthur Forman

CHARLOTTE SALOMON PAINTS HER LIFE

A NOVEL

PAMELA REITMAN

Truth is ugly.
We possess art lest we perish of the truth.

Friedrich Nietzsche,
The Will to Power

PART I

—

1939-40

CHAPTER 1

———

BERLIN TO PARIS AND POINTS SOUTH

JANUARY

A rolling motion jolted her. The carriage began clattering on the track of rail, setting her teeth to chatter. Charlotte Salomon watched her dearest ones, family and friends, and then the city where she had been born and lived all her twenty-one years—everything she had known and everything she loved—slide away. She was unable to raise a hand to wave back. She did not smile. She would have cried, but her eyes were dry and grainy.

I'm leaving you, Mama.

A reflection remained steady in the glass, a young German woman—tense temples, wary eyes, tight jaw. Also Jewish, but one who could pass.

A snappy rap on the door startled her. It slid open and slammed shut behind a short, white-mustachioed official.

"Tickets! Papers, *mademoiselle*!"

He stared at Charlotte's identity card. Suddenly she wished she'd paid more attention to her stepmother Katharina's instructions. *You know how naive you are, Lotte. You mustn't be dreamy or let your mind float away. Stay alert. Your life could depend upon it.*

When he asked for her passport, her voice faltered before she could speak.

"I—I don't need one. I don't turn twenty-two until April." She repeated the story Katharina had drilled into her about visiting her sick grandmother, whose letter was among her papers. He perused the papers, stared at the letter, presumably reading it, and then pointed to the pine case on the bunk.

"Open that."

Charlotte's fingers fumbled with the latch. She forced herself to hold his gaze.

At the sight of the contents, he said, "Artist's tools. You're working in France?"

You're not to reveal, Lotte, under any circumstances, that you're an artist.

Her voice gained strength as she remembered who she was, that part of herself she must keep hidden. "No!"

You must act a role. Like in the theater. Smile, sweet-like. Even though there was too much sorrow in her heart for a sweet smile, she did her best.

"I'm going to paint pictures for my grandmother. To cheer her up."

He thrust the papers back at her. The door opened; he departed, and it closed with a brutal clank. Her eardrums reverberated with the sound of total rupture, announcing the end of a world, an era, a history, a life. She was mute, her body aching to the point of numbness, her mind blank.

AT THE PARIS STATION, the commotion awakened her from stasis. A smart couple hurried to board. The woman with the posture of a ballerina wore a white coat with a Hermès scarf, red and blue, knotted with one tail streaming over her shoulder. Even in this time of scarcity, the French dressed in style. A red-and-white muffler topped the man's well-cut blue overcoat. Together, they were a scrambled version of the French flag. Charlotte was curious to see this woman, perhaps a good subject for a sketch.

She recalled Katharina's warning. *Stay in your compartment. Don't talk to anyone who's not an official. That should happen once. At the border. Then you're free.*

Not free. Cast out. Her destiny decided for her. The seams of her mind were loosening. She could let the whole cloth of it give way. But no, alone, she must make her own decisions. Charlotte stepped into the passageway, the pine case in her grip.

She roamed through carriage connections to the observation car, which was filled with hushed chatter. Lush potted palms spread their branches, creating conversational groupings. Under the shelter of one, she spotted them—the French-flag couple who'd boarded at Paris. She slipped into a chair by the window opposite and returned their polite acknowledgement with a nod.

Charlotte sat for a moment with her case on her lap, then lifted the pine lid. At the sight of her brushes in protective slipcovers, an invisible mantle of peace fell gently upon her shoulders.

It was too close quarters, she decided, for her to sketch the woman. Instead, she made a sketch of the bed she'd slept in all her life in the bedroom she'd left behind in Berlin, and upon it she drew an empty valise, gaping open. With the pencil lead at an angle, she darkened its coffin-like recesses. *Quickly now, before she's gone*; in one motion, Charlotte drew a vertical oblong for the upper body, added one line to sweep a small sad oval, the back of her head on bent neck. Shaded in most of the oval with hair. Added a "c" to indicate the ear. Left a sliver of face, the profile nearly indistinguishable. Below, she drew a horizontal oblong for the lower body, seated on a second valise, closed, the one containing the things to which her life had been reduced.

Here I am. She whispered her name to herself. *Lotte.*

Charlotte looked out the train's window and saw her reflection, a face—hers—sucked into the past.

She returned to her drawing and added pillows on the bed, shoes on the rug.

A poster of Van Gogh's sunflowers hung on the wall of her Berlin bedroom. Her father had given it to her, but she didn't include it in the drawing. Also omitted, the window where she had waited for a letter from Mama while weeping and whispering to God. She whispered now. *Mama.*

To those left standing on the platform in Berlin—the people who were hers, to whom she belonged forever—Lotte had disappeared. They were there. She was here. Her father had been bent, his hands behind his back, barely recovered from his imprisonment in Sachsenhausen. Sporting a red hat, Katharina assured her she would get them out of Germany. She and their housekeeper, Astrid, had stood erect, both clutching their purses in front of them. Forced smiles held fast on all their faces. Only Wolf looked truly hopeful.

Wolf Abrams. Who had he been to her? Charlotte supposed some thought that because he was almost twenty years older than she, he was like an uncle. Others perhaps suspected he was her lover. Only she knew he was neither. He understood her and her work. He believed in her as an artist. And because she was sure he held the key to the great mystery, the meaning of life, she'd allowed him to become the source of her belief in herself. Standing on the platform, he had appeared almost gratified, waving a white handkerchief.

Some final shading here and there with the side of the pencil. But she had her now, sitting in her bedroom, staring into the grave-dark interior of her valise.

Charlotte took a more objective look. It would be better in color.

The train made an unexpected stop. Charlotte could see police on the platform. The French-flag man rose and crossed the aisle. He peered out her window. Behind his rimless spectacles, his brows drew together. She packed up her drawing and materials as fast as she could and stood.

"My papers are in my compartment," she said in broken French.

He put a hand on her shoulder. His soft gaze held her.

"It'll be okay." His German was near perfect. "Better to sit. Can you play-act?" She nodded. "Good. Pretend you can't hear or speak." Then he returned to his seat and spoke to his wife, who looked anxious, but his voice was too soft for Charlotte to hear.

The door of the observation car opened. Men in blue uniforms and kepis entered, gendarmes, officers of the French police.

They approached the travelers one by one, looking at papers, asking each about destination, purpose, and length of stay. They stopped at the couple across from Charlotte.

"Jews!" One officer spat the word loud enough for the entire car to hear. Heads down, no one looked.

When the gendarmes were satisfied with the couple's papers, they turned and asked for Charlotte's, first in French, then German, then English. She clamped her hands to her ears, which stilled the nervous flutter, then pressed her fingers to her lips. The French man came to her side and addressed the officers.

"She's deaf-mute, my niece, and a little—" Here, he tapped his temple with one index finger and delivered a knowing look to the officers. "She left her papers in her compartment. We're just going back there. Shall you join us, and we'll help her retrieve them?"

Charlotte held her breath, hearing the thump of her heart in her ears.

The officers exchanged derisive smiles. "Never mind. She's dismissed."

Charlotte's heartbeat began to slow as the man lifted her by her elbow and ushered her out, along with his wife. Her savior. In the vestibule, he said, "Well, now, the dining car is this way. Please be our guest."

A real meal was an unimagined luxury. Katharina would prefer she decline in favor of the bread and turnip spread Astrid had packed, but the man had saved her just now. Didn't she owe him? And as long as the gendarmes were on the train, she felt she'd be safer with this couple.

STILL SHAKEN, Charlotte sat in a dark-green leather booth opposite the man and his wife. On the white linen tablecloth, one yellow rosebud, closed tight, peeked from a small vase.

The man made the introduction. "Raymond-Raoul Lambert and my wife, Simone."

The name meant something to her, but the experience in the observation car had made it so Charlotte had not quite caught up with herself, and she couldn't place it.

He was a thin man, prematurely bald, in his mid-forties. His wife's features were delicate—oval face and small, straight nose—combined with exceptionally large eyes, dark and smoky, rouged lips, and an intelligent mien. Charlotte took each extended hand a little tentatively, aware that her palms were overly wet from the run-in with the gendarmes.

"Charlotte Salomon. I'm indebted."

The introductions complete, Madame Lambert turned to her husband. "What do you think that was?"

"Most likely, they had a tip. On a crime. Looking for some person in particular."

When the waiter arrived, Monsieur Lambert ordered *boeuf bourguignon* and a burgundy, after asking Charlotte if that would please her. Her mind clearing, she accepted his choice graciously, and then, recalling his name, she said, "You are the editor of a French newspaper, *L'Univers israélite*? Am I right?'

He nodded, half impressed, half curious.

"My grandmother reads your paper religiously. She cuts out and sends us your editorials. Or else she summarizes your latest opinion in her letters to us."

His slight smile broadened at the news of a great fan.

"He also heads a large Jewish charity that aids refugees," said Madame Lambert. "We live in Paris with our three children."

Monsieur chimed in. "Now in the care of Simone's parents."

"On our way to Nice for a holiday."

When the braised stew arrived, the smell of onions, carrots, mushrooms, and beef—all redolent of garlic and herbs—was so heady that at first Charlotte was unable to take a bite. She told them her destination was not far from Nice and then—though it was so unlike her, she could not help herself—she poured out everything: how bad things had gotten for the Jews in Germany with the pogroms and new laws, how her father could no longer practice as a surgeon and his research was stalled, and how Katharina, a renowned opera singer, could perform only on the stages of Jewish theater. She even admitted how afraid she was for her own future as an artist.

Was she burdening them? She needed to stop.

Madame Lambert said, "You're fleeing. It must've torn your parents apart to send you off." Her eyes were filled with sympathy. "Hordes of German refugees are pouring into France. But we wonder now: With Blum out and Daladier in, it's not out of the question, a German takeover. Because Hitler's facing east doesn't mean he won't turn west."

"God forbid," Monsieur Lambert said. "We French wouldn't cede our country. And the Germans can extend themselves only so far. An occupation would never last."

"It doesn't have to last long for the French Jews to be in danger. As our friend Charlotte, a Jew, was in danger in Germany."

The waiter brought small bottles of mineral water and burgundy and removed the empties.

"We're Jews," Madame Lambert continued, "and however we regard our religion and our nationality, our fate may not be determined by our own view. We may have only two choices: stay to face our deaths, or flee to save our lives. Provided we have foresight. Apparently, your parents had it, Charlotte."

"Yes. My stepmother did. She was the forceful one." She paused. "My mother died when I was a child. From influenza."

The Lamberts glanced at each other and looked back at her with solemn expressions.

Madame Lambert said, "Oh, dear. Influenza, such a scourge, even after the epidemic. We are so sorry."

Monsieur Lambert said, "Yes. A terrible loss for you, I'm sure."

But Charlotte's heart raced in response to the opinion Madame Lambert had expressed about what might be in store for Jews in France. Was it possible she might be no safer here than in Germany? This thought disturbed her all through the chocolate mousse. But by the time she'd finished it off, a new thought had arrived: Papa and Katharina would meet her in Marseille, and they would sail to America as planned.

When the dessert plates had been cleared and napkins folded, Charlotte thanked her benefactors but slid from the booth with a rising wave of apprehension she could not suppress, and so declined their offer to see her to her compartment.

Back inside her private chamber, a butterfly of fear set up in her throat as she contemplated again what dormant danger lurked in France. Her grandmother had begged her father to send her.

Katharina had shared the news articles that her grandmother had enclosed in her letters, declaring that refugees in France were being provided for. Many times, she had said with her unshakeable confidence, "You will be safe." Charlotte repeated the phrase to herself over and over as the wheels of the train rolled through the night.

CHAPTER 2

————

NICE

Outside the Nice train station, Charlotte said goodbye to the Lambert couple, who hurried toward the lineup of taxis. The fronds of palm trees waved a bottle-green welcome. The air smelled of the sea. She tipped her head toward the sky, cloudless and startling blue, and the southern sun fell fully on her face. For a moment, she let the delicious warmth seep into her and spread throughout her body.

Her grandmother had written that a man, "mid to late twenties," would pick her up. Then she heard him.

"Fräulein Salomon?" The man spoke German with an Austrian accent. "Henri Nagel, from Olive Miller's household. Come to fetch you."

She stood agape while Henri Nagel, taller than her by half a foot, loaded her luggage into the trunk of a canary-yellow Peugeot roadster with its top down. She slid into the rich, cocoa-brown, crocodile-leather seat, feeling like she'd emerged onto an eerie theatrical set. But then, no more eerie than Berlin with its streets of shattered glass and burning synagogues.

"This is quite a car," she said, grateful to speak her own language.

"Belongs to a racing-car driver. He's out of the country this year and needed someone to keep it running. He's a patient of Dr. Mercier—you'll meet him. He's at the chateau now. Anyway, the doctor tapped me."

The ignition exploded in start-up, then leveled off to a hum. When he stepped on the accelerator, the car seemed to leap forward without her.

The brilliant light in Nice made the town look as though it was created that very morning. Belle Époque mansions commanded the architectural landscape, trimmed like wedding cakes with garlands of carved flowers. The car glided down a wide boulevard where mature palms marched along.

"The famed Promenade des Anglais," he said.

On her side, whitecaps tickled the shore. Sparkling aquamarine waters stretched to the horizon, turning indigo.

"Bay of Angels. You can walk the entire length."

Charlotte would have liked simply to sit and stare. With her easel on her lap and her brush in her hand.

In profile, Henri Nagel's rumpled brown hair rose above a high forehead and stood up to the wind. With high, sculpted cheekbones and a strong but not obtrusive nose, he was handsome by any standard, except for a scar near his right ear. Fascinating. But she looked away in order not to stare.

The car sang as it careened along the curvy road. He pulled off abruptly and braked to full stop in an overlook. He came around to open her door. On their way to the viewpoint, his left foot scraped the gravel in a pronounced limp.

"We've been looking forward to your arrival," he said, his smile making a long, vertical dimple in one cheek. He was one of those people who stood uncomfortably close. She took a step back.

"Thank you for that welcome, but honestly, from what I've heard, I can't imagine why Olive Miller wants another stranger in an already crowded household."

"I'll be frank, Charlotte. Your grandparents haven't been the easiest refugees to board. In the six years they've been here, Olive's focus has changed—away from them and onto the orphan children. She's providing them with education and regular physical activity. She oversees every aspect of their lives like they are her very own. Frankly, she hasn't the time for the many demands your grandparents make upon her. Olive hopes your presence will help."

Indeed, her grandparents both possessed trying natures. They took offense with ease and announced their insult whenever they decided others did not understand their fabricated claims to entitlement. On the verge of reentering her grandparents' lives, Charlotte felt dread rising. For a moment, even though the air was clear and clean and plentiful, she could not take a breath. She felt what it might be like to suffocate. Then she let her lungs fill with the pure air and pulled herself together.

"They're saving me, Herr Nagel, and I'm obligated to their kindness."

She had not taken in the view. Before they turned away, she did. Something moved inside her, something she could never have known in Berlin. The sea was so vast. There was room for life.

VILLEFRANCHE-SUR-MER WAS A PRISTINE little village stacked on a hillside with peach-kissed dwellings. Fishing boats studded the deep-blue harbor, rocking in the gentle ripples. Henri Nagel turned the car up Rue Cauvin, where dense shrubbery, wood fences, and tall eucalyptus provided privacy for luxurious properties. Passing through an open iron gate, the roadster kicked up a spray of gravel as it braked to a stop in front of a grand stone chateau covered in ivy and climbing vines.

From the balcony, a woman was waving madly. She called down in German, "Charlotte! Welcome!" The next moment, that woman, large-bodied but nimble, was flying down the front steps. The full skirt of her pale-yellow dress patterned with large white daisies swished around her tan, muscular legs. Her wide-open smile bloomed with bonhomie.

She took Charlotte in her arms and then released a barrage. "You got out okay? Did you find Henri right away? Did you sleep? Are you hungry?"

Questioned into dumb silence, Charlotte finally said, "You must be Mademoiselle Miller."

"Oh, call me Olive."

A man, late middle-aged with thick, iron-gray hair, who was not small but looked so in comparison to Olive, came forward. Olive introduced Dr. Phillipe Mercier, lean and trim like someone who did a great deal of hiking. Holding onto Charlotte's hand with both of his, he said, "You'll find many subjects for your painting in Villefranche, even here within the walls of l'Ermitage."

Ill at ease and self-conscious that a stranger knew she was an artist, her reply was a mumble even she couldn't parse. He wished her well settling in, begged off to continue his morning agenda, and left her feeling completely excused for her social shortcomings, as though he'd taken no notice whatsoever.

Henri said, "Well, back to the children." Then he was gone too.

Olive lifted Charlotte's luggage with little effort. "Let me take you to your grandparents."

Flashing a smile of perfectly formed large, white teeth, she walked with a bounce in her stride across the drive and along a path. Charlotte was staggering from the warmth of her reception and thrown off-kilter by how natural, intimate, and unselfconscious everyone was. Along the way, Olive explained that Henri was teaching woodwork this morning. The children were building a clubhouse. Her German was excellent, and she was a nonstop talker, which suited Charlotte just fine.

The path forked up to a knoll. At the top, a small cottage seemed half-buried under the shadow of an ancient oak. It was a one-story affair, stone, more than a bit ramshackle, and sunk into the ground on one side. Olive set down the luggage.

"I do mean to have it shored up. Too many mistrals, too many rains. Henri could do it, but with the children, well—" Olive paused, then looked Charlotte directly in the eye. "I want you to know that they could've had a grand suite in the Great House. But they refused it. So, okay, they have their privacy here."

Olive didn't sound fed up. Perhaps she was hiding it for Charlotte's sake.

"Anyway—" She clapped her hands and in a cheerier tone announced, "Supper at eight. Rest up, Charlotte. I've a surprise for you." Charlotte watched her stride back along the path.

A FEW FLECKS OF BLACK PAINT clung to the weathered wood of the door gone as gray as the stone. Charlotte knocked, waited, and knocked again. She tried the latch; the door opened. She took a tentative step inside. The small room was crammed from one side to the other with so much furniture, it resembled an antique store. She recognized the hefty, gray velvet sofa, the imposing cherrywood dining table, and the massive glass-paned bookcase stuffed with classics of German philosophy and her grandmother's knickknacks.

From a doorway on the left, her grandfather glared at her with cold, blue eyes. His long, pinched face was buried in a cloud of white hair, the mustache indistinguishable from the beard spread upon his black coat like a bib—an Old-World German, through and through.

"Marina claims to be ill. You get her up. I can't. Noon already. Shameful."

Charlotte winced. No greeting? No welcome? A fleeting but profound loneliness mixed with a flash of anger rolled through her body. Though privy to his running condemnation of outsiders, she'd never heard her grandfather speak so harshly of his wife. She dropped her bags, suddenly exhausted.

In the bedroom off the main room, her grandmother sat propped up in bed against a pile of pillows edged in wilted lace and embroidered with faded threads.

"What took you so long?" Her voice squeaked with misery.

Charlotte cringed. Was she really ready for this? She planted a kiss on her grandmother's forehead, where the skin was stretched back by the tight pull of her white-haired bun. When Charlotte told her how she had met the editor of *L'Univers israélite* on the train, she warmed a little and slipped from bed to show Charlotte to her room. Her grandfather picked up her pine case.

"Heavy. What's this?"

"Art supplies, Grosspapa."

"You hauled these all the way from Berlin? You'll have no leisure for silly pastimes here. You're to be useful." He lumbered ahead of her, muttering, "Art! Pssh!"

Taken aback, she wondered, when had her grandfather acquired a stand against art? And what had he meant by being useful? They left her at the door to her room. She heard them whispering as they retreated.

More than her grandparents' less-than-gracious welcome, the first sight of her room beyond the narrow kitchen deflated her. Of wood-plank construction the size and shape of a jail cell, it appeared to have been built as an add-on pantry or gardening shed. A shelf was fixed into the wall abutting the kitchen. On it was a thin, bare, single mattress with a stack of bedding on the edge. The dank smell of a cellar permeated the air. Worst of all, there was no window, and the only light was what squeezed between the slats. The window had been the essential feature of her bedroom in Berlin, and the tall drawing-room windows had been the essential feature of Charlotte's memory of her mother. They were framed by sapphire-blue velvet drapes spilling into round puddles on the carpet.

Eva Salomon had occupied the spot between them for long stretches of time every day, not looking down four floors to Wielandstrasse or up into the gray sky, but staring blankly, as though the window opened onto nothing, seeming to wait for a necessary weeping that never came. One day, Lotte returned from grammar school to the refined district of Charlottenburg and the family flat, Number 15. She could almost taste the creamy filling and the almond topping, sweet and crunchy, of the *Bienenstich* her mother had promised, her favorite treat. When she'd found her mother standing in her spot with her back to her, Lotte did not enter the drawing room, but from the doorway reminded her. "May I, Mama?" Eva hadn't answered, seeming incapable of turning from the window.

Staring at the dark wall, Charlotte's understanding of her mother's need for that window was vivid but inchoate.

Mama always had crawled into Lotte's bed to say goodnight, and Lotte always had nestled into the cozy burrow of her arms. One time, her mother had said, "Imagine me as a glorious angel with delicate wings." She'd added, "The souls in heaven are with God, and being with God, they are the happiest they've ever been, and the colors there are beautiful beyond all on Earth."

Lotte's doctor father saw many patients who'd survived influenza. More than anything, Lotte didn't want her mother to die from it. Couldn't Papa save her?

Lotte made her mother promise to write a letter from heaven, describing the special colors. "You must leave it on my windowsill." Eva Salomon had said she would, then kissed Lotte on the cheek, sealing a mama's promise.

In her mother's parents' dingy little cottage, Charlotte sank onto the hard seat of the straight-backed chair and swallowed a cry. What was clear was her own need. For a window. For light and air. Her body heated with a flush—something gone wild inside.

She stood, flung her suitcase onto the plank bed, and snapped open the latches. She draped her coat over the back of the chair, feeling in the pockets to make sure she still had her two gloves. There, she found a piece of paper. It was in his hand.

Rejoice—now you are saved! Wolf

IN THE EVENING, on the way to the Great House, Charlotte and her grandparents stopped at the fork in the path. Her grandfather said, "The short way takes you to the kitchen garden. This way goes to the front entrance."

"Which is always the way *we* go, Lotte," her grandmother added.

They complained about Olive Miller right up to the impressive, carved wooden door. Charlotte dreaded discovering that Henri Nagel was right about her grandparents' difficult behavior. She hoped that they wouldn't display it on this, her first night.

The dining room accommodated a table for twenty, two sideboards, and two enormous glass-cabinet breakfronts displaying soup tureens, punch bowls, and tea services, yet the room felt open and congenial. The children stood behind their chairs. The younger ones were sandwiched between the older. Olive's eyes twinkled in the candlelight.

"My dear Charlotte, welcome to l'Ermitage. Take this seat beside me." In a barely perceptible cooler tone, she said, "Welcome, Herr Doktor, Frau Gruenstein," and pointed to two empty chairs on her other side.

A good foot shorter than Olive, Charlotte's grandmother pulled herself up to her full height. "We prefer our usual."

Olive sighed. "I only thought with Charlotte's arrival you might—"

"Quite the opposite."

Olive motioned to the maid. "Delmira, please."

At the far end of the room, Delmira set up a small table and three chairs within the deep bay of windows, which were framed with tasseled drapery that created the effect of a darkened stage. Reluctantly, Charlotte joined her grandparents there.

Once settled she took notice of the many beautiful objects: painted ceiling panels in the Italian style, fabric wall panels, and a magnificent chandelier ending in a rain shower of crystals. A vase of Brockwitz cut glass displayed the first of the season's mimosas with their little balls of fluff spilling this way and that. Charlotte was surprised also to see a tapestry by a fellow countryman. It was German Art Nouveau, but after the Japanese hanging scroll: swans afloat on an abstract vertical river, bold and geometric in design. What a delight! Olive appreciated German artistry.

After Olive toasted Charlotte's arrival, she introduced the newcomer to everyone as the illustrious art student from Berlin.

"The annual award at the Berlin Art Academy was stolen from her only because she is a Jew. How lucky we are to have her in our midst."

Immediately, the older children wanted to know how that happened. The younger ones chimed in, "Oh, please tell us."

Charlotte felt her face flushing. She had no idea that Olive knew, and she was not used to the spotlight shining on her. She felt compelled to respond to the question on every face. They were all too sweet and earnest for her to continue to feel flustered, but it was dinnertime, and her grandparents looked impatient.

"I'll tell you some other time. I promise." That seemed to satisfy them for the moment.

Light chatter and great merriment ruled the big table and rose to a crescendo when the rabbit dish arrived. Henri came late, took the seat next to Olive, and nodded Charlotte's way, as if to say he understood it was her grandparents' doing that she wasn't the one at Olive's side.

While she longed to be under the chandelier and among the laughter, her grandparents ate rapidly, refusing to be infected by the gaiety in the room at large.

Why did her grandparents have to be so somber? They were in their late seventies; why couldn't they enjoy life? It annoyed her to be cast out with them and their self-imposed isolation.

Though she did not want to relive that painful experience—the stolen award Olive had just mentioned—seated in the dimly lit bay and sequestered in the dead silence of the meal with her grandparents, she could not help remembering how, after many tries at composing a still life, which had been the theme for the contest, she'd finally had a breakthrough, not only for herself but for what paint could do. It was monumental, and it had come to naught.

All the contest entries had been on display in the Berlin Art Academy's great hall. The whispered remarks, which ran through the student body and among the teachers, were that one work was unique, no question—in a league so far beyond the others that it nullified the competition. *It's irides-cent! Astonishing, daring! Impossible!* These were the words that popped from the mouths of those who'd surveyed the blind competition.

For the awards ceremony, the entire school of art students gathered in the oak-paneled assembly hall. While dressing for the event, Lotte had had to swat Katharina with a hairbrush for fussing with her white collar. At the assembly hall, she sat between her and her father. The prize-winning pieces on stage were propped on easels covered with black cloths.

Almost every seat was filled. The room smelled of furniture oil, damp wool, and the faint odor of turpentine vapor that always hovered throughout the building. Lotte felt waves of nausea. She had not eaten all day. Why could they not simply post the winners? Why must an artist parade herself upon a stage for all to gape at? She eyed the exit.

The headmaster mounted the stairs to the stage and took a place behind the podium. Lotte's heart palpitated as though a hummingbird, desperate to find a more fruitful place to land, was trapped there. In an inflated tone of voice, he made remarks Lotte was far too nervous to follow. She spotted Professor Beck a few rows behind her, his lips pressed together, suppressing his usual ear-to-ear smile. In the last row was Wolf Abrams, just taking his seat. He smiled broadly.

As each prize came up on the program, the headmaster's assistant withdrew the black cloth, and the headmaster himself called the name: first honorable mention, then the third and second places. Lotte watched as each student climbed the stairs on the left of the stage, walked across, took the award certificate with one hand, and offered the other to shake. It was an unimaginable journey. Katharina settled a hand on Lotte's bouncing knee.

"And now, for first place," said the headmaster. A few students turned to smile at Lotte, who was too frozen to react. Perhaps Katharina might go up for her. Lotte flexed her fingers, curling and uncurling them in her lap, thinking only, *I can't go up*, and seeing herself tripping, falling flat on her face.

"The winner, I am honored to announce, is—" The headmaster scanned the crowd, looking for the recipient. Lotte recalled Wolf saying that only her work was visionary. She remembered the sound of her name being whispered around the halls of the Berlin Art Academy. *How did she do it?* The one astounding, truly original work had to be hers. Now her name would be spoken aloud in front of the entire student body and their relatives.

The assistant pulled off the cover to expose the winning painting—a loaf of peasant bread, a hunk of cheese, and an earthenware jug, all on a red-checkered cloth. Propped against the jug was a small, framed portrait of the Führer, so obviously in the style of Arthur Rackham's fairy-tale illustrations.

"Ah, here she is. The winner is Nadja Kappel."

For one long moment, the hall was filled with silence, a void into which nothing of reason or logic could enter. Many heads turned toward Lotte. Hers drew back stiffly. She tightened her arms against her sides. Her core grew cold. It was her father who began clapping slowly. The rest of the audience picked up a little more enthusiastically. But what had happened? It made no sense. Her stomach hardened as though cast in plaster.

What she wanted most was to disappear. As she realized that, no, in fact, a kind of erasure had just occurred, she wanted to scream. People began to move. Buoyant, the Kappels escorted Nadja down the aisle, the look on her face pure triumph. As Lotte stood, she lost her legs and started to sag. Katharina and her father caught her and guided her along. She heard whispers of "unfair" and "you should have won." She kept her head down, like a criminal refusing to be gawked at, and made it to the door without uttering a word.

The next two days, there was no school. Lotte had withdrawn into her bedroom and did not touch the food that Astrid brought to her. On Monday morning, she dressed. She ate black bread with margarine, drank a cup of barley coffee, and buttoned up her two-tone gray herringbone coat. Katharina intercepted her at the door, still in her emerald-green dressing gown, her hair not yet fixed and floating loosely over her shoulders, her voice fluttery, tentative, conveying maternal obligation.

"Look, Lotte, you can hold your head high. It was just a contest."

Lotte flashed back, "It was everything."

She arrived at the Berlin Art Academy early. Professor Beck took her to an alcove with a built-in bench under a tall window, a standard spot for conversations between teachers and students. She was wary. She didn't want to be consoled for her loss.

His silver hair shone in the light streaming through the window. The smell of his tobacco was as familiar as when he leaned over her shoulder in class and offered words of praise and encouragement. His look was unguarded, his eyes full of compassion.

"Charlotte, the headmaster wants to see you, but before he does, I want you to know what a superior artist you are. Your talent is immense, and no one can take that from you."

His words had a softening effect. "Why does he want to see me?"

Professor Beck made her promise to keep the appointment if he told her, and she agreed.

"Someone must inform you. An awful injustice was done. You, not Nadja Kappel, should have received that award. It was your work that was chosen for first place."

Lotte felt a little shock tighten her neck into a tilt and then her brows knit together. "I won?"

"I was on the judging committee. When we lifted the blind on the winning painting and found it was yours, someone on the committee mentioned your Jewish heritage. If the press reported a Jew had won the prize at the Berlin Art Academy, especially so close to Hitler's *Degenerate Art* exhibit being in town, well, it could be"—Professor Beck took a deep breath—"detrimental to the school." He continued with a pained expression. "I made the best case I could for you, but in the end, they felt it was too chancy. And there was Nadja, her father a curator of *Degenerate Art*. It was just as easy to give it to her. And so much better for the school."

Never had Lotte considered that because she was a Jew, it would not matter what she had accomplished. She blurted out, "But I won."

"You did. And you are the best artist here. By far. You are the one we wait for. You are the reason we teach—to find the one who can teach us. Your vision is thrilling. Never give up."

She had done it. And she knew it. Everyone knew it.

"And the headmaster?"

"They can't let you go because then the school will fall below Jewish quota. But unfortunately, you won't be able to associate with other students. You'll have to work in the attic space."

THOUGH SHE'D BEEN DEPRIVED of her award, and her position as well, Lotte vowed she would find a way to keep on working. She had arrived at the conclusion that the artist only existed in the creation, not the recognition. Still, it was nice to have recognition here at l'Ermitage.

During a dessert of apple tart, Olive tapped her wine glass until the room was quiet and she had everyone's attention.

"After the meal, the children will provide musical entertainment."

Just as Charlotte was about to express her interest, her grandparents motioned her to leave with them.

In the reception hall, Olive said, "Charlotte, do stay."

Her grandfather said, "She needs her rest."

She wanted badly to remain among the lively group, but because it was her first night, she felt obliged to defer to her grandparents.

"Then come for breakfast tomorrow. We'll get acquainted. Show up as it suits you."

"Lotte!" The call came from the top of the grand staircase. She looked up, dumbfounded to see a face she recognized. It was Anneliese Eltmann, her school chum who had moved to Austria when they were thirteen, at the same time her father married Katharina.

Anneliese descended the stairs. "Sorry I missed supper. Rui was too fussy."

There she was, her friend, with her same small-boned figure, ivory skin, and mass of dark, almost black, curls. The contrast gave an illusion of fragility, but Charlotte recalled her as strong of mind, down-to-earth, and practical. She fell into her friend's embrace and inhaled her pleasant, earthy scent which flooded her with images of afternoons swimming in the sea, weekends riding horses in the forest, winters ice-skating on the lake, and their foreheads pressed together in the exchange of many secrets now long forgotten.

Olive said, "Anneliese Nagel, the surprise I promised."

Anneliese explained, no, Henri was not her husband. She had married his brother, Max. "He'll be down in a minute."

Rui was her infant son. Charlotte said, "You, a mother? Imagine."

When her grandparents repeated the need to leave, Anneliese invited her to visit in the afternoon.

They were barely out the door when Charlotte's grandmother criticized Olive for carrying on with Henri.

Charlotte said, "I noticed nothing of the kind."

"Oh, we've seen plenty of chicanery. Disgusting. She's much too old for him."

Her grandfather said, "The nerve. Inviting you to breakfast. We leave them to the Great House. And we stick to our cottage. You must do as we do, Lotte."

LONG AFTER CHARLOTTE had bedded down in the grave-like darkness of her room, her grandparents' behavior continued to bother her. She felt embarrassed for them. She'd seen how irritated they made Olive, and she'd noted the effort Olive made to conceal it for the sake of civility.

She thought of them at her age—what she knew from her grandmother's telling during one regular Sunday visit when she was a child. A *Schwarzwälder Kirschtorte* had been served. Lotte had held a whole cherry in her mouth while she listened.

"Your grandfather was left fatherless at eleven," her grandmother had said. He had grown up on his grandparents' sugar-beet farm in Ukraine. "His mother took him there, but they were banished to a hut. With a straw floor." Here, she had waved her hand in a gesture of dismissal. "They were slaves, they were. To farm work." Lotte had bitten down on the cherry to protect herself from such an impoverished life.

Her grandfather eventually made it off the farm and into university. He was introduced to Jewish bourgeois society by his father's friend, an ophthalmologist. "Without him," her grandmother had said, "Luitger would never have been able to marry me."

Lotte asked why. Mama, a willowy figure with cup in hand at the window, turned and said, "Grossmama was the daughter of a very prosperous Berlin family, Lotte. She was a refined woman. A poetess and cultured linguist. All Grosspapa had was his good looks."

"But what happened to Grosspapa's papa?"

In response, her grandmother had pointed to the tall pine tree in her drawing room, nearly grazing the ceiling. Like many assimilated German Jews, the Gruensteins and the Salomons always had a Christmas tree. "How about we get out the ornaments?"

Thinking now about her grandparents' lives didn't, after all, help Charlotte figure out how she was going to live with them today here in France, cooped up in this overstuffed, dark cottage, with the impossible pull between them and Olive Miller. She felt frustrated and restless and irritated that she had never gotten a straight answer. Why not just say her great-grandfather left his family? Or he died?

To calm herself, she conjured Wolf. He had not occupied the role of teacher, barely of mentor. She had been too contrary in his presence to allow it. She was, however, obsessed by him in his absence and wholly dependent upon his opinion of her work. For years, she had wanted him badly and discounted his engagement to a woman she felt was silly and not his equal. Having pursued him on the boulevards and into the cafés, she hung onto his every word, whether of philosophy, literature, myth, music, or art. He viewed her work with serious eyes, lauded her talent, encouraged her effort, and became her lifeline. Some might have called him an angel. Though she did not believe in such things, she had to admit that he had been divinely delivered to her.

A small smile crept over her face. She recalled the first winter that Wolf arrived from the Jewish Kulturbund. Katharina had yielded the piano and drawing room to him so he could take on students. Sometimes he worked with Katharina, training her voice. One day, when Katharina was practicing Orfeo—a male role scored for a female voice—Charlotte had overheard Wolf speaking. She had stepped closer to the open door, careful not to reveal herself.

"It's not entirely mine. I give credit to Jung. But it is my own application of his theory. We've always thought of it as a story of a lover risking all for his beloved. However, on a deeper level, Eurydice represents his voice. Which is his soul. That is, his anima, the other half of his soul. And the underworld he must traverse to reclaim it? That's his inner landscape of darkness."

Both male and female together within oneself? The idea still had meaning for Charlotte, and she missed Wolf. She imagined him in one of the new Austrian cafés, enjoying his dark coffee and writing his book. If she were there, he would take the time to look at her latest work and share with her his dark history. Her limbs began to relax. After a time, she drifted to sleep, wondering just how she was going to paint.

CHAPTER 3

VILLEFRANCHE-SUR-MER

Disregarding her grandparents' protests, Charlotte finally decided to take up Olive Miller's offer for breakfast. The sky was crystal clear, and she reveled in the feeling of being under the dome of it in a way she had never experienced in Berlin. It was like wandering inside an upside-down blue teacup. A row of cypress trees broke the bluster of a stormy airstream. In the kitchen garden, Delmira, wearing a crisp white apron over a faded black dress, was pulling out some plants along the stone wall.

"Good morning, Mademoiselle Salomon! Pretty, these winter roses. But toxic to children. Mademoiselle Miller says we must get rid of them, plant something else. She is upstairs. Come."

Charlotte followed Delmira into the kitchen with its expansive wooden block in the center, a multitude of pots and pans and utensils stacked on shelves, and a ferocious black stove-and-oven combination. They passed through a cozy breakfast room, the dining room, and the receiving hall, then went up the semicircular staircase. She caught a glimpse into the grand salon, a rustling concord of violet and azure accented by gilded woods.

She wondered whether envy might be at the root of her grandparents' querulous attitude toward l'Ermitage. It might be that they felt it was their due to own a grand chateau, which only some quirk of fate had mysteriously denied them. If they couldn't be the gentry, then they would be the peasants, thus diminishing themselves as a form of camouflage. From that vantage point, they were entitled to find fault with everything.

Wallpaper and furnishings in Olive's suite glowed rose and golden cream in the morning sunshine, colors merging to create the impression of a perfectly ripe peach. An Art Deco bed was unmade, half its silk and satin bedclothes adorning the floor.

In a turquoise shirtwaist with lime-green polka dots, Olive looked as fresh and vibrant as the morning Mediterranean. Charlotte clicked her teeth together softly, a tic she'd picked up in childhood. Did Olive sense her nervousness? She refrained from hugging. Instead, she kissed both cheeks while inviting Charlotte into a sitting room with a view of the back garden.

A table was set for two. Olive offered a plate of croissants. "Pastry flour from the States, if you're wondering."

Charlotte was too uneasy to wonder. And tongue-tied. Physically quivering, though not noticeably, her body attempted to synchronize with the beauty and harmony of the surroundings.

Olive asked, "Tell me, how do you like it here?"

Fortunately, Charlotte was able to talk about how magical the chateau was, how stunning the Mediterranean coast, and how captivating the light and colors.

"Even so, one can be lonely," Olive replied. "I'm thirty-two. A good ten years older than you. It may seem a great gap, but you're the single woman closest in age to me here. I'm delighted to have you."

To be firmly planted so centrally in the chateau's constellation was disturbing. Charlotte wondered what Olive expected from her. Then a small voice spoke to her from within: *She may be a friend.* Like an actor about to set foot on stage for the first time, Charlotte peeked out through the curtains of herself to assess the receptivity of the audience.

Olive said, "I'd love to see your work."

Charlotte mentally scanned the drawings she'd made on the train, wondering if she had something worth showing.

"Anything?" Olive asked. After pouring real coffee into fine porcelain cups, she went on in a rush. "Well, I understand. Artists need to protect their work. The time and the viewer must be right. The work must be ready. Meanwhile, did you happen to see Hitler's *Degenerate Art* exhibit? I'm so curious."

"I attended the opening. In Munich." Blocked windows, narrow spaces. The press of bodies. Sweltering heat. "I had to see everything at the earliest possible moment."

Charlotte had taken a big risk when she set out alone, defying her father, to attend the largest modern-art show ever staged. She needed to see the assembled masterpieces even before they came to Berlin. The most important works in Germany had been condemned, and viewing them would give her a leg up on her contest entry.

Charlotte described some of the works. When she discovered that Olive not only loved Chagall as she did, but also felt that his work had a profound effect on her soul, "lifting it into the sphere of the mystical," her tension unwound. She was not strange to her.

Charlotte picked at the flakes of the croissant, marveling at the real butter and raspberry preserves, too excited to eat.

Just then, Henri and all the children trooped through the trees onto the garden lawn. He drove two tall stakes into the ground and, with the help of the tallest child, strung a wire between.

"What's that?"

"He's going to hang a sheet." Olive explained that they were photographing the children for identity papers and to document who had been at l'Ermitage.

These little ones needed papers? Charlotte wanted to ask about their parents, but Olive was back on the exhibit.

"I understand there were horrid slogans all over the place." Olive plucked a purple grape from the fruit bowl. Charlotte was glad to see it wasn't just a decorative centerpiece and took a grape for herself. "How were the Jews represented there?"

Charlotte's throat constricted, and the beat of her heart picked up, partly because Olive's question felt like an invitation to know her better and partly because she'd remembered the Führer's speech. How lost she had felt in that vast audience. No reference point for her within the thunderous ovation. All this seemed like too much to convey to someone who hadn't experienced it firsthand.

"The Jews are considered responsible for destroying German art and culture. I think I can quote Hitler's words. If you really want to know."

"I do."

"He said, 'I don't want to leave a shadow of a doubt as to the fact that sooner or later'—now, how did he put it? Oh, yes—'the hour of liquidation'—yes, that's what he said—'the hour of liquidation will strike for those who have participated in this corruption.' He mentioned especially those with what he called 'eye disease.'"

Olive's hand went to her mouth. "How did you—?"

"Honestly? It put me in a panic."

Olive held Charlotte in her stabilizing gaze. During a long silence, she felt Olive's attempt to penetrate the experience while she herself became less fearful by virtue of the telling. In that nebulous sense, she felt the two of them grow closer.

By the end of their last cup of coffee, a thrill went up in her. She'd found a like-minded person.

When she stood to go, Olive invited her to return the next day. As they passed back through the bedroom, Charlotte noticed a man's black sock in the tangle of bedclothes.

"As an artist, Charlotte, here in France you're no longer subject to the censoring you were in Germany. I'd really love to see your work. When you're ready to show it, of course."

She managed to squeak out a modest, "Thank you for your interest."

Charlotte left Olive in her room and descended the great staircase. Just as she was walking out the front door, Henri was walking in. And—it happened too quickly to avoid—they brushed up against each other. In the middle of her chest, she felt a shifting motion, as though her heart moved a centimeter off its place and rocked back.

"Good morning, Charlotte." He was wearing a tan knit polo shirt, and his eyes were more brown than green. His hair had yet to be combed. "Coming from Olive? I hope you agreed to show her your work. You should, you know. She's quite a patron."

She tossed her head, as if to brush aside his inquiry as none of his business. Ignoring the remark, she gave him a quick greeting and down the steps she went, bristling with irritation and something else, which was distinctive but, before it could be identified, immediately dismissed.

She found a new path that led to an enclosed, manicured garden with a fountain in the center. She stood before a bench, hesitating to take the seat, searching for the sign that read, *No Jews Allowed*. But there was no sign. She was in France. She was free. As a Jew, she could sit.

She did sit, at first gingerly, then completely, with a sigh. The sun was reaching its zenith. The gurgle of water was pleasant, bubbling up memories of Munich.

IN THE ANHALTER BAHNHOF, waiting to board the train, Charlotte had un-fortuitously run into Nadja Kappel, Ginger-Rogers-gorgeous with cheeks like plums, an illustrator of children's fairy tales and, outrageously, then considered the school's best artist. She was with her mother, who insisted that Charlotte join them, be their guest, and share Nadja's room at the Hotel Torbräu. The two days Charlotte spent with them were excruciating. She'd had to keep her Jewish identity hidden, which became increasingly difficult beginning with the first morning when Herr Kappel joined them for breakfast sporting the uniform of the SS. Not only that, but he was also on the staff of Adolf Zeigler, Hitler's organizer of the *Degenerate Art* exhibit. Charlotte had upset her cup of coffee, the brown stain blossoming its way across the white tablecloth.

She had trudged with the Kappel family through Hitler's spanking-new House of German Art. More like: House of Atrocious German Art. She'd dined with them, attended the big parade, and sat with them in their choice front-row seats for Hitler's speech. Charlotte heard again that day's stomping of feet, the hollering and cheering and roaring of "Heil Hitler!" Had she been the sole Jew in that sea of deafening humanity stretching infinitely behind her? There had been no escape that would not draw down upon her the incriminating stares of thousands. Hitler had foamed like a rabid dog. Runnels of perspiration had flowed from her armpits. She had sat still and dug her fingers into her palms.

Finally, the next day, she was able to free herself from the Kappels with the excuse that she'd run into a friend and would be attending the *Degenerate Art* exhibit with her. They would head back to Berlin together. After turning her valise over to the hotel's luggage check-room and then standing for hours in a crowd of crushing humanity, she finally gained access to the exhibit she had longed so much to see.

She entered the first crowded room. Temporary walls blocked the windows and further closed in an already narrow space. Substandard lighting dimmed her sight until her eyes adjusted. The congestion—the way they were packed in together, more like herded cattle than art enthusiasts—made it so she was unable to see anything. The next room was a little better, suffused with gray light, murky yet penetrable. A banner proclaimed: *REVELATION OF THE JEWISH RACIAL SOUL.*

Here was Marc Chagall, whose works filled Charlotte with wonder. The Russian figure in "A Pinch of Snuff Rabbi," with his sidelocks and phylacteries so unlike the modern German rabbis. Why had Chagall given him two left hands?

She claimed a spot in front of the much smaller "Winter," hung beneath the rabbi. She crouched to better examine the mixture of watercolor and gouache techniques. The flattening-out of space and the multiplicity of smaller scenes within the whole astonished her. Here was a method with which she might experiment. She pulled a jotter from her purse and made a note: *Divided surface makes spaces for linear story.*

"What does this have to do with being Jewish?" A male voice came from directly behind her, along with a waft of undigested onions.

His female companion responded, "Read the card."

The man poked his head over Charlotte's shoulder.

"It says, *Marc Chagall, Jew.*"

"Exactly," the woman said. "The artist is a Jew. So, as art, the work is fraudulent."

"A-a-ah." His reply rang with the hauteur of the falsely enlightened.

More people pushed their way in. Too cramped, Charlotte moved into the next room. On her left, the first painting quickened her pulse. It was the striking "Yellow Dancer" by Ernst Ludwig Kirchner. That gesture! The dancer's hand lifted her skirts and displayed her spread legs. With thrilling, thick applications of color, bright clothing was made flamboyant and red lips lurid. A slogan ran across the wall: *AN INSULT TO GERMAN WOMANHOOD.*

Onlookers shook their heads or stole a glance, then averted their eyes. Charlotte liked how uncomfortable it made them. She loved the bold questioning of conventional morality in the liveliness and beauty of a woman, perhaps a Romani or prostitute—in any case, not a housewife, as most of the viewers seemed to be. She noted: *Areas of intense pure color dynamic. Like Fauves. Body in motion adds to effect.*

There had been no coat check, and the press of bodies heated the room. The brim of every hat toggled its neighbor's. Faces took on the grimace of physical discomfort mixed with revulsion. Charlotte's skin itched. Ahead were slogans on war: *AN INSULT TO THE GERMAN HEROES OF THE GREAT WAR*, and *DELIBERATE SABOTAGE OF NATIONAL DEFENSE.*

Coming face to face with a decimated village, Charlotte had reeled back a step and winced at the mishmash of houses, corpses, trees, body parts—splintered, destroyed, isolated, decomposed. A soldier's bare legs in stark white paint riveted her. Part of the left foot was blasted away, and blood gushed from bullet holes. Ammunition had riddled his blanket. The head hung with open mouth. At top left, steel girders skewered a corpse. It was "The War" by Otto Dix.

Charlotte had wanted to weep. A young woman standing next to her suppressed an outcry. Unlike the German *housfrauen* in their hats and flowered dresses, she, like Charlotte, was hatless and wearing plain gray.

Someone said, "Big public protest in Cologne. They got it removed from the museum."

Another chimed in, "They should have burned it."

Having recovered her composure, the young woman leaned Charlotte's way and spoke in a low tone. "Some prefer not to think of their soldiers rotting in trenches."

Charlotte nodded and matched her pitch. "No glory here."

"Because," the young woman was whispering now, "these images do not support a state that is mobilizing for war."

She wrote: *Expresses strong emotion and evokes it in the viewer.*

Charlotte made it through all six rooms. Her head was spinning, her body weary and clammy with sweat, and her right baby toe abraded from rubbing against a split in the leather of her shoe. Needing air, she descended the main staircase. On the first floor, she noticed a hallway with works she hadn't seen. Saturated with images but hating to miss anything, she drifted into the long corridor.

Under a low, arched ceiling hung portraits by Kandinsky, Grosz, Kokoschka, and Dix. In the vitrines below were pages from Hans Prinzhorn's book, *Artistry by the Mentally Ill.* They depicted photographs of mental patients, people who had not developed normally, and those with facial deformities. Side by side with them were displayed the works of artists like Modigliani.

Charlotte became dizzy and confused; her vision blurred. As the strength went out of her, she collapsed.

When she came to, a cool cloth was on her forehead. A severe-faced, middle-aged woman squatted before her in the uniform and cap of the Nazi Party. Charlotte recoiled.

"You fainted." The woman's voice was neutral. "You seemed to be alone. I was called."

Charlotte felt her temple, tender. She was sitting on a stool and propped against the wall in a tiny closet with a slanted ceiling and smelling of lye. A mop and bucket stood next to her. "I…" She stared into the open interior of her handbag on the floor and strained to clear her head.

"Charlotte Salomon. Berlin." The woman held her student card. "Salomon. A Jew?"

A wave of dizziness mixed with terror sent her mind reeling toward panic. She struggled to keep focus. "I—I'm not alone," she spluttered. "I'm with the Wilhelm Kappel family. At the Hotel Torbräu."

"Hmm?" She eyed the identification card, flicking its edge with one thumb.

"His daughter, Nadja, and I are fellow students at the Berlin Art Academy. And friends."

The Party woman looked back and forth from the card to Charlotte. She stood up.

"Well, I'm sure Herr Kappel would not host a Jew. Especially not a Jew artist. You all right to stand?"

A trifle unsteady, Charlotte got to her feet unaided. The woman returned her handbag. The closet door she held open led into the front foyer. Shielding her face from full view in the brighter light, Charlotte said a stiff thank-you. Quickly she pushed against the incoming crowd and went out into the street.

She shook uncontrollably. Would she crumple right there in broad daylight? She willed her brain to reason. She had to get out of Munich as fast as possible. She headed straight to the station. Her valise would have to remain behind at the hotel.

Before long, she had a window seat and was moving toward the outskirts of town. After her fright had subsided, she stewed for a long while in an uncomfortable state of overload. For the first time, she was genuinely afraid for herself as a Jew. And as an artist.

She looked out the window but took no notice of the landscape.

Yes, she had had a brush with danger. She knew now where she stood in regard to this world: on the outside looking in, where she had always stood. Only now she knew the world saw her there too.

But paintings were imbedded in her brain. A visit to this one exhibition felt like a full education in modern art. When Jewish artists were not tolerated even painting innocuous winter scenes or making abstract canvases, how could it be that she had a place at the Berlin Art Academy, the lone Jew? It was some kind of miracle. She must seize the advantage.

The train rocked. Her thoughts seemed to arise from the rhythm of the wheels.

She had found something of inestimable value. She could not quite name it. In some strange way, what made her an outcast might in the long run become a benefit. It felt like a seed had been planted—in her imagination, her body, her sense of herself—which someday would blossom into her own special "degeneracy."

The train entered a tunnel. In the dark, she caught her true and satisfied face reflected in the glass.

Katharina would chide her for abandoning her valise. A small price to pay to beat Nadja Kappel. First place—it would be hers.

Even as she had this thought, a new excitement had sparked inside and made her smile. She realized that excelling, winning, had little to do with Nadja or the other students. Its meaning would be a fulfillment of the same inner urging that had set her off on this journey. Which was what, exactly? A mystery she couldn't fathom but needed to understand. It seemed as close and intimate as her own breath, and as distant and obscure as the farthest star.

THE *DEGENERATE ART* EXHIBIT was followed by her lost award and expulsion from the Berlin Art Academy. Then, the terrible Night of Broken Glass and the arrest of her father. It seemed inevitable she had been forced to leave Berlin. The fountain murmured, and in it, she heard her good fortune.

Olive was right. She was not censored here. She vowed to make new work. Not only because she'd been asked, and not simply in return for her gracious refuge, but because here she was free to do so.

They were waiting for her when she walked in, both heavily clad in black, looking like furniture among furniture, and drinking tea out of dainty china cups. Her grandmother was absorbed in writing poetry, her grandfather in reading Schiller. The air bristled with a lack of conviviality. Charlotte let them know of Olive's interest in her work.

Her grandfather shot a piercing look over the top of his reading spectacles. "Olive Miller knows many rich people. She should find you a position."

"Position?"

"As a housemaid."

Charlotte's jaw dropped. "You mean making beds and scrubbing?"

Her grandmother put down her pen. "No, not that, Luitger. She must get married. She's almost an old maid. Lotte hasn't a clue about love. Olive should introduce her."

"Who says Olive knows anyone suitable? And courtship takes forever. Meanwhile, Marina, your jewels are running low."

Charlotte put her hands on her hips. She had not left everything behind and made the journey for this. Where had these ideas come from? Hadn't Katharina communicated what had happened to her, losing her position at the Berlin Art Academy and needing to be able to paint?

"Olive should make me a housemaid? Olive should make me a housewife?"

"Now, Lotte. Don't get worked up." Her grandmother stood and took her hand. "You're too sensitive. We're trying to help you live a normal life, which was impossible for you in Berlin."

Charlotte shook free. "Pardon me, but with all due respect, my normal life in Berlin was as an art student."

Her grandfather barked, "You were expelled!"

"I was not!" Her voice had risen too. "My position was annulled. It had nothing to do with my talent or performance. I had to leave because I'm a Jew. You should support me to pursue my painting."

Her grandfather slammed his book closed. "That's not possible here. Following idle dreams. Out of the question. That woman your father married—Katrina?"

"Katharina."

If only her stepmother were with her now. For five years after her mother died, Charlotte had had no motherly attention. She'd always felt glad when the weekly visit to her grandparents was over, relieved to be free from constant criticism—of her imperfect posture, her unpolished manners, her outspoken speech. It got worse as she became older, until Katharina arrived. Straight off, Katharina had claimed her. "I'm in charge now, darling," she had told her new husband whenever his mother-in-law tried to meddle. "I will not raise her to be a frivolous person."

Charlotte had been thirteen at the time and fawned over Katharina. Each night, she had waited in bed for her new, beloved stepmother to come and enfold her in her arms and kiss her on her cheeks and brow.

Katharina had protected her for three years, and then her grandparents moved to the South of France. Secret gladness came out into the open when Katharina said, "Gone at last!" Even her father hadn't been able to suppress a smirk. However, as Charlotte began to assert herself as an artist, her feelings toward Katharina had shifted.

One day, Wolf had praised her drawing of "Death and the Maiden," and she had agreed to let him borrow it. Later, she heard Katharina speaking with him in the drawing room.

"I don't understand how any drawing of Death is a good sign for a young woman," Katharina had said.

Charlotte recalled how she'd depicted the figure: from behind, cloaked, and topped with a skull. The bony joints of one hand curved over the maiden's crown of long, luxurious hair, swept back to reveal an exquisite forehead. Death's other hand rested on her bared shoulder.

"There's nothing of the usual horror about Death," she heard Wolf say. "He's smiling at her. This is a warm embrace. Almost a blessing. She accepts this skull, this figure, without fear, and the secrets she can't be told."

Charlotte had been mystified by his talk of secrets, which had had nothing to do with her making of the work. She could only surmise he meant that Death was the greatest secret.

"Don't you see?" he went on. "The maiden all dream and beauty. She's the artist's inner world. Death, so ugly, is her outer world. Despite her sheltered life, this artist—"

Katharina interrupted. "You mean our little Lotte?"

"Of course, that's who I mean. I'm interpreting this outstanding work for you. And what I'm saying is that she understands what's happening in Germany. But look, it's not a submissive gaze she returns. See the eyes? She searches for some meaning—trust, even."

"Ridiculous!" said Katharina. "It's just a drawing."

Hearing Katharina dismiss her work in such a demeaning way, Charlotte's hands had folded into fists. Her neck and face heated up. She wanted to lunge at her, grab her by the shoulders, and shout every hateful thing. *You prima donna! You think you are the only artist?*

Now her grandfather was speaking. "She's a prima donna, that Katrina. She indulged you. Spoiled you. They should have told you. You're here to be of help. To take care of us."

"No. What? Stop. I'm not. I'm in exile, just as you are. I do appreciate having a place to wait things out, and I will do my part. But I intend to paint. As in Berlin."

Her grandfather stood up. He took his spectacles in one hand and shook them at her. "There are only two choices, Lotte, and for either one you'll need to be a skilled home-maker. You'll start by doing the housework. It's too much for Marina." He dropped his spectacles on his book and strode out the door.

Anger swiftly spun Charlotte into a windstorm. She wanted to throw their effete teacups against the wall, hear them crack, and watch them splinter.

"This was to be a happy reunion," her grandmother cried. "Look what's become of it."

Charlotte paced and fumed. These two had taken her to Rome for her seventeenth birthday, where she discovered Michelangelo, Bernini, and all the best classical art collections in the world; where she had decided that she, too, would become an artist. And now they wanted her to clean houses, get married? It took a monumental effort to suppress the savage inside.

"Lotte, I know how much you want to paint. I do. Please understand, I can't contradict that man."

Charlotte, too, left the cottage for some fresh air, which, after some minutes, calmed her.

Her grandparents' years were gone. She must not waste hers. She didn't want to end up regretful, embittered by work undone.

She needed to put some distance between herself and them. Find a place to paint.

No sooner did she make this vow than they were pummeled by bad weather.

CHAPTER 4

VILLEFRANCHE-SUR-MER

In the month following, a mistral blew with extraordinary fury. Stretched out with bolsters on the Persian rug, Charlotte spent every morning with Olive, who remained in bed, wrapped in her sumptuous Japanese dressing gown. Thus arranged, they drank massive amounts of coffee and picked at croissants or brioches, licking l'Ermitage's marmalade from their fingers.

Over the days, Charlotte sketched Olive in her robe of ivory silk with large cabbage roses in variegated shades of pink amidst sage-green foliage. Olive told her how her uneducated mother had been determined her daughter not become a debutante, and so Olive had enrolled in the University of Pennsylvania. Her parents had been killed in the crash of a small commercial airplane during a tour of Europe to her grandfather's hometown of Ulm. He had been in the meatpacking business and made a fortune with the invention of the hot dog. The tragedy had made Olive an heiress. She chose to study art history, then worked at the

Rodin Museum when it opened in 1929. With her inheritance she had purchased l'Ermitage, "to have a foothold" in her favorite country. In the mid-1930s, she quit the museum to rescue orphaned children, then, with the rise of the Third Reich next door, to provide a haven for refugees.

"And here I am."

Charlotte wanted the morning to go on forever and asked how Olive came to know her grandparents.

"I first met them in 1932 while traveling in Spain. The following year, I was in Berlin and saw the Nazi parade. They were very troubled by Hitler's rise, and I invited them to stay if ever they wished to leave Germany. They came very soon after."

When Charlotte showed her sketch, Olive cried with delight.

"Surely in that dreary cottage you can't even see your pencil in front of your face. Wander the Great House. Really. It's yours."

With her sketch pad under her arm, Charlotte did wander. In one salon, Henri was distributing musical instruments to the children. He shot her a dimpled smile and winked. Was that a silent, discreet hello? Or something flirtatious? Which would be outrageous, given his special relationship with Olive. It put her in a shudder, either of excitement or need—of physical animation, at least.

She found a library, all ash wood, light and airy, complete with ladders to the upper shelves. Her eyes scanned hundreds of titles on art movements, artists, art history; also works of literature and history. She'd just settled into a comfortable chair when the children came. "*Bonjour*, Charlotte!" They tramped through the library, into the solarium, and out the garden door. This house, huge as it was, wasn't going to be a place where she could work.

By the third week in February, it was over, the mistral. Charlotte had reached her absolute limit of toleration of her grandmother's permanent state of nerves—incessant muttering, frequent pacing, and intermittent shrieking. Her grandfather made clumsy attempts to calm her and then cursed her when it didn't help, starting her up all over again.

Outside clouds began to gather, black and ominous, and the falling rain drove them back inside. Now water was rushing down the knoll the way the wind had been before. In a few hours, the sky dumped as much rain as Berlin might get in a year.

THE FIRST AFTERNOON of a new calm, Anneliese was outside the kitchen door in the graveled back garden. The rains had left behind the greening of nature. Her baby son, Rui, slept in a woven basket. At the sight of him, Charlotte's breath stalled. His face was as serene as a fine white beach that never bore a footprint.

While Anneliese unraveled the yarn of an old sweater, they sat under the oak and waited for the garden mint tea, which was steeping in a chipped ceramic teapot. Charlotte asked her how they'd arrived here.

The elder Nagels had been friends with Olive's parents for many years, and the Nagel family had spent many delightful vacations at l'Ermitage. The parents were arrested in Vienna on Pogromnacht. The brothers, Henri and Max, knew that if they could make it over the Alps to l'Ermitage, they'd be safe with Olive.

"You came across in winter? With the baby?"

"Strapped to my chest. Inside one of my father-in-law's coats." She poured the tea and told of trudging the steep paths in the freezing cold, with driving winds and snow, little to eat.

They had become confused about the route but luckily found an abandoned shack. Henri went out on his own to scout and came back with a broken femur. He'd slid off a precipice onto an outcrop.

Anneliese had been a nurse before marrying Max, so she sewed up a wound on Henri's face. Max took down a small tree with a rusty axe and split a log into flat splints. They cut a cabin blanket into strips to encase Henri's leg and fashioned crutches out of branches.

"It was all very makeshift, but he could move."

So this was the story behind Henri's limp and the scar on his face.

"Henri is a man of good strength," Anneliese went on, "but the kind who took his mortality for granted. No more. Anyway, he'll come back. Not physically, of course, but every other way."

A wave of gratitude came over Charlotte. Here she had come from Berlin in a luxurious, private compartment with a valise full of belongings. Her heart softened, and she felt kinder toward Henri.

"You're all very brave, and Rui's a lucky little one. I can see that motherhood suits you. Marriage, too, I suppose."

"We're very like-minded, Max and me. It's a partnership."

Charlotte found this odd, unfamiliar. Perhaps marriage wasn't necessarily a form of death. Perhaps it was the bourgeois life, one of habit and predictability, that was so stifling.

"Did you have anyone, Lotte?"

Her thoughts went to Wolf. She didn't "have" him in any conventional sense. Anneliese might not understand about an older man—philosopher, author, teacher—with an ailing mother, a sister who cared for their mother, and a shallow fiancée he brought to the Salomon apartment when he was invited to join in family celebrations.

Wolf cared, and all through the spring of 1938, Charlotte had seen him outside the apartment during the day, dreamed of him at night, and daydreamed about him in between times. She was enthralled by his learning and insight. She had sent paintings to him when she was in Tuscany with her grand-parents, and when she returned, she sought him out in the new Austrian cafés he haunted to show him her latest work. Listening to his teachings while picking off the lattice pastry from his Linzer torte, she'd lost track of time and had to face Katharina's ire. She was in heaven when he asked her to il-lustrate his book and in hell when he took ages to respond to her work. She even ambushed him at the station at two a.m., when she could be sure to catch him leaving the apartment of his absurd fiancée for the last train home.

About her "Death and the Maiden," he had said, "Those two figures are you and I." But those two figures had come to her in a dream. How could they have anything to do with her and him? Too mystified to ask what he meant and too electri-fied by his reference to the two of them as linked in any way, she gave him a painting of a meadow, but only agreed to let him borrow the drawing.

One time, at the Station Café where he took her after she'd waited for him into the wee hours, he had pushed aside their dark amber beers with the foam on top, and reached both arms across the red-checkered oilcloth, palms up. She placed her hands, roughened by the studio, into his silky ones.

"Your paintings," he said, "many of them are excellent, really, quite excellent."

On Wolf's face was a grin. It seemed to hold secret knowl-edge, which she wanted, more than anything, for him to reveal.

He said, "The world will know us, we two. Some day." His modulated voice had not a speck of drama, but to Charlotte it had the ring of an oracle.

The only thing she knew for sure was that in his eyes, she was an artist. Her mind drifted away from the steeping tea to the day she'd left Berlin, when he had helped her onto the train.

HER PARENTS HAD SACRIFICED black-market extras to scrape together the funds for a private compartment. Standing inside it, he had held her close, tightening his arms around her. Then he loosened his embrace and held her at arm's length.

"You are a sensitive young artist. And you have had to grow up without your mother, grieving an endless loss. It hasn't been easy, I'm sure. Yet you have made something from it. You are not who you have thought you are. You are something more. Much, much more."

Much, much more. The words had dropped to her core as into the bottom of a well, not dry but containing stagnant water, and they purified it. The water-words spread through her like watercolor, washing out as far as she could imagine, saturating her idea of herself—fragile of mind, unworthy of the life she had been given. And that old notion began to dissolve.

"Knowing that you are so much more than your suffering—that is how you will do it."

She heard the words without understanding, yet she felt them to be true.

"Now I will tell you something you are to remember always, dear Charlotte." In silent inquiry she looked up into his eyes, black as coal, warm as embers. He spoke slowly. "You are a genius. And I believe in you."

CHARLOTTE BELIEVED THEIR two souls were entwined, which was a valid marriage, perhaps the most valid. She thought Anneliese sensed she had something too complicated to share, because she was looking at her with that warm, accepting smile, scooping her into her heart.

Dr. Mercier emerged into the garden after having checked on a child with fever. "Be sure to keep baby Rui away from the children until the illness passes." They chitchatted a bit, then watched him saunter off, satchel in hand.

When Anneliese asked about Charlotte's grandparents, she admitted how trying they were.

"It's anyone's guess how long they'll last here," Anneliese said. "So many pleasant people seeking refuge. You could move in here, I'm quite sure."

"What I really need is a place to paint. Outside, away from their hubbub."

Max appeared, Henri a half-step behind with his bad leg. Their trousers were covered with soil from the knees down, their hands loamy. Behind them trailed the children, their loose body-to-body contact part of their natural sociability. They all washed up at the outside basin. Delmira burst through the door with cups, teapots, and a plate piled high with cookies.

So much activity was unsettling. Charlotte stood to leave.

"Lotte, wait," Anneliese said, then asked the men about a secluded place to paint.

Henri said, "The carnation tree."

Anneliese said, "Of course! Here, Lotte, I'll show you."

Henri flashed a wry, conspiratorial smile, suggestive and disconcerting. Though she had no idea what it was he seemed to be drawing her into, she felt drawn.

"Anneliese?" Charlotte asked when they were out of sight. "Is Henri having an affair with Olive?"

She nodded her head with vigor and explained it was the best thing after that miserable crossing. "Isn't it obvious?"

"I don't know. I thought he'd been…"

"Giving you looks? It's that dimpled smile of his. He can't help himself!" Anneliese gave Charlotte directions to the spot. "It's a Japanese cherry. You can't miss it."

Along an ancient wall and through an arbor, a path of footplates with colonized thyme led to a glade, and in it a cushioned chair under a large tree with clusters of clear pink blooms, which did look like carnations. She sank into the chair that appeared less like it had been placed there than it had sprouted and grown up from the ground. She gazed skyward at glossy, red-barked branches reaching up into a rosy cloud of blushing flowers set against the slate of periwinkle sky. Looking earthward again, she noticed a large stump next to her, from a tree that must've been cut down to create this clearing. Except for the rustling, the little crackles and crunches of nature, it was so quiet.

Astonishing, daring! New! She drifted into the memory of those who had viewed her contest entry and commented publicly on her altogether new approach toward light by way of the breakthrough she'd made in the composition of pigment.

She had studied the objects for her still life one by one. The more she'd looked, the more she'd seen a life force in each, vibrating with the essence of its own color, shape, material, and function. She observed how everything changed: flowers wilted; fruit rotted; clear wine grew cloudy; or a barb fell, leaving vacant its place in the vane of the feather. It was all process and movement—everything was burning itself up with its own inner passion. There was no such thing as still life.

She needed a different kind of pigment, one that would reveal the inner fire of things. She had experimented with ground glass, then fish scales. She procured some broken pearls from a jeweler and crushed them. With some successful begging on her part, her father obtained a bit of metal oxide from a chemist. Mica. She had worked toward developing a new dimension to color, something never before seen in painting, a very different effect from traditional light reflected from a single point. She fiddled with the application—a gradient of colors in the light areas, a gradient of colors in the shadows—until she was able to reveal ceaselessly shifting motion inherent to each object. Depending upon the angle from which it was viewed, the color miraculously changed.

Charlotte had been out of her mind with excitement, and though she'd shared her find with nobody, not even Wolf, who had taught her about the soul and the artist, finally the day came when she could contain herself no longer. She let Wolf go to view her work, and he reported back to her.

"The viewer moves, and the painted objects move. Move! Unbelievable! Charlotte, this is my honest and true opinion: your work is visionary."

The night before the awards ceremony, she stood by her bedroom window, still waiting there at the age of twenty-one, no longer for a letter from her mother but for some sign. The feeling that usually came over her of expectation, of sharp breathlessness in anticipation of an arrival, had waned. In its place was a flowing feeling. Some kind of arriving had just begun, but she could not yet know what it was.

Then, after the award was stolen from her and her position was annulled, there were the weeks of feeling lost. No longer was she a student of the Berlin Art Academy. She was used to feeling herself on the periphery of her peer group, but now that there was no group, there was no periphery. Her loneliness had grown more profound every day.

At the time, the nations called to an international conference at Evian had decided not to admit large numbers of Jewish refugees. America was limiting the number of Jews from Germany. No-one-wants-the-Jews became the theme of the headlines in German papers. She had known her situation was the result of her being Jewish. Still, she felt unworthy.

The days had stretched endlessly before her. She'd stayed behind the door of her bedroom or darted into the streets.

She'd gazed upon groups of people where they gathered in parks or cafés and longed to be among them. She spied and eavesdropped. Afterward, she talked to herself, making up conversations with the people who had just upped and left.

Now, seated under the carnation tree, a wave of sadness arose. Would it ever pass?

She watched a ladybug crawl up her arm, then recalled Wolf's words: "Human beings must find meaning in life by a path out of ugliness and into light."

The noisy cicadas sounded like rippling water and wind woven together, dissolving her sadness. From within rose a small voice: *Use water.*

Suddenly she was wide-awake, staring up into the pink feathery umbrella. Forget new pigments. Others will invent them. Forget still life. Forget all artifice. This was a land of sky and water. The place to paint nature. The place for watercolor. And here, this stump was the perfect surface upon which to spread out her tools.

Warmth radiated throughout her body. She felt her face break into a wide smile. There was nowhere to look that was not happiness. A bright green pierid, more like a leaf than a butterfly, fluttered from petal to bloom.

CHAPTER 5

___

VILLEFRANCHE-SUR-MER

SEPTEMBER 1939

All through the spring and summer, Charlotte worked under the cooling shade of the Japanese cherry while it snowed pink petals on her and its leaves grew light green and glossy, tinged with red; then turned to brilliant copper. She went unexpectedly in the direction of pastels.

Anneliese was fully occupied with Rui. When Charlotte walked him in her arms under the olive trees, leaves flickering their silvery light, she could almost imagine being a mother. Anneliese called her Tante Lotte.

Henri was always hanging around Olive whenever Max and he were not in search of homes willing to take in orphans, or whatever else they were doing. The men were at times evasive or vague about their activities. Olive, a marvel, taught the children sports, music, and gardening. The stout little clubhouse had been finished in time for Bastille Day, and they had hung lanterns from the fig trees. The children had danced around it, singing "The Marseillaise."

Later in the summer, Olive made a trip to Switzerland to visit relatives. When she returned, she and Charlotte celebrated with Delmira's little éclairs and a whole bottle of champagne, drunk between cups of coffee. Olive delivered horrendous news—art burned by the Nazis in Berlin.

"Five thousand pieces. On an enormous pyre. In the spring."

Charlotte was speechless. But she had to know, the way a person must know how it was her loved one had died.

It rose in her mind's eye: broken frames taking the flames, paint bubbling, bursting, melting, and dripping. While Olive had gone on about how she might've never known had she not gone to Switzerland, Charlotte could think only of how huge the pile of ash must have been.

For the first time, Charlotte realized that even though at twenty-two she was in France as an illegal person, she had an obligation to something greater than herself—to art, to history—if that didn't sound too high. Determination plowed under her grief. She would bring new work into this broken world. She had realized, too, that no matter how clean the cottage with a pot of soup simmering on the stove, her grandparents were never going to say, "Go, Charlotte, sit in the garden and paint."

Then Olive asked if she had any watercolors. She had a friend who was looking to buy.

LATELY, MARINA had given up her writing to listen to the radio. Whenever there was bad news, a new downturn of spirits seized her. Charlotte distracted her by asking for stories. That was how she finally found out how her grandfather had become fatherless: his father, the elder Gruenstein, the lens maker of Konigsberg, had committed suicide.

"Grosspapa's father killed himself?"

"He'd taken his brother's advice to invest heavily. But then in 1873 came economic panic. The firm had to declare bankruptcy. And your grandfather's father, your great-grandfather, Lotte, well, he…" Her grandmother closed her eyes. When she opened them, she continued, "Your grandfather was only eleven."

A suicide in the family? But Jews, she'd been taught, did not commit suicide, and indeed the only time she'd ever known of it was when she'd overheard Katharina talking to her father about a friend of hers in the Jewish Kulturbund. Lotte's eavesdropping was discovered, and her stepmother had sworn her to secrecy.

Charlotte was at first too stunned by her grandmother's revelation to respond, lest the stigma adhere to her. Then she cried, "Oh, how terrible!" Her grandfather only waved his hand without looking up from his soup in a gesture that dismissed the topic.

They were still at the dinner table when the air raid siren went off. Even though it was only a test, her grandmother, more agitated, cried out, "Germany's invaded Poland. Their wooden houses are burning up!"

The German invasion had been sudden. Nervous energy was palpable on the streets and in the shops. There was not nearly the enthusiasm there had been for the Great War. Nonetheless, Olive, who did her best to have her pulse on politics, reported requisitions going out for lodgings and transportation. Emergency appropriations were being made for schools and airfields, one on the western side of Nice.

"Calm yourself, Marina. We're eating." Her grandfather laid a hand on hers, not to comfort but to quiet her. She snatched it away.

"Great Britain and France declared war on Germany. Two days ago. Our country of refuge is waging war on our homeland. And here we sit, nationless."

Nationless? That couldn't be. They were only in France due to conditions. They were still Germans, weren't they? Nationhood was a matter of birth. And soul. Charlotte kept her thoughts to herself. But what if Germany were to defeat France? The idea of it made her afraid.

After dinner, her grandfather said it was Charlotte's job to quiet Marina for sleep. She spotted his doctor's bag by the sofa, at the ready even though in all his years in Villefranche, he had not been called to a single bedside. "Really, who would want him," Olive had once said, "when you could have Dr. Mercier?" Charlotte unearthed the bottle of veronal, which would soothe her grandmother's nerves.

"Put that back and tend to her," he said. "She just needs a little attention."

It took her a moment to decide what to do, and then Charlotte placed the bottle into his palm, saying, "You tend to her." And she walked out.

At the Great House, she was in time for the setup of the evening's recital. Too agitated to sit, she helped with the rearrangement of furniture.

Henri said, "Difficult night?"

She rolled her eyes, pleased by the understanding, then sat with Dr. Mercier and his wife, Matilde. With them, she felt safe and comfortable, and was reminded of the feeling at her family's Shabbat table in Berlin. She missed the ritual candle-lighting and prayers and the stillness that fell over the apartment at the end of the week.

The cottage was quiet when she returned. She had gotten used to the dark booth of her room as a refuge, where she would lie down to think through her day, turn over her dilemmas, make her decisions, and envision new work. She missed her father and Katharina terribly and prayed they were safe. She thought of Wolf, and doing so reminded her of who she was and gave her courage. She fell asleep thinking only of the next day's hours under the Japanese cherry.

CHARLOTTE WAS HAVING the nightmare about her eight-year-old self, running as fast as she could, breathless, down the whole length of the hall in the Berlin apartment—a monstrous, tall skeleton chasing her, its bones rattling, its skull knocking against the ceiling. The hanging light fixtures swung wildly, casting a pulsing chiaroscuro of light and shadow on the walls. A push woke her. A hand closed over her mouth.

"Hush!"

It was her grandfather. He had climbed into the bed and wedged her against the wall. His beard scratched her neck. The hot air of his breath flooded her ear, smelled of decay. She tried to cry stop, but it came out as a grunt. His hardness dug into the small of her back. He rocked against her. She struggled to free herself, kicked her legs back. He clamped the fingers of his other hand around her throat, cutting off air. She couldn't move. He was a hog rooting in the mud behind her. Then he went limp and let go.

She rolled backward to push him off the bed, kicking with all her might. But she was pinned, her thin nightgown soggy with his emission.

"Get out!" She felt she was shouting, but it was only a croak.

He rallied and grabbed her around the neck again, making it difficult for her to move.

"You, young lady, don't seem to understand why you've been summoned from Berlin." Spittle in her ear. "Or what your duty is."

His thumb dug into her throat. Her heart was pounding.

"Your grandmother's going down fast. And you, selfish impudent, you ignore her. And go about on your own whims."

He put a pinch on her windpipe. She could barely breathe.

"I want you by her side from the moment she wakes until she goes to sleep. You're to cook every meal. Keep house. See to it she's calm at all times." He intensified the pinch. "Do you understand?"

Her innards twisted. The outskirts of her mind blurred.

"Do you?" He let up. She was just barely able to nod. He released completely and stood. She choked, gulped in air, coughed. In the dark, the whiteness of his beard, like a ghostly vapor, spread over his nightshirt. Underneath were his spindly, pale legs.

"Speak. So that we're understood."

What she understood was that he was despicable. She could barely struggle to her feet, bent over, still coughing. Then she managed to pull herself to full height, which nearly matched his. She cleared her throat.

"I understand."

Fury roiled beyond her control from the inside out, from the top of her head down to her foot, which kicked him in the shin. He stumbled back against the wall. Did she dare? Stepping forward, she breathed into his face.

"On one condition."

"Pssh-ah! Who are you to have a condition?" Still, he stepped to one side to avoid another kick. "You're here entirely by our good graces."

She sidled all the way up to him, toe to toe, and planted her arms akimbo. "I'm here by Olive Miller's good graces, not yours. Every day, she offers me a room in the Great House. Olive would've kicked you out by now had I not arrived. Then where would you be? You wouldn't survive two days out there on your own."

He started to sputter. "Who does she think—"

"No! Who do *you* think you are? I'll tell you what—a twisted, repellent old man. Who needs me a lot more than I need him."

He said nothing. Charlotte sensed he was stunned by her audacity and the truth of her assertion.

"Now it's your turn to listen. I'll do what I can to help Grossmama." He huffed a nonverbal protest. "But if you ever attempt this again, I'll tell her, and it'll be her end. I'll tell Olive too. She'll call the gendarmes. And you'll rot in a French prison."

In the bathroom, she vomited into the toilet bowl and flushed, once, twice. She ripped off her sticky nightgown, her heart still pounding. Shaking, she ran a bath. Her female body, the fact of it—she would have foisted it off if she could. She climbed into the tub. The sound of water running from the faucets called out her degradation, and with it, her tears.

The frustration and anger she'd been feeling toward her grandparents, toward him in his raw power and her in her manipulative ways, was nothing compared to this white-hot rage in which Charlotte could envision taking him by the neck, as he'd taken her. She trembled so hard; the water sloshed over the top of the tub. Were she to dare, she wouldn't let go.

She sank up to her chin, inviting emptiness. But first came the soundless tears. She saw Wolf's dark eyes and kind face, and remembered when he'd held her afloat in the waters of Wannsee while the sky exploded in a cacophony of thunder, lightning, and cleansing rain.

THE DARK-BLUE WATERS, calm and hospitable, were dotted with sailboats and colorful tour cruisers. Wolf's muscular stroke of the paddle displaced enough water to pull them forward one full length of the canoe and more as it glided under a cloudless sky, its blue a never-ending allure. With languorous wrist, Charlotte let one hand trail alongside the canoe, defining their path, while the parted waters flowed back together, leaving no trace of it.

Despite the peacefulness of the day, she was wild with a kind of wanting that was new to her. While he talked of the book he was beginning, of a new religion he was creating that would end suffering, she imagined a frothy union awaited them, something elevated, transcendent. Meanwhile, the brutish side of sensuality overwhelmed her—the thrumming heat of the day, the water of the limpid lake. As they'd emerged from the dressing rooms clad only in bathing suits, she had been acutely aware of their age difference—nearly two decades. The fleshiness of their bodies was initially shocking, and the shock repeated itself each time her eyes landed on the curly, dark hair all over his stocky frame. He was not rugged, but strong and thick. She looked away, let her eyes roam over her own whiteness and smoothness. The extreme contrast between them was strange, fascinating, and a bit frightening.

How would they reach the mystical dissolve she imagined? A vast gap must be traversed from here, this dense, weighty corporeality, to there, the realm of spiritual distillation. The effort of imagining just how this might be accomplished whipped up an internal frenzy, a tornado-like funnel of passion, which she hoped would lift her off somehow.

Wolf paddled into a cove partially sheltered by a dense stand of reeds and beached the canoe on its sandy shore. They lay in the sand for a good, long rest, both quiet. She peered at him when he had his eyes closed. He looked younger without his glasses. His lips were relaxed.

There was something so familiar about him. If she were a man, she felt she would be him. She was sure that this was love like there had never been before. She drifted into a daydream: he lay on top of her, his arms encircling her head. In his lips, the current of his ardor urged her to consent.

Wolf opened his eyes. "Looks like rain," he said. The sky had gone from clear to overcast to dark and threatening in the time they had been lying there. "Let's swim."

He ran and she followed, kicking up the hot sand with their bare feet. They picked their way past the reeds. He glided through the water as she splattered her way in. They swam toward each other, away, and in circles, an arm sliding along a leg in passing, fingers grazing toes. He held her afloat on her back. Her pale knees, then her feet, broke the lake's surface. Her hair streamed behind her. The waves picked up. The rain came, light for a moment, then steady, building, peaking, and in another instant, torrential. The blackened sky rumbled. He pulled her, still horizontal, toward him until the side of her body pressed against his chest. Her breath caught in her throat. She looked at him, searching for his gaze. He was looking beyond her. Her eyes followed his. On the distant shore, lightning cracked the sky in two. His face lit up in a momentary white radiance. A clap of thunder exploded like a bomb had gone off. Her body tensed in terror, then shuddered. Suddenly he let her collapse under her own weight. He motioned to her to head for shore, where together they turned the canoe upside-down to drain the water.

"I wasn't expecting lightning. Fortunately, it didn't hit the water. We should not have gone in. Were you scared?" He draped a wet towel over her shoulders.

"No," she said. She meant that she would never be scared while being held by him, but she could not say it. They took to the shelter of the reeds and sat silently, their heels pulled into their bodies, their arms wrapped around their knees, letting the rain rinse away the afternoon.

When the storm had subsided, they righted the canoe and paddled back to their starting point under a clearing sky.

CHARLOTTE SURRENDERED to the bathwater. It lifted her body up and away from the thought of what her grandfather had done to her. She spoke to herself: *I will not let that man destroy me.*

In the morning, she drank glass after glass of water, standing at the kitchen window, staring out. While she dried the glass, the swirling dish towel stirred up the memory of her mother.

Straight-backed at a window, had her mother been looking outward or in? Either way, a vast abyss claimed her. Sometimes Lotte waited until she turned. Her mother's eyes used to grow wide with alarm, as though she'd forgotten she had a child.

Always, at every window, it was there, this image of her. And something hovering. Just beyond reach. Charlotte wondered what it might be like had influenza not torn her mother from her young life. She would have saved her from her grandfather's clutches. She was sure of it. Now, Eva Salomon was known to her not only as her dear mother who had died of a terrible illness, but as a daughter of a disgusting and hateful man.

Outside this cottage window, Charlotte could make out a parallelogram of distant sea, calm under diamond-clear skies.

On the pretext of going to market to shop, she smuggled out her supply case with a jam jar of water and mounted one of the bicycles always available behind the kitchen door of the Great House. She scooted out the driveway, flew down Rue Cauvin, and took the road to Nice.

The sun was white-hot. Even with a brimmed straw hat, she squinted. She pedaled eight kilometers to the bay. A few motor yachts at lazy anchor volleyed the afternoon light back and forth. She clattered down the rocky shore to sit on a pebbly patch, away from strewn seaweed. Nearby, a young boy flew a kite, a bright-yellow rhombus floating in the blue high above. The colors of the sea were changing shades of aquamarine, lime, turquoise, emerald, azure, and cerulean. Waves rolled gently in and splashed away the colors, scrubbing the water to complete transparency. Her inner tides merged with the sea.

Just seeing her tools for watercolor spread on the rocks lifted her up and away from the horror of the previous night. Her time was short, but watercolor went quickly. She started two paintings by applying a wash to the second while the first dried.

She knew she hadn't yet found her ultimate subject. For now, the sea. Tricky to catch a subject in ceaseless movement. When she'd finished the two paintings, she let her work dry while she lay down, looked up at the sky, and allowed herself to be transported. When she returned to l'Ermitage, she left her paintings on Olive's bed, then rushed to the cottage to make supper.

A WEEK PASSED, and Charlotte hadn't seen Olive to find out how she liked her paintings. Nights were restless, with feelings of vengeance. Images of her grandfather in his death mask, sometimes with blood on her hands, helped her finally to sleep. Days she was on the beach, where she felt she belonged. She missed Wolf's input and Professor Beck's comments, and even those of the other students. But here by the sea, lonesome feelings drifted out toward the horizon.

She'd been working on a single painting using a technique new to her—casein as the underlayer in dark tones, then a buildup with watercolors in progressively lighter ones. Each application needed to dry completely, or it would all turn to mud. Today she finished with a strong white for the foam.

While she was sitting on the rocks, a man approached, a hat shadowing his face. As he got closer, she spotted his limp and saw who it was.

"Henri! What are you doing here?"

"Out for a stroll. Olive gave me some time off today."

He found a seat next to her and craned his neck to look at her lap easel. She wasn't attuned to people viewing her work but supposed it couldn't be helped when one painted in public.

"Remarkable."

He entered a state of absorption. Then he emerged.

"Most artists here are after the dazzling surface. You've caught the depth of the sea not as playground, but as the sequester of losses. Hmm…" He paused. "It's like something threatens to surface. Needs to be retrieved."

He looked at her with full regard and appreciation. In an inner space, Charlotte felt an opening, as though an underwater sea creature were leaving off its camouflage.

He spoke about his refugee work, which made her wonder whether her father and Katharina would be able to get to France. Her father had explained their plan to meet her in the South of France and sail to America just as soon as the papers were in order. She recalled his promise.

"Someday we will return. Or perhaps we'll have made new lives, happy and full, where it's safe to be a Jew. I can research and practice as a doctor. Katharina can sing on any stage. And a Jewish artist may show her work in a gallery, a show, even a museum. Where you, Lotte, will enroll in an American art academy."

She tuned back into Henri. "Though the borders are closed," he said, "the police don't send people back. The unfortunate German Jews of the SS *St. Louis* were lucky that France agreed to take a couple hundred of them in."

Charlotte recalled the terrible news this summer when more than nine hundred Jews remained aboard the ship after two months, having crossed the Atlantic twice. With dwindling rations and unhygienic conditions, they had waited in extreme desperation for asylum back in Europe. The incident had given Charlotte some pause—great was her gratitude that she had gotten out and avoided that fate. It wasn't until she heard from her parents that she was able to have some relief. Thankfully, they had not been on the SS *St. Louis*, but they were still in Germany.

Henri said, "Those poor souls might have been the last refugees admitted. And now decree laws make them illegal, criminals no country really wants. All the refugees are stuck. The whole thing is a mess."

He was speaking politics while his gaze was personal, enjoying her. For a moment she felt confused, sitting alone with a man. Well, hardly alone. They were, after all, on a public beach, and he was speaking with perfect propriety. Yet the genuineness of his smile, the warmth in his eyes, the confessional tone in his voice—all felt like an invitation of sorts. Was she just so starved for attention and companionship that she needed to think so?

They both rubbed their hands over the stones between them, feeling their differing shapes, their warm surfaces. She mused a moment, thinking of his work caring for children—Olive's too—and of Max trying to find homes for them. Since she'd arrived at l'Ermitage, she'd often thought about why she didn't do something more immediately useful. She'd concluded she was too inclined to make pictures, too dreamy to trust herself with the lives of others. She wanted Henri to know how much she admired his work.

"Action, especially the kind that's aimed at the welfare of others—that's what keeps the world turning. Art, by comparison, is selfish. A kind of surrender. To escape the loneliness."

"Ah! But art may save your life." He paused. "And others' too."

"I'd like to think that. My hope is that someday I'll have a meaningful place in the world. Instead of standing apart, I'll belong to humanity."

The rhythm of their voices, back and forth like the gentle waves rolling up the shore and sliding back to sea, left space for contemplation. And in these quiet moments—much more so than in what was said—she felt the birthing of a genuine rapport. Then, when he asked her how she felt about the war, her heart went leaden.

"The country of my refuge at war with the country of my origin? What's wrong with people that they need to kill each other en masse? What's to become of Germany and France when this is over? What's to become of my family?" She picked up a small rock and massaged it with her thumb. "It's the most difficult thing to know what to think about humanity. About being a human being. To know how to live each day. When I think of soldiers going to war—young men, like you and Max—no one should be expendable. And I'm afraid I may be, too."

He looked a little dazed by her onslaught of words. "It's certainly put an end to progress the French were making on getting the decrees against refugees revoked," he said. "The government was developing programs for them to participate in the economy. Now there's only short-term help. Food, clothing, a place to sleep. What's to become of these forty thousand souls who thought they had made it to safety within France's borders?"

They looked at each other without speaking. Charlotte believed that he, too, was aware that the refugees were not only some others. The two of them were refugees, and though their life at l'Ermitage was without the hardship of so many, as Jews they were equally unsafe.

The pall that had fallen over them grew denser, heavier, sadder. It seemed neither would ever speak. Suddenly cheering up with unflappable surety, Henri said, "The good news? This war won't last long."

She was about to ask him on what grounds he could say something like that when she realized she'd stayed an hour longer than intended. They rose, brushed bits of tiny rock from their clothing, and bid each other farewell. Gone their separate ways—he to continue his walk down the beach, she back to Villefranche—in the same moment, they happened to glance back. It was as if Charlotte just now recognized a person she'd known a very long time.

CHAPTER 6

VILLEFRANCHE-SUR-MER

DECEMBER 1939

Charlotte's loneliness during the winter was extreme. She avoided long mornings with Olive for fear she would ask about her grandparents, setting off the memory of her grandfather in her bed.

Olive did sell two of Charlotte's paintings for five hundred francs. She promised Charlotte more buyers and indicated a possible commission for creating greeting cards. She even offered to procure pigments and paper. Charlotte's grandparents claimed that Olive was bribing her, that she would take her away from them. Her grandmother staged a fit at the front door of the Great House, demanding that Olive's "girl" sweep the path to their cottage. Olive retrieved a broom, walked Charlotte's grandmother around back toward the cypresses, put the broom in her hand, and said, "Here, Princess Marina. Sweep it yourself."

It had become clear: Charlotte had to get them to agree to move before Olive threw them out. When, finally, she was able to extract their grudging consent, she informed Olive, who made clear once again that Charlotte was welcome to stay and move into the Great House. Charlotte toyed with the idea only briefly. Life at the chateau had insulated her grandparents from the outside world for over six years. Charlotte wasn't sure of their ability to survive on their own.

One day, she had a moment with Henri after he and Max had returned from foraging for nettles, wild onions, and acorns. Anneliese had already indicated that he and Olive had "run their course," and Charlotte had become more at ease with him, admiring his way with the children, his skills at carpentry and mechanical things, and his readiness to take any job offered by Dr. Mercier, who seemed a father figure. Despite his limp, Henri walked through life light and buoyant, without false optimism nor a dour outlook, yet at times she detected a deep sadness tamped down.

Aware of the gap between him and Olive, Charlotte couldn't help wanting more of his attention. He drew a garden chair disturbingly close, stretched out his bad leg, and urged her to let her grandparents go.

"You must move into the Great House. They managed all right before you arrived." His scar had receded into a face ruddy and moist from hours of labor. "Olive has asked you for some work."

It was true. Olive had asked her to paint the gardens at l'Ermitage.

"There's space and light, and she'll provide you with any tools you need. She'll be sorry if you don't."

"It can't be helped. I'm duty-bound." Though Henri's sincerity touched her, the idea of Olive and Henri still talking about her started up the mixer of her emotions—disappointment, irritation, loneliness—and she couldn't help exclaiming, "What do you care what I do?"

"I care because I don't want you to become enslaved when you're clearly meant to be an artist." Then he leaned forward and looked straight at her. "Correction there. *Are* an artist."

Charlotte reeled from the shock of how his eyes searched hers, how well he understood her. For an odd moment, perhaps because the sun flashed through the bare oak in a certain way, his eyes blazed as limpid a green as shore-bound waters. She let them find hers. There was something vast, like the sea between the continents, that both connected them and kept them apart.

IT TOOK CHARLOTTE a month to find a place for the three of them, because refugees from Eastern Europe, who had flocked to Paris during the 1937 World's Fair, had then gravitated south from Paris to avoid costly rents. The new apartment was on Rue Neuscheller in the old quarter of Nice, in a turret at the top of a centuries-old mansion, the whole of which recently had been divided into apartments. Their small vestibule had two doors. One door went to the bathroom; the other led to the kitchen, beyond which was the main room, which served as both drawing room and dining room. In the vestibule, a narrow, wrought-iron, circular staircase led to the upper floor. At the top, under sloping eaves, was a single space that Charlotte coveted. With tall double windows that opened outward four stories above the courtyard, this large room had the best light. But it would be her grandparents' bedroom. The downstairs was neither airy nor light. They were all crammed in together during the day because Charlotte's room, on the far side of the main room, was too small for anything but sleep.

While unpacking, she had come across francs from the sale of her seascapes, and she remembered Olive's warning: *That's the important thing: to paint, no matter what's going on.* And about her earnings: *Save them. You never know when life may depend on a nest egg.*

It wasn't until the fourth day in the new apartment that Charlotte first heard the music. Beethoven. The slow opening strains of *Heiliger Dankgesang*. Somewhere in the building, a string quartet had gathered—two violins, a viola, and a cello. Chamber music. One saving grace.

Charlotte shopped for their food and other necessities, hauling everything up the steep lane. Rumors of rationing caused her, along with many others, to stockpile sugar, coffee, soap, rice, and oil. It was her job to scrub and scour and sweep. Hers, too, was the formidable and near-impossible task of keeping her grandmother in good spirits, especially in the face of terrifying news bulletins.

Germany was taking town after town in Poland. The anniversary of Pogromnacht followed an attempt on Hitler's life, which was in turn followed by SS Chief Heinrich Himmler issuing the death penalty for Jews who didn't report for deportation. At least—finally, she'd heard—her father and Katharina had made it out of Germany and into Amsterdam. But Charlotte did not know whether they were safe. Their letters, which were becoming fewer and farther in between and taking longer to reach her because they came by way of friends of the Salomons' in Switzerland who were willing to forward them, were always a bit too cheerful when she knew her father had lost all good cheer after his weeks of hard labor in freezing-cold Sachsenhausen.

The man who had returned after being required to walk the thirty-three kilometers from Oranienburg, who had stood in the doorway, had not at first appeared to be someone she knew. It had taken a moment for it to sink in. This man was of much smaller stature. This man was so thin, his clothes looked like they were on a hanger. His head and mustache had been shaved. Where both had been thick and dark, a little gray stubble had grown up. Pallor had taken possession of his face, marked by the hand of death.

Charlotte had thought then, as she did now: he was still her father, but something vital had been stolen from him.

The high point of her grandmother's week was *L'Univers israélite*, even though it upset her to read that her favorite editor, Raymond-Raoul Lambert, had gone off track. The muscles in her neck protruded as her manic, arthritic fingers paged through the paper.

"Psh! He's agreed to provisional asylum for foreigners." She pounded a gnarled fist on the table. "They should have full asylum. Full."

Her grandfather changed for the worse too. He didn't hesitate to give her grandmother a push. More than once, Charlotte had found her on the staircase, knocked down by him.

It was January, a month after the move and over a year since Charlotte had left Berlin. One day, Henri Nagel showed up at the apartment unannounced, panting from the climb up Rue Neuscheller. He was carrying a box of books that Luitger had left behind.

After wiping his brow with a handkerchief and rubbing the thigh of his bad leg, he told her that Max had enlisted in the Foreign Legion to ensure he wouldn't be arrested as an illegal, and that he himself was departing on a long trip to find safe housing for children. He would be traveling with Gabrielle on false identity papers provided by Dr. Mercier. Gabrielle was Delmira's niece, younger than Charlotte by five years, a mesmerizing French beauty with glowing skin and sleek, short hair, who bubbled endless good cheer. Posing as siblings—he as a Frenchman and Christian—they would travel to Catholic parishes, where Gabrielle's mother had in the past done housework for the Church. Thus, Gabrielle knew priests all along the coast.

The news unmoored Charlotte. Though she'd seen Henri only a few times since the move, times when she had been able to break away on the excuse of scavenging for food, it gave her some security to know he—and Anneliese and Max and Olive—were all there at l'Ermitage. Now that he was going off, she would not only be farther from him but not even know exactly where he was.

"Charlotte, there are a good many of us helping refugees, Jews and Christians together, who—"

But Charlotte barely heard him as she tried to think through what "posing as siblings" really meant. Was there something between Henri and Gabrielle? Her stomach hardened, and she clenched her teeth.

While they were conversing in the kitchen, a scuffle broke out on the stairs. Her grandfather, upon seeing the books, called Olive "that witch." Her grandmother stumbled into the kitchen, shouting at Henri. "Skirt chaser! Womanizer!"

Charlotte followed Henri out into the hall. He stepped close to her.

"I hope they're not treating you badly," he said. With her eyes cast down, she fought the feeling that everything was unbearable. She began to shake, her tears held in. Henri circled her with his arms. She softened against his chest and closed her eyes. Her cheek detected a lingering dampness under his shirt. She smelled the masculine odor of his sweat. The feeling of being soothed gave way to disturbing arousal. She shouldn't have confessed to him.

She pulled back and brushed away her tears with the back of her hand. "It's not your worry. I'll manage."

"But it is my worry." His lips pressed against her forehead. "Take care of yourself, Charlotte. Find a way out."

That night, her thoughts returned to Henri's imploring words. Had he meant that she should move back to l'Ermitage? How many nights had she sworn she'd go, let her grandparents fend for themselves? But they were not the sturdy people they once had been. Exile had diminished them. Despite much about them she disliked, even abhorred, she couldn't bring herself to walk out. Her grandfather barely managed the hill, and her grandmother wouldn't attempt it. They were incapable of shopping, cooking, and cleaning. How would they take care of themselves? But most of all, they were the parents of her mother—her poor mother, cut down by the flu before her time, and their poor daughter. And though she'd been bound to them in a circle of grief during all the time she'd been in France, she'd looked for her mother in them the way she used to look for a sign from her mother at the window. She'd found nothing, yet she could not tear her eyes away.

For them, there was only her. If something happened, to her grandmother especially, how could she ever face her father? She thought it through every which way, but it always came down to this: *No, I couldn't live with myself.*

CHAPTER 7

NICE

MARCH 1940

Katharina wrote that Wolf had moved to London and hoped to bring his sister and mother out soon. Off the continent, he might as well have been on another planet.

A month after Henri's visit, Marina took to bed. She had been wearing the same white nightdress for a week, dingy and stained with dribbles of soup and tea. The flow of her soul was despair, and she cried out. "Oh, the pain!"

This day was particularly difficult. She begged for morphine, and Luitger refused. When Charlotte called the doctor, he sent him away.

"You're so heartless, Grosspapa. Can't you hear her desperation?"

From his position on the sofa, he said, "We're doomed. I did my best to save us. She is beyond help. And I don't deserve this." He stood, fetched his hat, and brushed the lint from the brim. "I need a breath of fresh air. I'm going to visit Emmet."

Emmet Schatzman was a friend of Luitger's from Berlin, much milder in manner, even sweet of temperament. It was hard for Charlotte to understand how he could put up with Luitger. They had recently run into each other in the Cours Saleya market, and Luitger discovered that his old friend was living just down the street from them on Rue Neuscheller.

Charlotte went upstairs and flung the windows wide open. The quartet was playing Mozart, the adagio of a quintet. Minus one viola, it still managed to capture the deep melancholy of the piece.

The sky was gloriously clear, a blue that didn't exist in Germany, a blue that crackled and was at the same time serene. Charlotte took in a breath, imagined her blank white sheet of paper. How did one paint the unbounded? The way she painted the sea—no boats, no bathers, only water—that was how she would paint the sky. She would start with a rich blue wash, then apply multiple layers, each progressively lighter than the one before. Would this catch it? She wouldn't know until she tried.

"Life is wonderful, Grossmama. Do you ever wonder how we come to be here? I can't help but believe in the great mystery. You must too."

"Don't be a moron." The rasp of her voice grated, and her words pressed Charlotte beyond her limit.

The previous week, her grandfather had delivered a stunning blow by blurting to her in private, "You should know, Lotte, Marina has attempted to hang herself four times."

His tone had been flat, as though he were reading a news brief about a stranger. Charlotte hadn't been able to speak. The wind had gone out of her. After a moment of disbelief, she'd understood. Her grandmother's condition was so much worse than she'd imagined. She recalled her own inclination to throw herself onto the train tracks of the Anhalter Bahnhof rather than leave Berlin. She knew that hopelessness.

She had not wanted to board the train, to be sent out of Germany, to leave her family, her home, her country. She had longed to lie between the rails, arms clamped to her sides, staring up at the roof of iron arches where a pigeon flapped, frantic, from pane to pane, uncomprehending, seeking a way out.

But here was the blue sky, the resurrection that was possible. How could her grandmother believe her world was disappearing when Charlotte believed it would be restored?

After his declaration about Marina's suicide attempts, Charlotte's grandfather started spending long hours away. At home, he would cry, "I'm tougher than you, old bag!"

When Charlotte brought up his cruelty to her grandmother, she replied only, "He's an old man, an old, old man." A sigh of feigned compassion followed, but in that out-breath, Charlotte detected a loyalty beyond her comprehension.

THE NEXT DAY, the windows in the upper bedroom were open all the way out on their hinges, and her grandmother stood with her back to Charlotte in her thin nightdress, so tiny, shrunken, and frail, looking weightless and insubstantial, like something from the spirit world that might slowly rise off the ground and drift out the window. Without turning, Marina spoke into the air above the courtyard.

"Germany's going to invade France. I feel it in my bones." Her voice was toneless. "I lived through one war. I can't take another."

Charlotte had to get her away from the window. She would say anything.

"I burned the porridge, Grossmama. Come with me. I've some ground acorn and chicory. We'll brew some ersatz coffee."

After slowly negotiating the spiral staircase together, they settled at the dining table.

"I've lost everything. Everyone. My friends. My Jewish life. The Berlin poetry circles."

Her grandmother's pain was so palpable, a wave of nausea came over Charlotte, but she summoned the strength to speak. "That war ended. This one will too. The Americans will have to enter. You'll go back with your books and paintings, your poetry."

Her grandmother's eyes were cast down, her whole being swirling in the murky brown of her cup. Then she looked at Charlotte.

"The Jews are lost."

"Oh, Grossmama, the Jews have never been lost. Exiled, yes. They've had to wander. Hide. Lie low. But endured. Look. Here we are. Jews. In the middle of these horrors, we live."

"Germany will never welcome us back. The Nazis have poisoned the people. Dear Lotte, you must let me go. Even if there's a future in Berlin, I don't have it in me to get there."

The more intimate their exchange, the more Charlotte felt a great chasm between them.

"My darling, listen," her grandmother continued. "I'm on the verge of madness. I know this all too well, and I accept it. You must too."

Charlotte had tried to be a boulder rolled over the cave of her grandmother's despair. But all along, the despair had been more like rushing water—ignoring boulders, finding its own course, and flowing around.

Charlotte took her grandmother's cool, bony hands in hers, looking into eyes that were two pits of torment—bottomless, dark, and unfathomable. She was not a boulder, but a pebble thrown into the river of sorrow. She was sinking under the great weight of having to hold them both up.

"Depend on me, Grossmama, to pull you through this."

"No. I can't tie my life to yours, Lotte. You've too much yourself to deal with in exile. You're the one who must go on. Because you're the one who has something to offer the world."

Charlotte's heart skidded in her regret: She had no tools to save her grandmother. As she sensed the unstoppable, she ached in her helplessness.

"Leave Luitger. That man is bent on doing you in. It doesn't matter to him that you are his granddaughter. I guarantee it. He will destroy you." Marina's cup held the dregs. "Go, Lotte. Become an artist."

THE FOLLOWING DAY, Charlotte was sketching the disarray on the dining table. Her grandfather was out. Her grandmother sat opposite, holding pen and paper. How long could this delicate stability last?

Her grandfather returned with a letter for her grandmother.

"This came to you in care of Emmet."

She read it, the paper rustling in her shaky hand.

"Oh, no! Gertrude Mahlick died!" She screeched.

Her grandfather said, "Dead? Who, then, has written?"

"A relative. A cousin, she says." She looked up at Luitger. "Someone Emmet must know?" He shrugged.

"But you haven't seen Gertrude in, what? Forty years?"

"She was once a dear friend. The last left in Germany. Amazing that it found its way."

A second letter was enclosed within the first. Her grandmother fingered the onion-skin stationery. As she read, she became still. Then she bent over, crying, "Aiiiii!"

He walked to the window, stared down into the courtyard. Marina marched upstairs.

THAT NIGHT, there was shouting from above, both voices; also the sounds of a tussle, clunking noises, possibly books knocked off the nightstand. Charlotte was on her way up the staircase to intervene when it all stopped. She retreated. In the morning, she found her grandfather sleeping on the sofa. As soon as he became aware of her, he got up and went out.

Upstairs her grandmother lay in bed, curled tight, chin to chest. She pulled a hand from under the covers and shoved the letter at Charlotte, saying, "From Gertrude."

> *Marina: My lovely daughter, Eugenia, you remember her? Your Eva's friend? Before I die, I want you to know that Luitger molested her and, as a result, she has spent her entire adult life in an insane asylum.*
> *— G.*

Charlotte's hand flew to her heart, and her palm pressed against her breastbone.

Her grandmother whispered, "He visited our daughters' beds." She started with a jerk, then cried out her shame. "I knew what he was doing!" Her fierce eyes were within inches of Charlotte's. She grabbed the neckline of Charlotte's blouse, her breath hot and fusty. "Oh, mercy! I could have saved them."

All Charlotte could think of was how she had held her grandfather at bay with the threat of telling her grandmother what he'd done to her, while all along Marina had known his vileness. Her flesh went to steel, trying to keep out the thoughts of Aunt Charlotte. And her mother.

Charlotte stretched out beside her grandmother and stroked her loose hair. Long, thin, damp strands spread over the pillow like seaweed on the surface of the ocean. The old woman reeked with the off smell of a curdled spirit. They lay silent, still, and tearless.

After a long while, agony gave way.

"Make him tell you," her grandmother said. "Because— mark my words—something happened."

"Something happened? What, Grossmama? What happened?"

She drifted. "Never mind."

Coming from the courtyard, Tchaikovsky's first quartet began. Sorrow needed no buttressing, so before the second movement, Charlotte got up and shut the windows.

Marina wanted to put on her black day dress with buttons from collar to hem, and even her sturdy black boots. She asked Charlotte to fix her hair, and when it was all pinned, she agreed to some scrambled eggs.

"You'll feel better if you eat something."

Charlotte watched the eggs firm up in the pan while wanting to dart out of the apartment and straight into the middle of town, screaming. Then she remembered Wolf saying how we must face our suffering. "It is the only path to freedom." Still, she was cheered, though apprehensive, by her grandmother's sudden readiness for this day. Resolve gelled as she imagined walking arm in arm through the stately, manicured Massena gardens among the bobbing heads of roses. Taking the awkward, upward curve into the dark stairwell, she decided to propose this plan to her grandmother.

The rumpled bed was empty, the windows flung open.

The tray fell, egg bits flying, cutlery clattering. She rushed across the room. Below, on the cobblestone, a black heap of ruin. A tangle of white hair. A flow of dark crimson.

In a haze, she made for the narrow staircase, ran out the apartment door, spun down three more flights, and flew into the courtyard.

The limbs were unnaturally rotated by the torque of the fall. It had to be a broken thigh bone protruding, making the black dress stand up tentlike, exposing a leg. Head to one side, one eye like a fish on ice.

Now she was seeing it. This was death.

CHAPTER 8

─────

NICE

The corpse was removed to the synagogue on Boulevard Dubouchage. The congregation took care of the ritual washing and burial rites. While Charlotte stood over the grave, staring into the bottomless gullet of death, she ceased to think of the old man standing next to her as her grandfather.

The courtyard had been scrubbed to a gleam. Neighbors left a pot of soup, a basket of boiled eggs. Luitger's friend, Emmet Schatzman, who had come to the grave-site, brought a tin of ersatz coffee and black-market chocolate. Her grandmother's insistent words haunted her: *something happened.*

She notified Luitger, "I'm not cleaning or cooking until you tell me."

She retreated to her room, took out her sketch pad and charcoal. His eyes came first—Wolf's—soft and attentive, almond-shaped. His face was oval with pudgy cheeks, his thin lips gently parted. Lightly there. Lines in his forehead, two horizontal, two more standing vertical in the space between his eyes, thick-rimmed glasses perched beneath. She filled in the outline. Bushy eyebrows so wild, they appeared to be looking for a trellis to climb, and black waves brushed back from the perfect S-curve of his hairline.

The pounding came. She opened her door. His arms hung by his side; his posture sagged.

"Marina lost a daughter. We did. Together. Lost her." His voice was barely audible. "Charlotte, your aunt."

Charlotte backed up a step.

Then he exploded with more volume. "I never approved of your being kept in the dark. Never. Damn it! And now it's fallen to me."

When they were seated on the sofa, he dropped his head, an old man sunken into sorrow. A big gulp of breath braced him. "One day, our Charlotte walked out of the house and slipped into the river."

Charlotte gasped. Her aunt. Her namesake. Eighteen years old. A willful act, not an accident. *Slipped into the river.* Her mind slipping, as a shiver ran through her.

"Your grandmother lost eight relatives." His tone was pitiless, his expression opaque.

Her throat caught, dry. A whole family's worth of people.

"First her brother, Willi. An ambitious young man with talent, studying law. He began to show signs."

"What kind of signs?" The signs seemed all-important.

"He laughed at inappropriate moments. Loudly. His mother, your great-grandmother, had a garden house where he lived. With an actual guard. No visitors. He finished his studies. He married on the advice of his doctors. For stability. But his mother was a formidable woman. She'd insisted on a girl of class and wealth over the one he loved. He was weak. He yielded and became an unhappy man. He couldn't bear to live in his own home. He came to us." Her grandfather wheezed, the telling taking him to the end of his breath. "The distress this caused Marina—every day, it was: what could she do, what could she do? Then he drowned himself. Which is when his mother, drenched in guilt, tried to take her own life. It fell on us to hire nurses. Eight years. In the end, she died a natural death. Only because she was watched over and never left alone."

This was the history of Charlotte's family, yet it felt like it had nothing to do with her. She made a storybook by putting the pictures in her mind onto pages—the young law student, the rich girl, the garden house, the domineering mother.

"Why have I never been told?"

"Your grandmother was very close to her Uncle Scheinfeld. A melancholy man. She could cheer him up. But then one day, right before her eyes, he leaped out the window."

Charlotte's body jerked violently, like an electric jolt had been applied. Her grandfather licked his lips in a kind of relish at how his words assaulted her.

"Impossible, you think? So many in one family?"

Inside her, a paroxysm. She closed her eyes, ran her hands through her hair, grabbing and pulling hard at her scalp, as if she could extract the knowledge right out of her brain, herself out of this reality—make it all unsaid.

"I don't believe you. Or understand why you're making up this wild tale."

He walked over to the window. His syncopated, halting limbs reminded her of a puppet's. The sound of a ball being kicked around rose from the courtyard. "Children. Ach!" Then he adopted a pedagogical air. "Most likely the cause is a brain disorder, a mental imbalance. Commonly runs in families. It's in the psychiatric literature. No matter what you do—believe me, I tried."

She was as undone by his rehearsed manner as by this monumental revelation. She said, "But there are five more."

He returned to the sofa and explained how Marina's sister and her sister's husband both overdosed on veronal—together. How her brother Willi had had two children, and one of them, the girl—"See what I mean?"

Charlotte saw. And she did not see.

He went on. "Lately, there've been outside factors. Germany at war. Jews living in exile. I don't have to tell you. Finally, the boy too, Marina's nephew. She'd just gotten word from Berlin. It all compounds in a person with her history."

It all compounds? "You said eight. I count only seven."

He dropped his arms, covered his mouth, stared at the rug.

Her teeth, which had been clicking ever since he had appeared at her bedroom door, stopped. It dawned on her. She whispered, "My mother."

He looked up. His eyes glowed, blue neon. "Your mother didn't die of the flu, Lotte. Eva threw herself out the window."

Charlotte's heart picked up, thumping in her ears. Not influenza? But she had been sick in bed. Meaning what? She had not had that horrid illness?

All Charlotte saw were windows. She had killed herself? Windows released from walls, the frames simply afloat. And beckoning.

She clutched her throat. Mama had jumped? From which window had she—? The drawing-room window, where she always stood? The one by her bed? Her own, where she'd waited for the promised letter?

She pressed her fingers against her closed eyes, trying to blot out what she already knew. It couldn't have been. No. But it was. Suicide?

She couldn't move. Her whole body was numb. She must herself be dead.

"You're the last remaining in the maternal line. Now you know your inheritance." He put an index finger on her clavicle and tapped three times. "Mark my words. It's your destiny too."

Her chest collapsed. She could barely breathe. She ran to her room, shut the door, and threw herself on the bed, stuffing the pillow into her mouth, muffling the sound of her howl. Her body rocked. And it kept coming, the eerie, unearthly sound and the motion of her body as a fit seized her. She bolted upright to throw it off. It would not throw.

Her window. Right there. Opened, to air the room. She looked down into the courtyard. She'd always known. Standing by every window, what she'd felt hovering just outside, the unnamable thing beyond—it wasn't nothing. It was real all along, this colossal secret.

Below, housewives and mothers jabbered as though here, yesterday, nothing had happened. A toy wagon rattled its wheels on the pavement right where her grandmother had lain. Charlotte felt the despair from her grandmother's soul flow into hers.

A rope dangled from the window pull and coiled on the floor, far more length than needed to open the window to a tilt. Her body was numb, her head light. She could hear her own shallow, rapid breathing.

She dragged the chair as far away from the window as possible and wrapped the free end of the rope around the leg of the bed and then the leg of the chair. She sat and bound her own leg to both. No matter the terrors of the night to come, at least she'd be alive in the morning.

She picked up the drawing of Wolf and held it to her chest, remembering his story of the Great War.

"WE WERE WITHOUT ORDERS. The bottom half of my body was sunk into the sludge of earth, water, blood, entrails, and excrement. A comrade called for help—my help. 'Wolf, help me!' I cut off my boots with a bayonet to save myself from sinking into the mud and dying. I was crawling away just as something went off. I awoke under a pile of corpses. I heard the cries of the dying calling for God or their mothers, sounds that were inhuman. They were, in fact, deeply human. Utterances at the extreme end of emotion, at the breaking point of the soul."

He had talked of his days in a sanitarium in Italy where he went to recover from war, from having left a comrade to die in a trench. A veil had come over his face, as though he had gone elsewhere while talking. Charlotte had started to understand the inner sadness she'd observed in him from the day he'd first arrived at the apartment.

"One day," he told her, "I climbed Vesuvius. When I got to the summit, I could see the sky and sea, where they came together, the horizon, blue to blue dissolving into union. What I saw, I heard as musical harmony: one single, sustained note. It still vibrates within me. It is me. The secret of sight and sound, music and me, everything."

This struck her as familiar—in theory, anyway. "Synesthesia. Like Kandinsky."

"Listen to what I'm saying. I was saved. From death and the destruction of war. The way was music. Which is why I became a voice teacher. Do you see why I tell you?"

She hadn't answered. She was waking up to something of immense importance.

"My sphinx? Because we all must come to know ourselves. No matter how bad our suffering. It is our job to tread through the dark underbelly of our consciousness and experiences and the world we live in, and find the path through. And the most important thing is not to pose, not to pretend to others or to ourselves. To completely love life, one must embrace and understand the other side—death and suffering."

A FIRE ROARED INSIDE HER. The air was stifling hot, the atmosphere in the room blazing orange. She prayed.

"Please, God, let me not also go mad."

CHAPTER 9

NICE

MAY 1940

It had been two months since her grandmother's suicide. Each day had been a slow, underwater somersault through time. For weeks she had lain limp on her bed, unable to push up against the weight on her chest, to throw it off and claim the day. Her mind wandered into speculation about madness. Or contemplated Luitger's grotesque violations. Her stomach went into a state beyond nausea, as though the pouch of it was turned inside out. Recalling what he had done to her—of course, she believed her grandmother. It bled into her, her grandmother's shame.

Occasionally the outside world came to her through a newspaper, like the day Luitger brought home *Le Petit Niçois*. It seemed the French believed that the Germans didn't have either the means or the stomach for war. It was unclear. But the sentiment was that the French were winning: *and Warsaw will ring the bells of resurrection*, the paper proclaimed. Charlotte became optimistic in one moment, but in the next, suspicious that this kind of talk reflected a mere lull in hostilities. The worst part was that there was no way to know, and this not knowing added to her anxiety and ennui.

She was alone with her grandfather, and his bony fingers gripped her shoulder from behind. She flinched, and her entire body recoiled. She would not become his Eugenia Mahlick. Her shoulders rolled back, and she whipped around. The look in his blue eyes was cool and fierce.

She needed to confront him and decided not to be cowed. Restrictions had been instituted, a whole system of them, which limited what foods were available. It had become difficult to find olive oil or butter. She could not find a bakery that was permitted to make rolls. Baguettes were very dear. Even the hotels were having problems with procurement. Everything was going to the troops in the field. Luitger's miserliness was not helping.

"Why are you giving me less money for shopping?"

He claimed that they'd run short, and he'd had to sell Marina's jewels.

"Nothing. They amounted to nothing. On the black market. Pfft!"

She didn't believe him. But it hadn't taken her long this morning, while he was out, to determine that the jewels were gone. The amethyst ring. The emerald brooch. She wished she'd taken possession of them while she had had the chance.

She walked the five kilometers to Villefranche to see Olive about that job making greeting cards, which she hoped would save their situation.

Olive said, "The woman in Nice who was looking to sell cards made by local artists was American, and she's picked up stakes. Gone home."

CHARLOTTE SAT on the beach, watching a barefoot man amble along. He was carrying his shoes the way Wolf had on the shore of Wannsee, slung over his shoulders. His stocky stature, large head, and curly black hair also reminded her of Wolf.

When the chestnut trees were in flower—with their feathery white stalks drooping every which way, their musky odor thick and damp—she had met Wolf in cafés in the Tiergarten and Lietzenseepark. Her throat thickened. She wanted to be sitting next to him on a park bench, listening to his interpretation of the Orpheus myth and the nature of the human soul.

She missed her father. She wanted to be in his study after Shabbat dinner, with Katharina, curled up on the sofa opposite them, bundled in a knit blanket, sipping the last of the deep-red wine and staring into the fire, watching the flames leap and smelling the smoke of a fresh-hewn log being consumed while they discussed important political matters.

All afternoon she remained on the beach, thinking over the last twenty-four hours.

A scattering of fully dressed people, neither tourists nor natives—people like herself, other refugees—sat on the rocks and stared at the horizon. Thoughts of her family members who took their lives arrived, ghostlike. Who exactly were they? She opened her pad and began to build a family tree. She named each person in relation to herself. She didn't know all the names. In some cases, she didn't even know the manner of suicide. Yet collectively, they were nearly her whole family, thrown into the fire of the past, their lives consumed. Nothing passed along—not a letter or diary, nor a ring or pocket watch. Nothing. Except their absence. And the horrifying determination to end their lives.

The last spot, she left blank. She stared back into the moment of dawning knowledge. *Eva threw herself out the window.*

The waves, though merely lapping, suddenly sounded with a roar. All those years she believed the influenza story— She twitched, scratching the palms of her hands over the rough rock, wanting to blame her father and Katharina. Why had she not been told? She could have kept it a secret. She imagined them saying they had only tried to protect her. But it was her mother. She had had a right to know.

Exhausted and feeling lost, she slept awhile. When she woke, she sensed something important had been delivered to her in a dream. But the dream escaped her.

The sun descended, handsome yellow orb, tossing up pink and apricot streaks into the fading blue sky, casting purplish-mauve shadows onto the underside of clouds. Then it sank, leaving a more intense orange above, blending into magenta at the horizon, both colors reflected in the calm aquamarine water of the bay. Soon it would be dark.

What was it that must be averted? How should she protect herself? Against what—a mood, a thought, a person, a shadow? Or was she, too, doomed?

The surface of the sea turned deep teal. It dimmed and drained away. A dark-blue hue seemed to push up from below, unable to survive against the black seeping from the depths and gaining on it, as though a source of ink had been loosed from the ocean floor. She whispered, "Dream, speak to me." The sky tried to survive in sudden turquoise before light finally leaked out of the world.

THEN SHE KNEW. She could refuse this inheritance.

Many a young man tossed off his father's wealth to make his own way in the world. She breathed the soft sea air. The bracing salt quickened her lungs.

Yes. She refused her destiny. Even here alone, in exile, with war raging on the continent and without vision of the future, still there remained vision—beauty in the world, nearly unbearable, and tenderness in living, hardly endurable, both holding her fast to the promise that she could retrieve life itself from this inheritance. What she had not witnessed, she would remember and make manifest in shape and color.

Curiously, the night's shroud brought ease. Only a few people strolled, wearing their meditative states like shawls.

The water rolled back from the shore, pulling up into a long, gentle curl. Aloud, as though the sea's wave was a rising, listening ear, she whispered into it, "I will live for them all."

CHAPTER 10

———

NICE

JUNE 1940

Charlotte was unlatching the window over the sink when Luitger walked in and dropped a newspaper on the butcher block with a *thap*. Then a hand on her behind was like a sickly pink, segmented, parasitic worm had slid down her throat. She whirled around and stepped sideways.

"Armistice!" He pointed to a copy of *L'Eclaireur de Nice et du Sud-Est*. "Three days to come into effect."

Her insides still shuddering, she waited for him to leave so she could read.

Less than a month before, she had spotted a public notice in the Nice papers announcing that all female German nationals must present themselves at the Gurs center in the Pyrenées. But who would freely go? Explosions had been resounding from the high ground down into the valleys, caused by the French blowing up essential military infrastructure—bridges, tunnels, roads. Apparently, this preventive maneuver hadn't worked. Now France had fallen to the Third Reich. A dizzy, nauseous sensation dragged her into a whirlpool of fear and confusion. Had it all been for nothing—her escape from Germany, her failure to save her grandmother, her daily endurance of Luitger?

Were the Nazis coming to Nice? Should they flee? She had the urge to go to l'Ermitage, talk to Olive or Anneliese or Henri, who for sure would have a good idea of what it all meant. But she was too afraid and stayed put. She even thought of consulting Luitger's friend, Emmet, who kept abreast of things and had good sense, but she was afraid that would arouse her grandfather's ire. In order to not go mad with fear, she returned to her project of the last month: approaching the lives of her family's suicides in paint. She looked on the act of painting as the making of memory for them.

One was of her great-uncle. She had divided the sheet in the way of Chagall, except she created discrete panels. In the first, she put the figure of the ambitious young lawyer Willi, suited up, attaché case in hand, ascending the steps to the courts. He must have felt such promise about his future. In the next panel, he faced forward, eyes wild, mouth twisted bizarrely wide open in a laugh. Was he as disturbed as everyone else by what was happening to his mind? In the third panel, a man in uniform stood guard near the door of a little cottage. In the window was Willi, no longer laughing. Next was sad Willi at his marriage ceremony, with the woman he did not love beside him in white bridal lace. His true love was in the shadows. In the last scene, a turbulent sky, black and brown, moved over roiling river waters, brown and dark green, without much distinction between the sky and water. The viewer might just make out the faint outline of a bridge and, in the air, a small figure—it could almost be a bird, but it was him. Her great-uncle. Willi. He had leapt.

She painted Willi's mother, her great-grandmother, with a look of shock permanently imprinted upon her face, two nurses holding her up.

And one of her grandmother's sister and her sister's husband lying in bed, his arm outstretched toward the floor, where lay the empty bottle marked with a V for veronal. How was it they were not able to pull each other through?

The latest was Grossmama's Uncle Scheinfeld stepping out the window. But Charlotte felt she hadn't gotten it right yet.

Luitger barged into her room uninvited. "The apartment's filthy. Marina is gone two months. Enough wallowing. It's time you started taking care of things."

Charlotte put aside her work, swung her legs to the floor, and stood.

"I'm not a housekeeper, a washwoman, or a cook. And I'm not 'wallowing.' I'm an artist. You continually deny that fact, but your denial does not alter the truth. My job is to paint—"

"This isn't painting." He surveyed the work taped to the wall. "Horrifying circumstances. Terribly rendered. It's sickness. Obsession."

"Obsession? Perhaps. But certainly not sickness. If you don't leave me alone, I'll return to l'Ermitage. Might I remind you, that's a place where you aren't welcome."

At night she drifted toward sleep, imagining, after having said it aloud that very day, that she might return to l'Ermitage, then in that liminal state, deciding yes, she would go because she had had enough of him. A person did have limits. She would not tell him—simply pack her bag and walk out. Best when he was out. A slight smile crossed her face when she thought of him returning and finding her gone. Then she slid away into a dream of the Tiergarten in Berlin, where she sat on a bench with Wolf, and another dream, lying in bed in her room in Berlin. She heard the pounding of fists upon wood. In her dream she cried, *No! Not Papa, not Katharina!*

She woke to night terror. The pounding grew strident, resolute. An unmoored fear seized her, so much worse than fear of any particular thing or person. Lacking form, it took possession of her whole body and spirit until both became a scream that could tear out her throat and force her heart to burst its rib cage. But she held it in, listening, hoping whoever was pounding would go away while remembering the ones who came for her father, plainclothes police in trench coats and hats with their brims turned up in menacing grins. Astrid storming in at six a.m., the hem of her coat airborne. "They're taking the Jews. You must hide!" Papa going off to his scheduled surgery anyway. Katharina doing her best to stall the police.

Now, from the other side of their door, Charlotte heard a man's baritone yell, "Open up!"

She ran to it and flung it open. Four men in uniform stood as one. She took some courage from the sight of the tall kepi, rimmed with the thin braid of the local police rather than the thick, braided cross of the military gendarmerie. The most forward one spoke.

"We're looking for the Jew, Dr. Luitger Gruenstein. We're taking him into custody."

Her throat caught.

Katharina agreeing—all right, she'd take the police to the hospital. She needed her coat. But the coat was an excuse to warn Astrid to leave quickly by the back way out, lest she be found in the house of Jews, and to instruct Charlotte to go to police headquarters to see what she could find out.

"There must be some mistake. My grandfather is almost eighty."

"Our orders are to take all foreign nationals, regardless of age. Get him up. You too. Hurry up about it."

"Me?" Her heart was beating fast.

"Women, children, everyone. You may each take a blanket."

She stood paralyzed, the sound of her heartbeat now pounding in her ears.

"Get to it." He gave her a push toward the main room.

Luitger was asleep on the sofa. "Wake up." She shook him. "The police are here."

He sat up straight. "What?" His sleepiness disappeared in an instant, and he was trembling.

"We're being arrested."

He was standing now and turning from side to side, bewildered, disoriented. "But why? That can't be. What's going on?" He put one hand to his throat, then his chest.

"They said to hurry."

He sat back down on the sofa. She pulled at him to get up.

"You need to get dressed." Charlotte tossed him his trousers. "You can bring the blanket."

In her room, she paced frantically back and forth from the window to the opposite wall. What would happen to her and Luitger? Her muscles tensed, and her breathing became short and shallow. She wanted to run but it would be of no use. She would not be able to get past four gendarmes. She was terrified. The window was the only way out, but she would not survive.

"Hurry up in there!" one of the gendarmes called from the kitchen.

She pulled on two dresses, one on top of the other. She stuffed pencils, ink, brushes, and a sketch pad into one patch pocket of the dress underneath. In the other pocket, clean linen. Then she rolled up her blanket. There was nowhere to go but into the hands of the police.

She felt dizzy and had to sit on the edge of her bed for a few moments before leaving her room. Maybe there would be an opportunity for escape on the way. She had to count on that.

Luitger was dressed. From the bowl full of pears on the dining table, she picked two yellow ones and placed them in her pockets. It was much too warm for a coat, but Luitger insisted upon it. His hands were trembling so hard now, she had to help him with the buttons. She stuffed two more pears into his pockets, rolled his blanket, and crammed it under his arm.

She looked into his eyes, which were beseeching and rageful. As she returned his gaze, she felt her own rage mixed with terror in a singular moment of connection between them that immediately passed.

The streets of Old Town were dark. Even though the fighting was far away, new blackout rules forbid nighttime lighting. More gendarmes were leading more Jews similarly roused from sleep. A woman had flung her blanket over her shoulder, one triangular edge sweeping the cobblestones.

The civilized trample through the streets was nothing like the mobs of young men with crowbars and bricks who had raced down Wielandstrasse, right under the Salomons' Number 15. A thousand boots had clapped the pavement, one rolling brown tempest of a wave. In faces, frenzied savagery. Strong, gleeful, purposeful shouts of vengeance. "Die, Jews!"

The balconies of the Nice-Ville Train Station, away from the center of the city, smiled with their opulent decorations, a vacation-gay façade even in the dark. Charlotte and her grandfather were thrown into a crowd of hundreds. And there they stood, not permitted to sit, for hours. They inquired through their ranks, but no one knew where they were going.

FINALLY, AT DAWN, the crowd was loaded onto the train. The carriage cars had been stripped of their seats so that everyone had to sit on the floor. Charlotte and Luitger secured a spot under a window. In the abrupt seizure, a filament of Charlotte's mind had come loose. She was yanked back into the past, to a dreary, cold Berlin morning.

The boulevard eerily empty of the usual throngs. A few dark figures moving hurriedly and with purpose. On sidewalk and street, broken glass in glittering heaps. The morning's cinereous vapor floated through open doorways, hung ghost-like in the dark caverns of abandoned stores. Streams of elegant gowns—lilac crêpe de chine, indigo velvet, cerulean silk, peach organdy, and fuchsia satin—trailed from a vandalized dress shop. No dead bodies. No one injured. Simply no one.

In the Wittenbergplatz, the great Fasanenstrasse synagogue exploded right before her eyes into a blazing inferno. Lotte grabbed her head in her hands to prevent her mind from flying out.

Now it dangled—this loose filament of mind—like a worm cast out on the end of a hook into an empty brook to be caught by nothing. Luitger was cursing. Charlotte held back her tears, refusing to let him see her emotion.

The train rose above the steep cliffs. She stood up and stared out the window at the landscape rushing past. She took out her sketch pad and pencil, and divided the page vertically and horizontally, creating four panels to make her paper last. Leaning one side of her body against the window for support, she sketched the sheer drops, the grassy clifftops dotted with square-tiled roofs, the round clouds in receding rows from sea to horizon, stepping-stones to the beyond. And the dangle of her mind looped its way back toward its base.

With the water on their left, they were going west. Cars peopled by the careless and carefree took the mountain roads, with convertible tops down in the fresh morning air. She wanted to cry out: *Stop. Please, stop for us.* But they were already gone. Then the vast sea disappeared, causing another unraveling of mind. Tempting to let it float away to wherever the sea had gone; instead, with more ferocity, she drew.

Back on the floor, sketching: a shoe with a broken lace knotted at a grommet. Now, a crowd of women in winter coats gathered on Prinz-Albrecht-Strasse in front of police headquarters. She lined out a figure of herself with a bag of apples because Katharina had commanded her to get food into jail for Papa and apples had been all she could find. She threaded her way among the small groups and heard stories. The insides of homes destroyed with axes. Men carted away without explanation. An official came to the door. "Go home! The men have been taken. You'll get a notice in the mail."

She started crying. Other women were not. Their ashen faces, contorted in agony and in anticipation of the worst, turned to steel, as if to say they wouldn't be stopped from finding their men. Police peeled them away from each other to hasten the dispersal. A guttural moan came from her. "Papa!"

Luitger's eyes moved from her face to her pad, and he flashed a look of thorough disgust. She closed her eyes, let her head roll back on her shoulders.

There was a lurch. Had she slept? She unearthed her pencil, which had fallen and rolled under her hip. Floor sketch: a bent head hidden by a wrap. A gnarled hand held it together under the chin. The folds fell like a rabbi's prayer shawl.

Charlotte drew herself as she walked away that day, looking down at the heel of her shoe where something dragged. It was difficult to draw a shudder, so she drew the handbill stuck to her heel. It read, "Führer, free us of the Jewish Plague!" In her next drawing, Lotte was headed home, carrying her bag of ripe red apples. On the bottom, she wrote: *Where has he been taken?*

Packed together, the people were beyond weary. They moaned. And the train rumbled on: we have our lives, we have our lives, we have our lives.

The pears were eaten. The stench was indescribable. Sleep was impossible. She kept drawing. A baby's curled fist. Luitger's ear flap, the skin encrusted with brown wax, gray hairs growing from the lobe.

Marseille. Brakes hissed. Might they get off and stretch their legs? Doors stayed shut. The train juddered in place, then rolled.

A medieval town in the distance. Golden stone houses. Rows of them winding around the mountaintop.

Floor sketch: two middle-aged women, one leaning her head on the other's shoulder, her face carved by care and worry. The other defiant, even in repose.

Woodlands of oak and stone pine clung to the steep slopes of a coastal range. Cultivated olive orchards and almond groves. Castles coming and going. Rivers, too. Fields of sunflowers already starting to bloom. Then, shrub lands of maquis plants growing low, bulbous, like looking down on a dense crowd of green bowler hats.

Rain began and seemed never to increase or decrease. Down, down, steady and apathetic.

Along a plateau, the train jolted to a halt, brakes screeching.

DISEMBARKING IN OLORON-SAINTE-MARIE in the early evening when the light of this one interminable day lingered on, they were loaded immediately onto uncovered lorries, packed together like cows or pigs. They passed through the town's imposing architecture of castles and stone fortifications from centuries past, then lurched through a valley of the Pyrenées. Snow-capped mountains rose on both sides. Rain blurred their vision. Charlotte kept her blanket rolled tight with her sketch pad inside, held against her belly under two layers of dresses. Luitger, too, kept his blanket rolled, relying on his overcoat, which was not such a bad idea after all.

In less than an hour, they arrived at wooden gates on the top of a hill, which flattened into a plateau running to the horizon and along with it, barbed wire at least a mile out—fencing for hundreds of identical structures like military barracks, built in straight rows and converging in the distance. The buildings were black. No vegetation interrupted the scene, not one tree. Rain had saturated the clay of the barren earth. As far as the eye could see—mud.

Dragging their weary bodies, burdened with water-logged clothes, they trudged down the single street, which spanned the length of the camp. *Îlots* was the French term for the parcels on both sides blocked off by barbed wire. The men headed for the *îlots* on one side of the road.

Luitger's mangled beard, like a wet rug, came to a point and hosed water down the front of his coat. Without a backward glance, off he went. Though she was relieved to be rid of him, Charlotte felt a pang. He'd be alone because he was too unpleasant for anyone to take pity.

Up close, the outer walls of the women's cabins took their black color from a tarred fabric cover. Inside, the roof sloped down to the floor, forcing everyone to the middle to stand. There were no windows. Charlotte's eyes adjusted to the shadowy atmosphere of the one room, about twenty-five square meters. Forty of them needed to squeeze in. Many languages comingled.

One woman said, "No insulation. We'll freeze."

Looking up at the sockets in the ceiling, another said, "No bulbs."

Rainwater dribbled in through the deteriorated tar. It stained the thin wood-plank walls with vertical patterns of flow and puddled on the floor. A rat ran the length of the cabin and disappeared. Charlotte recoiled and suppressed a cry.

"Here's an old stove." This proclamation generated a wave of excitement, but nothing burnable was found.

"There's not a stick of furniture."

"Surely they'll bring beds."

Grateful for shelter, most lay down to spread their limbs. Charlotte couldn't go a step farther from the door, and so sank to the bare floor there. After a while, the door opened. Two men entered, speaking Spanish. They offered food at black-market prices. Women who had money bought bread, hard-boiled eggs, and canned juice. The sight of food made Charlotte aware of her light head, the hollow in her stomach. She thought about her hidden francs in Nice, then decided it was better not to think of them because it only made her hungrier.

She awoke in the night with the need to go. A woman was just leaving by the door.

"Follow me. I've been shown the way."

Under a full moon, the mud glistened slimy brown-gray. A path of planks floated on the surface, sliding beneath their feet. "Hold on." Charlotte grabbed the wire strung from one cabin to the next. With the barbs stripped, it served as a railing. Leaping out from under a cabin, rats streamed across their path. Charlotte held her breath while the never-ending tails slithered past, black and whiplike.

They approached a two-story cabin. The stench of excrement was suffocating. Up the stairs and inside, a platform was cut with holes along the length. Underneath were troughs. They lifted their dresses and sat.

All through the night, the door to the cabin opened and closed with numerous trips to the latrine. Each time, a rush of frigid air blew through Charlotte. Otherwise, inside was dark as a grave and, without insulation, as cold.

The next morning, a wail came from the adjacent cabin. Soon word arrived: One woman hadn't made the return trip from the latrine. She had fallen into the wet, unctuous clay, which was now up to the knees. She was found face down, having choked to death on the mud.

CHAPTER 11

GURS CAMP, PYRENÉES

A routine emerged. At dawn, a loaf of heavy, dark bread flew in the door. One woman divided the loaf without the benefit of a knife.

Twice a day, a woman entered with a wooden pole riding her shoulders, a bucket hung on each end. Charlotte used a discarded can for the watery "soup." Floating sometimes— one chickpea, particles of yellow beets, or a bit of horsemeat so tough it had to be spat out.

Six or so coffins a day passed down the main road to the cemetery beyond the *îlots*. Under the guise of attending a funeral, women frequently claimed relation to the dead so that they might meet their husbands at the grave site. The French guards were too lackadaisical to check.

At the communal basin, the water was icy, soap scarce. Charlotte found a towel she'd normally regard as too filthy to mop up a spill.

During dry spells, they paired up for chores. A strong emphasis was put on order and cleanliness. It didn't take long for her to figure out she must do her part. They shook out the bedding. By now, sacks and a bit of straw to fill them had arrived. They fetched water, washed, and hung laundry. Charlotte sent one dress and set of linens at a time, and thus maintained minimal hygiene. After years of conflict with Katharina, then her grandmother, Charlotte was amazed women could live in such harmony.

After chores, they were free because there was no labor. They were merely interned. They sat in groups according to nationality and spoke in their native tongues. Charlotte discovered the camp was originally for the Brigadists and Basques, many of whom remained. Germans like herself, Jews who escaped the Nazis, were the "undesirables." Also detained were Austrians, Poles, Italians, Czecho-Slovakians, French communists, others considered dangerous to the government, and ordinary prisoners awaiting trial. Despite efforts to stay clean and well ordered, a grim despair resided on many faces. Blank eyes stared into an unknown future.

Charlotte preferred to sit apart. Without a mother, she didn't know how to join in. At a very early age, she'd lost her point of departure, that essential place from which she could risk leave-taking and to which she could safely return. Remaining separate, silent, and still had become a habit of being.

Her spot was near the fence. Occasionally, a guard sauntered by.

She drew what she saw: the cabins, the flat land, jaunty undergarments drying on the line, two women carrying a bucket, four sitting at an outdoor table conversing, even the rats. Incessantly she drew. She would not go mad.

Today, a middle-aged woman approached, carrying a sketch pad. Charlotte had noticed her, daily wandering the *îlot* in a wide-brimmed hat and a rainbow-striped scarf. Uninvited, she sat.

"I'm Lou, an artist." Her skin was olive, her lips mahogany, sensuous. She asked to see Charlotte's drawing. Charlotte shook her head and turned over her pad.

"At night, we artists meet and share our work. No obligation to show."

Lou asked her name and described the way to her cabin. When she was gone, Charlotte sensed herself materializing, as though she were made of something dissolved in water, now precipitating into an observable solid.

A GROUP OF NEW ARRIVALS trudged down the long street looking weary and defeated, stiff in their bodies from the journey. One was a little straighter, a little taller, clutching a bundle to her chest. Charlotte ran to the wire.

"Anneliese! Here! It's me, Charlotte!" Madly, she waved. "In that cabin." She pointed.

The bundle Anneliese carried was Rui. Charlotte embraced them.

"Where's your assignment?"

"Here. This is where they told me to go."

Anneliese looked worn, as all who entered were. Her skin was sallow. Her black curls had lost their luster. In her eyes was utter bafflement. Charlotte was so sorry for her, and at the same time, her heart burst with joy.

They sat on a mat with Rui between. Anneliese told how after Max left to join the French Foreign Legion and Henri went in search of homes for the children, she no longer had her finger on the pulse of what was happening, so she took to going into the village of Villefranche. She met up with a group of Jews who urged her to go to a haven in the Pyrenées, where she was told there were garden chalets. Olive had offered her bus fare.

Charlotte had never seen tears in her friend's eyes. Now they were wide and wet but did not spill.

"I can't believe I came of my own free will. I've made myself a prisoner. My son too."

Charlotte told how she and Luitger were shipped by train. When Charlotte asked, Anneliese said there was no danger Henri would follow. Someone had to care for the children.

After the evening ration, Anneliese and Rui fell asleep. Charlotte used a whole page to draw them—Anneliese with worry lines that clung to her forehead, Rui limp and blissful in her arms. Then she picked up her pad, which she always kept with her, safe from the rats, and she walked outside for some air.

There was no moon. The sky was deeply purple, like the velvety skin of a black plum, and lit by countless stars.

At the other end of this same *îlot*, a group of women artists was gathering. Her stomach went from rock-hard to fluttery and back again, the way it had whenever she'd entered the classroom at the Berlin Art Academy, with fear that she didn't belong there, hope that she did, fear that her work was horrid, hope that it was original.

She set off in the direction of Lou's cabin.

THE INSIDE GLOWED with candlelight. Lou sat, commanding a group of fifteen. Swept up from a broad forehead, her hair was dark and glossy with dramatic gray patches at the temples framing an oblong face. She motioned Charlotte in.

"Group, meet Charlotte."

Their greeting was murmured in deference to the women who were asleep, but it was also quietly enthusiastic. The circle widened in a rustling movement, creating a space for her. She hesitated, then took the empty spot.

Lou said, "Who wants to go first?"

The sketch held up was a view through the fence bordering the road over to the other side. Through the wire a man reached his hand, which held out a loaf of bread. A passing guard was seizing it. Foregrounded on the left, top to bottom, was the headless profile of a pregnant woman's torso. The artist was herself quite large with child.

Lou said, "I like the beseeching look on the man's face and how you omitted the woman's. We know how she feels. Wonderfully executed."

Charlotte's turn arrived. The others' work had been compelling compositions that conveyed the harsh and the quotidian. What did she have to show except the rotten fruits of the journey? And in camp, nothing but scribbles of a mind trying to hold itself together. She passed.

Next was an ink drawing of three women at a makeshift stove. Seen from behind, they peered at slices of bread toasting. Their postures conveyed intense anticipation of the meager meal. Charlotte looked from the drawing to the artist on the other side of the circle. It was Lili Rilik-Andrieux from Berlin, who'd been a class ahead of her at the Berlin Art Academy. The sight of her put a pleasant buzz in Charlotte's head and resurrected a past that felt too far away to have been real. She was flooded with memories: the stone façade; the gray light of Berlin coming in through the hall windows; the smell of turpentine, linseed oil, and bratwurst sandwiches; a particularly fleshy nude model; the rustle of the students preparing to work; and the intense absorption in their drawing.

Then Lou said, "Well, that's almost it for the night. Before we go, Charlotte, you have another chance."

Everyone looked expectant. Lili smiled encouragement. Could she bear the exposure? If only the work could be seen while she could be elsewhere. She quickly flipped open her sketch pad and held it in front of her face. Small gasps erupted.

Lou said, "Today's work?"

"My friend. And her little boy." She spoke from behind the pad. "They just arrived."

Lou nodded and said, "Beautiful contrast between the two faces." Charlotte's insides danced in delight. Lou continued, "We feel like we know these people. A little more shading in the neck, perhaps?"

Charlotte looked lovingly at her drawing before putting it aside. Then Lou reminded the group of the importance of what they were doing: documenting their experience and supporting each other's efforts.

"We're developing our vision of the world here, who we are in it. This place means to erase our identities. In our work, we defy that effort and reclaim ourselves."

Defying the erasure of identity. This idea grabbed Charlotte, echoed the violent deletion of the suicides from her family's spoken culture, and with it, their unlived lives, a heritage to which she had an unclaimable right.

As they filed out, Lili found Charlotte. "Charlotte Salomon, the real Berlin Art Academy competition winner, whose prize was stolen."

"But you had graduated and gone on to Paris, Lili. To the Academie Ranson. How did you know?"

"News travels."

Their cabins were in the same direction. They walked together, at the rescue should one of them slip in the mud.

"Paris is where I met Lou. She was once in Berlin, a member of the Novembergruppe."

Recalling that Kandinsky had once been in the Novembergruppe, Charlotte stopped and looked at Lili. "That woman is Lou Albert-Lasard?"

Charlotte had perused the old exhibition catalogs of the Novembergruppe. She recalled a particular quality in Lou's portraits of women who stared straight at the viewer, revealing their inner states. Soft eyes managing to convey hard determination. Inspiring, daring depictions.

"Lately she's in the Montparnasse group. She's introduced me around. It's a good place to be an artist, Paris." Lili shook her head. Below her brown bangs, her big eyes looked sad. "Actually, I should say *was*."

"Oh, no. Don't say that. You'll return. I'm sure of it."

That night, Charlotte lay awake in a state of thrill. She reviewed every moment of the evening, seeing all the drawings and the faces, and feeling again the seriousness mixed with good humor—a company of artists, and herself among them. She tried to imagine what Paris was like. And vowed to see Lili again and ask for every detail: where she painted, where she lived, how she met up with people, who were the artists she admired, and how she got by. Beyond the mud, there was something to live for.

CHAPTER 12

GURS CAMP, PYRENÉES

JUNE 1940

Little more than two weeks later, they were approaching nine thousand in the women's camp, all the barracks filled beyond capacity, sixty in Charlotte's cabin. Some had been released back into France, others shipped elsewhere; no one knew where. Not knowing one's fate was more unbearable than hunger by far.

Charlotte observed how difficult it was to be a person there. The camp's purpose was to strip down everyone—from whatever walk of life, of whatever political persuasion, criminals and innocents alike—to something less than their naked selves, to a state of nonbeing. No subsistence to the nonexistent. Robbed of identity, the "nobodies" wasted away.

Who was running this place? This question received much debate. Ostensibly the French, though there were now two Frances. The northern zone was clearly under German occupation. A new regime in Vichy, which looked French but felt German, ran the south. Why were all German nationals being rounded up?

While the questions remained unanswered, Charlotte witnessed many who deteriorated from dysentery. Others succumbed to typhus, tuberculosis, anemia, and edemas. Some rocked on their straw mats all day, muttering and crying, their nervous systems ruined beyond repair. Then there were those who endured all the deprivation by keeping busy. They organized the community, visited the sickbeds, and soothed those who suffered. Charlotte learned that looking for what needed to be done and doing it was a way to survive. She helped Anneliese with Rui, because of her friend's need and the baby's. And her own, Charlotte discovered. Over the days, she began to feel that with humility and dignity, hardship could be endured.

Charlotte saw how the artists in camp were lucky to have a reliable way to defend against dispossession and despair. At the nightly meetings, Lou distributed art supplies brought to camp by the charities. Always, there was new work. Paper was scarce, so people used wrapping paper, camp flyers and notices, or the backs of posters, even toilet paper.

She had time to think about herself, who she had been and who she was now. She saw how she had tended to rest her thoughts—and it was not rest, it was agitation—on the woeful things that had happened to her. Her mother had died when she was eight. Her father had been too absorbed in work to pay her much attention. Katharina was too strict. Her instructors too weak to refuse to teach race science, the Berlin Art Academy too willing to abolish her. She reviewed how she had become captive to the light and colors of the Mediterranean coast and the beauty of l'Ermitage, and now understood how that had been a way to turn away from her suffering.

Hardly had she begun to grieve her grandmother and digest the legacy of suicides when she had been arrested. She thought she would go mad with what was going on inside her until she arrived in Gurs camp and understood the war that was raging, the chaos it had created—the snatching away of thousands of loved ones from their homes, their towns; the wrenching apart of husbands and wives. The whole world was falling apart. Humanity was destroying what it had built over millennia—its own educational institutions, social systems, cultures, and civilizations. Itself!

How could the culture not be reflected in the family? One was as integral to the other as a branch to the tree, as an arm or leg to the whole body. What was happening inside her, she saw now, was happening outside. The insanity of suicide was the insanity of humanicide, driven like a stake straight through the tender spirit of the individual.

At Gurs, the only light that made it through the perpetually overcast sky and penetrated the sheets of rain was graybrown. Everything was cast in this brume: the clay mud of the earth, the tar-covered barracks splashed with char-colored slush, the cloudy wash water, the slosh of bucketed provisions, and the faces of every human soul.

How would they survive when in this gloom they were all reduced to the noncolor of ash?

Then someone in Lou's group painted a picture of the barracks and added an impossible sunflower, standing straight and tall, shining yellow.

One night, Charlotte woke to Anneliese crying, "Rosemarie's labor has started."

Another German-Jewish "undesirable," Rosemarie was a few years younger than Charlotte. As a former nurse, Anneliese felt responsible for the birth because no woman doctor could be found in their *îlot*. She'd attended a funeral expressly to speak to a male doctor who was able to tell her how to handle complications. In the pitch dark of the cabin, with quiet urgency, she issued instructions.

"We need clean, hot water. And clean cloths. Ask women with babies for napkins. The water is more important. Do that first."

Charlotte's eye twitched, spasmodic. Clean water? It couldn't be gotten. And hot? She had no idea. But she grabbed two buckets, and after making her way to Lili's cabin and waking her friend, they headed toward the cabin where women made toast. The sky was hidden behind a thick layer of dark clouds. No star shone, and rain was falling, lightly but ice cold. The women with the stove responded, "We can heat water. And we'll find wood even if we need to pry a plank from every cabin. Get the crow!"

Before long, they'd fetched water and returned to Lili's cabin to find a good fire going. Lili stayed to collect more water while Charlotte went on her way with a wooden pole over her shoulders, one full bucket of hot water on each end. Water sloshed over the top, scalding her legs. The planks were so slippery under her feet that she was afraid she might skid out like a car on Berlin black ice. She thought of Rosemarie's need for her to return with clean water, and of Anneliese, who knew all too well how inept Charlotte was at all things practical. Water streamed down her face and soaked her shoulders. Out of the corner of her eye, she marked her progress as one cabin faded into the watery oblivion behind her and the sidewall of the next slowly emerged. Back at the cabin, she bloomed inside with secret pride for her small accomplishment.

A candle and glass hurricane protector had been found. Many were awake, blankets pulled tight around shoulders, hair disheveled and thick with stalks of straw. The light illuminated Rosemarie, who was propped upon a pile of sacks, unclothed. Her great belly overwhelmed her form. The skin was taut, smooth, and shiny, as though rubbed with oil.

Rosemarie emitted animal-like sounds. In between the pains, Anneliese rubbed her neck and shoulders, encouraging her to relax. This went on for hours, Rosemarie's face damp, her long blond hair matted with sweat. Then she collapsed and fell off her sacks.

Charlotte thought she had fainted. But, no, she was between contractions. Anneliese said. "Let's get her up and walking."

Rosemarie looked like she'd never get up. Her face bore that kind of gone. They roused her and helped her rise to standing.

Anneliese put the candle in Charlotte's hand and took Rosemarie's arm. The three began to walk the length of the filthy, mean shelter while Charlotte shed light on a meandering path among the muddy puddles pooling at intervals.

Rosemarie's gravid, naked body was like the most spectacular float in a parade. The candlelight made her skin translucent. Something became pronounced and visible for a few moments, stretching the skin to reveal its tiny shape. A foot! As though the baby was showing off, saying, *well, of course there's a foot.*

The door opened and in came Lili and her cabin mates, carrying loads of wood. "We finally figured it would be much easier to carry wood than hot water. We'll start a fire here."

Rosemarie stopped, cried out.

Anneliese said, "Breathe."

Charlotte tried to imagine what it was, this thing called a contraction. She could see only how Rosemarie's slim shoulders rose to her ears, her lithe limbs took twisted shapes like the arms and legs of a puppet on a string, her eyes shut tight, her mouth opened wide to bare her teeth, and her face became contorted in the furthest extremity of agony. Charlotte's own body tensed in response.

"Sit me down!" Rosemarie yelled. According to the one wristwatch in the cabin, they'd been walking for two hours.

They lowered Rosemarie to the straw mat, which had been covered with clean towels.

Anneliese washed her hands with a chip of soap. Soup bowls and empty juice cans had been rinsed and stacked. One bowl was used to ladle hot water from a bucket. One was for washing, another rinsing, another for waste, which was removed and replaced with an empty.

Charlotte felt faint. She rose, wanting to step back in search of an observation post. Anneliese said, "Stay."

Charlotte's teeth were clicking uncontrollably. "I don't know anything. I'm not trustworthy." She looked around for someone else to present herself in her place, but no one did.

"Nonetheless, I'm trusting you. You're simply a little afraid. That's natural."

Finally, Charlotte tightened her jaw to stop her tic and gave a slight nod.

"A napkin, then," Anneliese said without a trace of chastisement.

Charlotte handed her a fresh cloth. Anneliese washed Rosemarie, taking special care with the belly. Charlotte dipped the next napkin. Gently separating Rosemarie's legs, Anneliese washed her inner thighs.

The tuft on the mound was blond. Anneliese nudged Rosemarie's legs farther apart until the mound parted, like two curtains opening to reveal inner fleshy lips. Charlotte was riveted to what she'd never seen—a woman's most private part, sequestered even away from her own eyes. A stringy, blood-tinged mucous oozed out. Anneliese swabbed it away with considered strokes that said this was a necessary prelude but not the main act, and handed Charlotte the cloth. In her palm, it was like the juice of a plum or the sap of a tree, sending up a shiver for what it announced. She passed it on for disposal.

The next pain came with terrible force. Rosemarie sounded out at a pitch that, but for the rain beating down on all the rooftops, could have been heard—might have actually been heard—all the way across the camp. It might have been taken for the howl of a mountain wolf perched on an outcrop over the plateau of this hellish swamp. A shudder went up and down the line of women, and Charlotte could barely stand it. She was sure Rosemarie was going to die.

HOURS WENT BY. Several women took up posts at the spots where rats entered the barrack, and they either blocked the openings with whatever they could find or beat them back. Water and fresh cloths arrived by way of Lili. A replacement candle appeared. Every detail unfolded like a seamlessly choreographed production.

Charlotte wiped Rosemarie's forehead with a steady hand. She badly wanted Rosemarie to feel that everything was fine, even though she herself was not convinced.

Suddenly, a gutteral expulsion of sound and air flew from Rosemarie.

"Up," Anneliese said. "You're ready. You must do this work now. Think, I'm pushing the baby out."

Rosemarie's face was absent of will. "I can't go on."

What would happen if Rosemarie could not go on? Would the baby die inside of her?

Anneliese was matter-of-fact. "You're doing a good job. Your body will push the baby out. When you feel the pressure, bear down."

Women who'd slept through the night were awake now. One very old woman named Edith was wasted and weakened by malnutrition. Wizened and bald, her body was no longer able to sustain even the spun-sugar wisps of hair she had had when she arrived. Seeing her so took the wind out of Charlotte. Her limbs ached. She wanted only to lie down.

Anneliese gave an order. "Grab her behind the knees and pull her legs up to her chest."

Two women moved in, one on each side of Rosemarie, who took a deep breath, closed her eyes tight, and screwed up her whole face. She gave it her best, which appeared to fall short of what was needed.

Anneliese cried out, "I see the head."

Charlotte's eyes popped as a little circle of glossy golden hair became visible in the aperture between Rosemarie's legs. Her heart raced. The damp cap slipped back inside, out of sight. Terror slammed Charlotte's breath into the rear of her throat.

"Come now, once again."

They were all holding their one breath.

Rosemarie puffed and went limp. "Can't."

The women started to chant softly. "Yes, you can. Yes, you can." In German, French, Polish, Hungarian, Italian, Czech, and Spanish, it was a babble of encouragement and belief, understanding, support, and commitment. Anneliese interjected, "Push. Push. Push." The chanting grew stronger while maintaining the steadiness of a solid drumbeat.

"You're doing it. One more now."

Rosemarie took a long breath, deep into her lungs. Her shoulders dropped from her ears toward her rib cage as she bore down with one sustained, moaning effort that was so intense and extended, it seemed it would never end.

The birth opening stretched bright red, and sparkled like a ruby tiara. Suddenly it was there, the entire head. It turned itself to the side, and Anneliese took it in her hands.

"I have the little face. Your baby. You've waited so long. And worked so hard. Now. Once more. And it's yours."

Anxiety for the outcome reached a pitch in the wide eyes around the circle. Chanting stopped. In an eternal moment of waiting, no breath was expelled. The flimsy walls of the cabin fell away. There was no Gurs, no camp. There was no mud. Charlotte felt them all disappearing, along with this terrible world. Even the great maternal hillock disappeared, even the reaching receptive hands, as a rotund body, arms pressed to chest and belly, emerged with pinky-white flesh glistening, legs slithering out with gushes of blood and fluid, all of it wrinkled and slimy, its cord of connection spiraled and pulsating blue. A brand-new cry rang loud and clear, sounding the bell of life. And the whole universe—from this bright point to that of the farthest star—expanded to embrace it.

Held breaths released in one great sigh. Anneliese tied and cut the cord. "A daughter," she said, wrapping the infant in a towel.

Women still on their mats rose and came forth, making a circle behind the circle, until all were gathered except for Edith, whose ancient, decrepit body was indistinguishable from the mat she lay upon. Anneliese, eyes moist, placed the bundle in Rosemarie's arms. Mother and newborn radiated light. A beam of need leapt between them, suffused outwards onto faces struck by wonder and streaming tears of relief and liberation.

CHAPTER 13

———

GURS CAMP, PYRENÉES

JULY 1940

Charlotte stood in front of the wood-gated exit at the end of the long street that divided camp, with her eyes on Luitger stumbling toward her. His coat, once coal-black and now faded to dusty pewter, appeared to shuffle along on its own. His cheekbones rose in bony protrusions from the top of his thin and scraggly beard the color of dirty snow. His eyes had faded to blue-gray, but the whole of his expression was fierce, a mixture of suffering dismissed and determination to prevail.

Like a punctured tire, Charlotte's body deflated. To her dismay, he'd survived.

"Just get me to Nice." His words rattled in his throat.

Two days before, a committee from Germany had arrived and reviewed all prisoners' records. They had decided to let Luitger go because of his age and the fact that he had a residence in Nice.

"I begged for you—begged, little lady. And now you'll take care of me. If you don't, you'll be hauled back here."

They gave Charlotte a certificate of legal status, stating her condition of release: *to care for Doctor Luitger Gruenstein, the German-Jewish national, residing on Rue Neuscheller, Nice.*

They were going out the way they came, with only the clothes on their backs now gone half to rags. He was without his blanket. Charlotte had hers, and in her pocket was her sketch pad. There was nothing to do but start walking.

He took hold of her arm for support. He told her the Italians had taken the Alpes-Maritimes region, which included Nice.

"Mussolini's mistress is a Jew," he said. "We'll be safe."

She had no idea how to make it across an entire country with an old man leaning on her. His weight, flopping this way and that, was more than a burden. It was a curse.

A river known as Gave d'Aspe ran down from a peak in Spain, and she'd been told that it was not far from this road.

She said, "Before it bends away, we must drink."

Through a path among the trees, they reached the river's bank. She unwrapped her blanket and produced two empty cans. There was not the least acknowledgement of her practical forethought.

"Wait here." She climbed over the rocky shore onto a peninsula of slab jutting into the river. The mountain's torrent rolled swiftly, cold and crystalline from its descent. She scooped from the bubbling top, aerated and shot through with sunlight. They drank in greedy gulps.

She said, "We grew ill on contaminated water while this abundant source was nearby." He only grunted. When they'd drunk their fill, they returned to the road, passing quaint farmhouses and, in town, a white stucco church with a stone bell tower. They drew withering looks from villagers. Dirty, ragged, thin—their needs announced that they had been prisoners at the camp. Charlotte stopped an old woman with a market basket and asked how they might head toward Nice.

"Follow this road to Oloron-Sainte-Marie, eighteen kilometers, and ask from there."

Alone, Charlotte figured she could make it within the day. Looking them up and down, the old woman added, "Or you could follow the Gave d'Aspe. Longer, but you'd be protected from unfriendly sorts. It goes right through the town of Oloron-Sainte-Marie." With "God bless," she tore the heel off her loaf of bread, which they devoured before she was out of sight.

A MILLION HUES of green were in the foliage, the low-lying ground cover, and the moss growing on the trunks of fir, beech, and oak. The unending sight of verdant nature in its lush color quenched a different kind of thirst. The sound of the river was reassuring; even without food, they would drink.

First Charlotte found Luitger a suitable walking stick. Where the ground was flat, now he could go on his own. Mountains rose on both sides. Where the bank became steep, they were forced to climb. Luitger hung onto her, wheezing and tugging so erratically she feared at treacherous points they'd take a steep fall into the whipping waters. As the sun passed its zenith, she realized that by leaving the road, they'd given up being taken in for the night.

Their once-sturdy shoes had lost their stiff support from days marinated in mud. How easily an ankle might turn on the sloping terrain. They went even more slowly. While stopping to rest, they spotted a man standing in quiet water with a fishing pole. They picked their way down, Luitger clutching her, sometimes losing his footing and slamming into her.

When they were on flat terrain and within earshot, Charlotte called to the fisherman. "Excuse me, sir. We're still on the Gave d'Aspe? Headed for Oloron-Sainte-Marie?"

In his pail were several speckled fish, quiescent or expired. "You are," he shouted from midstream. His line suddenly tautened, and he hauled in a thrashing one, its silver scales like glittering diamonds in the sunlight.

As the fisherman slogged his way to the shore, Luitger ambled downstream toward a rocky place. The fisherman unhooked the fish. It flailed on the sandy bar.

"Brown trout. A kilo, a little over. Most of these are three, four, by now."

He regarded them—a young, emaciated woman and an old man who had wandered some distance. The fish gave its last effort and became still.

"There," he said, pointing to the trout. "I got more than my wife and I can eat." Charlotte thanked him and waved him off as he made to leave.

Luitger was squatting, his back to her. When Charlotte caught up to him, carrying their good fortune, she saw he had a fish twice the size of the one in her hands. He was using a sharp-edged rock to scrape away the scales.

"You took that from his pail?"

"He wasn't going to give us two. We're a whole lot hungrier than he."

He returned to his scraping. There was nothing to do but find a suitable stone and do the same. They sat side by side, eating their bounty raw. Charlotte spit out the first bite—too cold, wet, fresh to the tongue. Then she tore with her teeth and swallowed a great gulp. Afraid she'd get sick and lose it all, she slowed down. Then the cold fish was refreshing, its wet quenching, the satiation glorious.

Two hours later, it was time to figure out how to survive the cold night. Charlotte set Luitger on a chair-like ledge of a boulder while she scouted.

"Don't you dare run off on me! I'll go right back to Gurs and call the police."

He didn't have the strength to retrace this day's path on his own, yet the threat disturbed her. She was not free. She and Luitger were trapped together, as though surrounded by an invisible barrier of barbed wire.

She found a place where the trees thinned to form a clearing. She gathered leaves into two mounds. By now it was dusk. She half wished Luitger had somehow disappeared, but he was exactly where she had left him.

"Lie down there," she instructed when they reached the overnight site. "Hold your hands over your chest."

After her sketch pad, her blanket was her most prized possession, yet she covered him with it, then piled a thick layer of undergrowth over the blanket, patting it close around his body, even up over his bald forehead. She'd nearly buried him.

"I'm going to die."

"Calm down. You won't die. Go to sleep."

CHARLOTTE WOKE, amazed to be alive. The river gurgled somewhere below. The sun filtered through the forest canopy, making the morning light soft, golden green in which the leaves fluttered with the movement of birds flitting from branch to branch. Rustling sounds announced small mammals scampering. The smell of pine was fresh and bracing. She was not separate. She was flesh, embedded in this world.

Before long, they were moving again. It rained on and off. Suddenly, she realized she didn't have her sketch pad. She kept feeling her pockets, as if one more check would make the sketch pad materialize. Five good remaining sheets of paper, gone, and there was no going back. They trudged on, the rain heavier, her weeks of work disintegrating into the earth.

They came upon the backsides of houses built four or five centuries before, crossed a bridge, and went along a pleasant promenade with long views across the countryside to the higher peaks. Aware of how people recoiled and gave large berth, it took some daring to ask. The next major town, Pau, was twice the distance they'd come. They hadn't lost much altitude. She feared another night outside.

At the arched, Romanesque portal of a cathedral, they entered through one side of the double wooden doors. Inside, the smells of candle wax, incense, and wood oil lingered. They crouched in the shadow of a stone staircase until they heard the barreling sound of the doors being shut. For fear of being discovered during the night, they slept on the stone floor rather than on the pews. It was like trying to sleep on a block of ice.

In the morning, she woke to a tangy smell. On the pew sat a black lacquered tray with a hunk of ewe's cheese, two buttered rolls, and two cups of "coffee" made from a roasted grain. Where had this bounty come from? Had the priest brought it? A monk? A church worker? Although she was not one to pray before eating, this morning she held the cup between her hands to warm them and gave thanks to whomever had provided this nourishment.

WEEKS WENT BY. They passed through Pau, then Tarbes and Saint-Girons. She decided to avoid Toulouse. They were managing in the woods and occasionally braving backcountry roads. Charlotte feared that without resources, they might be arrested. So they went by way of Foix, then headed toward Narbonne on the coast.

The slopes grew progressively softer into undulating hills with meadows covered in showy wild iris and the humbler blue thistle. They walked under azure skies, the rain behind them, the cold subsiding with each hour.

Luitger was in constant pain. He frequently cried, "Stop." Whenever he sat, it took a great effort to right him again. She imagined herself as Gertrude Mahlick's daughter, Eugenia, or one of Luitger's own daughters, letting him topple to the ground and stomping him. Her thoughts horrified her. Well brought up German girls didn't think such things. But maybe, she ventured, they did have to *think* them, even if they did not *do* them, in order to avoid killing themselves.

She'd managed to find them morsels to eat, clean water to drink, and places to sleep, meeting these tests by not thinking too far into the future, only of the one next thing required. Amazingly, what they needed had been provided—not plentifully, but enough to move them a little farther toward home.

Then a more familiar climate greeted them, sunny and hot. Their clothes dried out. But every day, Luitger had a new complaint: shooting pains in his legs, a wobbly knee, and an aching back. He was near breathless on the slightest inclines. She dreaded how she'd have to nurse him when they got home and wondered how she was ever going to paint again.

Something was taking shape within her. It had started a few nights earlier, when she'd felt a terrible longing for her friends in the camp. She saw again, in her mind's eye, the plunging forth of an eager new being into this world. Whatever she had imagined birthing to be, she couldn't have been more wrong. Whatever she had imagined the limits of strength, she had had no idea. Whatever she had imagined being alive meant, she had not known. If Rosemarie had had it in her to give birth, the baby to make it through to this side, Anneliese to midwife, the other women to provide support under the most unhygienic conditions, and herself to rise to the occasion, then, she thought, *I am a woman among women. I, too, am life.*

She remembered each of the women artists, their paintings and drawings. She had promised Lili that they would meet again. Lou had cast her coal-black eyes directly into Charlotte's.

"When the war is over, come to the City of Light. I'll introduce you to Picasso, Delaunay, Giacometti, show you all of bohemian Paris."

Paris. Even though she'd listened to Lili's Left Bank stories, for herself it was inconceivable—but for the memory of Lou and what felt like a summons she must answer.

CHAPTER 14

NEAR PERPIGNAN

AUGUST 1940

Their first real shelter was an unheated outbuilding on the property of an abandoned villa not far from Perpignan. Charlotte had meant to go to Narbonne, not Perpignan. The groundskeeper's wife explained that Narbonne was sixty-five kilometers northeast along the coast. Charlotte's heart sank. They'd gone the opposite way. She accepted a sliver of pine soap and a half loaf of bread, grateful for the invitation to take fallen apples from the orchard.

Beyond the orchard, a meadow looked toward the impressive peak of Mount Canigou. They took turns at the trough. She splashed freezing-cold rainwater on her legs—torn from walking through brush—cleansed the sores and washed one dress.

The only furniture was a narrow, old, iron bedstead with a saggy mattress. After they'd eaten their bread and apples, Charlotte lay down in near collapse on the bare floor. Cold came from the earth below, tempered by layers of air and wood planks. She pushed aside the question of how they had gotten so off course. Instead, she imagined fingering the silky sable tip of her paintbrush waiting for her in Nice.

"Come here, Lotte."

Luitger's voice dragged Charlotte off the path to slumber. It was much softer than usual, almost conciliatory. In the darkness, he held up one corner of the filthy, threadbare blanket.

"Why don't you share the only bed with me? Please, crawl in. It's only natural." Onto his plea, he spun a note of self-pity. "I've had no warmth since your grandmother died."

Suddenly Charlotte was wide awake. Her skin felt as though it were being attacked by a thousand small spiders. Did he think she didn't see through his ploy? Didn't recall his hands on her throat while he jabbed at the small of her back with rigid thrusts? Bile seeped its acrid ooze upward into her throat.

"My grandmother had no warmth for you." Now. She would tell him. "And for good reason." She kept her voice level. "She told me the truth about Gertrude Mahlick's daughter, Eugenia."

She couldn't hear a sound. He must have been breathing from the shallow of his chest, wondering how much his wife had revealed. Charlotte felt a surge of energy, the power of knowing the black of his soul.

"And I know what you did to your own daughters. My aunt. My mother, for God's sake. You were the one who drove them to their ends."

A suppressed sound, like the whimper of a dog fearing the lash. She sensed his urge for flight.

They lay a long time in tense silence. Her head filled with images of the women he'd wronged. She recalled how he listed them, dispatching each, like ticking off a list of items missing after a burglary but with less sense of loss. The suicides hung about, ghostly, asking an elusive question.

The smell of apples giving off their rot from the heat of the day permeated the night air. The sound of a plucked guitar accompanied by a mournful woodwind floated from the far side of the meadow. The terrible things people did to each other rushed through her mind. The Great War. Millions of dead, all the young and beautiful boys. Trenches that Wolf endured. Pogromnacht—the roundup of Jewish men throughout the Reich. Poles fleeing Hitler. Crimes of the Nazis, which her grandmother had read to them every day. Spaniards fleeing Franco. Their own arrest. The hideous hellhole of Gurs. Disgusted as she was with him, her grandfather's individual life came into focus in minute profile set against the evils of the world, orders of magnitude greater.

She stopped asking why he was who he was. Others who had had greater losses weren't so twisted. It was a choice, a succession of choices—to become a human being or not.

Charlotte absolved him of nothing, but possessed by thoughts ranging wider, far outside their twisted circle, she let out a doleful cry.

"Luitger, all humanity is stained and broken. But it doesn't have to be."

His reply came—loud, abrupt—with the permanent croak the camp had left in his voice. "Oh, stop your foolish talk. Just get it over with and kill yourself too!"

It was night in the countryside. The chorus of stridulating bush crickets, aggressive, insistent, might have egged her on in the direction Luitger wanted her to take. She had carried him from tree to river to farm—he, who with exquisite talent, had stolen cherished innocence, all the while thinking himself a decent person. The more entwined their every movement, the more indifferent she was to his fate. She fell asleep cradling her treasure, the spark of well-gotten hatred in her heart.

When she woke, she padded out to the yard, saw the apricot sky with a promising rosy blush, and stretched the muscles of her legs. She lifted her arms toward the day. Uncontained, her whole being reached across the meadow into the mountains and beyond, right into the sky.

She wanted to create something extraordinary, beyond the mind's eye, outside of any categorization, genre, or movement. A thing fierce and unique, alarming in its newness. She had a life never lived before, belonging to no one else, unique, wholly hers. And she would paint it.

CHAPTER 15

───────

PERPIGNAN

AUGUST 1940

By the time they reached Perpignan's town center, the rays of the sun had warmed their bones, and Charlotte had conceived a new strategy.

Sprawled around a broadly curved corner, an open-air restaurant caught her eye. A canopy of white umbrellas shaded the tables, most of which were occupied for the midday meal. She left Luitger standing on the sidewalk while she took a table away from the street, directly in the path of the busy waiters, who looked askance at her.

"I'd like to speak with the owner, please," she said, taking the proffered menu.

He went off a little huffy and returned with a middle-aged woman in a white apron.

"We've nothing to eat." Charlotte's voice was low. She pointed to Luitger. "My grandfather is very frail. We must get to Nice."

The woman took the measure of Luitger, who looked like an ancient golem, made more of earth than flesh. She mouthed: Jews?

Charlotte risked a nod. The woman made her way out to the sidewalk, where she took Luitger by the arm. He offered no resistance, and as diners averted their eyes, she steered him back among the tables to the spot where Charlotte was sitting.

"Follow me," she said to Charlotte, her arm still guiding Luitger.

She deposited them at a table in a small garden. A mishmash of colorfully painted fanciful pots displayed red geraniums, blue lobelia, and sweet white alyssum. The beds on one side were dedicated to vegetables, and on the other, herbs. From above, bright birdsong.

Soon the proprietor returned with cassoulets in small clay pots. The aroma of tomatoes, onions, garlic, and herbs made Charlotte want to cry. Luitger stuffed his mouth too full and expelled pieces of half-chewed morsels back into the bowl while precious broth dripped onto his beard and disappeared. They'd finished wiping their plates clean with country bread when the owner returned.

"Louis is trucking his cork and olive oil to Marseille. Hurry, now. Out this way."

She led them through the garden door to the side street. Next thing they knew, they were in the cab of Louis's truck, rambling along the road at great speed with windows rolled down, breathing salty air, learning how cork was harvested from cork oaks growing around Perpignan. In less than an hour, they sailed through Narbonne, Charlotte's huge mistake undone.

"How far from Marseille to Nice?" she asked Louis.

"Around two hundred kilometers."

Two or three more hours by car. They could make it this day if they were lucky enough to pick up another ride.

When they arrived in Marseille, Luitger instructed Louis to drop them at the railway station. Charlotte followed as he marched up to a window and asked the price of a ticket to Nice. He reached inside his coat, ripped the frayed lining open, and pulled out franc notes.

Charlotte blinked and squinted, trying to verify what she saw. "You have francs?"

"Of course. Your grandmother sewed them inside. 'If they come for you,' she said, 'take this coat. No matter what the weather, take it.'"

Charlotte's whole body seized up, twisted into a contorted question. How dare he have withheld this? But she was speechless. A tremendous wave of relief passed through her. It was the end of this walking ordeal.

"A ticket to Nice," he said to the man behind the window.

Charlotte said, "One?"

"It's all I can afford. You're young. A woman. You'll find your way. And I expect you in Nice by tomorrow night."

She wanted to shout scathing words or stomp off in a flaming whirl. But she just stood with scorn roaring in her ears and venom bubbling in her throat, not in disbelief but as dumb observer. She watched him turn his back and head toward the waiting train. His dusky figure moved away from her with halting steps. He'd just as soon be rid of her as she of him. Who wanted to live with one who knew the truth of you—like peering into a looking glass daily, reflecting one's baseness—the truth you thought you had squelched?

PART II

—

1941-42

CHAPTER 16

NICE

AUGUST 1941

After Luitger left her in Marseille, Charlotte had inquired at a synagogue. A congregant family housed her for a week and found her a safe ride across the coast. All the way, she dreamed of painting again, and of living: eating real food, being free to go to the sea. But the first thing she wanted was to sleep for a long, long time. Half of her couldn't wait to be back in the apartment, tucked into her bed. Half of her dreaded seeing Luitger again and wished—she was not even ashamed to have thought it—that he'd perished.

What she found on the sofa was a heap of fragile bones in a pile of raggedy clothes. She wanted to shriek him out of existence, but there he was. His skin was sallow, the circles under his eyes dark purple and yellow, his mouth a dry scummy slit in a filthy beard. But his blue eyes were as frigid as ever, and he was quite capable of making demands.

Charlotte, too, had lost an enormous amount of strength. Her soft, rounded belly had turned concave, like a bowl between protruding hip bones. Immediately she was thrown into the tedium of caretaking.

The burden of Luitger included taking him to visit Emmet Schatzman halfway down steep Rue Neuscheller, which he claimed was too dangerous for him to navigate on his own, and then picking him up at the end of his visit. But Charlotte thought he simply enjoyed issuing orders and watching her carry them out.

Indistinguishable one from the other, the days turned over. They gurgled down the drain in the suds, evaporated into the air from washed linen. They marched down the hill, labored back up, brewed five hundred pots of tea, and sliced innumerable loaves of bran and coarse rye bread, usually stale. They sewed up the holes in old clothes and sheets with thread from the hems and knitted together unraveling sweaters with found yarn. The days washed away, each like a drop of pigment disappearing into the sea. *Gone*, she said to herself each night, gone and gone again, until all together, they stole a year of her life.

As she began to recover, she found a brief respite from misery. Henri had brought her a bicycle, compliments of Olive, so she sometimes made the trip to l'Ermitage, but it made her jealous all over again when she heard he was off once more with Gabrielle, looking to place the children. The wasting of her body, the loss of her youthful bloom, didn't make that any easier. Neither did the limited allotment of only three potatoes per month per person.

Life had resumed at the chateau. Meanwhile, Olive was arranging through the consulate to take the orphaned children to America.

Anneliese and Rui had been released shortly after Charlotte. Her year of days lost to Luitger was for Anneliese a year of days gained in renewal. By the time summer rolled around again, she seemed no worse for her ordeal in the camp. Her skin had grown pale and fresh again, her black

curls bouncy. She looked very much the capable young mother to a sturdy two-year-old that she was, and she was patient
in listening to Charlotte's woes.

For some months after her return, Charlotte had not had
a menstrual period, but Dr. Mercier had assured her that
was normal for young women living in deprived conditions
such as Gurs. Touching her with gentle respect and giving so
much comfort, he promised better nutrition would promote
a normal cycle. With the garden vegetables and eggs from
l'Ermitage, it did.

Charlotte became well, robust but sinewy, able again to
easily lift a basket of laundry, and this resilience was remarkable. She had looked out at the world to find beauty. Oddly,
it had been conferred upon her innermost self. Or maybe her
experience cleared her inner vision, letting her see what had
always been there.

These visits to l'Ermitage, though, were but a bit of
breathing space. The time of her real life was in her painting. Not long after she first returned from Gurs, Henri had
built a latched storage container for her bicycle, big enough
for her art-supply box. Dr. Mercier told her she had suffered
multiple traumas: leaving Berlin, her grandmother's suicide,
the burden of discovering all the family suicides—which she
had blurted out to him in her desperation—not to mention
the internment.

"Take up painting again, Charlotte," he said. "It will help
to heal you."

A word from him to Henri, for they were very close, might
well have produced the pretty box, sanded and oiled, that
made it possible for Charlotte to paint on the beach. There
she made small seascapes, which she then sold to the tourists
on the promenade, where bicycle rickshaws were beginning
to appear, and the hotel lawns were turning into gardens. She

would not spend her francs on those vegetables, even had they been for sale to the public. She was saving them and adding to her dream of escaping Luitger.

It was August again, a year after her release. On this warm day, she finished cleaning up their breakfast of tea and eggs and apricots. As she often did while busy with housekeeping, she thought about her father and Katharina. Though they had escaped Berlin for Amsterdam, Rotterdam had now stopped issuing visas. She hadn't heard from them since Germany invaded the Netherlands, since before she and Luitger were taken to Gurs. Fifteen, sixteen months? Her whole being floated on the hope they would appear, then sank with the puncturing thought that more likely, they'd been arrested.

Many days, Luitger was out the door at midmorning to spend an hour or two with Emmet. Clearly, she realized, he could handle the walk up and down Rue Neuscheller if he chose. She didn't challenge him on this point. She was happy enough that he was out of the apartment. She swiped the crumbs from the butcher block and took out her supplies and little easel. Chores could wait.

Today, she decided to look at all the paintings she had made in the last year. But there wasn't the space to lay them all out. Then she got the idea to go where she hadn't gone since before their arrest—out the kitchen, five steps across the tiny foyer, and up the narrow staircase. The door at the top was closed. She opened it.

As she stepped inside, a powerful odor made her gag. It was the smell of rotting fabric and long-enclosed space, of claustrophobia and the untouched disarray despair trails in its wake. She left footprints on floorboards shrouded by a film of dust. Still, there were three bare walls, and the large windows, though dingy, flooded the room with a better light by far than the kitchen. How had she not discovered it this whole year? Right under her nose, or more precisely, above her head—an art studio.

While packing up her grandmother's belongings to take to the Boulevard Dubouchage synagogue, she discovered in the hem of a long black coat what felt like a bunch of pebbles that turned out to be pearls—perfectly round, smooth, and luminous—a handful of them, and five small diamonds. She stared at the gems in a state of uplift akin to awe. These jewels were meant for escape. Her grandmother had urged her to survive. *You are the one who has it to go on, Lotte. Go. Become an artist.*

She tucked them into a purple velvet drawstring pouch and went downstairs, where she placed the pouch into the bottom of her art-supply case, along with her earned francs. A thrill rose to her throat, made her heady. With her next sigh, she raised her palms together in gratitude.

When the upstairs room was spotless and fully aired out, she taped her paintings to the walls. There was a series honoring her grandmother. Pictures with multiple scenes: her marriage; domestic life; the birth of Charlotte's mother, Eva; even Luitger rocking the cradle; and the two of them dressed up for an evening out.

Willi's drowning had a picture all its own. His figure, an uneven blend of dark blue and dark red but for a white triangle of shirt, repeated six times, diagonally from top left; then, in the opposite direction, twenty-one more squeezed up against each other with bluish faces of no distinction. In the bottom third of the picture—brown and blue, green and dark red—the menacing waters of the river swirled.

She especially liked a painting of her grandmother sitting with her aunt Charlotte as a bundled baby, the brushstroke unifying mother and baby as one. Looking on but separated by a distinct distance was a little girl. She was Eva. Many more paintings along these lines—madness and the urge to suicide in the merry whirl of domestic life.

She counted fifty, almost one for each week since Gurs. Some were in the form of multi-panel narratives. Others showed a single dramatic event. Still others were simple portraits of her female relatives—face forward, in the style of Lou Albert-Lasard. In Charlotte's, the women appeared startled or expressionless, revealing their inner desolation. Then there were scenes from her own childhood and a good number of Wolf.

Charlotte shifted them around, created groupings. Something started to rise within her, as though the deep sea had loosened a sunken hulk long anchored to the ocean floor. She could feel it lifting and moving, and the subtle wave pushing upward against resistance.

People killed themselves. And a whole theater of life got created so no one would know. It was like something occurring backstage that the audience would never see, but explained what the play was about. In her case, so many of the events and people belonged to a past beyond the bounds of her memory, her existence. But something—more insistent, incorporeal, a shadow of it all—had remained to make itself known through her.

From the courtyard, the sound of drums. Then trumpets. Someone was playing a wire recording of Beethoven's *Wellington's Victory*. Full orchestra. Percussion mimicking artillery. Exciting crescendos. Both sides, French and British, fighting to the death for victory.

Only this remained: a resurrection, these paintings, on these three walls, one after another, right up to the windows—each one, all together—more her life than her actual life.

After carrying her supplies upstairs, she made her palette fresh, dipped her wide brush into blue, and diluted it until the water was as pale as a robin's egg. The brush was poised above the blank paper, ready to deliver the first stroke of wash, when she blinked and looked about the sparkling room, swooping the paintings into a whole she didn't understand but believed in. Her eyes felt hot. Her vision blurred. One hand went to her chest to stay a sudden aching.

For all the scrubbing, the inner picture would not erase. The rumpled bed. Streams of white hair on the damp pillow. Her eyes were leaking tears, shut against the image of her grandmother crying out for morphine. When Charlotte opened them, the life had gone out of her paintings. This was not a place she would be able to work.

CHAPTER 17

VILLEFRANCHE-SUR-MER

Henri decided it best to stay in the Italian zone, so he took Charlotte north from Nice to La Trinité. On this unusually warm day, he'd folded down the convertible top on the fancy yellow roadster.

They'd just made a sad farewell to Olive, who had pulled away from l'Ermitage in a beat-up Renault break de chasse, loaded with ten children, a pig, and two goats, bound for New York via southern France, Spain, and Lisbon. Through the American Joint Committee's generosity, she had obtained a large quantity of chocolate plus powdered milk to supplement any short supply from the goats. Dr. Mercier had provided health certificates for the children. Henri had promised to find homes for four remaining behind.

All had gathered for this farewell. Matilde was there. Delmira and Gabrielle. Max and Anneliese with Rui in her arms. Delmira openly sobbed. Henri slipped his arm around Charlotte's waist. They were all holding on to one another, and at the same time, waving goodbye with brave smiles on their faces.

"Take care of Charlotte too!" Olive had called out the window. A wave of warm appreciation washed over Charlotte for this moment of belonging, and subsided in the wistful thought that this was really the beginning of dispersion. The children to new, strange homes. Delmira back to her farm. The Merciers to town. And for the refugees, who knew? But that melancholy faded when Henri drew her toward him until his hip pressed against hers. His heat penetrated her tense muscles, making them soften. That was when he asked her to go for a spin.

A carefree hour from Luitger, from the children, excited her. It also made her uneasy. Did she know how to enjoy herself? Her nerves vibrated throughout her body, but like the plucked strings of a violin, sweetly.

They sped around the curved mountain roads and stopped at a *village perché*—one of the walled villages perched on top of a cliff. Henri bought cheese and paid dearly for a real baguette, "compliments of excessive compensation for keeping the car in the pink."

They picnicked in the roadster at an overlook. Deftly uncorking a bottle of l'Ermitage wine from the trunk, Henri admitted to a hankering for a German sausage.

"Me too," Charlotte said as he held his thumb under a piece of baguette and his index finger over the cheese in a manner that was precise in its awareness of the pleasure this morsel would deliver. She accepted it with an open mouth as he popped it in.

He began to talk about his family, and she relaxed into listening. Happy family times dominated his memory: hiking together in the Austrian Alps, high enough to get an eagle's view of the world; resting by tranquil mountain lakes; and staying in picturesque villages. His talk reminded her of her own family treks, and she told him about finding her governess in the Dolomites.

"She could see my frozen tears and made sure my motherless childhood was filled with happy times. Horseback riding on the beach at the North Sea. Playing the lute. Drawing. Tennis."

She told him how her father was rounded up and then returned from Sachsenhausen, and of his surgical practice and research. And about Katharina's magnificent voice, how they became more observant as Jews, went to synagogue on her mother's *yahrtzeit* and on Yom Kippur when Katharina chanted "Kol Nidre."

"I even had a bat mitzvah."

She almost mentioned Wolf Abrams in their apartment too, how he found employment through the Kulturbund as Katharina's voice teacher. But when she thought of who Wolf had been to her—her unquenchable longing for his gaze and so much more, her dire need for his approval of her sketches and drawings, her craving to understand his perplexing and mysterious thoughts, and her obsession with him night and day for years—she felt even less able to explain him to Henri than she had been to Anneliese.

"It was the place I liked best to be on wintry Sundays." Henri was now speaking of his father's small carpentry shop at home, where he liked to tinker and make small carvings. "Max preferred the outdoors, especially ice hockey."

Charlotte's heart raced. She would ask.

"How did it happen?"

He closed his eyes for a moment. When he opened them, he took a long breath.

"It was sheer luck for me. I happened to be out." He paused. "I was spared."

He had at the time only a few years in the import-export business. He enjoyed the give and take of trade, meeting people from other countries and cultures, and beginning to make a good living. That morning, his mother was preparing his favorite Wiener schnitzel for dinner.

"I said my usual goodbye. I liked to pull at her apron strings a little, egg her away from the stove. She said what she always said when I left the house in the morning: 'In whatever you do today, be happy, my son.'"

Charlotte knew this pit in her stomach, what it felt like to have a parent taken. Her father had returned, but Henri had never heard from either of his parents. His hand resting on his thigh twitched so subtly. She laid her hand on his. She wanted him to have hope.

After a while, Henri asked about her experience in Gurs camp. She hadn't talked about it to anyone—never with Luitger and not even Anneliese.

"I don't mean to pry." He seemed only to want to know her better. At least, his eyes said so, clear as a fine peridot this cloudless day.

She left out everything ugly and told him about Lou, Lili, and the artists' group, and the decision she had made to become more directed in her work.

He peeled an orange. A little spritz effervesced, releasing a citrusy tang into the air. His brown hair was blown about from the car ride, making him look boyish, even intriguing with the scar by his right ear, which had grown less garish and frightful over the years, blending into his skin like a fine white line of someone starting to draw…what?

She said, "I want to believe I can walk right back into it. When this is all over. And I know I can't. I don't know anything about what will be. There. Here. Or even, sometimes, which is real. That? Or this?"

"I, too, wonder. Did I ever really have a featherbed in Salzburg, or sit by the river Salzach with friends in the evening, drinking beer and watching the sun set over the city's spires? Maybe just as real as sitting here, drinking wine and looking out at the Mediterranean. Maybe not a question of reality but of time. Past. And present."

"In a normal life, the present rises out of a shaping, an effort," she said. "But we're flotsam and jetsam, randomly afloat on the sea, not knowing where we're going."

"Flotsam and jetsam? Hardly! We've been delivered conditions. We still have choices. And one choice is to develop a toleration of the unknown while continuing to make the effort."

She ruminated for a moment. Yes. Exactly as she should think.

She wanted to kiss him but didn't dare. If Olive had ended it with him, he might be looking to soothe his broken heart with her. If he'd been the one to end it, well, then Olive's fate might become hers too. Anneliese said not every affair was about the heart. Perhaps that was true for him and Olive. But it would not be true for her.

He asked about her current work. She explained that she was on to something of weight, scale, and import; also, she told him why she couldn't work in the apartment.

"I want to move out."

"Hurrah! Even you don't believe the flotsam-and-jetsam nonsense you espouse." His smile said he'd been waiting to hear this a long time. "Come back to l'Ermitage. Leave that old troll to his own devices."

For a moment, she felt shame over Luitger's disgusting behavior toward her. No matter how vigorously she cast it off, it kept a hook in, like an obdurate parasite, and when she was least aware, it grew from its hooked stump a new body within her. Now she felt its sickly thickness in her throat, something she couldn't reveal to Henri for fear it would drive him away.

"I'm legally bound to take care of him. If I leave, he'll hunt me down. L'Ermitage will be the first place he looks."

"We certainly won't let Luitger prowl the Great House."

"But he might send the police. I can't let you take that risk."

Henri pulled himself up, broadening his shoulders. The look on his face was like that of a soldier standing on guard with orders he wouldn't violate.

"We've taken measures. Everyone in the house, including the remaining children, now has Swiss papers. Provided by Dr. Mercier. Delmira, of course, is still Delmira. She answers the door by day. Max, Anneliese, and Rui have new identities. They are now the Rochat family. Anneliese answers at night, as Madame Rochat."

"A very good development."

"Luitger won't turn you in. You're all he has. If he did, he would lose you for good. He would have no one to whom he might appeal. If you're only away somewhere, he can hope you'll return. He can try as he might to get you back. That would be more in his interest than to have you arrested."

Her heart pounded with the thrill and fear of freedom.

"No. I know him. He would have me arrested. Out of revenge. If I go, I must be well hidden."

Charlotte told him of the found jewels, the francs she'd saved, and the hefty sum Olive left her. "I'm looking for a room to let on the other side of town, or in Villefranche. So far? No luck."

"But you'll be completely alone. And without identity papers. You'll be subject to arrest and internment. Possibly deportation."

"I know. Should I be afraid? I don't feel afraid."

"At the moment, no, because the Italians aren't looking to capture Jews. But if you won't come to l'Ermitage, you might try moving more out of the way, farther east. To a sleepy place. Saint-Jean-Cap-Ferrat, perhaps."

Then they stepped out of the car to enjoy the view. There was something in the smell of the atmosphere, perhaps a heavier salt and something earthier, as though it were the mushrooms' turn now in the mountains to fragrance the air with their nutty essence. It was a day that hearkened back to late summer and hung onto autumn, suggesting time could be suspended long enough to be embedded in memory. She'd paint it true blue and shimmering golden yellow with a ribbon of wine red, a light spray of orange and pink and violet, exclamations on the moment.

Henri stood close to her. He stared out at the horizon. Charlotte stole glances, appreciating the mix of strong features, especially his cheekbones, which were very fine without lending arrogance—in fact, adding to his sensitivity. Then she took in the sea with him.

She closed her eyes for a second, then opened them to see anew. At first sight, the blue was shocking. The water sparkled, and her body attuned to the quiver of its surface. Maybe it was the beauty of this place that assuaged her longing for everything she missed. Or because Henri and she had shared their losses. Anyway, she felt lighter.

"I'm just thinking," he said, "if you move, we must know where you are so we can warn you. Because I see you're right. The police would come to l'Ermitage first."

Her heart swelled. She turned to him so he could see her gratitude. Because he stood so near, it was only his face she saw.

"And so that I might find you when I return."

When he returned? He was going off again? The very moment Olive had left? The very moment they were standing here like this? She backed up a step.

"Oh?"

He laid his hands on her shoulders. His touch awakened a fresh yearning, not for what was lost, what couldn't be had, but for what was right there and might be had. Or not—she didn't know.

"Gabrielle and I need to line up four more homes. We're leaving in the morning. I could be gone for months."

With that girl? Night and day?

Charlotte's voice had an edge of hysteria to it. "Months?"

He pressed down on her shoulders. "I'll be doing some work with refugees as well. Jews from Eastern Europe."

She wanted to flip away and make for the coast downhill on foot, not caring if it took her until nightfall to reach Nice. But she stood frozen. When she couldn't help but let him hold her gaze, he said, "I will find you, Charlotte, when I return."

She didn't want him to go, and there was nothing she could do about it. They hadn't had even one chaste pressing-together of their lips. She found herself lifting onto her toes. Her body had made a decision not quite signed on for, and her mind simply had to follow.

She kissed him.

She'd imagined the wanting extinguished in the fulfillment. But the feel of his lips with their lingering taste of cheese, oak of wine, hint of orange, made her want more. She took more, then sank down onto her feet again, breath quickening.

She reached out to touch his scar. His face went dark, and he took her hand in his. Something had come over him, but what?

His arms reached all the way around her. He pulled her into him, and her head went light. His whole mouth covered hers. Giving in to the flooding warmth, she closed her eyes. Then she felt it—all of him, their meeting. He was holding her tight so none of her could escape. She didn't know whether she was lost or had been found.

She blinked—breathless, stirred, bewildered.

Henri said, "Perhaps this wasn't fair. With me leaving. But I'll return. It's a promise."

Promises made her afraid, sent up a butterfly of panic.

"I'll be back in the spring to take over the car again. We'll drive the Route d'Or up to Tanneron to see the mimosa trees in bloom."

"That sounds lovely," Charlotte replied, aware of her heart rocking in her chest, shifting about for its old place to settle, which was gone.

CHAPTER 18

NICE

More than a month after Henri's departure, Charlotte rolled into the tiny town of Saint-Jean-Cap-Ferrat, its harbor crammed with yachts and sailboats. The reflection of the white masts undulated on the water's surface. After walking her bicycle through a street stuffed with stalls selling practical wares and books, into another flanked by archways hung with signs that read *Bar* and *Tabac*, she headed uphill. Wild explosions of magenta bougainvillea hung above doorways. As she climbed, tall fences and giant cypress hedges created fortresses for unseen villas.

When she was well above the posh seaside, what looked like a small white *pension* sparkled in the sunlight, its garden wall adorned with a citron tree. An attractive woman, fortyish, stood on its terrace, looking down.

Charlotte didn't see a sign and wanted badly to ask. Her heart started to pound. She stammered at first, summoned her courage, and started again. "*Bonjour, madame*! You wouldn't happen to have a room available?"

"I do! I'll be right down."

Charlotte tried not to get her hopes up. There was bound to be something wrong with it.

The woman was naturally slim, wearing a striped shirt-waist dress open at the throat the way Olive wore hers, fresh-looking but in a French way. A barrette secured her bobbed brown hair above one temple, making her look businesslike but not severe. She introduced herself with out-stretched hand.

"Madame Piché."

Charlotte followed her up to Room Number 1. Right away, a shower of glittering white light poured in from two opposing windows. The room wasn't large, but adequate, with a brass bed and a white, tufted spread; a small wardrobe with a mirror atop; and, near one window, an armchair in a slipcover the color of butter. She looked out at the terrace below, from which Madame Piché had spotted her. A few steps down led to a pretty walled garden running the length of the building.

The view out the other window was over red-tiled roof-tops stacked down the hillside and the green-covered hills to the west toward Villefranche. It was quiet. Charlotte felt like she was floating above it all. In the distance, under the vault of pale-blue sky, a sliver of sea lay undisturbed—oval and shining, like a polished sapphire just cut, not yet set.

"It's very pretty," she said. The carpet was a true pink, like the blossoms of her Japanese cherry.

The weekly rent was affordable. Her francs would go far. Discreet and nonintrusive, Madame Piché was open to an in-determinate length of stay. Charlotte would decline the meals because she needed to be frugal to a fault. Her attention to her work would be ardent and uninterrupted.

"So? You think it's right for you, *mademoiselle*?"

It was the perfect place. But something held her back.

Charlotte asked her to hold it until the next day. Madame Piché said, "Someone else may—"

"I understand. Of course, you'd have to—"

Charlotte could tell the landlady was assessing her. A single woman. German. Possibly a refugee. Clean dress, hair only slightly awry from cycling.

"I'm an artist. In need of a bright room in which to work." It was as if she was not speaking of herself but of another person standing beside her. In the next moment, she stepped inside that person. Now there was one. It was her, and it was true. "I didn't set out today with the intention. And I've nothing to leave down."

This wasn't true. In one hand she held her purse with enough francs. Her free hand was not free. Luitger had it.

"Oh, but you do want it, I see. I'll hold it until ten in the morning."

On the street, Charlotte noticed the *pension's* sign: *La Belle Aurore*. The Beautiful Dawn.

Charlotte cycled back to Nice. There was no longer a moral point: she was being mistreated. That freed her from obligation. Somehow Luitger would manage. If he could swallow his pride, there was always the soup kitchen run by the Jewish assistance committee. There was no longer fear; he wouldn't be able to find her. She'd be safe. Yet she was unable to convince herself.

Aimless and agitated, she left her bicycle to walk along Rue France. In the shopping district, the beautiful people from all over Europe filled the sidewalk cafés. Spoons clinked against glass, stirring pale-yellow *citrons pressés*. The prattle and gossip were lurid and cheerful. Such freedom and festivity seemed bizarre when the continent was aflame with war and the country had been invaded.

She longed to sit with her brushes by the window of Room Number 1. The clarity of today's light reminded her of the impossibility of the work. And the necessity. The series she'd begun would be a monument to her life. Monument? Perhaps she *was* truly mad, because that was too great a word for any endeavor of hers. But she knew no other way to discover if this was a delusion than by devotion to making it manifest. And it was not wholly hers. A driving power had taken her by force on the road from Gurs, like a tornado of intense energy committed by nature to sweeping away everything obstructive.

She left the town for the beach and found the very spot where she felt at home to sit. A hundred shades of blue filled her field of vision. Darker indigo patches dotted the cerulean surface of the sea. Above the water, the sky began blue-gray. Rising, it gathered strata into one vast dome of cobalt from which the sun sent its blinding sparkle down to the water's surface. She studied it with intensity, begging for an answer.

A tern separated itself from the noisy colony on the beach. As it ascended, the flock got quiet. The bird dived, plunged into the water, and came up with a fish, which it carried aloft, its wingspan and belly a white dazzle against the sky.

Suddenly Charlotte felt sad for her mother, for what had happened to her and her need to end her life. Sad for herself, too, that she didn't have her mother to turn to for advice and support in this moment. Sad, then, for what never could've been. Melancholy constricted her heart and tightened it around…nothing.

She realized she'd come to think of herself as immune to Luitger's arthritic hands reaching for her. Yet it was a continuous betrayal because every day she must slide away from his unnerving advances, which sent icy shudders up her spine. In that betrayal and the pleasure he took in her recoiling, there was possession. She remained his.

She rubbed her hands over the rocks. What would Wolf have her do? He would say she had not, after a year and a half, come to terms with the family suicides. Even though she'd survived Gurs and the journey home, she was still threatened by them. Living with Luitger was a form of self-imposed death. But the purpose of facing death, he would say, was to confront life. Could he have known of all the suicides in her family? Perhaps Katharina had told him?

She recalled giving Wolf her drawing, "Death and the Maiden." She had thought she was drawing a dream. Now she saw that based on what he had taught her, she had drawn her own means of survival.

HAVING FOREGONE the day's rations, Charlotte returned ready for Luitger's rebuke. He moved quietly from the kitchen into the parlor, grazing her hip with his fingertips as if by accident. At the cleared end of the dining table on the polished wood surface were her brushes, not upright in their glass jar, not smoothed to the point, as she'd left them in her bedroom, but tossed about. Splayed, the fine hairs stood out in all directions like the shocked fur of an antagonistic cat. The sight slapped her cold.

Her voice crackled. "You—You—What have you done?"

He stared at her, smug, like he'd gotten the better of her.

"You discarded Marina's belongings. Her brush and mirror, inlaid with mother-of-pearl, I gave her for an anniversary. Her good coat."

He had to have been upstairs. Charlotte turned and took the stairs in twos. The walls were bare. On the floor lay her paintings in heaps. Some were mostly whole, torn only where he had ripped them from the wall. Others were scraps: a half sheet, a ragged quarter. Her stomach seized in a violent contraction. Luitger let out an obstreperous guffaw from below.

He appeared in the doorway. The grinding of her teeth echoed in the bones of her skull.

"Why did you do this?"

"Because you stole from me."

"They were her things. Not yours. She's dead. I gave them to the needy."

"Without my permission. You took over our room. You're finished here. I've moved back up."

A pile of books dominated the night table. Charlotte shouted and paced and pulled her hair.

"This is my work. The one thing in all the world that matters to me!"

"Stupefied faces. Figures without form. Clothing without buttons. Pfft! Grow up. Make my bed. Clean the kitchen. And get some decent food into this apartment."

He stood, both divested of his anger and agitated from expressing it, his dry lips parted in a slight smile. The quivering in her body mounted into uncontrollable convulsing and launched her forward at him. She grabbed his thin shoulders.

"You!" She shook him hard. She was stunned by what she was doing. "You...you...old bastard!"

Over and over, she cursed while his head jerked on his skinny chicken neck. She wanted to bash him against the wall. He cried out so loudly, she stopped.

She released him. He stumbled off to a corner of the room. Sinking to her knees, she raked the brittle pieces—like fallen leaves in no way resembling the tree—around her folded body. Without her paintings, she was nobody. Being nobody, she could not even weep.

Certainty now pounded in her breast. Betrayal. Not only his of her, but her of herself if she even considered staying now.

What if he'd gone into her things? She scrambled to her feet and swept past him down the stairs into her room. She opened her pine case and checked: francs, the purple velvet pouch—treasure, all there. With relish and fervor, she packed—dresses, nightgowns, linen. She sat on the valise, snapped it shut. She carried it to the front door along with her pine case and the rope, which she'd detached from the window. She opened the door.

He shouted from the upper bedroom. "I'm an old man."

Knowing exactly how much she despised him, she felt alive. She relished her hatred. It spurred her on. Only one step to the other side.

His feet padded across the floor above. "I need you."

She took the step. She was in the hall. She heard his footfalls descending.

"The state's ordered you. It'll be your fault if anything happens to me."

She wouldn't be torn by his pleas. She didn't want to be captured by the Vichy. She knew it was a distinct possibility, and that was why she needed first, before that ever occurred, to finish the work. She took the three flights without once looking back and went directly into the courtyard to her bicycle. She put the pine case in the storage box and, with the rope, tied the valise on top. Was he watching her? She didn't look up. Was he coming after her? She would mow him down. She hopped on and pedaled out of the courtyard.

Charlotte Salomon barreled down Rue Neuscheller and out of Nice, away from her grandfather, freeing herself of his misery. She left the cobbled streets of Old Town, skirting the city's fringes, reaching back in time for what would thrust her out, carry her aloft. Barely discernible, the piano keys, dim tinkle of pine forests, small hills, and lakes of her native countryside. Then, propelled on by the familiar road to Villefranche, she swung past a blur of café tables, *brasserie*, *créperie*, potted palms and ferns, taking an upright position on the hills. She shifted her weight, heavy on one pedal, then the other, side to side, chest heaving. Inhaling salt, citrus, a mélange of fragrances, she crested, then coasted the down-hills, leg muscles loosening, hearing the words of Katharina's song, faint, rising from the round-and-round hum and rhythm of spokes and wheels: *There's a signpost in that hollow that I clearly now discern*. Onward, she delivered herself to the full exertion of body—sinews and flesh—to her own capacity, which promised dreams without measure, to a place where he would never find her.

She arrived in tiny Saint-Jean-Cap-Ferrat while the day was feathery mauve—*There's a pathway I must follow from which no mortal shall return*—and from there went straight up again, all the way to La Belle Aurore.

CHAPTER 19

SAINT-JEAN-CAP-FERRAT

NOVEMBER 1941

With Charlotte's few things hung in the wardrobe, her hairbrush on the dresser, and her pine case on the small desk Madame Piché had added under one of the windows of Room Number 1, at last her work had begun.

It had been a couple of weeks since she'd left Luitger, and she'd painted in order to catch up, trying to remember what she'd created that he'd destroyed. But it was impossible. Her vision was different, just as one's memory of an event at one point in time can differ from the memory of the same event at another point. She'd originally depicted her parents' wedding as a gala affair. On one wall of her room, she'd hung the new version.

This time around she revealed more of the truth or, more accurately, hinted at the mystery—two grim faces in the gay crowd. The bride's parents had already lost one daughter. Their sole other child, Eva, was leaving them now. Charlotte stared at the new version. *Leaving them before she leaves the world.*

She'd come to prefer gouache, watercolor made dense with more pigment, rendering the colors opaque. As for the newlyweds, snug under a snowy-white quilt in their blue nuptial chamber, the couple looked out the grand windows at the full moon. Where did the shadow come from, the one she'd thrown upon the bed and the floor? In a painting, a shadow can come from the future.

Charlotte had no contact with other boarders. Now that she needed to shrink from sight for self-preservation, feeling unseen made her lonelier than ever. She did run across Madame Piché on occasion and gave her most cheery hello, though one that telegraphed that she needed no more of an exchange. She went out once during the day to stave off hunger, rarely to a restaurant. She ate by the seaside. A boiled egg or a turnip was sufficient.

Henri was still gone. She reminded herself of his promise to return. Was she naive to believe in that promise? She did not like imagining him with Gabrielle, who was nineteen, just a child compared to him at almost thirty. He wouldn't take advantage of her, would he? Delmira would not have consented to her niece taking off on a long journey with Henri if she didn't trust him. But then, being an aunt does not confer the same insight or authority as being a parent does, and Gabrielle did have a strong independent streak. Anything could happen on the road. Charlotte would tell herself it really wasn't her business. But then she made it her business by turning it over and over in her mind, especially on days when she was aware that she had no contact with anyone who really knew her.

She wanted badly to go to l'Ermitage, to find herself in the comfortable companionship of Anneliese. Two in the afternoon of a fall day was mild enough to enjoy the out-of-doors. She would like to sit with her friend and confidante in the graveled area of the garden under the great oak. Garden mint would be steeping in a chipped ceramic teapot, the release port emitting a thin thread of steam visible in the cool air. The olive, fig, mulberry, and Brandywine crabapple trees would allow the weak autumn rays to fall through their web of branches. The light would tint some of the windows recessed into the wall of the stone villa. They would talk about everything until the sun had gone to a slant, a chill had slipped into the air, and the windows gleamed gold, then bronze, then gold again.

But she dared not go. Instead she sent Anneliese her new address, asking her to memorize it and then burn it. Perhaps her friend would find a way to stay in touch.

One morning, Charlotte received a letter from an anonymous courier via Dr. Mercier. It was from Luitger. He'd written her at l'Ermitage. In it, he railed at her audacity in abandoning him. He reminded her that she was legally bound to care for him. He demanded she return to Nice immediately. There was no "or else," but it was implied.

With Luitger's letter still in hand, she heard heavy footsteps coming up the stairs. They did not disappear down the hall toward the other rooms. They came closer to hers, the only room on her side of the staircase. Her heart was pounding. Luitger had done it. He'd discovered her at La Belle Aurore and had sent the police. Her throat pinched tight.

Charlotte edged toward the street-side window. She would surely break a leg, at least. And there might be a gendarme outside the building. She pressed her back against the wall, barely breathing.

Only one pair of feet, and they were coming straight up to her door. A pregnant silence followed. It felt as though someone was listening to determine whether she was in. Surely Madame Piché would be accompanying the gendarme, and they'd be talking. She held her breath for the knock, but it didn't come.

Images of mud-soaked Gurs overwhelmed her vision. Her skin prickled the way it did when a piece of straw had penetrated the layers of ragged dress. At least, when they were taken from the apartment in Nice, it had been swift.

A knock—not loud, not demanding. She would not answer it. She girded herself. They would have to break in. Then a rattling sound on the floorboard right outside her door. Receding footsteps. After a long silence, she looked out the window. Finding nothing there, she opened the door a crack, scanned the hall. At her feet was a tray with a bowl of soup, a spoon, and a pristine white napkin.

EVERY DAY NOW in the early evening, after the boarders had finished their meal, something to eat appeared outside Charlotte's door—a bowl of stew, soup, porridge, or custard. Since she was not paying for meals, she felt guilty accepting this kindness. She asked Madame Piché what she might do in return, and Madame Piché said, "Everything is well taken care of. But thank you. You just keep at your painting, Charlotte." The arrangement did help preserve her store of francs. It also saved her a trip out, and as a result, she had that much more time to work.

Something new began to emerge in the way a painting evolved. First—a tune sprang from nowhere. She hummed it. As it looped around in her mind, she would recall a piece of her past, an event, an incident, and that started to take the shape of an image. Her humming became louder—strident, even. The image was sometimes fully formed, and she simply painted what had appeared in her inner vision. Or it was dim, like an undeveloped photograph, which she brought up and then filled in. Or it was partial, and she would start with what she "saw," getting that down, and as she went, the rest blossomed onto the paper, part by part. But always now, a vital, shaping tune began the work, seemed to draw out her brushstrokes.

She was satisfied with her works and at the same time knew they were only the prelude to rendering the tragedy. Her painting would be a testimony after the fact. Could that be authentic? True? Wasn't testimony confined to eyewitnesses, those present? She had not borne witness. She had been a child. Didn't that fact alone rule out her testimony?

These thoughts slid quietly through her mind because she had no doubt that, even having been offered the lie of influenza as a child, she had known. The apartment had remained gloomy on sunny days, the atmosphere heavy with unnatural sorrow, on and on for many years after her mother's death. Her father had disappeared into his practice, his teaching, his research, even after he married Katharina. There was something that could not be spoken—maybe whispered, but never in Lotte's presence. When Luitger had come out with it, his words had given shape to something she realized she already knew. So yes, her testimony would be valid, sound, even authoritative.

The day that she was ready, she began with a new palette. The ritual was preparatory but stunted: she had only black, white, and the primary colors. Yellow at the top, yellow always. Counterclockwise, she skipped a space, applied a dollop of red, then went back between the two and mixed her orange. The semicircle was bright, cheerful, and intense, stirring the shining memories of her childhood.

Setting up her palette was so automatic her thoughts could drift, today to avenues of escape she might've overlooked, not because she seriously contemplated escape but only because this was the talk that she overheard from other refugees she happened to sit near on the beach.

She could never get out without a passport. Even if she had one, where would she go? Besides, she needed to wait for her father and Katharina. What would they think if, when they arrived, she was nowhere to be found? They would be frantic. Her father might collapse and never recover.

White to the right of the yellow. Green (mixed), blue, and purple (also mixed) defined the semicircle sweeping clockwise—deep, sinister, and severe—tolling the legacy of family secrets. Ending in black, the palette was complete.

There was no escape, and it dawned on her it would be better if her father and Katharina did not come to France. Did they know the situation here?

She heard Luitger: *How can you paint when they're doing this to the Jews?*

As long as I'm free, how can I not?

The washbasin served for water. She filled it in the *salle de bain*. The feel of the brush in her hand soothed her anxious feelings about a future she could not envision, about the possibility she would not see her father and Katharina again. Its tip swirled her longing into the water and began the inner turning.

Tune without surcease. *I am visiting Mama.* With the supposed onset of influenza, her mother had gone to live with her parents. Lotte wore her cheerful red dress and carried flowers. Her father was in his blue doctor suit. She had to know: Why couldn't Mama get well in their apartment? Her father had said that with her in school and him with his patients, "Mama needs someone to take care of her. Grossmama can look after her much better, Lotte. This way you won't get influenza too." But her grandmother wasn't looking after her mother. A nurse in white uniform was. Why couldn't the nurse take care of Mama in her own home? But the nurse's eyes were narrow, her lips straight, mean-looking. Lotte wouldn't want those eyes in their home.

Quickly, Charlotte made two paintings. A page divided vertically in half. On the left side, Lotte next to the bed, Mama hugging her. On the right, a picture of Lotte waving goodbye at the end of the visit. Another page divided. On the left, her father on the phone, his face dark and strange. On the right, he sat on the bed with the red quilt, head in his hands. "I've lost her. My happiness, my love. Gone." A little black mixed into the red defined the squares of the quilt.

The day of the funeral. At her grandparents', where her father had dropped her. Sitting on the sofa between them, her grandmother had cried out, "We've lost her." Her grandfather had cried out too. Lotte hadn't cried. She'd told them, "Mama's an angel in Heaven now, and we should all be happy." In the painting, Lotte did look happy, but her grandparents did not. Their mouths she painted as crescents, upside down.

Charlotte stood and pushed out the shuttered windows. She loved the fresh air but didn't always leave the window open because voices carried up from the terrace below and disturbed the dream-trance of her work. But she was done for now. The clean, minty fragrance of the eucalyptus opened her air passages.

Monsieur Piché, the landlady's husband, was in the garden below the terrace. He was a trim, attractive Frenchman with a wide forehead, hair gone white at the temples, typically dressed, as he was today, in a short-sleeve shirt, revealing his tanned and hairy arms and chest. A friend had arrived. Charlotte looked directly down upon the visitor's navy-blue beret.

"Terrifying rumors coming from Russia," the friend said. "The Jews are being shot. En masse."

Charlotte felt her eyes grow wide. She listened while he told how the Jews were being forced into ghettos, everything taken from them—their identification papers, food, everything.

The melodious song of a blackbird filled a brief silence. She spotted its orange beak in the eucalyptus and wanted to tell it to shut up so she could hear.

"The woman didn't look Jewish, and she'd torn up her papers, so she was set aside." He told Monsieur Piché how that woman watched the Nazis march the Jews, who were totally naked, into the ravine at Babi Yar near Kiev. "At the end of the day, an order came to shoot every last one. She threw herself onto the heap of dead ones. She waited for soldiers to finish shoveling the soil to cover the bodies. When she believed it safe, she crawled out. Ran naked under cover of night. And this is how we know."

Charlotte suddenly felt cold and dizzy. She moved away from the window and shrank into herself, squeezing her eyes shut, as though that could block out the impossible report. But no, she had to hear it all, and she went back.

"But that's monstrous!" Monsieur Piché said. "An exaggeration, Paul, perhaps?"

"No, it's true. But very difficult to accept, I know. There are more reports. Too many to be rumors."

The men strolled the full length of the garden and went out of earshot. Charlotte leaned out the window, but she could hear only indistinct speech. Perhaps Paul was wrong. Russia was a long way away. Information could become distorted, traveling such a distance.

When they returned, Charlotte heard Monsieur Piché. "Here, we think it's bad—criminal, really—that your people must report into the prefecture."

"I saw Raymond-Raoul Lambert, back from Vichy," Paul said. "He says soon there'll be no difference between French Jews and foreigners. There will be no way out."

No way out?

He continued, "We have six children just arrived from Paris. I came to ask a favor. I heard you know the American woman, Mademoiselle Miller, at Villefranche. Might you ask on the children's behalf?"

"Paul, my friend, I'm sorry to say she's left. Taken the little ones and gone to America."

Monsieur Piché knew Olive? And Monsieur Lambert, the journalist? The comfort Charlotte took in the smallness of the world was dampened by Paul's terrible message. She wanted to tell him that Henri and Gabrielle would be back and perhaps they might help, but she was afraid to reveal her identity.

Monsieur Piché put his hand on his friend's shoulder. "If what you report is true, we can't live with that knowledge. We'll go insane. But listen, if you ever have need of an apartment in Nice, my wife has one to lend on the west side of town. You just let me know."

The two French friends, Jew and non-Jew, stood a moment in silence, looking at each other. Paul touched his beret and waved goodbye.

Charlotte's stomach turned over. Paul seemed so sure. That woman, naked and lying upon the dead, soil falling by the shovelful upon her back, did everything she could not to move a hair's breadth while being buried alive. Even as Charlotte strained to imagine, it was beyond imagination. Remembering Wolf's experience being buried alive in a trench on a battlefield of the Great War now released her from doubt, bound her to the truth of Paul's story.

While Monsieur Piché remained on the spot, looking distraught, Madame Piché appeared and asked her husband if he was all right. After hearing the report about Babi Yar, Madame Piché exclaimed her disbelief.

"My dear," she said, "I'm worried for our new boarder, Charlotte. She's very quiet, doesn't offer anything about herself. She may be Jewish."

Charlotte pulled away from the window, keeping an ear cocked.

"You didn't ask her?"

"No, no, no."

"And we won't. We can't be in trouble for what we don't know. Vichy cannot last. If she is a Jewish refugee, consider it providence she found us."

A grip of panic sent a rush of blood thumping into Charlotte's ears. Nearly overwhelmed by the need to flee, she paced, clicking her teeth and breathing heavily with elbows cinched to her side. Her brain was like the static of a bad radio broadcast. Every muscle in her body wanted to propel her out the door. It was all she could do to keep herself inside. Each time she reached the door, she turned and leaned against it, holding one balled fist tightly inside the other palm, then pushed off again. What did this mean? Jews being shot in mass graves?

Minutes passed and her pace slowed. She could take a deeper breath. Should she try to get a fake passport? Or should she do nothing and stay put?

Through the barrage of questions riding upon slower waves of fear, her bit of good fortune made itself known. At least, she was not boarding with antisemites. The fact calmed her. Eventually she was able to stop pacing, but her mind spun. What separated her from the woman who'd crawled naked out of the ravine? She wanted to say she was different; it wouldn't happen to her. But they were too similar. Women who didn't look Jewish but were. Without identity cards. She wanted to find one thing different but could not.

Charlotte fixed a clean sheet to her board. What separated her from the mass of dead bodies? The distance from here to Kiev? A string of indifferent moments?

Perhaps only a series of urgent brushstrokes.

CHAPTER 20

SAINT-JEAN-CAP-FERRAT

DECEMBER 1941

The month turned over, and the world truly went mad with Japan's surprise attack on Pearl Harbor and America's declaration of war on Japan. Madame Piché informed Charlotte that Germany and Italy had declared war on America, and America in return on those two countries. She shook her head. "Have we not learned anything from the Great War?"

Charlotte said, "Is humanity really this stupid? We are all people. Can't we agree to live in peace? Why not? Really, why not?"

Luitger's letters piled up, sent first by post to l'Ermitage and from there by courier to La Belle Aurore. He had softened his tone, repeating his complaint that the apartment was a mess, housekeeping was unmanageable, he needed her to return, and he was sorry about what he had done to her work. She knew this last was not true. He wanted her to take pity on him, to believe he was contrite, but she saw through his stratagem. He was trying to manipulate her, and the minute she stepped foot back into that apartment, it would all be the same—intimidation accompanied by creepy hands. Just thinking about it sent chills up her spine. She would not relent.

The last letter, however, was worrisome. He knew she had not registered for the census. He was explicit. If she did not return, he would turn her in. He claimed to have made an acquaintance among the Vichy police, whom he referred to only as Officer X. Still, Charlotte was determined not to be disturbed. She had left him in order to preserve herself and to work, and she forced herself to lay aside her concerns. She was safe at La Belle Aurore. Other than Luitger, there was no disturbance.

The seclusion; the assurance of her absolute safety; the quiet, undisturbed hours—these conditions allowed her at last to think about her dead relatives—first her aunt Charlotte, what Luitger had done to her, how she had ended her life. A startling painting of her suicide was pinned on her wall. In it, lamps still pierced the dark just before dawn. A woman with a long, anemic face, her arms wrapped around her brown torso, descended the rust-colored steps from her home. The city streets were a watery aqua-gray, and the ghost of this figure glided through, repeating itself, tracing an S-curve across the painting. She entered the park, its shrubbery and trees ominous in the night, sat by a river, and disappeared into the molten red-black deep. Eighteen years old. Charlotte marked the painting with the date: 1913. In her family, a historical event.

Contemplating it on the wall, her thoughts turned to her mother. She'd produced so many paintings of her, bits of what she recalled: Mama in the kitchen with a wooden spoon, stirring a batter; Mama dressed to go shopping in a blue coat and hat with her stiff purse in the crook of her elbow; and Mama folding a knit afghan in the study where red coals smoldered in the fireplace. These showed her false, busy side.

Charlotte liked best the ones of the two of them in bed to-gether. That was real. And this one, face front. Had her moth-er blamed herself for her sister Charlotte's suicide? In other paintings, she'd rendered her mother's sad face in profile. Had she wondered why she was alive? Yearning for what? The one that broke Charlotte's heart to have to paint was an extreme close-up of an open window in an empty room where her mother had stood, the floorboards bare.

Today Charlotte heard Katharina singing the lyrics to Von Weber's *Der Freischütz* as clearly as if she had a front seat at the opera: *We twine for thee the maiden's wreath with violet-colored ribbon.* On stage, Agathe appeared in dazzling white bridal dress decorated with a green ribbon. Oh-so-soft horns. Four bars of charming oboe melody. The on-stage scene dissolved. Another flashed once in her mind's eye. It never came up all the way. It came up only on the blank white sheet exactly the size of her lap easel. There and nowhere else.

She hummed as she mixed pigment in water. The tune of-fered the color. She liked violet for its ethereal quality, found in fleeting things like lilacs and the underside of clouds at sun-set. Brush twirled a bit of cadmium red and cerulean blue into water. Too brownish. A dab of cadmium yellow light. From the saved end of a tube of dioxazine violet, she added a speck. Short strokes on the paper. Translucent application. A round-ed violet shape took form—not the perfect round of a sphere, but humped like a fluffed-up pillow, only more substantial, with the density and give of a loaf of bread. This round, violet shape occupied most of the center space.

She worked what was on the sheet while her mind was transported back to the operatic stage. Bridesmaids entered, fes-tooned in their local costumes, to announce to Agathe the arrival of her wreath with violet-blue silk, which the hermit had prom-ised would protect her against a danger. What was the danger if not the black bird of prey Agathe had dreamed of?

Return to the palette to make the background. Brighter colors first, topped by darker. That done, outline one broken leg, with its foot turned inward. Another leg? No. Somewhere unseen under the round violet shape, which was now—clearly—the rise of a human body.

She didn't see it in her mind and then transfer it to the paper. It was not so simple as that. The painting made its way through orchestras playing in her inner ear; elaborate, detailed memories of stage performances; and emotion-filled memories of real-life events.

Bridesmaids danced around Agathe. Strings and first soprano alternated. Folk song of rural love. Apply red next to the violet shape, off center to the left. Red. Like blood. Running out from under the violet shape.

Lilting song, bouncy good cheer. She hummed loudly. Her brain, the whole room, was booming with song. *Lovely green, lovely green maiden's wreath! Violet-blue silk! Violet-blue silk!* Annchen, the bride's cousin, entered the stage in her finery, carrying a round hatbox. The tune coiled through her mind even as Annchen opened the box and found inside, to everyone's horror, a silver funeral wreath.

Louder, even. Forceful. More red. Below the violet shape. A patch of blood. A puddle of blood. A pool, shapeless, uncontained. This was all she had of the blood—the blood she could make on the sheet with her brush—real, horrifying, and lovely.

Now, draw. Directly underneath the round violet shape. Loose wrist. Strong but fluid lines. Suggest two arms folded at elbows. Now, the head resting on arms. Face down. Auburn hair—apply many colors—flowing over one wrist.

Enough.

Charlotte held the finished painting at arm's length, her heart pounding, every cell in her body pulsing with awareness, understanding, acceptance. She propped it against the back of the low armchair and took a few steps back. Yes, the arms had transformed the generic round shape into the rise of a woman's body, her back in violet dress.

Charlotte heaved the deepest sigh. This woman—not the dead one or the one of memory, but the one to which she had just given birth—she belonged to her more than to anyone else in the world.

Mama. As she might have been seen by someone looking out from the fourth-floor window just after she had jumped. *Not influenza. No.* A secret guarded by the family for these many years, and now it was out. *Suicide.* Charlotte gazed as she would at her own child.

In the upper right-hand corner, she added: *CS.*

CHAPTER 21

BEAULIEU-SUR-MER

FEBRUARY 1942

The walk from St. Jean around the southern tip of the Cap to Beaulieu was the wildest and most remote. Whenever Charlotte went out to breathe the fresh sea air, she preferred it, but today she felt anxious and so took the level paved walk shaded by umbrella pines. Though there had been rain and squalls earlier in the month, this last week the weather had been fair, and today, too, the sky was clear with a bit of wind from the northeast. She found this miniature coastal town the most charming, wedged in as it was between Villefranche and Èze into an inward curve of land protected by gray slabs of rocky cliffs. It was an even quieter, more timeless paradise with small clothing boutiques, galleries, florists, and cafés.

Early for her meeting with Anneliese, she walked through the Provençal market. The smell of lavender permeated the air. If she had had the will to dip into her funds for a small luxury, she would have bought a bar of soap. Even though it was unlikely by the greatest stretch of her imagination that Luitger or his agent would look for her here, she felt she should not be wandering about. But having been cooped up in her room, she was drawn now to the seafront gardens, shaded by tall palms. She roamed, and the tangled roots of ancient magnolia trees spoke to her in a language she understood—the language of the half hidden.

The trees soothed her anxious, lonely soul, but only so much. Lately she had been toying with going back to l'Ermitage. The winter had been depressing. Being so entirely alone was taking a toll on her. She missed her cherry tree, the gardens, and the chateau's happy domestic life. Surely the chateau was big enough to provide a hidden corner for her. She would ask Anneliese.

Along the promenade, past a parade of Belle-Époque resorts—white villas decked with turquoise balustrades and ceramic friezes—fit for crowned heads of state, she wondered. How many who vacationed here—as in Nice, as in Villefranche—were otherwise occupied with waging war? What evil plans and strategies were being cooked up behind these grand façades?

Finally, it was time, and she made her way to the eleventh-century Saint-Hospice Chapel, up a hill and off the beaten track. Anneliese (now known as Madame Rochat, she reminded herself) was exactly where her message said she would be, right next to the entrance to the Belgian cemetery for their soldiers of the Great War. She wore a sun hat with a floppy brim and carried a bouquet of carnations. Without speaking, they entered the cemetery and wandered as though in search of a particular grave site. Potted plants and flowers dotted nearly every headstone. It was a colorful and fragrant place, and well visited. At the moment, they found themselves alone.

Charlotte said, "Tell me. It must be serious."

Anneliese repositioned herself so that she was facing the entrance, then began.

"Two officers of the Vichy police in Nice came to l'Ermitage. Three days ago. Looking for you. Delmira answered the door and said you had moved out more than two years ago. And no, she didn't know where you were. They wanted to search the house. Delmira said she had to get permission from the lady of the house. They said they needed no permission but would be good enough to wait."

Charlotte's heart was beating hard. How ridiculous that she had been entertaining a return when even her distance, her hiddenness, had failed to protect the household from disturbance. "Is everyone all right?"

Anneliese placed a hand on her arm, which was trembling. "Everyone's fine. They were very genteel. They asked to see identity papers. It was just Delmira, myself, and the children. They accepted our papers, but they wanted to make a search."

Charlotte envisioned the scene Anneliese was describing, and though her voice was calm and Charlotte's heart had quieted, the wind there on the hill felt too sharp, and her stomach churned. Anneliese told her that they had walked through every room, "very methodical, always looking first at the walls."

"For evidence of my work?"

"Possibly, yes. They asked about every hung painting. Yours, I explained, had been purchased and framed by Olive. I told them you'd left before my arrival. I said I'd never met you and had no idea even what you looked like."

Charlotte smiled at her friend's cleverness, and Anneliese broke a smile too.

"It was Luitger, wasn't it, who sent them? Did they say?"

"They didn't offer it until I asked what the problem was. But yes, they said he's looking for you. Should I see or hear from you, I'm to tell you to return to him at once. If you're not inclined to comply, I'm to let them know of your whereabouts."

"He writes to implore me to return. Who leaves an old man alone like that? Maybe I should go back."

Anneliese stepped back in alarm. Her voice pitched upward. "He—and your grandmother—they both pressed you beyond endurance from the day you arrived, not to mention everyone else in the household. They should have been ashamed. You don't need to pay attention. You have only just gotten free of him."

"He says he can't manage."

"Well, he must be managing, as it has already been a few months since you left Nice. You are much better off where you are now."

Charlotte considered. Yes, of course, this had to be true. Somehow, he had figured out how to do for himself.

When she recounted his threat to turn her in, Anneliese leveled a stern gaze upon her.

"It's blackmail. He won't turn you in."

"Then why the police?"

"You're all he has. He thinks he can force you to return. What's the likelihood you would be found? None, really. Only I know your whereabouts."

An older couple entered the cemetery. With her head bowed and Anneliese's hand on her shoulder, and both in obvious distress, they looked like real mourners. They waited to see where the couple was headed, and when it was clear they were far enough away, Anneliese laid her bouquet on the nearest grave and together they left, not too quickly. Outside and some distance away from the cemetery toward the cliff, they found a bench that afforded privacy.

"OTHER NEWS? How are you? And Max, too, since he returned from the Foreign Legion."

Charlotte had never felt particularly close to Max when she was at l'Ermitage. He was pleasant enough but remote, frequently preoccupied, but always, whether present or absent, the head of household, the strongest, the clearest of mind, the true leader of his family. His well-being was of the utmost importance to all of them.

Far below the cliff, the view through the cypresses revealed the Mediterranean, the dotted white terraces of the seaside village and the little harbor, the boats too small to see clearly from this distance.

Anneliese stood and looked back toward the cemetery and chapel, then sat. "All clear. I suppose I can tell you. You have no one to tell. So here it is. After decommissioning, Max found his way into the Rue Amelot movement in Paris."

"Rue Amelot?"

"It's a group of welfare organizations. Recently joined together. Medical dispensary. Clothing. Several canteens. Legal aid. Those sorts of services. He says it's become much worse for Jews in Paris. The Vichy has established one large organization for all Jews. *Union Générale d'Israélites de France.* Known as U-G-I-F. Max says it's a trap."

"Meaning?"

"An umbrella organization like that for all other Jewish organizations? It's a good organ for control. Possibly the basis for creating ghettos. In fact, the police have cracked down. They're now confining the Jews to the Seine area. Rue Amelot has gone semi-clandestine. Max thinks they'll become an armed force."

Hungry for news, Charlotte listened attentively. Anneliese looked around again and continued.

"The children in the north are under the care of the UGIF. But because they've kept lists, their whole setup is now becoming less viable. Rue Amelot is creating new identities for the children and bringing them south. Max, like Henri, will begin scouting out Christian farm families in remote locations willing to adopt Jewish children."

This was the first time Charlotte had heard any details of child rescue. Her heart swelled with admiration for Henri and Max. At the same time, she was gripped by fear for their safety.

"If another wave comes from Paris, will you take them into l'Ermitage?"

"We cannot. We're here by Olive's good graces. She has agreed to pay Delmira to keep house just for us. It is too risky. Besides, there is hardly enough food. We would only be bringing them here to starve. But we can ask Delmira if she knows of any families."

Charlotte once thought motherhood made women weak because that was how she saw her own mother. But Gurs had changed that perception—Gurs, where the mothers were the strongest among the women, and Anneliese was among the strongest of mothers. Yet her outer appearance—her delicate features, the whimsical curl of her black hair, her flowered dress—all gave the impression of fragility and grace, camouflaging the tensile intelligence and competence just under the surface. Charlotte suspected she had something more to say.

"There've been releases from Drancy. Max heard from UGIF North. An epidemic broke out. Dysentery. Only sixty toilets for the whole camp. They queued up, but imagine, many could not help themselves. The yard was a mess. No way to clean up. The stench unbearable."

"What do you mean by 'releases?' To where?"

The two women locked eyes. Anneliese didn't answer. She just shrugged, sighed, and shook her head. Charlotte winced and convulsed, wrapping her arms around herself, and rocked back and forth, sharing in the sorrow and anxiety of not knowing.

"I should go." Anneliese stood. "If I've been followed or even spotted by anyone I know, it could be dangerous for you."

Charlotte didn't want her friend to leave. She remained seated, stuffing her hands under her thighs.

"Did they say whether they'd be back, the police?"

"No. And anyway, they won't find you. You're safe." Annaleise's eyes surveyed the terrain. "But you needed to know."

Still seated, Charlotte's voice became squeaky. "What do I do now?"

"Do nothing. Under no circumstances come to l'Ermitage." She turned to leave, pulling the brim of her hat down to shade her face.

"Wait, Anneliese. Henri?"

"Back mid-April. Be careful now, going home."

CHAPTER 22

SAINT-JEAN-CAP-FERRAT

APRIL 1942

*D*ress for your birthday dinner!

The letter was from Henri, the rendezvous the same little cemetery where Charlotte had met Anneliese. Her heart went a little wild. What could he mean? No one went to dinner anymore but tourists.

Her hands were encrusted with paint. She found her nailbrush and ran hot water into the tub—in the middle of the afternoon, no less.

She couldn't believe she was going to see him again. It had been more than six months. Although she'd been engrossed in her work, a little voice inside her had asked at least once every day: *When?*

She tried on an outfit she'd never worn, one that Olive left her. The long, gray skirt was fitted through the hips, and the pale-blue angora sweater was nicely snug across the chest. She had shoes, too, black pumps with toe and heel caps of shiny patent leather. She rummaged among Olive's treasures for the tube of lipstick. Too slippery. She wiped it off.

She wondered what Olive had been thinking when she said, "Someday you may need these." Certainly she hadn't meant for Charlotte to dine with her own ex-lover.

Charlotte couldn't stop wondering what had happened between Henri and Gabrielle. Would he be asking her to dinner if he'd been with her in that way? She hoped not. But how could she know? For sure?

Charlotte brushed her hair until it was full and loose. She tied it back with a blue ribbon to keep it from falling into her eyes. An unfamiliar reflection stared back at her from the mirror. She could have been on the cover of *Le Petit Echo de la Mode*. Well, not quite. But was this really her? Perhaps.

It WASN'T SAFE TO LOITER, but she couldn't help arriving early. Did she look suspicious, standing in the chapel's parking lot? The sky was lavender with streaks of hot pink. The early-evening air was still. Then came the unmistakable revved engine of the Peugeot roadster making its way up the hill. It appeared, top down, canary yellow, and gleaming. Here he was, Henri Nagel, his wavy hair every which way from the drive.

"Hop in." The mellow tenor of his voice was the sound of warm caramel. His eyes darted about to determine whether they were being seen. The owners of the parked cars were either in the cemetery or the chapel. The minute she was seated in the brown crocodile interior, he took off.

He flashed a smile at her now. The long, vertical dimple in one cheek, the one facing her, gave her the same delight it had the day he'd picked her up from the train station in Nice. She couldn't take her eyes off him. She drank in the high forehead, the strong facial features, and just there, by his ear, the trace of scar that gave her comfort. It was his grand imperfection on display. It also made her aware of a hidden pain she occasionally detected. She was pleased to see he was dressed up, too, in a white shirt open at the neck and a navy jacket.

The roadster took the curves, each upward swing expanding their view of the ocean, which lay calm and jewellike, reflecting a hint of golden light. They were high in the cliffs when Henri came to a stop at an intersection. She watched his gaze travel the length of her body, and curiously, what came to mind were the paintings of Katharina she'd made lately. She had always wanted to acquire something of her stepmother. Her femininity. Her desirability. Some quality of the eternal. Charlotte wanted to embody all of that for Henri now.

"You look lovely."

This was not her true self, but she thought she might like it better. This self didn't brood. Her fingers needed to touch the back of his hands, which were bare of hair, the nails cut short and clean, but she was not so bold. She wanted to close this distance, but she didn't know how. Her arms felt an impulse to circle his neck. Her body wanted to press up against him and feel the great wall of his. Maybe this was, after all, her true self—a part of it, anyway, that she hadn't known. The idea that she might be more than she had imagined thrilled her.

THE RESTAURANT WAS an old farmhouse. Antique kitchen tools—including eggbeaters of every size, shape, and color— hung on the whitewashed walls. The back wall was red brick and housed an open fire. A little woman with wispy hair introduced herself as Pauline. Piled before her in great mounds were cabbages, leeks, onions, mushrooms, carrots, and garlic. She cooked everything herself in plain sight. Everyone in the small restaurant was served the same plates. First a *pissladière*, a tart topped with anchovies, onions, and Niçoise olives. It was so intensely flavored that Charlotte could barely think and eat at the same time.

Four people at the neighboring table addressed them in German. They all exchanged pleasant greetings. Though she and Henri were naturally concerned that their dining companions might be Nazis, they feigned the excitement peculiar to travelers who discover others from their native land and demonstrate a familiarity they never would were they to meet at home. Charlotte and Henri exchanged winks of enjoyment at their successful charade. When Henri toasted Charlotte's twenty-fifth birthday, all the patrons sang "Happy Birthday" in German. Henri belted it out with them while Charlotte blushed.

They ate socca and ravioli with Swiss chard and ricotta. A braised veal shoulder arrived.

"Henri, how can you afford this?"

During the owner's last absence, there had been a break-in and burglary. The owner was paying Henri double for taking care of the car while he was in Algeria because this time Henri was staying in the owner's cottage, as well, to keep watch on the chateau.

"I'm perfectly aware," he said, "that people in Nice are starving, that recently a delivery cart headed to the prefecture with pastries upended. Sweets all over the streets. You wouldn't believe how many women came running, calling for bread and milk. I know it because I saw it. I'm on daily rations. But I've had this good fortune, so I gave my rations for that day to a woman carrying a baby. And some of my good fortune I wanted to share with you on your birthday."

Charlotte ate slowly and not too much, to enjoy the meal without getting ill. She told him the details of how she'd taken his advice, gone to Saint-Jean-Cap-Ferrat and found La Belle Aurore, how Luitger destroyed her work and she finally left him.

"I have the peace and solitude I need. I'm making good progress. Hundreds of paintings."

"Hundreds? That's impressive. You must not be doing anything else."

"Not much. And I don't care. The paintings will tie together in some way. And it'll be a grand work." She was impressed by a confidence she didn't know she had. "A pictorial expression of Wolf Abrams's ideas."

She had said this without recalling that Henri had no idea who Wolf was—to Katharina, yes, but not to her. Because it made her nervous that she might betray the strength of her feelings for Wolf, she launched into his life story, relating how during the Great War, he'd been buried under dead and dying bodies in a trench and been poisoned by mustard gas.

"He emerged shell-shocked. Unable even to speak. It took over ten years for him to recover at a sanitarium in Italy. But while he was there, he discovered the relationship between voice and psyche. Voice and body. Eros and Thanatos, the essence of creativity in the individual."

The words from her mouth sounded bizarre, especially spoken in a restaurant to a man who was looking at her with a definite longing. She couldn't help herself. She persisted.

"He had a death mask made. By a sculptor. I was there, watched him apply the plaster to Wolf's face."

She was not sure she'd conveyed the real import of this. At the time it was, for her, extraordinary. Why would someone do such a thing? Yet something about his obsession with death intrigued her. She, too, had wondered what it was like, the great unknown. Maybe the creation of a death mask really was a path to knowing.

She added, "He thought he could discover the transition from life to death this way."

Henri raised an eyebrow, not with skepticism but genuine curiosity. "And did he?"

"Wolf understood death."

Charlotte felt Henri trying through his perplexity to make sense of it. "You revered his philosophy."

"I did."

"Who is he to you?"

Charlotte thought back through her fantasies, her obsessions, her unrequited teenage love, and arrived at what she had been unable to share with Anneliese: that their two souls, Wolf's and hers, were bound as one. It would be too cruel to tell Henri.

"Wolf's influence on me remains. He was a champion of my talent and ambition. His devotion has saved me from my loneliness. It's been my solace. Because...well, as I said, he understood death."

She could see this explanation didn't make her the most appealing of women, and it was in direct opposition to the yearning she felt for Henri. She hoped he could understand, even as she was creating more confusion for herself.

With a little hesitation, he said, "He was central to your artistic development."

She pressed a palm to her heart. Henri understood. "My intellectual education too."

She changed the subject, asking Henri about his travels. He said that they had lined up homes for three children. She wondered how it could take so long to accomplish this. There had been times when he had seemed purposely vague about his doings and whereabouts. All along, she'd suspected that he must be involved in something more than he was willing to reveal, but she never asked. It might be better not to know.

She couldn't help wanting to know the all-important thing, but it made her feel vulnerable to ask. She might look petty or come across as overly needy or even nosy about something that was none of her business. If she didn't like the answer, she would not be able to hide hurt. Beads of perspiration bloomed on her chest, making her sweater stick. Still, she had to know. "And you and Gabrielle?"

"Yes, the two of us." He joshed. "Haven't you been listening? We're a first-rate team."

When Charlotte remained silent, he clapped one hand to his forehead.

"Oh! Oh, no! Not that. She's a child, and Delmira's niece. And besides—no!"

He put down his fork and reached across the table for her hand, which she let him take. He closed his eyes for a moment. When he opened them, they were soft and moist.

"I wanted only to get back here to you as quickly as possible." His words reassured her. "Don't you remember? I promised." He was squeezing her hand, and she squeezed back and nodded to say, yes, she did.

She sighed, lighter, knowing her doubts had been unfounded. In the next instant, they dissolved, leaving her mind free. Her heart opened.

Suddenly she was seized with a hunger to possess this man, to know the ultimate act everyone waits for and hadn't yet arrived for her. The feel of his hands excited her. The articulation of his fingers moved her. She wanted them on her body, stroking the length of it.

THE NIGHT AIR WAS COOL, but Henri left the top down.

The moon was out, and his face flickered in the light and shadow of its beams peeking through the trees as he floored the accelerator and raced a straightaway. In an opening among the trees, blue-white moonlight poured down upon them and seemed to ignite an inner, mysterious source of warmth, amber and liquid, flowing from her center out through her limbs. Henri took a hairpin curve at a reckless speed that was sure to send them flying off the cliff, sailing through the air like a magic carpet to some distant, enchanted land. Charlotte was flung against him, and as they came right through what seemed like the danger point, she felt his hand on her skirted knee, steadying her. But nothing could steady her urgent need.

Henri pulled into a lookout and turned off the engine, then drew her toward him. The black sky was made indigo by the full moon. The sea was ultramarine with a surface shimmer of silver. She could almost believe that the world was at peace. He gave her the news to which she'd had no access and they dared not discuss at dinner.

Since Pearl Harbor, America had virtually stopped issuing visas to refugees in France. Vichy had been diligent in searching for places to which Jews might immigrate, but without success. A scheme to send Jews to Madagascar had fallen apart. A pitiful couple of thousand had made it to Algeria. The Germans were pressuring France, Poland, and Czechoslovakia to return German foreigners.

"All Laval wants at this point is to get rid of the foreigners. If the Germans are willing to help when no other country is... well, you can see his point of view. Why not send them back?"

"But I thought Pierre Laval was a socialist."

"Once was. But after the Armistice, he took a position under Pétain. A vice-something of the Vichy regime. Now prime minister."

"That's a hundred-and-eighty-degree turn."

"Politicians do that."

"You're saying we'll be deported back to Germany?" He nodded. "And then what? We go back to our homes?"

"We wish. There was a deportation in March. Those Jews are not back in their homes."

"Where are they?"

"No one knows. There were a few people at the synagogue on Boulevard Dubouchage who were seized. The committee there has tried to track them down. They have not been able to contact a single one."

"They've disappeared? Like that? How do you know this?"

"I'm living in the world, Charlotte. The work I do brings me in contact with news." He paused and then asked, "Do you want to know more?"

Did she? Already she felt so much more afraid for herself and Henri. But there was comfort in his arms.

"Yes. Tell me."

"Okay, but brace yourself. This is gruesome. The London press reported a town in the Ukraine —I can't remember the name of it—in which all the Jews have been killed."

Her throat caught. She told him about Monsieur Piché's friend, Paul, and the news he brought about a mass grave. Once again, she felt carried away by a swollen river of dread.

Henri strengthened his hold on her. She wrapped an arm around his waist. They sat entwined.

"The good news," he said, "is that ever since the communist groups joined forces last year, the Resistance has become more effective. Dozens of attacks on the rail lines every month. And a few days ago in Arras, there was an attack on German headquarters."

This seemed rather pitiful, considering mass graves and whole towns full of Jews wiped out, but Henri was so much closer to the real situation than she. If he had hope, it must be well founded. A trickle of hope seeped into her.

"Luitger's detectives have been spotted following us at l'Ermitage. He's hoping we'll lead them to you. The chances we take now are risky."

Charlotte was a tiny bit woozy from the food and wine, the wind and the thrill of the ride, and the heaviness of the state of the world. Henri tilted his head and leaned his face toward hers until their lips touched. She could hear his breathing and felt little balmy gusts on her face. Her eagerness for him was tinged with anxiety because she knew the next thing he was going to say, and she didn't have a prepared response.

"I've missed you so much, Charlotte. Let me take you to the cottage."

She pulled away from him and crumpled into her seat. What if he laughed at her inexperience? But if she didn't speak up, then what? It would only be more difficult in the moment. She took a deep breath and released a great sigh.

"Henri, I have to tell you something." A worried look came over his face, which a moment ago was so enamored. Charlotte's voice was a whisper. "I...I've never—"

His face relaxed and a slight smile emerged. He pulled her to him and tucked her head under his chin. He pressed his mouth onto the crown of her head.

He said, "We're meant to be. It will come naturally for us."

Charlotte leaned into his chest, felt the rise and fall of it. She wanted to remain still and quiet and let a great spaciousness fill the night.

"Trust me to take care."

She did.

HE WAS DRIVING AGAIN, ticking off several kilometers while Charlotte tried to figure out how to prepare for something this momentous, a point of no return, a passage to some kind of belonging—her own womanhood. He pulled into the driveway of a large chateau, and there seemed nothing to do but be excited and a little nervous. A nightingale released its powerful trill and gurgle, a male calling to a female. He took her hand. Her lack of skill walking in pumps slowed her into perfect pace with his limp. Bright-white lilies of the valley nodded their heads, visible against their dark-green foliage, their perfume sweet and heady. Columns of stately cypresses marched up the terraced orchards of gnarled, old olive trees. Along a path through a darker, wooded area, they slowed down to see the way to a door and through it into a tiny room with a bed.

The window faced the moon and through the transparent tulle curtains, they were bathed in a haze of blue-gray light. He searched her eyes, and she nodded. He pulled the ribbon from her hair, lifted her sweater over her head, and unzipped her skirt, which fell to the floor. These he placed on the chair. He reached down and slid his hands under her chemise, up the length of her thighs, over her hips, and removed the filmy garment. She stepped out of her shoes and removed her stockings while she watched him take off his jacket, shirt, and trousers.

They were standing naked before each other. Unabashed, she looked him up and down. He was strong in the torso, muscular. She was expecting him to take her fully into his arms, but when she saw how much one leg was atrophied, she fell to her knees, wrapped her arms around it, pressed her lips to it, and made a track of kisses along its length.

Henri lifted her to standing and stretched her out upon the bed's patchwork quilt. Lying on top of her, his hair fell forward from his forehead. She ran her fingers through it and held his head up to see his face. His wide-open eyes in the night were like dark moss and flecked with copper. She understood they were not merely looking into each other deeply, but in this moment discovering the whole of one another. An intense wave of feeling flooded her chest, her entire body. She was alert to every spot where he now lay his lips—her cheekbones, her neck, her collarbone, her nipples, her belly—bringing skin to awareness of itself. Then his body, so warm, hot, sliding against hers, pressure and sigh, murmur and stroke. She was drawn along and following. She let herself go. In the midst of surrender, a small sharp thrust of pain. Was she all right? She went still. She *was* all right. Then a new movement started, mounting a flood of feeling upon feeling, her breath catching in her throat, losing track of who he was and who she was—the wild loss of everything. Her breath abandoned to a moan that became a cry. Then his too.

CHAPTER 23

NICE

JULY, 1942

After their first time at the end of April, Charlotte and Henri had a month of cliffside drives and frequent, though risky, rendezvous at the cottage until its owner returned. She wanted to know everything about Henri. What made him happy? What had he endured? What was the story behind the occasional cloud that came over him in the form of a faraway, sad gaze, notably—it seemed, she wasn't sure—when he spoke of Max?

Her new, tumultuous, and thrilling feelings for Henri fell into a whirlpool with those for Wolf. She had never loved anyone as she'd loved Wolf, as she still loved him and would love him to her dying day. They were soulmates. She didn't believe a person could have two soulmates. What, then, was this powerful thing she felt with Henri? She had wanted a philosopher and someone who thoroughly understood her, but she came to realize that what she really needed was something else. Whatever it was with Henri, it was equally authentic. Their bodies were like two magnetized pieces of a puzzlc. They seemed always to want to be together, fitted to each other to a T. When separated, she felt an intense sense of belonging to someone, deliciously warmed through and through, cherished from head to toe, made whole, and, at the same time, a half that sought its other again and again. Her conclusion was this: Though Henri was not her soulmate, he was her lovemate.

During June they'd been able to see each other only in public places and briefly. Now it was too dangerous for them to see each other at all, though he usually wrote her once or twice a week.

His last letter told how many thousands of Parisian Jews had been rounded up, crammed into a stadium. No toilets, people having to go along the wall, and only two water faucets, which you would lose your life trying to get to. Unrelenting, hysterical screaming and people throwing themselves off the top of bleachers. As she read this, Charlotte put her hand over her heart, which had clenched in pain. Those poor souls. She would have rather been back in Gurs than in that stadium.

She'd followed the news as best she could. Opposition to the Vichy regime was growing. The French were fed up with Pétain. His reputation had remained tarnished ever since he'd met with Hitler in 1940. She overheard the Pichés in the garden: Hundreds had gathered in Place Masséna on Bastille Day chanting, "*Vive de Gaulle.*"

In a follow-up letter, Henri told her the Paris Jews had been deported. Now the foreign Jews were also being deported out of the Free Zone.

Free, hah! Though the prospect of this was so frightening, thankfully she was still able to disappear into her paints and images.

Henri's next letter:

Dearest Charlotte,

Fourteen more Jewish children, their parents deport-
ed, arrived at l'Ermitage. It was a hasty drop-off and
unexpected, but we couldn't turn them away. We must
find them homes as soon as possible as they have no
papers and their presence here endangers those of us
who do. Dr. and Mrs. M are making trips into the
country twice a week for provisions. They're hoping
to procure more chickens, maybe a duck or two. The
rabbit population increased in the spring, and that
helps. The chateau can only sustain so many. Must go
in search of homes again. I'll miss you every moment
of every day.

Your Henri

P.S. Anneliese sends love. She'll write when she can,
but she has a big show to run here. Everyone else
sends kisses. Me too.

Alone in her room, Charlotte sat on the bed, her heart
sinking. She couldn't stand the thought of Henri going off
again, even if it was for the best of causes. Travel had grown
more dangerous. Placing fourteen children would take a very
long time. She wondered whether he was even telling the
truth. Perhaps he was engaged in activity in opposition to the
Vichy government.

She felt fortunate to have her little room and a few francs
tucked away, but she was so sick of how trapped she was.
Without Henri for who knew how long, she was unable to
pick up her brush again. It all seemed pointless. She lay down
on her bed and stared at the ceiling.

Henri had been working on getting forged papers for her, but it had been a slow process. In January, the principal clandestine lab for forgery in Nice had been discovered by the Vichy police. Everything had been smashed, the best forger murdered on the spot. A half-year later, it hadn't been possible to replace all the necessary machinery and specialized tools or the skill of that forger, who was considered a genius.

If she were to be stopped, or police were to come to La Belle Aurore during a general search, she had nothing to prove legal status but her certificate from Gurs. She would be returned to Luitger, if not deported. It was as simple as that.

In Nice, she figured, she could get an identity card. She'd been contemplating this ever since she'd first learned of the Paris roundups. An identity card might give her a slight edge. Ration coupons, too, might keep her alive. All this time, since the census decree went into effect over a year ago, she'd failed to report to the police, but she could report now, fill out a form, and come back with an identity card, one that would not tie her to Luitger. Who knew? One piece of paper might make the difference someday.

She would be saving Henri the trouble of obtaining one for her. She felt resourceful. Traveling to Nice seemed worth the risk.

DESPITE ITS NEARNESS to the sea, there was no relief from the heat in Nice. The central district was an oven in which people moved in slow motion, and the heat rising from the pavement could be seen as wavy distortions of the atmosphere. It had been a long time since Charlotte had been in Nice, and she was acutely aware of the posters and graffiti that called out for the annexation of Italy's lost fatherlands: *Vive l'Italie!* This, she knew, was a great threat to Vichy's Marshal Pétain. It couldn't possibly be anything but a cause for anxiety for the Nicois and the foreigners like herself living in the Italian-occupied zone. The slogans, screaming across the walls of vacant buildings and in the headlines of discarded handbills, pointed to greater social instability than she had understood existed in the shelter of La Belle Aurore. Sweat formed on her skin, which tingled with agitation. Her bicycle escaped her hold and clattered to the sidewalk before she finally was able to park it.

Inside the prefecture it was a bit cooler, and oddly there was no one in line. Charlotte approached the window. A young man, whose uniform had managed to stay crisp in the heat and whose bored look went straight at her but without the focus of actual eye contact, waited for her to speak.

"I'm a refugee from Germany. Here to report as a Jew. For the census."

"Please go to the door on your right. Someone will meet you there."

A burly gendarme ushered her through the door and hurried her down a long hall to the back of the building. A door opened onto a courtyard where buses were parked shoulder to shoulder in a row on the diagonal, a gendarme stationed at each. He delivered her into the hands of one, who pushed her aboard.

Bewildered, she stopped on the steps, went no farther, and turned around, clutching her purse to her chest.

"There's some mistake."

"No mistake."

Charlotte tried to debark. "I don't speak good French. I'm here to register only. Register."

He blocked her way with his baton across the steps. "Get back." His voice was gruff. She bit her lip. "The bus will take you to register."

Well, why hadn't he said so?

"Now get up there."

The bus was full. Her eyes darted about. Noisy foreigners. Polish, it sounded like, Hungarian, too; Russian, Czech, and, in the back, German. Side by side in the front row were the two remaining empty seats.

CHARLOTTE HAD BEEN SITTING for an hour. She was not allowed to open a window. It was stifling. She felt faint, not having eaten this day. At least, she needed water, but there was no going out for it. She'd tried. It was like being in prison. In prison for obeying the law! Why had she done this? She could be back in La Belle Aurore.

She decided to try the German couple. They were both gray-haired, with purplish bags under their eyes. The old woman fidgeted with her hands like she was washing up. Charlotte introduced herself and tried to verify what was going on. They had registered for the census some time ago. Husband and wife both had identity cards.

"Why, then, are you on this bus? If you've already complied with the census?"

The man's eyes were large and bulging behind his spectacles. "We were rounded up," he said quietly. "This is a deportation bus. Headed back to Germany."

Despite the heat, Charlotte's body went cold, her empty stomach felt heavy, her brain fuzzy. Katharina: *You know how naive you are, Lotte. You must not be dreamy. You must stay alert. Your life could depend upon it.*

She'd made a horrible mistake. She had to get off the bus. Right now. Grabbing onto the backs of the seats to keep her legs from folding under, she returned to the front. The air was unbreathable. She wanted to beat her hands against the doors until the gendarme, who stood coolly with his back to it, was forced to open. This, of course, was not a good idea. She'd already annoyed him with several requests. She sat down with her arms wrapped around her body, her chin to chest, shaking her head. She refused to feel trapped. Every minute they remained parked, there was a chance of reprieve. Then she sprang up with manic energy, asking herself what she should do. There was nothing to do.

THE BUS WAS GETTING HOTTER as the sun went over its midpoint and rays sliced through the window next to her, burning her cheeks. She went woozy and began to hear "*Eine kleine Nachtmusik*" playing in her head. Katharina was singing, Kurt Singer conducting.

A driver mounted behind the wheel, awakening Charlotte from her reverie. A gendarme climbed aboard; a young man no older than she. In him, she detected a soul too soft for police work or already done in by it. He surveyed the seats, saw the desperate, beseeching faces. His body bristled as though warding off any possible effect of these faces upon his professional duty. The doors closed. The driver turned the key in the ignition, and the engine roared to life. The gendarme took the empty seat beside Charlotte.

She asked, "Where are we going?"

He looked at her, not in that surveying way that he'd looked at the others, but really looked. She could not control the visible shaking in her limbs. The bus rumbled into an alley leading to the main street and stopped at the point where it was about to enter the traffic stream.

The gendarme issued the order. "Open the doors." He stood and pulled Charlotte up by her arm, speaking in a low voice. "Get out. Quickly, down the street that way." He pointed away from the front entrance of the prefecture. "Go home. Never come back. Never."

Before she knew it, she was on the street and running. Never, he said, never. She wanted to cry but kept running. Her bicycle. She forced her pace to slow, started around the block, turned the corners, walked normally.

She spotted it right in front of the prefecture. A gendarme emerged from the door, turned his head her way without seeming to take special notice, then sauntered off in the opposite direction. Quickly she strode to her bicycle, hopped on, and pedaled away as fast as she could.

Never once did she look back, all the way out of Nice, hot, sweating, on to Villefranche, then Cap de Ferrat and St. Jean. When she got back to La Belle Aurore, she was heaving. Her dress was soaked through. Madame Piché was leaning over the balustrade. Her eyebrows rose in alarm. She disappeared from her vantage point, reappeared at the garden gate, and ushered Charlotte off the street and straight up to the terrace. Charlotte was shaking and couldn't bring herself to speak.

"Here, sit down. I'll bring you a glass of water."

Charlotte popped up. She was still breathing hard.

Madame Piché returned with water. She set the glass on the wrought-iron table. The way her hands smoothed the skirt of her dress over her knees, slowly and thoughtfully, calmed Charlotte and helped her take a seat.

In her fright, she realized she might have revealed to Madame Piché who she was. Who but a Jew would be this crazed with fear? A new wave of panic came over her. True, the Pichés had their suspicions about her identity, but that was very different from knowing for sure. What would Madame Piché do if she knew the truth? Charlotte leapt from the chair, upsetting the glass, ignoring the water pouring onto the flagstone. Her face twitched. Her lips pressed together. Her eyes darted while her hands opened and closed at her sides.

"Don't worry, Charlotte. We suspected you were Jewish."

She recalled overhearing the Pichés' conversation, that perhaps it was "providence" that she had found her way to

La Belle Aurore. Even so, she felt a scream come into her throat and choked it back. If she admitted to her Jewishness, would they be obliged to call the police? And why wouldn't they? They were solid citizens of this little village, and they hardly knew her.

"We won't turn you in."

Stunned, Charlotte stared, wide-eyed, while gasping but managing to stand still even as she had the urge to run down into the garden and out the gate. She searched Madame Piché's face for a sign. Her eyes looked as vulnerable as Charlotte felt. In soft focus, they said, *It's all right.*

"We suspected. Almost from the first." She paused. "And then letters were arriving here, not by post but by courier, unaddressed, and, well…"

All this time, these nine months, they knew? Her heartbeat started to slow. She was able to sit. Neither spoke for a while, and Charlotte felt comfort come to her in that silence.

"So now you know?"

"Yes, I do. We do. How are you feeling? Do you want to tell me what happened?"

Charlotte told her about why she went to Nice. Seeing Madame Piché's sympathetic regard, she unreeled the whole story.

"Oh, my God, dear! You were nearly deported!"

Charlotte asked, "Is it true? Are they taking Jews right out of Nice?"

Madame Piché lowered her eyes. "I'm afraid so. It's a crime. It's wrong. But it's happening." Looking up, she caught Charlotte's gaze and held it. "And you must be vigilant."

"Where? Where are they taking us?" Her voice was half hysterical.

"I wish we knew. The Nazis want German foreigners in France returned to them."

"But I'm not German anymore. I've been denied citizenship there. I'm…without a country. First, they were trying to get us out. Now they want us back?"

Madame Piché shook her head. "I don't know. They're short on labor, we hear." She shrugged. "The main thing is not to get caught. You mustn't go back to Nice. Forget about registering. Don't even go out. Ever. Remain hidden right here, where you're safe."

With those words, Charlotte breathed a deep sigh of relief. Madame Piché righted the empty glass and put her hand on Charlotte's shoulder.

"Back in a minute."

She returned with the glass refilled. Charlotte drank the water down in one long gulp. Feeling calmed now, she stood. She could find no words to express the full measure of her gratitude, so she said a simple thank you, walked slowly inside, and up the stairs to Room Number 1 with its pink carpet, two windows, and glittering white light. Before removing her sticky clothes, she lay down on the white-tufted bedspread.

She was safe. She had to repeat that many times to convince herself of the truth of it. Still, it took more than a day to recover from the panic. No identity card. No way out. Furthermore, no right to any place in any country. By a miracle she'd been saved, and as long as she stayed within these walls, she could trust the Pichés.

She took up painting with new determination. Her attention tunneled down into bringing the work to completion as rapidly as possible. She had to keep going.

Days passed, and from time to time, fright would unexpectedly reverberate in her bones. When she paused in her work, Charlotte saw her foolishness and naiveté and how losing her mother had ended her childhood and at the same time left her stuck in it, crippled in her ability to respond to the situations she faced. Her father had sheltered her. Of course, he'd wanted to protect her after such a great loss. She did not fault him. She had been catered to by Katharina, who wanted to do so much for her rather than letting her do for herself and wanted to protect her from her grandparents, which now made so much more sense than it did when she was a young girl. Katharina had married into a family with secrets and had become complicit with them. Despite their best intentions, Charlotte had been prevented from growing up.

She had gone to register, knowing foreign Jews were being deported. So stupid! Having failed to connect that fact with herself, her own life, her habit of believing in her invisibility prevailed even as she was presenting herself to the police. She had not seen the danger, and wouldn't have had she not spoken with the German couple. A sympathetic gendarme had been sheer luck. Without him, she might be...?

She didn't want to think of where the Jews were being sent. There was no "there," no form of place, nothing. The terrifying unknown, unimaginable, remained shrouded in mystery; and the terror, unable to latch on to anything, which in its specificity might diminish its force and effect, was loosed from the nothingness of place, became free-floating, all-encompassing, and increased its grip on her, haunting her dreams. Madame Piché told her she sometimes cried out in the night, loud enough to be heard throughout La Belle Aurore.

When Charlotte asked whether any boarder had complained, Madame Piché said, "No, dear."

Everything was getting worse in this broken world. Charlotte decided she must cling to her life. She must guard it more carefully. She picked up her brush and palette and stared at the clean white sheet of paper on her easel. She would redeem this horrid experience with a sunny wash—yellow with a tinge of orange.

CHAPTER 24

SAINT-JEAN-CAP-FERRAT

DECEMBER 1942

Nothing from Henri since August.

After Charlotte's escape from deportation, tears welled up in Madame Piché's eyes as she informed her of subsequent roundups of Jews in Nice and environs. They were put on trains. A mother threw her infant out the window for someone to catch and protect. Charlotte's heart caved in when she heard.

She did take heed of these reports and had ventured no farther than the garden of La Belle Aurore, and then only into a corner unobservable by passersby or neighbors. Madame Piché was providing food and refusing to accept francs. Being so confined, Charlotte had no way to sell seascapes. This was the way it had to be.

In a mad fury, she made hundreds of paintings of Wolf: as voice teacher to Katharina, how he mooned over her stepmother when she sold her ruby ring so that he might eat; their arguments—Wolf's that the true artist roams the highest spheres of imagination, Katharina's that the artist must be firmly rooted in earthly occupations—his pigheaded bid for her attention, which he finally turned, with the very same obstinacy, onto Charlotte, waiting in the wings for him. Charlotte had managed to convey some of his philosophy in her paintings of Wolf: voice as the mirror of the soul and singing as the urge to freedom. He once expected life to love him until he realized that what really mattered was that he loved life.

Then she heard another melody. An aria from Stölzel's lost opera *Diomedes*.

"If it's lost, how can you sing it?" Lotte had asked her stepmother as she dressed for her performance. She was thirteen and had been watching Katharina in a peach satin slip at her vanity table. Brushing her hair. Spritzing her favorite and only perfume, 4711, in its ornately scrolled blue-and-gold bottle. Lotte stepped closer so the mist might land on her too. The air wafting citrus, also bergamot, neroli, and a hint of rosemary, made for a lovely swoon.

"Because, Lotte, it was recorded in the *Notebook for Anna Magdalena Bach*."

On Katharina's dressing table sat a reproduction of an eighteenth-century engraving of Bach and Anna Magdalena. Just then Lotte planned out the rest of her life: she would marry a painter, and they would work together all their years.

"Did she sing '*Bist du bei mir*'? Anna Magdalena?"

"Very well she might have. It was a popular song, even used in weddings."

"I wouldn't want that," Lotte said, "a song about death at my wedding."

Katharina rose from her vanity and dressed in her midnight-blue sleeveless velvet gown. Dr. Salomon helped her don a black beaver coat with its sumptuous, rolled collar. With her father at Katharina's side, smart in his felt hat, and Lotte not far behind in her good navy coat, they'd all set out.

Charlotte began with water. She coveted its clarity, though of itself it did not speak. On paper it was nothing. As was imagination and memory, until given color.

Add white. White water. Like the foam delivered to shore. Like whitecaps riding high. Snowcaps piercing the sky. Fields of daisies. Crystals of sugar.

A dab of yellow. Swirled until it turned to strands and the strands disappeared and so did the white. Not a true yellow. A white made sunny. A voice turned to light. Charlotte washed it over the whole sheet of paper with a broad square brush, leaving a pinpoint here and there of the bare white paper.

The air had flushed yellow in the opera house and smelled of evening dresses stored with sachets, the supple leather of glove and shoe, a potpourri of fine perfumes and hair balms, orange blossoms and lilies. Gliding over the carpet, women in floor-length gowns—wine burgundy, jade green, sparkling silver lamé—and men in black tails. Her arm laced inside her father's. Katharina had gone the other way to her dressing room. With each step, the plush carpet kissed her feet.

They moved along the wall, for there were no aisles, only long, curved rows of red velvet seats. As they picked their way to the middle of the third row, the entire opera house opened before them. A great commotion of people passed in toward their seats, standing and scanning the crowd, twiddling their fingers discreetly at spotted friends, chattering with others in neighboring rows, while the orchestra tuned up, plucking at their instruments, generating birdlike squeaks and cheeps, shuffling their chairs, their stands, an inch this way or that, flipping pages, smiling at each other, and making quips. In the boxes: here, a bare arm; there, mother-of-pearl opera glasses held to the face and adjusted. From above, an immense chandelier, together with the gleaming wall sconces, washed a golden bath over the whole house, which buzzed with the voices of pleasantries and the twitter of instruments so that everything altogether pulsed inside one glow of light.

Charlotte deepened the wash with more yellow. Brighter. Made broad strokes of it upon the upper half of the page. Added orange, stroked again, and the tiniest amount of brown to subdue it as she moved into the lower half.

Exploding from the wings, the conductor. Crossing to middle stage, bowing to the audience. Kurt Singer, the famed and revered. In tails and striped trousers. A protruding forehead, receding hairline leading up to an enormous mane, thick and snow white. Booming applause. Then—a tall, graceful woman. Glissading out from the wing and seeming to float to center. Trailing sapphire velvet train, blond hair in a chignon. Applause, thunderous.

Along the bottom third of the paper, Charlotte made humps of red ovals. Above each one, more ovals, either brown or dark green. She outlined the ovals with a thicker, darker red—then, with a dense black, began to draw. Red ovals became chairs. Brown and green ones, shoulders and heads. One blue hump, herself, in the lower left.

Two smooth diagonals like train tracks, just below mid-page, defined the front edge of the stage. Above, many small heads on the right, facing center. Many more on the left, facing center.

Kurt Singer, turning his back to the audience, had raised his arms to shoulder height, a baton in one hand, poised for the moment. And brought it down. The sweet melody entered, introduced by the oboe, accompanied by the smooth violins and viola, and supported by the continuo.

Charlotte returned to the red of the chairs. Darkened them with brown. To a rich chestnut. On the stage itself, she brushed on a T-shaped form, the conductor's body. Dabbed on a lighter color for the head and outlined in black the whole figure.

Beside him now, facing the audience, Katharina had clasped her hands in front of her, leaned slightly to her left with her blond head also tilted that way, and began.

Be thou with me and I'll go gladly unto my death and on to my repose.

Moving to the darkest blue, she pulled a dab of it to the middle of her palette, pasted into it a touch of black. And painted a form to the right of the conductor's, this one feminine in shape. Added a pale-blue face with tiny features and uncovered arms, a white lace collar extended to the length of a short shawl. A few tiny squiggles of bright yellow, the magnificent halo of the singer's hair.

She hummed. Pleased with the basics of the scene. Hummed on while hearing the lyrics as well. So simple. So affecting.

Ah, how my end would bring contentment, if, pressing with thy hands so lovely, thou wouldst my faithful eyes then close.

Katharina's voice, soaring. Lotte had had the sensation of ascending with it, being lifted high above the seated crowd, riding the voice to the upper regions of the hall, as if to the heavens, wheeling round, circling nether regions of exquisite emotion, and gliding down, coming to rest.

Charlotte aimlessly twirled her brush in plain water. Contemplated how to translate. In Nice, she had scrounged the beach and waste cans for smaller tins and amassed a collection. Now, in one, the slightest hint of red in water. In another tin—the same for blue. And yellow. Pale, watery. Now, the same colors in three more tins, each with added intensity.

She hummed again before beginning, allowing her body to sway to the music. Dipped into the tins and with short upward flips of her wrist, stroked red diluted to pink diagonally up. Her brush went flip, flip, flip. Then pale blue. Then yellow.

Flip went her wrist. Grazing the paper. Up went her heart. Pulling away. Fingering the wooden handle of the brush. Returning. Touch, sweep, lift. The brush kissing the paper.

Humming. From the beginning again. Dipping faster. Flipping faster. Increasing the intensity of the color here and there. Hardly looking. And again.

White. Touch. Lift. Brush. Lift. Dot. Done.

She dropped the brush and rose. Fell onto the bed, face up, arms spread.

Paper. Katharina. Water. The Voice. Color. Myself.

Charlotte drifted to sleep. When she woke, she was pleased to have a painting of Katharina singing on stage. She pinned it on the wall next to earlier portraits. All the upward brushstrokes, which she meant to be the burst of song rising to the rafters of the opera house, now also looked like the thunder of applause that rang out when Katharina's voice came to silence, breaking into colorful confetti, raining praise upon the one who sang.

Lotte had wondered then. Charlotte still did: What would it feel like to be heard?

An important painting like this in the series, when finished, typically left Charlotte feeling at peace, and she would be at peace now except for her worry over Henri. Back in November, Anneliese had reported the welcome news that the Allies had landed in French North Africa. Though the Germans had occupied Vichy France, the Italians had stood firm in the eastern section. In Nice, it seemed as though the Italian authorities were protecting the Jews.

That afternoon, another letter from Anneliese arrived. Vichy had decided to evacuate the Jews from the coast, north to German-occupied areas. The refugee committee at the synagogue on Boulevard Dubouchage in Nice had been working with the Italian authorities, and together they refused to hand over the Jews. Furthermore, their refusal was backed by the Italian Foreign Ministry, which had decided the French police could not expel Italian Jews, or any Jews, into areas occupied by the Germans.

> *But the best news is that eleven Allied governments signed a declaration with the Free French Committee denouncing Hitler's intention to exterminate the Jewish people of Europe. I know because Max has obtained a radio and we are listening to the broadcasts of the BBC and Radio London, which is the voice of the Free French. Plus reports from Max, who is privy to the workings of the Comité Dubouchage. Lotte, these governments have promised to punish the guilty parties. Such hope! We are almost afraid to feel it.*

Enough with politics. What about Henri? Anneliese had not mentioned him. Maybe she knew something that couldn't be put in writing.

Charlotte could stand it no longer, this complete dearth of information about Henri. Surely Anneliese had some word, however slight. She shouldn't be considering a trip to l'Ermitage, but she was. With the Italians in control, it must be safe. She watched herself put on her shoes, pick up her purse, and leave a note for Madame Piché saying that she needed a change of scene and would be back shortly.

Her bicycle, after these months, still stood outside the gate. She relished the familiar rhythm of pedaling, and the stretch and bend of her legs. The sun shone, but the air was mild, even a little cool, as she gained speed. The sight of Villefranche's little harbor with its fishing boats thrilled her.

As she pedaled up Rue Cauvin, she felt like she was heading home, even though l'Ermitage was not home and she would stay for only the shortest possible visit.

Inside the iron gate, pebbles crunched under her tires. She hopped off. L'Ermitage rose before her, the old stone chateau stately and serene. She recalled the day when Olive came down the front steps to greet her. Sweet memories flooded her mind: morning coffee and sumptuous pastries in Olive's suite, tea in the garden with Anneliese and Rui, and time alone to work under the Japanese cherry tree.

The crush and grind of gravel behind her woke her from her memories. A car had pulled in. The two front doors swung open, and a man and a woman stepped out onto the driveway with the ease and command of those in power. They were not wearing uniforms, but Charlotte was wary, recalling plainclothes officers who had arrived to take her father. She smelled stealth and stalking. And Luitger. How else could it be that the one time she ventured onto l'Ermitage in almost two years, the police arrived?

She asked, "May I help you?"

"We're looking for Madame Rochat," the woman said.

Anneliese's new surname. Charlotte said nothing. She would not admit that she knew her.

"Authorities." The man produced his badge. Vichy. Plainclothes. "You can give her my name. She knows us."

Charlotte's heart started beating faster. She needed to calm down. Anneliese had papers.

Just then, Anneliese appeared on the balcony. When she saw Charlotte, a stricken look flashed across her face.

The man said, "Ah, there she is."

"On my way," cried Anneliese, then appeared shortly out the front door, down the stone steps, and across the drive.

"Scoot now." Anneliese spoke to Charlotte in a harsh and scolding tone. "We don't need the likes of you prowling around here."

Anneliese was pointing a way out for her. She circled her bicycle and headed back toward the gate, her heart now in her throat.

"Excuse us, mademoiselle." It was the man's voice. Charlotte wanted to run. "May we see your papers?"

She had no papers. If she bolted, she'd look guilty. They would pursue her, and she would be easily overcome. For a moment she couldn't move, as though her feet were made of concrete. Her mind scrambled for a way out, finding nothing. Slowly she turned her bike around. The woman's shoes made a chomping sound on the gravel as she approached her. She lifted Charlotte's purse from the basket and handed it over to the man, who said, "May we?"

Charlotte grasped at the first thing that came into her head. "I left my papers at home today."

He pulled out her certificate from Gurs, which had become ragged over the years, and unfolded it.

"Charlotte Salomon."

She bit her lip, closed her eyes. He turned to Anneliese.

"Do you know this young woman?"

She lifted her nose in a haughty expression. "I do not. I've never seen her before."

To Charlotte, he said, "States here you're to be caring for your grandfather, a Jew in Nice. Which makes you, too, a Jew." He paused. Charlotte did not speak. "Is that so?"

She stammered. "Y-yes."

"Tell us what you're doing in Villefranche, a good eight kilometers from Nice."

She rubbed the toe of one shoe in the gravel. Her head felt like it was going to explode. What should she say? She wracked her brain for an excuse, anything plausible that would explain her presence.

"I used to live here. Years ago." Her voice was halting, and she was mumbling.

"Yes. Speak up."

"I thought I might prevail on someone here for something to eat. It's very hard for my grandfather and me to get by."

Anneliese looked entirely without sympathy, but Charlotte knew she was hoping just as much as she was that this story would pass muster.

"Good try," said the man, "but we have it from Monsieur Docteur Gruenstein that you abandoned him quite some time ago. You will come with us."

The woman took Charlotte by one arm, then the other, the bicycle crashing to the ground. She guided her into the back seat of the car.

Anneliese spoke up. "Officer! You were wanting to talk to me?"

The man replied, "We got what we came looking for."

Anneliese stood back. On her face was a look of satisfaction, aimed at the officers, in thanks for having taken care of the problem.

LUITGER'S FACE was flushed with the triumph of conquest, his smile gleeful, his blue eyes on fire, demonic. This couldn't be true. Charlotte couldn't be back here, standing in this kitchen. The smell was putrid, as though a dead animal lay rotting behind the wall. The officers explained her legal status exactly as it had been delivered to her in Gurs.

The woman said, "You understand that foreigners are being deported?"

The man said, "In particular, Jews. In particular, German Jews."

Charlotte was seething. She could hear her teeth grinding. If so much weren't at stake, she wouldn't be able to stop herself from pummeling one or the other of them, pummeling and clawing. But she was stumped. Why were they not taking her and Luitger away for deportation?

They made it clear they would be checking on her. She nodded. She was supposed to be grateful.

When Luitger showed them the door, he slipped something into the hand of the woman. It caught a glint of purple light. Grossmama's amethyst ring! And into the hand of the man, Luitger's own gold watch and chain.

An amateur pianist across the courtyard was mashing Chopin to bits.

PART III

—

1943

CHAPTER 25

NICE

MARCH 1943

Three months after Charlotte's capture, she began feeling as though she was disappearing again into another string of days of unending toil. That, combined with Luitger's screeching demands, was dragging her toward madness.

She had begun a great work. Her grandfather had destroyed it. She had begun again. Now it was aborted, all that effort beyond her reach. There was only the shopping, the cooking, the washing, and standing by the window, staring down into the courtyard.

Luitger had registered with the census. Because he could prove residence, he was able to obtain ration cards, but with the extreme shortage of food, the cards were nearly useless. Without deliveries from l'Ermitage's garden as in earlier years, the two grew thin and weak. Due to his growing frailty, Luitger left the apartment much less often. Charlotte went out every day, if for nothing else than to get away from him.

Meanwhile the Germans had renamed the Occupied Zone. Now it was the North Zone, and the Free Zone was now known as the South Zone. All of France was under German control, except the narrow strip of coast from Menton to Nice, where the Italians had expanded their occupation. Under the Italians, the Vichy police had lost some power. Their visits to the apartment fell off, and that meant Luitger's daily threats grew emptier. Sometimes Charlotte thought of leaving—how she longed to—but after her brush with deportation the previous summer, she wouldn't risk it.

On her daily excursion through town, she noticed that Nice had become overrun with those seeking safe haven. She passed a Judaic school that had opened and a training center specifically for Jews. The Jews sat, unafraid, in sidewalk cafés. The Italian soldiers were just as relaxed, sauntering along, lacking the spit and polish of the SS, or even the trim of the Vichy. Passing a café table, she overheard a representative from the Ashkenazi synagogue openly soliciting funds to send parcels to Jews.

"Jews where?"

"In the city prison. And in Vichy's camps. At Gurs and Les Milles."

Charlotte had heard of Les Milles from Max, who had once helped an aid organization there, where the agonizing separations of children from parents took place. Parents clung to their sons and daughters, stroking their backs, hugging them, caressing their cherubic faces, kissing the tops of their richly colored heads and their cheeks, peering deeply into their eyes to stamp upon them their own faces. They hugged them one last time, burying their faces in the hollows of their necks, inhaling their clean smell, oxygen of that wrenching moment. Then the children were loaded onto buses. Even the most distraught of fathers and mothers leapt to attention and stood waving with encouraging smiles on their faces. "As soon as the buses pulled away," Max had said, "the courtyard went dead of sound."

Down the street at another café, laughter erupted. The Italian soldiers were a sight to behold with their heads thrown back, their mouths open wide, their chests heaving in good humor. The same was true of the table's occupants—Jews, amazingly. How could this be when the other side of France, less than 150 kilometers away, was the end point for so many Jewish families?

"But the children," Max had wrapped it up, "they were delivered into the care of the OSE, the Children's Rescue, at the Hotel Bompard in Marseille."

The clink of glasses and shouts of Yiddish-accented "*Salut!*" dissolved Charlotte's memory. There was no longer a Free Zone, yet the Jews were still here.

But Henri was not here.

She wandered through the Cours Saleya market, the flower stands overflowing with bright mimosa flowers, splendid balls of golden-yellow fluff giving off a light perfume, harvested from the forests north of Nice near Tanneron. Henri had promised her a drive through the mimosa forest. The trees had kept their promise to herald the spring. But where was Henri?

On her way across the square, Charlotte spotted a familiar figure disembarking from a bicycle, lean and spry.

"Dr. Mercier?"

"Charlotte! How glad I am to see you!"

It was the gravelly voice she knew, the one that conveyed a confidence that no matter how bad things were, all was still well.

"Do you have a moment?" he asked.

"Of course!"

"Come with me where we can talk."

She went with him across the plaza. He parked his bicycle, and she accompanied him into the Church of Mercy. A woman was kneeling in the front row, her head thrown back, apparently looking up in devotion at her savior on the cross, who died for her sins that she might live. But what about all those who were dying on the battlefields of the continent? Multitudes of saviors. So that *they* might live.

They took seats in the rear and were quiet for a moment while their eyes adjusted to reveal the splendid architecture. Charlotte admired the Baroque angels swirling between gilt friezes under a domed ceiling covered in frescos. The smell of incense lingered and melded with the fragrance of oiled wood. A pleasant sensation of peace came over her, something she hadn't felt in a very long time, like the candle-lighting of a Berlin Shabbat or resting in her father's study or sitting under the Japanese cherry. Where had it been? But no matter; here it was. She gave herself over to it.

Charlotte hadn't seen Dr. Mercier since the day Olive left for America, almost a year and a half ago. With his iron-gray hair still thick in middle age and his wiry, athletic body, he hardly seemed changed. Then she noticed the pain in his eyes, an unspoken burden he carried—of sadness? of suppressed anger?—and the lines this burden had wrought in his face.

He had apparently kept up with developments in her life during his visits to l'Ermitage. He was aware of her year in hiding—he didn't know where—and the circumstances of her seizure by the police and return to Nice.

"I'm so sorry." His eyes filled with real feeling and an eagerness to reach her. "I know how impossible your grandfather is."

When he asked if there was anything he could do for her, Charlotte wanted to ask about Henri but didn't know if he knew why Henri was away. So she said no and asked him how he was getting on.

"Homes have been found for all the children, and many have been situated."

That puzzled her. She wasn't aware Dr. Mercier was involved in the same project as Henri and Max.

"Charlotte, I need to tell you that I'm running an operation along with others spread across the coast. There's more than one network involved, and Henri's in mine. That's the only reason I'm revealing my role. I know you two—"

Charlotte's stomach started churning with excitement. "Then you know where Henri is and when he'll be back."

He was quiet for a moment. "I'm afraid I don't."

A lump came into her throat.

"When the Germans came, Henri was in Marseille. We haven't heard from him since."

Not heard from him?

"He'd previously contacted me to say all the children were safe. He was alone at the time."

At the time of what?

"I thought he was with—"

"Gabrielle? No. She stayed behind this time because Anneliese was sick."

Why hadn't he come back? Where was he? What did this mean?

"Is he in a camp?"

"The situation in Marseille is not like it is here. Here, the Italians have managed to prevent the Nazis from deporting Jews. There—in Marseille—Jews are being deported in huge numbers. Thousands."

Dr. Mercier bowed his head in feigned prayer. Charlotte followed suit until a group of people passed their pew. He lowered his voice to a whisper. She had to stop her teeth from clicking to hear him.

"We've tried to find out. Believe me, every single one of us in the networks is precious, with knowledge and skills not easily replaced. We do our best to track people down. If one of ours is in a camp, we leave no stone unturned to enable release. But the camps aren't always willing to give out information. And our communication lines to the inside are often faulty. We are forced to work underground and sideways. With Henri, we just don't know."

Charlotte's mouth went dry. Her chest tightened. How could he not know? Wasn't it his job to know? Then she recalled how difficult it had been in Gurs to communicate with the outside. One might have slipped a message to aid workers who brought in supplies, but there was no assurance the message would reach its destination.

Charlotte threw her head back and took a deep breath. The throng of angels flying above had become no more than gold metal among imitation marble, hard stone, ungiving materials.

Dr. Mercier said, "There is some good news."

There was no good news aside from knowing Henri's whereabouts and the date of his safe return. But it would be rude not to listen.

"You know of Angelo Donati?"

She did not.

"He's an Italian banker here in Nice. A Jew. He's taken charge of helping the Jews by positioning himself close to the Italians. He has connections high up in the Italian government from his days in Paris. Since February, at least, members of the Comité Dubouchage have been meeting with him every day. You know them?"

"I know the synagogue. On Boulevard Dubouchage. I took my grandmother's belongings there to donate to the poor after she died. I've overheard Max and Henri mention the *comité*. Do you think the Comité Dubouchage could find Henri?"

"I've already gotten as much help as I can from them. They're focused primarily on protecting Jews right here in Nice."

Charlotte's heart sank.

"But listen, thanks to the *comité* and the synagogue's rabbi, Donati has had some influence getting the Italians to stop the French police from carrying out deportations."

Dr. Mercier was going on about the Germans having complained to Mussolini, and Mussolini having appointed an Inspector General of Racial Police, who was now in Nice and had met with Donati.

"Guido Lospinoso. Fully installed. Donati convinced him he was the most informed person in Nice, and Lospinoso appointed Donati as his councilor. Perhaps you've noticed recently all the restraint on the part of the Germans and the Vichy. Angelo Donati is behind it."

Charlotte listened but only partially heard. She should be grateful to this Donati character because Nice was probably one of the safest places in France for a Jew. What the doctor said fit with what she'd observed in the cafés. But she couldn't bring herself to engage in conversation.

"And it's clear now. The Germans lost at Stalingrad. They will be defeated."

She remained silent. He seemed to see her mind was on only one thing.

"Henri wouldn't fail to communicate with me. He's—" Dr. Mercier rolled his lips into a tight slit and pulled his eyes into a taut squint, pressing back a strong emotion. "Charlotte, Matilde and I weren't able to have children. Henri's been like a son to me. To us."

Her heart bent in curiosity. It made sense. It squared with everything she had known of Henri and the Merciers. Dr. Mercier had continually found work for Henri, periodically examined his injured leg, and clapped him on the back in that fatherly way.

He swallowed his emotion. "Unfortunately, yes, I'd have to say a camp. That's my best guess."

Her voice was a small cry. "But they're deporting people from the camps now."

Her fingers twitched. She grasped one hand in the other to stop it. Suddenly she was furious with Dr. Mercier. How dare he lose Henri? He hadn't tried hard enough. She thought that she would go to the camps, track him down herself. Then she realized the impossibility of that plan, how skewed her thinking was. Her hands dropped into her lap.

"I'm sorry." He laid a hand on her shoulder. "I know he was in love with you. If that's any consolation."

Was?

He looked into her eyes with so much sincerity and understanding. He'd done everything within his power, and by the tears that welled there, she knew that this was his loss too.

CHAPTER 26

NICE

MARCH 1943

D r. Mercier was still straddling his bicycle. "I'll let you know the minute we hear anything about Henri." He reached in his bike sack and handed her a copy of *Libération*.

Charlotte managed a smile because she was truly happy to have seen the kind doctor, but as soon as he waved her off, she felt deeply saddened. She tried not to think it—that she might never see Henri again—but it was right there in the forefront of her mind.

Instead of going directly back to the apartment, she found herself heading in the direction of the synagogue. Had Dr. Mercier said something about attacks on Jews in the synagogue by the Milice? She couldn't recall. In any case, here at the synagogue's door were Italians protecting Jews, four Carabinieri standing guard.

In the days that followed, by way of Dr. Mercier, Henri's feelings for Charlotte became strangely more tangible. It was as though love had its own existence in the world. Or, by Dr. Mercier pronouncing their love aloud, it flew from the confines of her heart, where she'd kept it precious and alive, and expanded into the world and breathed, happy and free.

Even with one bad leg, Henri was a hearty man. If she had survived a camp, he surely would. But the deportations—that was the horrible difference. The Vichy at Gurs were lackadaisical. But a camp in the hands of the Nazis—who knew what might happen to him there?

Charlotte would start over: Henri loved her. He would come back. But each time she repeated this to herself, belief lost a shade of its bloom. Deported persons weren't returning. They couldn't be located in their home countries, not by phone, mail, telegraph, or friends and family left behind. She read *Libération,* which made it clear that the deportations were continuing, and it gave advice:

> *What can you do not to fall into the hands of the German murderers? What can you do to accelerate their demise and save everyone's liberty? Here is how every Jew, man or woman, should act...*

> *Don't stay at home waiting for them to come and get you. Whatever it takes, hide. Hide the children first with the help of the French people who feel a sympathetic obligation. Look for every possible way to escape.*

She noted an article about Warsaw and was eager to read about conditions anywhere in Germany. The Jews had been gathered into a walled-in section of the city. They were starving and dying in the streets. The Germans were intending to clear the ghetto, and a small band of resisters meant to fight them.

Reading this, the world seemed to slow down, then spin. It was brave of them, of course. But it was fruitless, too, a small band against the whole German army. The journalist was full of admiration. "They will die with honor." The news of all who had died, as well as those remaining who were doomed, only made Charlotte sadder.

Luitger was out. He had probably steered himself down the hill to Emmet's. She stood in the salon, looking into the courtyard, staring at the spot where her grandmother had landed. Longing for escape, she knew for herself there was none. Charlotte saw her there still, her crumpled body lying in a bag of black garments, one leg at an impossible angle.

One day shortly after her grandmother had died, almost exactly three years ago, before she and Luitger were sent to Gurs, Charlotte had taken the three flights down, gone through the shadowed passageway into the bright courtyard, and examined the spot. No specks of dried blood were buried between the cobblestones; no single cobblestone was tinged pink. All had been scrubbed clean. Who would know that an old refugee woman had lost hope, thrown herself out the window, and landed there? It was as though here, nothing had happened.

She wondered now, as she stood staring down at that spot from the third-floor salon, what people in this building had said, especially the mothers to their children. Most likely they said nothing—silence as part of the complete erasure of not only the event but the personal history leading to it. Or perhaps they had said, "A woman fell from one of the courtyard windows and died. Stay away from the windowsill." Maybe not even that much. To the little ones who only had heard the thunderous impact of her grandmother's landing on their cobbled play surface but hadn't seen the fall and were ushered out of the courtyard, perhaps, "Nothing, little one, nothing happened. Let's go inside."

Dwelling on her grandmother's suicide led Charlotte naturally to the others. The women in her family—dead Eurydices all—who chose their fate. Why not join them?

The front door opened and closed, and Luitger interrupted her musings. She didn't like him to see her at the window, and it made her feel naked that he had caught her there. He was breathing heavily from the uphill climb and the stairs. His voice was thick with desire to be done with her.

"Do it. It'll be over in an instant. You will anyway. Eventually. Why not now?"

Then he was seated, making the point, as always, that she was late with his meal. As she placed his plate of Jerusalem artichokes and a maize baguette before him, the momentary nearness to him, the sight over his shoulder of his filthy beard, which was permanently the gray-brown of Gurs, looking like a perfect nest for vermin, made her stomach turn.

She could no longer bear to eat with him, and went to her room and shut the door.

Once, she had had the balm of painting. An illusion, or perhaps a delusion, that she might rise above it all—Hitler, the Nazis, the Vichy. As if her work meant anything, so puny in its little obsessive particulars of dead relatives, charismatic stepmother, illustrious doctor-father, callous grandparents. Didn't everyone have some version of this?

Again she stared out the window into the courtyard, this time out her bedroom window. The spot of her fixation was at more of a distance here than in the salon, but her eyes automatically scanned, searching for it in a methodical way. It wasn't good enough for her to gaze toward it in soft focus. She felt obliged to identify the exact location. There was one cobblestone that heaved a larger dome among significantly smaller ones. The stone came to signify her grandmother's rounded back. Charlotte's gaze, having settled on the precise, hallowed site, gave her a kind of relief. As long as that stone was there and she could locate it, something was saved from the horror of her grandmother's demise, something that might be of use, though she didn't yet know what it could be.

Across the courtyard, a mother was calling her little girl to come inside. The girl shook her head vigorously. Her blond braids flew out and swung around her face. Other children had minded their mothers and left the courtyard a quarter of an hour ago. This girl was alone and engrossed with her dolls. The mother finally lured her daughter with the promise of a bedtime story. Then the courtyard was empty.

The sacred stone, her grandmother's fallen body, reminded Charlotte of her painting of her own mother's fall, and then all the scenes she'd painted—over thirteen hundred; she had once counted. No one would see any of it. They were only smudges of the earth's mineral ores dissolved in water. Dirt, colored dirt. For a while it had worked; she had hung onto her sanity. But the truth was: she had nothing. Her mother—dead. All those many relatives—dead. Her father, Katharina, Wolf—they, too, possibly dead. And now Henri. Where was he?

Had he been sent back to Germany? To Austria? For being a Jew? That was what she was too: a Jew. Without those she loved, without her work, the fact of being a Jew—her life being reduced to just that and nothing more—it would kill her, she knew.

Everyone was dying. Dead or dying, those at Gurs. All over the battlefields of France. In the streets of Paris. In mass graves in Russia. In the face of which life and beauty appeared as jokes. Is that who she'd been? A jokester, making slurries all over the page in the name of art?

She heard a voice. Her throat was tight. Her hands over her ears would not block it out.

End it.

A PROFOUND ENNUI had crept into her body. In the mornings, her limbs didn't want to move. Her legs couldn't imagine swinging over the bed's edge or her feet gripping the floorboards. Her whole being was without the urge to lift itself to the day. On good days, she was able to fall back into the inky pool of sleep without dreams.

Only because she'd bought rutabagas, was she motivated on this day in March to make a large pot of soup. The chopping was laborious, the heat in the kitchen enervating, and the cleanup exhausting. The pot of soup would have to last forever. She would not be cleaning again. She would not be washing. She was done with all that. Instead, she was drawn over and over to stand by the window in a paralyzing state of gray dullness.

Now the little girl with blond braids in the courtyard was arranging her dolls and, even from this height above, her intense devotion penetrated Charlotte's fog and impressed her. Charlotte could distinguish the blues, reds, and yellows of the dolls' dresses. The little girl held each figure for a long interval and seemed to contemplate the best placement for it. Charlotte was too far away to discern the design—a semicircle, she thought. The girl made an adjustment by moving one doll into the place of another and then the displaced one into the position of a third and so on. Her fidelity to her vision, to the process of discovering it, sparked a new awareness.

The stone-cold nothingness inside of Charlotte gave way. In the cauldron of her belly, a bit of her innards was still warm and alive. Roused to move off, leaving the little girl to her work, she took up paper and pen. And she wrote:

Dear Dr. Mercier:

When we talked recently inside the Church of Mercy here in Nice, you offered me a favor. I'd be so grateful if you were able to collect my things from La Belle Aurore in Saint-Jean-Cap-Ferrat, assuming they're still there. And to keep them for the time being. Madame Piché is the landlady, and if, too, you could convey my apologies for having gone off despite her warning me to remain on the property for my own safety, I'd appreciate it. It was foolish of me. I regret not having heeded her warning, and any inconvenience or worry my sudden absence caused her and Monsieur Piché. And of course, I hope they are well. You too.

Yours sincerely,

Charlotte

P.S. Please reimburse her for the last three months. Francs in art-supply case.

SHE WAITED A WEEK after mailing the letter, figuring it would take at least that long for Dr. Mercier to receive it, contact Madame Piché, and write back. For fear Luitger might intercept Dr. Mercier's response, she took possession of the mailbox key from the cup on the dining table and went down to the ground floor herself. She could see through the brass slots that there was nothing inside, but she opened the box anyway. The inner, dark emptiness invoked her desolation. She thought of the delight with which she once received news from Berlin. *Papa. Katharina.* Almost two years ago now.

Fifteen days passed without word. On the sixteenth, a sliver of white shone through the mail slots. A bubble of hope rose to her throat. She turned the key.

She was halfway up the first flight of stairs with it in her hand. Suddenly, she was afraid. Possibly so much time had passed that Madame Piché had discarded her things, or that, bending over backward to protect her identity, she had refused to respond to Dr. Mercier. Before she could think of another worst case, she was back in the privacy of her room. Her heart was beating hard, and she had to read it twice before she could be sure of the meaning.

Dr. Mercier confirmed he had made good on her debt and he had her work in hand, and that in the process of collecting it side by side with Madame Piché, they both remarked on "the strangeness and wonder of it." He hoped she would soon find a way to work again. He assured her he would keep it safe until that day. His closing words reminded her of Wolf's. As she read them, her whole body radiated warmth. He'd written: *Charlotte, I believe in it.*

CHAPTER 27

———

NICE

APRIL 1943

Charlotte stood at the window with Dr. Mercier's letter in her pocket. What she wanted most was to live a real life, a free life—by which she meant free from Luitger, free to complete her work—and she had no idea how she could bring that about.

She asked herself, *What have I produced?* What do they say, what do they mean—those thirteen hundred paintings? In a flurry and a fury and with no sense of design, the images had flown onto the paper. She was convinced there was something in them but completely baffled, and without being able to look at them, there was no hope in figuring out what it was, what she had to say that had felt, and still felt, so urgent. She should be grateful her work was in safe hands, and she was. But the agony of separation, her inability to get to it, was the worst part of remaining alive. Her whole body felt heavy and numb, except for her aching heart. She kneaded her chest with the heel of one hand to make the pain go away, but her heart beat up into her throat as she struggled for a way to go on.

She was sure she had the courage of her mother and grandmother, who'd refused to dignify a meaningless life. A way to end it was right before her. It would be simple. She kept returning to the window, testing what it might feel like to take two bold steps over the sill or to sit on the sill and lean out over the courtyard, waiting for the moment when it felt right to tip out that speck further beyond the point of return, to let go and tumble.

Today, as every day, she saw her grandmother's corpse on the courtyard cobbles, broken limbs akimbo, a puddle the color of purple wine billowing outward around her white head. She also saw her mother, her auburn hair flung in four directions, her delicate face gone to stone. She could imagine, too, yes, herself having fallen, landed below, her blue dress hiked and twisted, her light hair soaked in her own lifeblood. The dread and lure of death pounded on Charlotte like the sea against an ancient wall that was doomed to crumble. *It'll only be a moment.*

Suddenly, Luitger was there. He must have entered quietly, stealthily.

In the last month, he had become truly unable to manage the hill on his own. Sometimes he'd take to standing on the sidewalk to get some air and watch the comings and goings. He spoke to passersby, tried to delay them along the way so they might listen to him. He was always careful to present himself as the civilized, cultured man. It was a performance Charlotte could not bear to witness. She expected him to demand she help with a visit to Emmet. This entailed accompanying him there, waiting an hour or so, and picking him up for the trudge back uphill. She would do it, but not without resentment.

With a look of disapproval on his face, he scanned the room. She hadn't lifted a finger. She did not now rush to tidy the clutter, but remained at the window while he rummaged in his doctor's bag.

"Here," he said, coming to her side with a brown bottle. "This was for Marina. I'll never use it. It's for weak people, and I'm certainly not weak." He grabbed Charlotte's hand, slapped the bottle into her palm, and folded her fingers over it. He lowered his voice, his stinking breath upon her. "There's plenty here to do you in."

The glass bottle was cold, the label in assured script: *veronal*. He was horrifying. She was not horrified. Instead, she pondered: Had he done her a favor? Offered an easier way?

He shook his head in disgust at her. Charlotte looked at him, bent and bony, his ratty beard covering half of his chest. He had not changed a whit since she had arrived in the South of France. He was ancient. He had always been ancient. Decrepit. She searched for his eyes. They were averted. When he looked at her, they were blank. She peered at them, but there was no feeling, no acknowledgement of who she was, his granddaughter, nothing. It was not a man who was standing there, but a human fiend. A shriek, long and silent, opened inside her. She needed to be free of him, and he had given her that out.

Through the window, the united D in fortissimo of all four instruments abruptly flowing into a soft, stately chorale. It was the hour of practice for the string quartet, and they'd jumped right into Schubert's *Death and the Maiden*. The violent mood shifts carried Charlotte far from this window, back to Berlin where she had often heard the piece played in small concert halls. To the wood carving in the Bode-Museum, of Death holding the naked maiden in an erotic embrace. To the ivory piece, a statue sculpted to display the two figures back to back. And Edvard Munch's erotic embrace in oil. Finally, to her own drawing, different from all of them, the one she had presented to Wolf.

At the time, his response resembled one of his opaque lectures. Because she hoped it would be a way into understanding, she'd memorized the words of the poem—it was Wolf who'd told her it was by Matthias Claudius. Death's stanza:

Give me your hand, you fair and tender form!
I am a friend; I do not come to punish.
Be of good cheer! I am not a savage.
You shall sleep gently in my arms.

She wondered how her own death mask would look. *You shall sleep gently.* Her heart quieted. A face serene in its final freedom.

Luitger stood there, expectant. Who would press someone to commit suicide? His own flesh and blood. The one who was caring for him and keeping him alive. She looked at the bottle of veronal in her hand. A sound came from her throat—taut, dry, and strangled. Then some small courage broke through the terror of what she might do to herself.

She said, "You're the one who should take these pills. Your father committed suicide. By your own reasoning, then, perhaps it's your destiny."

"You don't know what you're talking about."

"I do know. Grossmama told me. And you were present when she did." He looked doubtful. "I remember because it was that same night you paid my bed a visit. Shortly after I arrived. Four years ago." He lowered his eyes. "Furthermore, you're the one who made your own life worthless by stealing that of others."

"You know nothing. I gave this family everything. Education, culture, comfort, social status. I became a doctor. Years of study. Years. I sacrificed my own life for theirs. I gave them opportunity. Freedom. Berlin! And what did they do? They had no thanks. Marina, especially, a sniveling, complaining woman who spent her last years trying to do herself in. It was exhausting. Our daughter, Charlotte, was cut from the same cloth—already as a young woman, nothing was good enough for her. And your mother"—he pointed a finger at Charlotte—"she was the worst. A depressive, the most miserable specimen of femininity. Your father couldn't handle her, foisted her back on us! Imagine—our married daughter in our home. We had a nurse watch her. Ach! She did it anyway. Just as Marina stepped into her room. Out the window, right in front of her mother. This is the thanks I got. If it were not for Marina's breakdown, we would not have left Berlin. I, who deserved so much more, would not be here now."

His version of himself put Charlotte into a simmering rage. She could not passively walk away. The thought of facing him down made her insides churn. What was she afraid of? He was loathsome. Why should he have the privilege of escaping her wrath?

"What? You think you'd be living your cozy bourgeois life in your Berlin apartment? Do you miss the good times when your daughters were at home, and you could crawl into their beds?"

"I never did such a thing."

"You did. And I know. Grossmama told me. On one of those last days that I was nursing her. When you strolled the streets while she writhed in pain and misery. And you sent the doctor away with his morphine, morphine that could have soothed her, made it all bearable.

"Have Charlotte take care of her! As if I could relieve that kind of agony. But I stayed by her side. I did my best, and I'm glad I did because she told me everything. She was sick with shame that she did nothing for her daughters. That's what ate her alive. And you stand there and deny it?"

She shook her hand with the bottle in it at him. "You are a rapist and a filthy liar. You're the one deserving of a death-dose of veronal. You, Luitger, you."

Charlotte had never called her grandfather by his first name. It made her feel powerful to do so, to dissociate herself from the familial relationship that put him above her, that required her to submit to his will. It created an intimacy, this first-name basis, and the way he tried to stop his body from squirming told her he didn't like it.

"It was bad fortune. I married into a family with a history of mental disorder."

"You were a doctor. You had prominence. You had connections. You could have gotten the very best care for them. Instead, you took advantage of the young and innocent. You destroyed them. Along with Grossmama's best friend's daughter, Eugenia Mahlick. And who knows how many more? You, the lecher of Berlin. It was you who sent them to their deaths."

With her words came release, but she couldn't tell whether he knew what he had done.

"They were hysterics," he said.

She wanted him to take responsibility for those lost lives. He stood there stone-faced, implacable.

"You want me to take this poison?" she said. "Then state your crimes. Say what you did to their young bodies, how it drove them mad. Say how it was you who made their lives intolerable."

Charlotte stood in silence and heaved, waiting for an answer that might never come. If she moved, it would all be over. She held perfectly still. More than anything she wanted to run him down into an admission. Those women were dead. He was no longer in the country in which he'd enacted those deeds. He was no longer subject to those laws. There could be no real-world consequences. He had gotten away with it.

Even so, she was prepared to be—what? His confessor? His judge? No. A witness. That was it. She wanted him to break, right before her.

She stared at him. He started to turn to go and then stopped. His hands trembled loose by his sides, mangled and arthritic. The blank look in his eyes dissolved, replaced by beseeching, undone by shriveled pride. His voice was almost inaudible.

"I was a doctor. I thought I could heal them."

His response, finally, was not something Charlotte had expected. Though it threw her, she stood steady.

"Heal them how?"

"They were repressed girls." He paused and searched her face, presumably to see if she was following him. "In that way." He peered at her. She was not following. "Excitable. Excessively anxious. Like their mother. To be honest, because of her. They had lost touch with their essential vitality."

"Meaning what, exactly?"

"They needed guidance."

Charlotte struggled to follow his logic. She could feel her brows knit together in puzzlement.

"A malfunction. Specifically, if you must know, a sexual malfunction. I only wanted to unblock the flow of psychic energy, so they would be free of their nervous symptoms, of the damage Marina had done. Free from her. Free to be fully feminine grown women."

Charlotte had to draw a steadying breath.

"And better me than some strange psychiatrist," he added.

She was appalled but not surprised. It explained so much.

"The damage Grossmama had done?" Loudly, almost shouting, she repeated her accusation. His hands flew to his ears.

"What difference does it make who?" he shouted back. "Yes, they were ruined. The therapeutic treatment didn't work. But it was their decision, each of them individually, to take their own lives." He paused. She remained unwavering. "Their suicides were ridiculous female melodramas! Completely un-called for. Even Marina said husbands could be found who would not need to know of the hysteria before the wedding. Husbands who might be willing to live with it. As, by the way, your father was. But they would have been unhappy all their lives, so perhaps their choice, your aunt Charlotte's and your mother Eva's, was the best one for each of them."

A cold wind blew through her, seeming to have swept in from a desolate landscape far beyond her aunt's grave, her mother's grave. So that was it. He had disclosed his corrup-tion. He had abused them, driven them mad, one to drown herself, the other to leap out the window, and he had washed his hands of it all.

His admission brought Charlotte no satisfaction. She saw herself as a little girl of eight placing a wreath on the grave, nurse by her side, believing utterly in the bad fortune of her mother having contracted a terrible case of influenza. She stared at Luitger, the criminal. Could this possibly be the same man who'd tried to soothe her with a baby doll? Sitting on his lap then, had little Lotte been in the sights of his evil eye? Was he waiting for her to grow up and for circumstances to present themselves? She shuddered and surrendered to not knowing what to say next or what to do.

From across the courtyard, the lilting violin arrived in the first variation of the second movement, the pulling strains of the cello in the next, back to a charging fortissimo, breaking off into the deeply passionate in the fourth, and the fifth ris-ing forcibly again. Now Wolf's words came back to her with clarity: *She is in self-possession, contained and noble, a girl who has matured into womanhood, who has decided to make something of her life.*

Charlotte's eyes turned to the sky—endless, soothing blue. Her spirit was drawn up into it. The diabolical scherzo began.

She only half-noticed that Luitger had taken a step toward her. "It'll be over in half an hour. No pain. Like falling sleep." His voice attempted to break into her trance, but the music and the sky held her.

Did he imagine her swallowing the contents of the bottle right before his eyes?

All four instruments briskly. Syncopated, full of excitement and terror, leaping. A dramatic push and pull.

She gazed down into the courtyard again, where the evening ritual was underway, where mother lured daughter with a bedtime story. "'Cinderella' tonight, sweetheart." The irresistible pull of story.

Charlotte was whirling in a sea-storm of emotion, like a ship about to wreck, its mast creaking at the breaking point.

The little girl gathered her dolls into their basket, tossed her blond braids, and seduced by the story of a motherless child enslaved by a cruel stepmother, she went home.

Charlotte dropped the veronal into her pocket, plucking from her precarious state of mind the thorn of Luitger's demonic vitriol. He was trying to break her, and she would not let him. Only he had not realized it, and that was a power she would not yield to him at this moment. Her emotions blew through. Her mind settled.

A story. She became completely oblivious to the man who was bent on destroying her.

What she had not known for a year she now saw with the clarity of the shimmering light of Room Number 1. Her paintings, carefully culled for the best and thoughtfully arranged—they might tell a story. She could add an actual narrative, in words, snippets of dialogue, character details. Who was to say she couldn't add words? She could.

She could even add musical prompts. Schubert. Gluck, Mahler, Beethoven. And folk songs and children's ditties. All the tunes that had run through her mind as she'd painted.

Outside, the swirling rondo. Her heart synced with the shifting beats. Paint, words, music. These were all in the mix of making the work. And—this was what she saw—together, they could drive toward an extraordinary experience. An unmatched totality.

Her breathing picked up with the quickness of the tempo. The breath of life stabilized her. It felt like the ballasts taking hold, the ship righting itself again.

Suddenly Luitger lunged for her, and she stumbled backward against the windowsill. In the next moment he was upon her, trying to get his hands around her neck. She regained her footing and thrust her leg at him until he backed away. He came at her again, pushing, as though he meant for her to roll back out the window and plunge. There were shrieks and grunts in the tussle, his and hers, as they went back and forth along the window end of the room, knocking over a lamp, pulling down a panel of curtain. Then he had her down on the windowsill, bent backward over it. Her top half was outside, down to the bottom of her shoulder blades. She flailed about, trying to catch hold of the sash. He tucked an arm under her knees and lifted. He would flip her into a somersault. She caught hold of the sash, freed the leg nearest him, and kicked sideways. She'd struck him in the shoulder, and he went flying and hit the floor.

Major turned to minor just as Charlotte prevailed. Propelled by the musical crescendo coming from the courtyard, she was across the salon and into her own room, door shut, shaken but unhurt, and without need for any further clarification.

SHE LEVERED THE CHAIR against the doorknob to bar his entry. Breathless, she paced until her heart stopped pounding. She searched the pile of work she had brought from Berlin. There at the bottom it lay, her own version of "Death and the Maiden," the first of her works she had been sure, nine years ago, she knew not why, was original and true. Now she understood. *A girl who has matured into womanhood, who has decided to make something of her life.* Without understanding what she'd been doing at the time, she had made a drawing of her own future.

In one hand now was the drawing. In the other, pulled from her pocket, was the bottle of veronal. She looked back and forth from one to the other. He had tried to kill her. The atmosphere in the room thickened. It was as though a great fog had rolled into the room, becoming denser by the moment. The bed upon which she sat, the dresser, the chair—all appeared to be swallowed up into it so that there was less of a distinction among objects.

He would try again. Was she going to carry him through the war? She would have to remain aware at every moment of the threat he posed. Could she survive with that burden?

Then something gelled. She couldn't say what it was.

Slowly, one hand laid the drawing aside. Slowly, the other returned the bottle to her pocket. She reached through the fog, groped for the handle of the door, opened it, and stepped out. Silence in the courtyard. He was lying on the sofa now, reading a paper as though nothing had happened. She understood that was the way it had always been. As he pursued his perversity, family members did themselves in.

In Germany, among Jews, suicide had been frowned upon, reviled, regarded as a sign of weakness the community could not afford. Always, an excuse needed to be called on. She died of influenza. There was an accident. He and Marina, and under their sway, her father and mother, all went on as though no one had been abused, no one had been driven mad, as though nothing happened other than ordinary, unfortunate death.

In the kitchen, eggs in the hanging wire basket appeared as a cloud. Charlotte broke two into a bowl. Both she and Luitger could easily devour three or four, they had grown so thin and starved, but Charlotte did not think of their deprivation. If asked, she would have said she was not thinking of anything. She added a dribble of water. Began to whisk. In this strange state of fog and cloud and unboundedness, the sound of metal against metal was a distant, muffled discordance.

A shadow in her periphery—by its shape, Luitger—shuffled through the kitchen into the bathroom. She heard the click of the tongue in groove as he pulled the door closed.

She reached into her pocket and drew out the bottle. She twisted off the cap, imagining a rain of pure white grains, like miniature hailstones, floating down into the bowl. To disguise the bitter taste, she would scrape the last hardened specks from the bottom of the sugar bowl and add them to the eggs, along with some pungent fresh rosemary she'd grown in the windowsill. She would whip and whip. A beautiful pale froth.

She held the bottle aloft, her arm paralyzed in the air. Questions rolled through her mind: Was it not self-defense? Had she pushed him out the window at that moment, yes. But no, not in this moment. She was not in imminent danger. Was she willing to live the rest of her life as a murderess? No one would ever discover that she poisoned him. Who cared how an old Jew died in these times? But she would know.

She capped the bottle and dropped it back into her pocket.

Luitger emerged and wandered through to the salon. She heard the scratch of him pulling out the chair, then the scrape of him pulling himself to table.

She lit a match and turned on the stove's burner. The spark took the flame, making a circle of fire. She lay a pan on top. The fat bubbled and sizzled. She poured in the contents of the bowl. Slowly the eggs passed from liquid to soft solid. The moist, yellow envelope slid onto a plate—a perfect omelet.

In the salon, she set down the plate. She replaced the veronal in the doctor bag by the sofa.

He noticed and said, "Coward."

After he'd eaten, Luitger asked her to take him down to Emmet's. The heat of their physical struggle still burned inside her. She yearned to be able to walk out, and had she a place to hide from him, she would. She was stuck, but she was not going to be his handmaiden. He wasn't capable of the hill anymore, and for once he was not going to get his way. He wasn't going to get to run off to bad-mouth her to Emmet.

"Sorry," she said. She stood, crossed into her room, and closed the door. She sat on her bed with the small carriage clock in her lap and her hands under her thighs, her drawing beside her. Completely still, quieting her breath, she was alert to every sound in the other room.

The rasp of the chair as it was pushed away from the table. Footsteps. The door opening and closing. He was challenging her. He wanted her to come running after him, come to his aid. Well, she wouldn't. He would have to be content standing outside the door and watching people go by.

She would stay put. Her room was womblike, safe. She watched the big hand on the clock move minute by minute around the perimeter. She knew, but not how she knew, that he would go to Emmet's, to prove he could go on his own, to spite her.

She reclined. An hour passed. Another half hour. A knock at the door woke her from her trance-like state. She went to it and opened it. There stood Emmet.

"Your grandfather."

Several neighbors pushed their way in, carrying Luitger. Charlotte motioned them toward the salon. They laid him out on the sofa.

Emmet said, "He was making his way home from my place. It seems he collapsed on the street. I'd offered to see him up the hill, but he refused."

Luitger's eyes were open but fixed.

"Is he—?"

Emmet cast his eyes down. "I'm afraid so."

She caught herself not breathing while staring at Luitger as he lay on the sofa. The other neighbors slipped away, one by one.

"He was a great friend to me, your grandfather. So warm and understanding." He could not possibly be talking about Luitger. "I'll help you out tomorrow. We'll get in touch with the synagogue."

She could not react. His hand on her shoulder was heavy. "Would you like me to stay with you tonight?"

It was a question she was supposed to answer. She tried to remember what he asked. He repeated it. "Oh! No, no, thank you. I'll be fine."

After he'd gone, Charlotte sat in a chair some distance from the sofa. She allowed darkness to descend on the apartment. She felt nothing; numbness, maybe. She wondered if her blood was still circulating. Then she felt a delicate sigh move through her body.

She recalled the Maiden's words:

> *It's all over! Alas, it's all over now!*
> *Go, savage man of bone!*
> *I am still young—go devoted one!*
> *And do not molest me.*

His face was gaunt, cheekbones protruding bladelike. His eyes receded deep within bruised sockets. Bony fingers just touched each other across his chest, which failed to rise.

SHE TURNED ON A LAMP, slid the chair up beside him, and placed one of his large books on her lap. She had retrieved "Death and the Maiden," turned it over now, and on the blank back of that drawing, Charlotte began another.

CHAPTER 28

VILLEFRANCHE-SUR-MER

APRIL 1943

The synagogue at Boulevard Dubouchage took charge of the corpse. The death certificate stated: *natural causes.* Luitger had failed to claim the grave site adjacent to Marina. In a dark corner, under the menacing shadow of an overgrown sorb tree, Luitger lay alone, unmourned except by Emmet Schatzman, who accompanied Charlotte through the rites.

She had not slept, and only stood there because it was required by Jewish law. Her absence would have drawn unwanted attention to herself. Herr Schatzman let tears roll down his cheeks, but Charlotte's eyes were dry. She could not imagine ever shedding a tear for Luitger. She would not look Herr Schatzman in the eye for fear he would see that it was she who had caused the death of his friend. She tilted her head side to side in a rhythmic motion that matched the rabbi's intonation. She took the shovel in hand. The first clumps of earth landed on the coffin with a thud, resounding with her tiny remorse. The second rang a gong of freedom. It was the end of an era. Charlotte drew a deep breath and released it completely.

As they left the cemetery, she allowed Herr Schatzman to put his arm around her, only because he was a dear man and seemed badly in need of comforting her. She patted him on the back in return. They parted ways at the bottom of Rue Neuscheller, she choosing to "walk a bit with her thoughts." When he was out of sight, Charlotte continued on with an empty feeling inside, as though having been drained of a toxic substance, her arms swinging loosely in time with her pensive stride.

As QUICKLY as she could, Charlotte moved out of the Nice apartment and returned to l'Ermitage, her work retrieved from Dr. Mercier. "Originally a ballet studio," Anneliese said as she'd walked Charlotte around her new room. "Then our children's dormitory." The long, rectangular space opened at the far end into a bay of windows projecting out over a wooded portion of the property and with a view through to the sea. Next door was a bedroom and adjoining bathroom— all together, her own little suite. Each day, she awoke in a burning heat to nothing but the task: to choose and to shape.

On the two windowless walls, she'd pinned up her paintings, some in clear succession, running like a train track along the entire length at eye level; others helter-skelter above and below the main line, not yet placed but not yet eliminated. They fell loosely into three sections: Prelude, Main Section, and Epilogue.

She would stare at the arrangements, not knowing what to do next, waiting for the answer to come. Sometimes in these moments of passive incubation, an awful experience arrived, a bolt out of nowhere. Now, as she stood contemplating, it struck. The room and all the paintings failed to cohere, and the fog crept in, making them disappear behind a white veil. She saw the eggs, frothy like the fog, and the brown bottle of veronal grains, frozen in time. She saw herself sitting in her room, having refused to take Luitger to Emmet's and knowing that he likely would attempt the trip himself.

She became nauseated and sweaty. She couldn't swallow. No one knew she'd come close to poisoning her grandfather. No one knew she'd let Luitger go down the hill on his own, except Emmet, and he had not blamed her. But her grandfather—that odious man still had a stranglehold on her throat.

The crunch of a car on the driveway gravel wrested her from the secret that possessed her. When she turned from contemplating her wall, there, coming through the door, was Henri, a slow smile spreading across his shining face. Her whole body ignited and took flight straight into his arms. They hugged, rocking and squeezing, kissing necks, faces, eyes, and lips. He held her at arm's length, his smile wry and boundless.

"You left him?"

She didn't hesitate. "He died."

"Thank God!"

They made love quickly, and then again in long, slow verification of each other's presence. Charlotte lingered over her lover's form: his shoulder, his flank, his smell. This was the weight of him, the heat of him. *This is us.*

Afterward, he lit a eucalyptus cigarette. They propped the pillows and shared the smoke while he told what happened. He had never been in a camp.

"Dr. M warned me this trip would be very dangerous, with the Germans occupying the western departments. They were rounding up Jews straight out of the cafés. Right from a neighboring table."

The German presence disrupted the child-rescue mission. Luckily his children had been placed, but it was too risky to make the return trip and impossible to remain in Marseille. He took to the mountains and joined up with resistance fighters.

His eyes roved her face. It felt like he was assuring himself that it was true: They were finally together. Her heart swelled with the love she once knew, reborn here, by a miracle restored, like a lost object never lost, only obscured by being so far out of sight.

"I believed you would survive," she said. A pinch of shame reminded her how she had given up on him. She had despaired, and that despair had contributed to her considering suicide. But she couldn't tell him.

Henri had helped in tactical planning of actions. They wanted him to lead. But he was a dozen years older than most, and he hadn't signed up for that.

"I was afraid I'd die. I couldn't bear the thought of you being left not knowing what happened to me."

She couldn't imagine surviving in the mountains. She up and straddled him. Her thumbs smoothed his brows. Her fingers drew down his nose. She touched his scar. Sharply he turned his head to that side, forcing her to remove her hand. Melancholy took possession of his face. It was the private kind that refused to be questioned. She placed both hands on his head, and he relaxed.

They were quiet while a soft spring-afternoon breeze drifted through the open window. Her fingers lightly traced circles on his chest, rhythmically rising and falling. She pressed her hand over his heart, absorbed the heat of his body, making his presence more real.

His bad leg had gotten worse, which was why he couldn't fight. "A nurse assigned to a fighting unit told me, 'Too much nerve damage.'" His eyes welled up. He turned his head away to collect himself. She rested a hand on the bad leg.

"No more expeditions for you," she said, sad about his leg but glad he wouldn't be off.

They became silent, comfortably wandering around in each other's eyes for a while. Then she collapsed and pressed her whole torso against his, burying her face in his neck.

"I'm going on a kissing expedition," she said, and began where she was, at his neck.

LATER, THEY JOINED ANNELIESE, Max, and Rui for dinner. Max brought up a bottle of wine from the cellar.

"A very good Beaujolais," he said. They raised their glasses. "To Henri's safe return."

She looped her arm through Henri's and squeezed. A lock of brown hair grown long fell across his forehead. He flipped it away and smiled, looking content. His return enlivened all of them, seeming to cast a surrounding glow that made them whole again.

Max reported news of an uprising of Jews in the Warsaw ghetto, and they raised their glasses to those brave warriors willing to go directly up against the German army.

A few days later, Charlotte and Henri were lying on his bed in his old room down the hall from her quarters, protected from the sun's midday rays in the shadow of the bed's canopy. Slowly, what she had been holding back all came out. She described the times Luitger had begged her to kill herself. How she kept coming back to the feeling that he'd stolen her life. How he'd urged the veronal on her and how he'd tried to push her out the window.

Henri didn't seem to care how Luitger had met his end. He was so grateful she was no longer bound to him. There was no catch in his breath. He didn't even flinch. His arms held her in a tight embrace.

"I sat in my room and did nothing, knowing how treacherous that hill was for the feeble old man he had become." She felt her chin quivering. "And sure enough, he died trying to make it home."

Charlotte let Henri see her eyes full of tears, which she tried to restrain. Were they for Luitger, that horrid man? Or herself in her remorse? Or the terrible tangle of their relationship that was finally over? She couldn't say. But the tears needed to flow, and did so freely.

Henri's expression was grave, not full of disgust or showing judgment, but serious, solemn. Charlotte was alert to the slightest alteration. In the enveloping silence, in which even the breeze was still and the birds quiet, Henri's body softened and allowed hers to melt even more deeply into his as she grew calm. He sighed her sorrow, and his sigh was a shield against her darkest thoughts and most painful feelings, which receded until, for the moment, there was no thought, no feeling, but just the nakedness of her own being, quietly alive.

CHAPTER 29

VILLEFRANCHE-SUR-MER

JUNE 1943

After her confession, life took on a routine. Charlotte kept at it, organizing and shaping her paintings toward something coherent and whole. She could almost see it, then she couldn't, then she could almost. Meanwhile, when Henri wasn't out making friends with the Italian authorities, he began to build a hiding place in one of the outbuildings used for mechanical repairs and light carpentry. Old bicycle wheels and tools would hang on a fake wall. Behind it, he intended to erect a loft.

"Henri, I thought you believed we were safe under the Italians."

"Yes, but what if the Germans attack and the Italians don't hold out? You, for one, have no false papers. So this is just in case. And it gives me something useful to do."

Max was in and out on short trips to Nice and environs, leaving before dawn and returning after dark, sometimes gone a few days. Anneliese was rested and strong again, now that she had only Rui to care for.

Meanwhile, Charlotte had missed two monthlies. She wasn't sick, and she'd skipped before. She hoped she hadn't done something she wasn't ready for. She felt confused. In other moods, when she'd patched together a good sequence of paintings, she was elated.

Two weeks later, Anneliese told Charlotte that the tenderness in her breasts confirmed it, and she beseeched her to tell Henri already. She vowed to do so soon.

The afternoon she'd designated for her reveal to Henri, several Italian officers—bearing real cigars, not rolls of parched grape leaves; and real cigarettes, Gauloises—called on Henri at l'Ermitage for a private meeting. They all waited eagerly to hear about it. At dinner, Henri explained that thousands of Jews had flocked into Nice. The Vichy had banned them from the coast and were requiring them to go inland to enforced residences. The idea was to move them into the German-occupied territory.

"But," he said, "the Italians aren't so stupid as to position the Jews to be deported. They're moving Jews 'as ordered,' but within our zone, north of Nice, to the high country. Megève, Saint-Gervais, Vananson. For better protection."

There, the Jews were living in France's most lavish hotels and its ritziest spas, and were free to go about. The Jewish organizations were taking complete care of them.

All three exchanged looks of amazement and acknowledged Italian cleverness. They talked about whether these resettlements were for them. Maybe for Max and Anneliese, temporarily.

"With our passports, we want to get to Switzerland," Max said.

"How about you two?" Anneliese asked.

Charlotte and Henri had never claimed more than the one day they were living. With this practical question,

Charlotte realized her condition wasn't a mere curiosity, a mysterious collection of physical symptoms. It was one of becoming, and what was becoming was a child, Henri's very own as well as hers. All muddled inside, she felt how much simpler it was not to think of the future. She and Henri exchanged bewildered looks.

Henri said, "We'll need to discuss it."

While washing dishes, Anneliese said she was not going to keep sitting at meals while being the only one who knew.

"Come on, Charlotte. Life! What more could you want in these times?"

In the kitchen corner, Rui bounced in his wood-and-mesh playpen and squealed, "Rife!"

Anneliese shook her dripping, soapy hands at Charlotte, resulting in a bubbly shower. "What are you afraid of?"

Charlotte dipped her hands into the sink and returned the favor. Just then, Henri and Max entered and asked what was going on, and failing to get any answer other than laughter, they joined in the water fight. Henri took Charlotte's side and Max Anneliese's, and the play went on until they were all in hysterics—including Rui, who had received a few splashes—with their clothing soaked through, their hair matted to their scalps, and the kitchen floor a slippery disaster area.

Lying in bed with Henri the next morning while he still slept, Charlotte asked herself Anneliese's question, and the only thing that came to mind was: *Oh, no. I'm having a child.* Then her mind went blank with the overwhelming fact of it. Her body was flooded with the desire to keep it wholly to herself as long as possible, to savor it, fearing that it might, for some inexplicable reason, disappear. It was too intimate for anyone else, yet it was a person destined to belong to the world.

She was horrified—yes, horrified—that such a thing could happen in her body without her own design; but then, they had taken no precautions. Thinking they were immune? Were they caught in wishful thinking? If so, wishing what? Wanting? Not wanting? They'd never considered a child, a family. She was terrified of Henri's response. What if he became angry and blaming? What if something beautiful became suddenly hideous? She would wait for the perfect moment rather than create an imperfect one.

CHARLOTTE FELT SHE had overcome the obstacle that was Luitger—once by leaving him, once by managing to prevail—to live. The purpose of her life, even as she was aware of her pregnancy (and possibly that development made it more urgent), was to finish her work. The Italians were clever, but the Nazis were a formidable power. The Vichy at Gurs had tried to deny her identity. The Nazis, already in the south, might be on their way. This was how Charlotte saw the moment, and she worked with such fierce energy, intent, and speed that it was like living inside a tornado. Thus, she delayed telling Henri for another week. Some days, like today, he looked in at this hour of the afternoon to see if she'd like to take a break.

"Have a look," she said. She hadn't shown him her work for fear of losing hold of it, not knowing, she admitted, exactly what "it" was. Anyway, it was very private, and even as she was inviting him in, she wondered at herself. Then it was clear: This was a test. If he passed, she'd be able to tell him the news. How awful of her! Yet she couldn't help herself.

With eyebrows jauntily raised and a small smirk of a smile, he looked surprised, pleased, and interested. He squared his shoulders in readiness, as if he'd been waiting for this moment.

First, she showed him the paintings of her childhood in Berlin. He moved along the scenes, then broke out in a laugh.

"Look at you as a little girl! Skating! Just as carefree as could be. And with a blue muffler flying in the wind behind you!" His eyes were crinkled with laughter. "I could eat you up," he said, taking her chin in his hands and planting a kiss on her lips.

This was not exactly the artistic critique she had expected.

She walked along the wall, wanting to give him the big idea of it all. She introduced the main section devoted to Wolf and Katharina, explaining they had been her two most important people, maybe even more important than her father.

"They were entangled with each other—not as lovers, though. And each entangled with me as well. It was complicated. I'm still working it out."

He ambled, hands in the pockets of his work pants, head jutting forward, neck strained, and eyes concentrated on the work. He took in portraits of Katharina and called her "a formidable person," distilling her perfectly to a word. He seemed to be enjoying rather than judging.

She had to tell him, but she couldn't bring herself to open her mouth.

He noticed the references to tunes, raised his eyebrows in amazement while nodding in admiration. A fluttery panic in her throat sent her hurrying to the last section, an epilogue about her years in France. Just as she felt the moment had arrived, he crossed the room, returning to the prelude section. Another reprieve.

"What are those, with the writing on them?" He pointed to transparent sheets pinned above the paintings, which were overlays to attach to the paintings. The words written on them were the narrative that went with the pictures. He viewed a painting of Charlotte as a young girl at a desk, bent over and using a paintbrush. The words read: *I like doing this. Maybe I could learn to draw. It feels just right.*

The painting drew her back to her origins. She thought about how she had failed in fashion design—Katharina's choice for her—and how at first, the Berlin Art Academy turned her down. She had taken drawing lessons and resented her teacher, who forced her to faithfully copy every stalk of a cactus rather than draw what she saw.

"Scenes with words and dialogue? This is becoming quite a dramatic thing."

He'd failed to say whether it was good. Good and bad weren't, she saw, his parameters. He was looking at the work for what it was. He'd penetrated her realm.

She couldn't get the words out. She was mistress of the wall, but not her body. Then she summoned the courage and turned to face him.

"Henri," she murmured.

"Truly outstanding, Charlotte."

Finally, an opinion. And one she especially liked.

"You've given birth to something unusual...unique."

This had to be the moment. She put her hands on her belly, spreading her fingers.

"And something else as well."

His eyes locked on hers, and in two heartbeats his face exploded with surprise and incredulity.

"What? Really?"

"Well, not yet. But on its way."

His biggest smile burst forth. Charlotte knew that smile. It was the one reserved for her, her very own Henri smile, lighter and brighter than ever, electrifying every fiber in her body. Her limbs felt light, bouncy. Her head tingled.

She gave him a playful shove. He lifted her up, twirled her around, took her hands, and danced her up and down and around the studio, her paintings spinning around them in a kaleidoscope, flowing into one continuous piece. Henri's eyes flashed green sparks of joy. She threw her head back in frenzied bliss. She felt weightless, and then, in what must be like the exhilaration of flight, she went free. Her heart radiated heat, pumping out happiness. When he brought her to a stop, he held her and kissed her all over her face and hugged her to him and held her away again and kissed her long on the lips.

The kiss came to an abrupt halt. "We have to get married," he said.

The idea sent a thrill through her. She'd seen how it had worked for Max and Anneliese. Couples came to mind—under the canopy of a chuppah, being blessed by a rabbi and embraced by a joyful congregation. A wedding was hope that they all might endure. But…

She looked away. Her hands fidgeted. "I have to get back to work," she said.

"Are you kidding? We must talk."

Henri marched her out of the studio to a loveseat in the upper passageway overlooking the grand entrance hall. He sat her down. "What? Tell me."

"It's not the best idea."

He shook his head. All the merriment had gone out of him. "We'd have a place in the world," he said, looking a little like he couldn't believe he had to argue this point. More than anything, Charlotte didn't want to disappoint him in this moment.

"No. Actually, we would not have a place in the world. We're still refugees."

"We can do it quietly in the town hall, which is Italian now. It wouldn't be under the eyes of the Gestapo. Or even the Vichy." Always the first to point out risks and on guard for everyone's safety, he seemed completely sold on a path that might put them in danger.

"Why jeopardize ourselves by making a public show?"

"Because it's normal and right and natural and good."

It was hard to argue with that. He was a grown man, had lost his parents, had taken enormous risks to trek the dangerous coast, but the way his eyes had become dewy, he appeared as innocent as a child in this moment. Charlotte withdrew into her shell.

He picked up. "And because safety under the Italians isn't guaranteed. The Germans could move in. We could be torn from each other. And the child wouldn't have a name."

She considered this point. "You see it as a form of protection?"

"I do. Under worse circumstances, it might be the one thing that permits us to stay together." He paused. "If we were deport—if we were moved out."

He closed his eyes, presumably to get control over himself. She felt a tightening in her chest. A baby coming. Their status as refugees. The need to move or stay put. She'd only wanted to tell him the news. She hadn't wanted to become even more confused by having to figure out what to do. And now, public marriage?

He took her hands and waited for her to look at him. She wanted to pull away. She became intensely afraid of losing her most sacred inner life, her autonomy, control over her own destiny.

When she did look up, he said, "Don't you see how vulnerable you are? You can't have any security as an unmarried pregnant woman. And after the birth? You'd be a woman refugee with a child."

Then she saw what he was getting at, and her shoulders, which had been inching up toward her ears, dropped in surrender to this cold fact.

"We're having a child, Charlotte," he said, emphasizing *we*. "You and me, together. I can't live without doing what's right and honorable and what I want to do."

She realized she'd been too frightened to think of what it meant to have a child given their circumstances, too occupied trying to disentangle from Luitger, and too engrossed in bringing her work to completion. The one and only clear point she'd come to was that she must continue her work, finish this project, and go on to whatever was next.

When Henri beamed his earnest, hopeful, solid smile, she was bathed in its luminosity, and suddenly, for the first time since she'd left Berlin, that terrible, haunting, ultimate aloneness wholly disappeared. It dissolved to reveal the indisputable and inviolable connection she had to Henri. Also to Anneliese, Max, and Rui. It was a bit terrifying to have lost her familiar loneliness. She understood, though, that she was not disembodied, disconnected. Her life was embedded in this family and in the world. Amazingly she felt that, in this new view of things, she still did have her inner life, as Henri had his.

"You'll have to surrender your identity card," she said. As someone who trafficked in false papers and documents, who prized his "real" Swiss identity above all else and depended on it to carry him unscathed through the war, it would be no small matter.

"I've factored that in," he said with an unexpected look of delight, the kind arising from the offer of the ultimate gift, in a gesture of rare, resolute self-sacrifice. "We won't be able to stay here. Dr. M will help us."

The glow of his cheeks, the mischievous grin, the yearning so strong his whole body was pitched tight, leaning toward her, and barely restrained—all said how very much he wanted her to say yes. She was impressed he had thought this through and consulted Dr. Mercier. It made her feel cared for.

Charlotte pulsed with a new sensation, awash in exquisite love flowing from Henri to her, from her to him, from them both to their little one, and from that tiny life, she was sure, back to them. This proposal was not an indulgent romantic fantasy, but a practical, sensible move—and a risky one. The safeguards might well outweigh the risks. It was hard to know. But their circle of three seemed to have its own driving force and its own requirements, the one in this moment, that felt outside of time and sacred, being a leap of faith.

"All right, then," she said. "Let's have hope and courage."

CHARLOTTE BECAME OBSESSED, driven with all she had, to finish before the big day. She culled out five hundred paintings and was left with seven hundred sixty-nine. These were necessary. These told the story. They covered two entire walls of the studio, top to bottom, and most of the floor. Over and over them she went, making small adjustments, eyeing passages, sweeping through them all at once to sense whether they cohered as a whole. Then it happened: Her work came to an end.

And the end was also the beginning. The hundreds and hundreds of pictures were one—the story of coming to make the story, the story of a young woman becoming an artist. Charlotte threw her head back. Yes. She had done it. Then she couldn't help swinging in circles, her heart pounding in disbelief and relief. She was all emptiness and fulfillment.

When she came to stillness, she crossed to the enormous bay windows and opened all eight of them. She took a deep breath of the incoming fresh air. She was standing at a window differently—not paralyzed, not looking into the abyss. The day sparkled. Through the trees below, the gardens and terraces of l'Ermitage vibrated with their summer rainbow of colors and green, green lawns. The sky and sea twinkled at each other's unending blue across the horizon. Charlotte sighed long, hard, in gratitude for all this beauty and the time within which she'd been given the gift of retreating from the world to make her work.

LESS THAN TWO WEEKS after they'd first talked about marrying, Charlotte and Henri were lying in bed on the morning of their wedding day, June seventeenth. Each confessed to being a little nervous about the public ceremony. They decided to make a private, sacred vow.

"Never by our own will shall we be parted," Henri said with solemn face.

"Never," Charlotte said, floating on the wonder of such absolute certainty and her willingness to declare it.

Within the hour, they were standing in Nice's town hall in a tight little room with bars over the counter's window. Henri was in a blue suit and tie, his hair brushed and, it looked to Charlotte, pomaded to stay off his forehead. She had scrubbed the paint from under her nails and gotten out every last bit. She wore one of Olive's tea dresses, a Victorian empire style in translucent ivory layers. Delmira had pinned up her hair, revealing her elegant neck, leaving loose tendrils, and Anneliese had lent Charlotte her own mother's gold earrings set with pearls, gently clasping them onto her earlobes. Charlotte felt elevated out of present time, transported to an earlier, saner, more civilized, peaceful era.

They filled out the form with their full names, dates of birth, and the address of current residence on Rue Cauvin. Charlotte presented the German identity card she'd brought with her from Berlin five years ago, classifying her as a Jew. All was ready to go off smoothly when Henri presented his Swiss identity card to the official in charge.

"I'm sorry, but you're Aryan and cannot marry a Jew. Next!"

Henri grabbed Charlotte's hand. Standing tall, unmoving, he said, "I'm Jewish!"

"What?" The man looked baffled for a moment, then regained his official demeanor. "You must surrender this card at police headquarters. Immediately."

"Wait," Charlotte said. "Perhaps we should reconsider."

But Henri had already gone off. Charlotte had a moment of panic while waiting with Anneliese, Max, Rui, Gabrielle, and Delmira, who fluffed up the layers of her skirt. She should not have expressed doubts at the last minute, but Anneliese and Delmira said it was normal.

Henri was back by the time Emmet Schatzman and the Merciers arrived. He and Charlotte completed the paperwork by signing the registry. The group was sent into a smaller room with a bland-faced official. Charlotte's stomach felt all fluttery. *This is Henri*, she repeated, just to keep her two feet on the floor. After agreeing to take each other as husband and wife, they were pronounced united. Henri was grinning, his dimple deep with joy. Charlotte was shy to kiss him in public, but it needed to be done. He kissed her longer than she thought seemly in a town hall. When she opened her eyes to see everyone watching, she could feel her face blush bright pink. But the realness of what was in her heart, the overwhelming immediacy and goodness of their union, overrode her self-consciousness. Then they were off to l'Ermitage.

In the garden, the table was set with a lace cloth and studded with colorful bouquets of summer flowers. A champagne cork popped, bringing on the loud chirping and caws of the birds. A bowl of lemons, the centerpiece, was moved aside to make way for the succulent goat. Tender asparagus, cheesy potato gratin, and many side dishes appeared. Her husband had been trolling the black market for sure. Everything was as delectable as if there were no war, no Vichy, no Germans in the business of their lives. Too excited to eat, Charlotte rose and strolled around the table, feeling the warmth of the sun on her bare arms and the swish of her dress against her bare legs while laying a hand on every shoulder, inhaling each fragrant head.

A skid of gravel announced a carload of Italians in time for dessert, offering cigarettes, cigars, and Tuscan red wine. They removed their kepis and leather belts with their revolvers. Delmira had baked an Austrian Sacher torte, Henri's favorite chocolate-and-apricot delight, and a French lemon-raspberry cake. By dark they were all a bit too tipsy, Delmira included, to do anything but wander away from the gay debris.

In the morning, Charlotte and Henri were still among the sheets. Happiness flowed from her toes to her head and back. She luxuriated in the feeling, letting herself melt into it while trying to detect what this meant, marriage. Were they different? In here it felt the same. What it meant out there—was it anything more than a piece of paper filed away?

Henri reached into the drawer of the night table and brought forth a tarnished brass key.

"To Dr. Mercier's apartment in Monaco."

Charlotte did know it would come to this, but amidst the planning and festivities, her mind had always slid past the eventuality.

"We must leave. As soon as possible."

"Why so soon?"

They had both assumed they would have some leisure. But Dr. Mercier had taken Henri aside after the ceremony.

"He told me that Alois Brunner—the most brutal of all Hitler's men—has taken over Drancy camp near Paris. He has solid intelligence. German motorized divisions will arrive in Nice before the end of the month. There's going to be a return to German rule."

"What? No! That will be awful."

"Even worse for us, it could be fatal. We signed our names as Jews in the town hall, along with registering our residence here in Villefranche at l'Ermitage. They have our address. They can find us. We know what happened in Germany,

Austria, Poland. We have to expect they will come for us." He stubbed out his cigarette.

Henri stared into the distance, his eyes empty, blank, then becoming glazed and shiny. He stared at the key in his hands. It was the only path remaining to their survival. Now, fear on a rampage, pounding from head to toe like a mob of galloping wild horses, trampled the space vacated by Charlotte's happiness.

CHAPTER 30

———

MONACO

Dr. Mercier's tiny place in Monaco could hardly be called an apartment. It was a fifth-floor walk-up in an old building, one room under the eaves with a creaky old bed in one corner, a small icebox, a hot plate with one burner, and the bare necessities in terms of cook pots, dishware, and cutlery. A round table with two chairs was set in front of the only window, where one couldn't help but be happy just looking out across the street at buildings painted yellow, orange, coral, and fuchsia.

At first Charlotte and Henri explored the city, behaving like honeymooners. Without francs to spend freely, they walked the harbor, marveling at the yachts, and strolled the square of the casino admiring the Beaux-Arts architecture. Henri enjoyed eyeing the collection of the best cars the world had to offer: Mercedes-Benz, Bentley, and Rolls Royce. With an austere lunch in hand, they found a shaded bench in the Saint-Martin Gardens, where they could eat and while away the time.

The one radio at l'Ermitage belonged to Max, and they did not have funds to purchase another. Although they were only twenty-one kilometers from Nice, they felt alone and isolated, waiting every day for news from Anneliese.

They were able to obtain tidbits of information from Madame LaRoche, who lived across the hall. A woman advanced in age and living alone, she watched over the apartment for Dr. Mercier. He had assured Henri she was a safe person to talk to. They'd learned that Marseille was overrun with Nazis. The offices of the UGIF, the umbrella organization for all Jewish charities, had been raided, and Raymond-Raoul Lambert, the leader, had been deported, along with his wife and children. Operations had been driven underground. That had been in May. Ever since, Jews had been fleeing to the countryside or trying to get back into the Italian zone.

Lambert? The journalist? He had to be the same, Marina's favorite, and the one who had saved Charlotte from the French police on the train from Paris, the one who had taken her to dinner with his wife. He had been so sure the Germans would not be able to extend themselves into France. Charlotte recalled his wife's words: *We may have only two choices. Stay to face our deaths. Or flee to save our lives.*

They stayed. And now they had been deported.

"But the Nazis are out to catch all Jews trying to make it into the Italian zone," Madame LaRoche whispered to Henri in the hallway of their apartment building. "They're checking identity papers on the trains between Marseille and Nice."

The third week of July, they invited Madame LaRoche to tea. She sat at the table with Charlotte while Henri perched at the foot of the bed. She told them of a Polish man who had deliberately gone into the camps. "To witness what was going on." He escaped and made his way to London to report the unspeakable things he'd seen.

"Asphyxiation by gas. People being burned alive. Electrocuted."

"That can't be true," Charlotte said.

"Jan Karski presented direct testimony," she said. "The way I figure it, the BBC must have believed him. Or else, why broadcast it to the world?"

After Madame LaRoche had bid them goodnight, Charlotte said, "We need to contact Max and find out what to do."

In the first week of August, a telegram came from Max. As predicted, a German motorized division had arrived in Nice and was stationed locally in barracks.

> *We have left the Great House. Apartment in Nice.*
> *Rumors of large-scale roundups. Distinct possibility of*
> *escape for all of us. Come back. M*

THE NICE APARTMENT was in the western end of the city on Boulevard Gambetta, not far from the train station. With one bedroom, it was adequate for Max, Anneliese, and Rui, but with five occupants, it was cramped. It belonged to Madame Piché, who had offered it to Dr. Mercier on the day he came to see her about collecting Charlotte's work. She was concerned that one day Charlotte might need it. Although Charlotte knew there was a network of French people helping the Jews, perceiving how it operated in her own life bent her heart in gratitude.

Max, who was staying in close touch with the workings of the Comité Dubouchage at the synagogue, caught them up on changing conditions in Nice. "There's no doubt. There will be a switch back to German control."

"Jews here have been in a panic," Anneliese said. "Children are being scattered into the countryside. But we're hanging onto Rui."

Charlotte put a hand on her stomach, which had grown prominent in the last two months. "Germans. Roundups. Children in danger. Why, then, did you call us back?"

"Because there's some hope of escape," Max said. "Angelo Donati has cooked up a scheme."

Charlotte vaguely recalled Dr. Mercier mentioning a Donati who helped the Jews. Max explained that Donati had been meeting every morning with two leaders, Michel Topiol and Ignace Fink. He managed to restrain the Italian authorities and used his influence among important Jewish personalities to raise money for the Comité. Those funds helped to feed the poor people pouring into Nice.

"Anyway, he believes that all the Jews here on the Côte d'Azur can be saved. That all the refugees can be got into Italy. And he has asked Father Marie-Benoit if he wouldn't get the Vatican to put pressure on Mussolini."

Charlotte said, "That sounds mad. Getting all the Jews out of France and into Italy?" Yet she felt a flicker of excitement in the slight vibration of her insides. She took Henri's hand.

"He's envisioning something on an even larger scale. From Italy, the refugees will continue to North Africa." Max explained how the pope had already swung his support behind Donati's project. The pope's commitment, plus the fall of Mussolini, had made Donati very optimistic. "He's gone to the Vatican. As we speak, he's meeting with senior officials of the Italian Foreign Ministry. Also, representatives of Great Britain and the US. He means to transfer thirty thousand Jews from France to North Africa and Palestine."

Charlotte said, "That's wild! He couldn't possibly do that."

"He thinks he can. It's a serious plan. I happen to be privy to some of Fink's and Topiol's communications with Donati. The Italian government is going to provide four ships and transfer an additional twenty thousand Jews out of Italy."

Henri said, "But who can afford that? Not even a wealthy banker."

Max said, "The Jewish Joint."

It was starting to make sense. The international Jewish community, led by the Americans, was going to save the European Jews. The Italian government was supplying ships for the exodus, not out of beneficence; they were as antisemitic as ever. This plan had the advantage of ridding them of their own Jews, and a Jewish Italian banker was making the arrangements. But still, it was hard to believe.

"You two need to go to the synagogue and get identity cards, which will put you exclusively under safe Italian control and secure your places on the passenger list. Passports are being prepared in Rome."

CHAPTER 31

NICE

Charlotte and Henri approached the synagogue on Boulevard Dubouchage. Outside, four Carbinieri stood guard. "Around the clock," Max had said. In no time, they had identity cards. They were now under the protection of the Italian authorities. The official stamp attested to it. The Vichy could no longer touch them.

That evening, they turned over their cards to Max, who said he would get them to the Comité, which would verify them for transport out of France. Charlotte hated to let go of her card, afraid it might disappear.

Max had brought home a guest for dinner, Ignace Fink, one of the leaders of the Comité Dubouchage. He was a small man with a large presence, neat in his worn clothing, going slightly bald. He was humble and thankful for the invitation and seemed to tuck away his forcefulness for the duration of the meal, relaxed in knowing he was among friends.

Anneliese had procured cucumbers and tomatoes from a connection she'd made at the children's health clinic to a nearby farmer's wife who brought in vegetables from the country twice a week, which she sold in a friend's apartment. The salad, sprinkled with lemon and salt, was so delicious that everyone savored the treat in silence.

Henri finally opened the subject on everyone's mind. "When will the ships arrive?"

"No one is being told exactly," Fink said, sitting up straight and alert, his voice a bit rapid, seeming pleased to be getting down to business. "We're to get ready. A matter of days, I think. Maybe a week, according to what I heard today at the Comité."

There was a grave look on his face. Anneliese set out a plate of purple figs. She cut one into quarters and gave a piece to Rui, who smashed it into his mouth, leaving ripe, pink, seeded pulp on his chin. Fink smiled at the little boy before going serious again and speaking.

"We've been living in false security for a long time." He told of two men arrested in Nice over a year ago. They'd been deported to someplace in Poland, escaped, and found their way back to the synagogue.

"The first man's name was Honig. He told us about a camp called Auschwitz. Not a labor camp or transit camp, but a death camp."

Death camp? Charlotte did a double take and looked at Henri, who peered out from under his eyebrows at Max for verification. Max and Anneliese both stared wide-eyed at Fink, who paused with a big sigh. Before he could continue, Anneliese interrupted.

"Wait, please." She tilted her head toward Rui and mouthed, "Not for little ears." She picked up her son, settled him in the other room with the toy train Henri had carved for him, and then returned.

Fink picked up where he had left off. "This Honig, he said he saw Jews being gassed and their bodies burned in crematoria."

Charlotte's breath retreated and hung in the shallow of her chest while her thoughts scrambled to understand. *Gassed? Burned?*

"We at the synagogue thought he was mad. We determined that for his survival, he needed to leave the country. We shepherded him and his family on his way to Switzerland."

He paused for a bite of fig.

"And that was that?" Charlotte asked.

"That was that. We prided ourselves on having gotten a madman and his family out of the country. Out of harm's way. The way he was—ranting, hysterical—they never would've survived. But part of his story had included his escape plan from Auschwitz. He and another fellow were charged with going out for fresh supplies. That allowed them frequent excursions into the town of Oświęcim. They made connections with some of the townspeople, who provided them with clothing. And they were able to make their way—so Honig claimed—through Germany. Posing as foreign workmen. To Holland, then to Belgium, then Nice.

"The other man came later. Salomon. The same name as you, Charlotte. Haim Salomon. We put him up in a hotel. But that night, there was an identity check, and his papers were suspicious. He was arrested as a spy. It became a complicated thing. I approached Lospinoso, who has always been kind to the Jews."

Charlotte recalled Dr. Mercier telling her about Lospinoso, sent from Rome to work with the Nazis. Instead, he had set to work with the Comité Dubouchage.

Fink bit into another fig and wiped his forearm across his mouth to catch the juice from falling.

"And the second man, Salomon?" Anneliese asked.

"With Lospinoso's help, we were finally able to get the charges dropped. The upshot was that Salomon was finally freed and confided in Angelo Donati and eventually came to talk to us at the synagogue.

"'Jews are being exterminated.' That's what he said. He was raving. As with Honig, we thought he was crazy. We called a doctor."

Immediately a conversation broke out around the table about the meaning of these testimonies.

"Just like Jan Karski's story," Charlotte said, recalling Madame LaRoche's report in Monaco.

Henri said, "Extermination? One can't even conceive—"

Anneliese said, "It's possible, you know, that they mean to get rid of us. No more Jews. And there you go. The Jewish problem? Solved."

Max said, "So the deportations. Not for labor in Germany? The Jews are being taken to their death?" It was a question that was a statement that was an understanding struggling to dawn upon everyone.

Charlotte felt a necessary bewilderment and clung to it. She wanted to argue the assertion out of existence. "You can't get rid of a whole people."

Max said, "Who knows for sure? We had real homes and beautiful lives in other countries. Then the world changed. In a minute, it seemed. We were lucky to find a temporary home at l'Ermitage, where we could almost forget we were in exile. We assumed we would go back. Now look at us. Crowded into two borrowed rooms. Not much more than the clothes on our backs. We've lost everything but our lives."

Henri asked Fink, "What do you think of Donati's escape plan?"

"He's a good man. But he's somewhat of a dreamer. He has great faith in the Italians standing their ground here and backing him. Assuring us escape by sea. Word has it that Jews are being brought back down to Nice from the northern towns to board the ships. What can I say?" He looked at each one around the table. Charlotte saw a man, intense and calm, who had given his all to save the Jews and had the capacity to keep despair at bay. "It's our only hope."

CHAPTER 32

NICE

SEPTEMBER, 1943

The big day of departure was rumored to be set for the following morning, September ninth. Jews were seven to ten to a hotel room. On the beaches, people kept on the move at night to avoid arrest, or they caught some sleep under the watchful eye of a companion. By day the streets were almost impassable.

Charlotte and her family, crammed into their two-room apartment and happy to have a place indoors, were grateful beyond words. Angelo Donati. Taking the Jews to freedom by sea. A latter-day Moses. They were getting off this continent, away from this war and the long arm of the SS, leaving behind everything dark and ugly that had occurred here. She would have the baby in a safe place. Now, as they packed, she seemed to be the only one who was openly anxious.

"What if something goes wrong?" she asked.

Max said, "Nothing's going wrong." It sounded like a personal guarantee, but the way he fumbled around for his things wasn't characteristic of her brother-in-law.

Henri said, "The ships pull in. We mount the gangway. Off we go."

"What do you think, Anneliese?" Charlotte asked.

She stopped folding Rui's little things. "Honestly, Charlotte, let's think about something else. Like where we'll land in Italy."

"And where from there," Max said.

Charlotte wanted to stay in Italy, to be as close as possible to search for her father and Katharina. Thinking about reunion, she could smell 4711 perfume and feel her father's big arms around her. Henri favored Palestine as a place of honest labor, but he also yearned to go to America to explore contacts in the import-export business and meet up with Olive.

Henri held up a pair of trousers, the ones he wore for carpentry and gardening. "Perhaps I should leave behind?" He looked stumped in a way he never did, especially about small things.

Charlotte said, "Take them. Maybe there'll be a job as a gardener wherever we end up. Or we'll have a garden."

She'd wrapped her stacks of paintings in brown paper. The large bundles had traveled with her to Monaco and back, taking up a large portion of her suitcase. She placed her last piece of charcoal inside the pine box and snapped it shut. While she caressed the grain, made smooth by Henri's oiling of the wood, her chest ached.

"We're leaving Papa and Katharina behind."

Henry sat beside her. Her head was bent. Her eyelids felt gummy. He put his arm around her shoulder and lifted her chin with his free hand. There was determination in his eyes. "We *will* find them." His confident smile became a playful grin. "They're the grandparents, after all."

She let her head fall onto his chest. Henri would get along with her father. They were paired temperamentally as quiet, thoughtful types. Katharina would accept and respect Henri while finding him lacking charisma. She would be surprised to see that Charlotte had outgrown most, if not all, of her stubbornness. They would both be beside themselves with joy about the baby.

They stacked their few things in a corner—one bag each, plus her art supplies and Henri's toolbox. Anneliese seemed to be in good charge of her inventory. So Charlotte began to make soup out of the last of the turnips and greens.

When the soup was ready, they all sat at the table. They always turned on the radio in the evening to try to catch the BBC news. They ate in attentive silence, aware this was their last meal in this apartment, in Nice, in Europe. The newscaster introduced United States General Dwight D. Eisenhower for a special announcement. The signal was often weak, but tonight the general's voice was loud and clear.

"Today, the Italian government has surrendered its armed forces unconditionally."

Her body stiffened. The meaning was instantly unmistakable. The Germans would be charging into Nice. Her chin trembled uncontrollably. The Americans knew the Jews were about to be saved. They were party to it. Why could they not have let the Italians wait one more day?

Henri had his head in his hands. Anneliese had gone ashen.

Max stood and slammed down both hands on the table. "Don't anyone move. I'm going to scout." He grabbed his coat.

After Anneliese put Rui to bed, the three waited. Anneliese sewed. Charlotte drew. Henri paced, his bad leg making a rhythmic thump, until he wearied and took a chair. No one spoke. The air was thick with apprehension and the unsettling, acrid smell of bald fear.

THREE HOURS LATER, Max returned. He flipped the fourth chair and straddled it. His voice was devoid of emotion. "We must get out of here, all of us. Tonight."

He seemed to be speaking to the air and avoided looking directly at anyone. His mouth was twisted and grim.

Henri stood, leaning over the table toward Max. "What about the boats? Won't they come in for us anyway?"

Before Max could answer him, Charlotte leapt up. "We'll swim if we have to."

Anneliese cried, "Get out of here tonight? And go where?"

Max went to the window, parted a curtain with one thumb, and peered down into the street. Then he returned to his chair. Charlotte sat too. Henri stood against the wall.

Max spoke, "All the Jews who poured into town these last days, crammed into the hotels, just waiting for the ships? They were out celebrating. Dancing in the streets. I saw it."

Charlotte clicked her teeth and tapped her fingernails on the side of her chair, impatient to know what had happened. She could hear Henri's breathing growing heavier as he approached and stood behind her. She looked up and saw the tension in his face, his nostrils flared.

Across the table, Max's face was drawn tight and grave. He looked away, trying to hide the naked terror in his rapid blinking and jerky movements. Henri lit him a cigarette. More composed, Max told how the Italians had not joined the fun but whispered among themselves. In stealth and through shadows, he'd moved about town.

"I saw fewer and fewer of them. Then I passed the synagogue. Something was wrong." His speech became breathy. "The four guards who are always there—gone."

Charlotte's chest seized, without the Italians—the boats— where would they go?

On the main road, he saw Italian soldiers in retreat. Then black Citroëns on the cruise.

He crossed paths with two comrades. They compared notes.

"Gestapo agents. It's a roundup. Right off the streets. They're going into all the hotels, then the residences. Door to door. We must operate as if these reports about death camps are true."

Charlotte's chest felt like someone was standing on it. She, Henri, and Anneliese remained in stunned silence, staring at Max, muzzled by disbelief and horror.

Max added, "There will be no ships to save us."

Now Charlotte's heart vaulted in her chest from one side to the other. Still, no one said a word. Henri laid his hands on her shoulders and squeezed them. Charlotte's mind reeled. She thought she might faint.

Anneliese threw her head back, closed her eyes, and let out a sigh of lost hope.

Max continued, "The word is to scatter. We need to head up-country immediately."

A trek on foot into the mountains? Charlotte clasped her belly in both hands.

Max said, "Charlotte, you're as strong as we are. You'll make it."

She looked at Henri for reassurance. A forced smile flickered; then his face went slack.

He let go of her shoulders.

Of course. With his leg—impossible.

"Henri, I have a place for you a little outside Nice," Max said. "Essentially a false closet by day. They'll take only one. The best I could do."

Inwardly, Charlotte was furious. How dare Max suggest she go with them and leave Henri behind?

Outwardly, she suppressed her fury and tried to poke a hole in that plan. "But what if the Nazis broaden the raid? Outside Nice?"

Charlotte turned to see Henri's face, which was pale. His eyes were cast down, lips set together. He crossed to the window, stood staring at the curtain. With his back to them, he muttered, "L'Ermitage."

Max went straigh up to Henri, who remained unmoved. "Way too risky. Rue Cauvin is in black and white in Nice's marriage registry, which also, may I remind you, identifies you as Jews. Jews in Villefranche on Rue Cauvin. Above both your signatures."

Henri turned to face him, hands in his pockets, jaw firmed. "Villefranche is eight kilometers from Nice. A small, lazy town. The Nazis may not bother. If they do, there's the hideout."

Thank God for the hideout, for Henri's foresight.

Max asked, "You think it's safe?"

Henri nodded. "I do."

Max looked at Charlotte.

"L'Ermitage. With Henri."

Max expelled a breath, which marked the end of the conversation. "Well, all right, then. Get ready. Take only what's necessary."

He and Anneliese made off into the other room. So thoughtfully packed, the valises snapped open.

Henri fixed his sight on one corner of the ceiling. Softly, Charlotte pulled on his hands to get him to look at her. His voice, pitched lower, sounded resolute, but she detected the effort behind it.

"You need to go with them. They'll take care of you." He glanced at her, then away. "I want you to."

He couldn't mean this.

"That's not what being married means. That's not what we vowed in bed on the morning of our wedding day."

His face sagged. The mask of feigned courage fell away. His eyes were still avoiding hers, and his hands in hers were limp. Charlotte felt the commanding presence inside.

"You begged me to marry you. You were adamant I needed your protection. Now you're telling me to go? Besides, Max and Anneliese have their own burden."

"It's your only chance." His voice was flat, like he'd been delivered this line from the dark side of his heart.

He squeezed her hand, just slightly. Charlotte squeezed back until finally he looked straight at her. She searched and found in the deep, green wells his enormous need for her exposed. She saw he didn't want her to go, yet he wouldn't say so because, she was sure, telling her to go was what he thought was the right thing to do. But this was not theater, and she wouldn't let him play that part.

"I have the strength but not the status. A lone, Jewish, refugee woman, pregnant. No papers. Remember? I'm not going to make it. And I won't consider leaving you."

She lay her hand on the round of her belly. She looked into his eyes, and he looked back, both gazing directly at the unexpected persons they'd been to each other, mindful of the miracle given. He covered her hand with his.

One half-hour later, they were all at the door. Rui was in a harness Max had rigged up on his back. He also had a knapsack slung over each shoulder. Anneliese had two packs, which included the food she'd acquired for the journey by boat. Bound for Switzerland, they wore sturdy boots. Charlotte and Henri had their few things and, in short pants, posed as hikers.

Charlotte hugged Max, whose muscles were taut in readiness to take off. She planted a kiss on sleepy Rui's velvety forehead. Anneliese held on tight to her. The years they'd shared flew through her mind: school in Berlin, meeting again at Olive's, the many languid days passed in the extravagant luxury of l'Ermitage's gardens, the terrible times at Gurs, and these last hopeful days. From schoolmates to best friends to sisters-in-law. Her pale complexion was framed by dark curls, her delicate features belying her unflappable strength. Would Charlotte ever see them again, her new family?

"Give us five minutes. Then go," Max said and clasped his brother to him.

Max put a hand on Charlotte's cheek. "Get there as fast as you can. Give him a hand if he needs it." Turning to Henri, he said, "Don't be proud. She's carrying precious goods, but she's sturdy." They smiled and nodded. "As soon as the sun comes up, Nice is going to be a disaster area for Jews."

Max's and Anneliese's footsteps made a pattering sound down the staircase. The door of the building closed with a clunk. Five minutes later, Charlotte and Henri were at the same door, peeking out. The street was empty. In the dark before dawn, they hiked out of Nice northward and east, the steady thump of Henri's leg marking their way through a backcountry route that would return them, roundabout, to l'Ermitage.

CHAPTER 33

VILLEFRANCHE-SUR-MER

SEPTEMBER 1943

Charlotte loved to watch Henri asleep in the morning: the care lines of his face relaxed, his silky eyelashes sometimes twitching. On this day, a week or so after they'd arrived back at l'Ermitage, she waited for him to wake up so that she could tell him she was going into Villefranche. He would oppose her, but it was vital she go without delay.

It had taken her awhile to figure out what to do with her work, this vast project that had saved her through these times of uncertainty. She had to admit to hopes that one day it would be seen. She'd searched for a hiding place in the Great House until she realized that if the Nazis came, they would ransack every nook and cranny. She could bury it, but even inside a suitable container, it would suffer from exposure to the elements. Furthermore, it might never be found. So now she made her decision: because it had saved her all these years, in order to save it, she must let it go. She meant to take her work to Dr. Mercier, and to do so, she would have to elude the SS.

Charlotte was happy nestling with Henri under the coverlet at night and waking up to the solid mound of him in the morning. In their first days here, they'd had the shock of loss. Anneliese not in the kitchen? Rui, now four, not here with his endless questions? All Charlotte could do was sleep—early to bed and long naps in the afternoon. With her work complete, she was at loose ends. Her whole experience of being alive had been one enormous effort to make manifest what she thought was a great and worthy statement, a necessary one. She'd been purposeful; she'd known what to do. Now, she did not. Her body demanded an abrupt turning toward a deep and ever finer attunement to what was happening inside. She became rapt by the changes, her swollen breasts and rounded belly. There seemed nothing to do but watch. If it was a girl, they would name her Eva, of course. If a boy, Elias, after Henri's father.

Delmira had anticipated her intense desire for salty foods by stocking the kitchen with quarts of her pickles, which by now Charlotte had almost completely devoured. All in all, there was not much food. The few farms in the area suffered from the arid climate and produced small yields, most of which the occupying force claimed. According to Delmira, some contraband was being smuggled in from Italy, finding its way past German customs. There were still rutabagas enough and grapes from a bountiful harvest. Charlotte grew thinner when she should have been filling out. Henri hovered over her, sharing his portions with her, her slightest discomfort provoking concern.

One difference had emerged between them. She believed the two of them were most likely doomed. Henri believed in the safety of l'Ermitage and their sure survival. Maybe they only took sides to volley the worst and the best at each other, to make the uncertainty tolerable.

With Delmira's help, they had abandoned the upper floor, covered the furniture on the main floor with sheets, and confined themselves more and more to the solarium at the far end of the chateau. Curled up on the enormous chaise the size of a small bed, they warmed themselves by the parabolic copper-disk heater and read from the books in the library. They walked out and sat on the bench underneath the oak, a spot protected from the eyes of outsiders. They let time pass, wondering how bad it was in Nice.

It was on record that they lived here. Stupidly, but without another clear choice, here they resided. They couldn't have remained in the apartment. That was clear from the moment Max burst in with the news of the Germans moving at light speed through Nice. Even with Charlotte's aid, Henri couldn't have made the trip through the mountains again. Then there was the "closet" outside of Nice, promising no guarantee. They supposed, whenever they'd reviewed it, that Henri could've moved on from Nice by himself, but he would've had to hold to the coast—very risky. Perhaps she would've been lucky enough to make it with Max and Anneliese. The way they were cloistered here at l'Ermitage with no understanding of what was going on, their only hope was that the Nazis would be stopped before they reached them.

When Henri opened his eyes, Charlotte said, "I'm going to see Dr. M today."

He sprang into full wakefulness, blinking and swiping his hair off his forehead. "Why? Is something going wrong? Inside you? Is the baby okay?"

"No, no. Nothing like that. Though I should see him about a midwife." She sat up, steeling herself against expected resistance. When she explained her mission, Henri elbowed himself up to sitting and shook his head to rid himself of the last vestiges of sleep.

"I'll go with you."

She stepped out of the tangle of sheets and into the cool morning air. They both glanced at her swell and couldn't help but exchange wry smiles.

"No. I can go much faster on my own. Please don't insist."

He bared his teeth and raised his voice. "But I *am* insisting. Charlotte, no. You can't go out alone. We've no idea what's out there. You can't risk it." He had never spoken to her in such a sharp tone.

"You feel guilty, don't you, that I didn't go with Anneliese and Max? And take my work with me?"

The tension in his face yielded to a moment of admission, then he flung an arm toward the ceiling and raised his voice. "You could be whipped right off the street into a police van."

She considered that he might be right. "I don't think that'll happen."

He sprang out of bed and was brought up short. His leg was numb, and he needed to rotate it back and forth before he could move. Charlotte said nothing. After she put on her robe, he took her by the shoulders and squared her to him. His eyes shaped an earnest plea.

"Don't do this. There has to be another way."

"If we're captured here, the work is lost. I fought madness and suicide to make it. Now I must be willing to risk a run-in with the SS to save it."

Charlotte hated to see him so upset, especially because he hadn't had to face how ungovernable she could be. She could tell by his modulated tone he was trying to control his anger.

"It's my child you're carrying. And *you* who must be saved. It's my paramount duty. And you're not making it easy."

In the long silence that followed, he drew on his trousers, lit a cigarette, and sat back on the chaise, propped up against the pillows. She perched on the side of the chaise. He made no effort to move his legs to give her a little more room.

"It might be all that's left of me," she said. "For my own peace, I need to personally place the work in Dr. M's hands. And I must do it today. Immediately."

He looked away and blew smoke. Stumbling over his words, he said, "You w-would—? R-really? Do this?" Charlotte could feel he didn't want to diminish her work and understood that everything was at stake between them if he did. He stamped out the cigarette and looked at her with hard, accusing eyes. "You would put your work above your life? Above your child's life?"

She moved to place one hand on his bare chest, and he let her. She felt the heat of the night still there. "I understand how you see it. But let me assure you." He didn't avoid her eyes. "I do not, absolutely do not, believe that art is more important than life."

"Then why?"

"Because—" She halted. "No, I won't say why. You won't accept it. You're too sure of our survival."

"Tell me." His tone was challenging.

"Okay, then. Just remember, you asked." She took a deep breath before spitting it out. "Art is more enduring."

He blinked in surprise. His gaze went thoughtful. He sighed. It was so simple and true. It couldn't be disputed. But he wouldn't agree. And—she knew he understood that she was going.

"I need a bath and breakfast," she said. "I soaked the oats overnight."

Charlotte sank into the warm water, felt her own anxiety, and tried to let it dissolve. Thinking of going out, encountering SS in their raven-black uniforms, with their rifles, bludgeons, cars, and vans—the bath soothed her nerves hardly at all.

They had their porridge at the kitchen worktable. Charlotte consumed a double portion and was still hungry. The two tomes of her work wrapped in brown paper were on the counter. Henri wrote on them: *Property of Mrs. Olive Miller*. She put them in a market basket, covered them with a towel, and then filled the rest of the basket with flowers picked from the kitchen garden.

"Clever," Henri said, resigned but not calm about her venture. "You have to stay alert in every moment, but at the same time look normal, casual. Move along, but not too quickly. Definitely don't run. If you see a black Citroën, turn off. If Gestapo stop you, you'll say what?"

"I'll indicate my belly and say I'm on my way to the doctor."

"If they ask about the basket?"

"I always bring him fresh flowers."

"And if they remove the flowers?"

"Loaning him books."

"Books?"

Actually, the packages didn't look like books. "Encyclopedia of gardening. Two volumes."

"And if they ask for your papers? Your Italian identity card is no good anymore."

"Please. I'm aware." They both knew that at that point, it would all be over. But she gave it a shot. "I went out without. I live at La Belle Aurore. In St. Jean."

Henri looked beyond skeptical.

"We can't compromise Dr. M's networks. If they take me to St. Jean, Madame Piché will vouch for me."

"That's a best-case scenario if I ever heard one."

"Yes, I suppose the Gestapo aren't accompanying suspected Jews back to their supposed residences to retrieve their supposed papers."

"More likely they—"

"I know."

A glimmer of final hope that she would change her mind flickered in his eyes. When she didn't respond, his whole face made a downturn, and he slumped with sorrowful resignation. He took her into his arms and held her close. She heard his accelerated heartbeat.

"I'm waiting for you. And I'm very afraid."

"Don't be, Henri. Be brave for me. I need it."

CHARLOTTE LEFT THE GROUNDS of l'Ermitage and wound her way down Rue Cauvin. When a view of the sea appeared, a billowy feeling soothed her nerves. The weight of the basket in the crook of her arm reminded her of the making of the work, and she missed that intensity of focus and the good cheer a day's effort conferred. She kept telling herself that the risk had shifted. Once, she had hazarded everything to make these paintings. Now her exposure in the public record posed a threat to their survival. But no harm would come to them with the doctor.

By the time she reached Avenue de Grand-Bretagne, the traffic had thickened. She startled at the sight of a black Citroën whizzing by and disappearing around the street's loop. Should she proceed toward Villefranche? If the Gestapo were stopping in town, not just passing through, it would be best to turn around. But she'd come this far. And she was so close.

Behind her, she heard a car pulling over. *Keep walking,* she told herself.

"Mademoiselle!" The voice was broken French with a German accent. "Stop right there."

She did stop and turn around, only to face an SS officer standing next to the open curbside door of his Citroën. He slammed it shut, and the sound reverberated in Charlotte's chest and limbs. She did everything she could to stop quivering. He strolled toward her. He was neither old nor young. He was a blonde, excessively clean and groomed, but pumped up with excitement, his cheeks flushed.

She was shaking on the inside but on the outside managed to remain composed. Her brain was all jumbled. Though she couldn't recall what she was supposed to say, she felt maybe she could get the upper hand. Smile. She spoke first, in German. "So nice to see you, sir. What can I do for you? Do you need directions?"

He pulled back in a start, as though he were expecting a different response.

"What are you doing out, Mademois—Fräulein?"

Charlotte pulled her arm aside to reveal her belly. Should she say she was on the way to the doctor? What if he asked which doctor? She should have looked up another doctor, so she at least had a name. She would make up a name.

"On my way to the doctor."

"And what is a young German Fräulein—excuse me, Frau—with a Berlin accent doing in Villefranche in the first place?"

"I'm here with my husband. We were having a little holiday. Before baby."

"You shouldn't be out on the streets. We're rounding up Jews. It's very dangerous."

"Yes, we heard that." She gulped. "We're hoping for your great success."

"And the basket?"

She felt weak in the knees.

"Flowers and books."

He wrested the basket from her. She had an urge to grab it back. Only the dread of discovery prevented her from yelling *No!*

"Heavy," he said, a slow, diabolical smile building. He lifted the flowers, pulled aside the towel. He was staring at the top package wrapped in brown paper. "Books? Really?"

He shook the bouquet of flowers in his other hand. "Nice camouflage." He winked at her.

Just then, the driver got out of the car and before he could say anything, Charlotte shot out her arm in the "Heil Hitler" sign. Then she said, "Your partner."

The officer turned to see his partner responding in kind to Charlotte with an outstretched arm. The partner then called out, over the top of his open door, "Derek! Come on now. No time for pretty girls. We need to stay on course."

The officer dropped the flowers into the basket and handed it back.

"It's too dangerous out here, especially for a woman in your condition. You could get caught up in some nasty business. If you need to go out, keep your passport on you."

Charlotte nodded. He headed back to his car. He stopped and turned toward her. She made the "Heil Hitler" sign for a second time. He returned it.

"Watch out! Or you could be mistaken for a Jew."

The door closed, and the Citroën pulled away from the curb.

It was all she could do to stop heaving and catch a breath, all she could do to make her legs stop trembling and to walk normally along.

CHAPTER 34

VILLEFRANCHE-SUR-MER

SEPTEMBER 1943

In another five minutes, Dr. Mercier's stone cottage came into view, with its wooden door painted a bright teal and a brass knocker in the shape of a lion's head. Matilde answered.

"Charlotte?" she cried, hauling her inside. She looked both ways on the street and shut the door. "Thank God! With what's going on in Nice, we have been so very worried."

Charlotte nearly collapsed. In another wave of panic, her heart was racing, and she was having to make a special effort to breathe. Matilde guided her to the sofa in the small front room. She called out toward the back door.

"Phillipe! It's Charlotte Salomon!"

Matilde sat beside her until Dr. Mercier appeared from the garden, his face ruddy and moist, his iron-gray hair wild, and his trouser knees sporting dirt patches. Seeing her condition, he pulled up a chair and listened as she recounted her encounter with the SS. He asked Matilde to bring a glass of goat's milk.

"She's been to see country relatives, and we have lots. It'll be good for you."

Rich and creamy, the frothy milk slid down her throat and produced a sublime satisfaction. She finished it off in enormous gulps, a little embarrassed at her lack of manners.

After Charlotte explained how they had gotten out of Nice in time and were back at l'Ermitage, Dr. Mercier said, "Looks like you could use another one." After the second glass, she was fully restored from her fright.

"Now, what can I do for you?"

She paused, going back over her decision and its risks. There was not another safe option. Finally, she said, "I have a very great favor to ask."

She gave the flowers to Matilde and removed the brown paper packages, stacking one on top of the other on the low table in front of the sofa. His eyes widened, and his black brows knit with curiosity.

"My work. I need to get it into safekeeping. Again."

She recalled (perhaps he did too) past times when he had encouraged her work, going back to the very first day she'd arrived at l'Ermitage and he had recommended the gardens as a source of artistic inspiration. Especially, she recalled how he felt that painting would help her heal after Gurs, and how thankful she was when he retrieved her work from Madame Piché's boarding house, even more so for his comment at the time, that he believed in it and hoped she would finish.

She was delighted when he said, "You've completed it. Congratulations! Certainly I'll keep it for you." But she was surprised when he added, "May I have a look at the finished product?"

She was afraid to untie it. She might lose courage. With the tenderness that one would handle a newborn, she pulled the string and parted the paper. He looked at the title page with its red, yellow, and blue stripes running down the left side, like a binding. The words of her title in German she translated for him: *Life? Or Theater?* The subtitle: *A play with music.*

Here also were her initials, CS, in a tight circle. Jewish? Female? No one could tell. Not Charlotte the woman. Not Salomon the Jew. CS—the artist.

Topping it all, a bright-red heart floated like a cheerful punctuation mark. Only she knew this whole work was a testament to her feelings for Wolf.

"*Life? Or Theater?* Ah, an operetta," he said. He read the dedication to Olive Miller, followed by the cast of characters. "Like a theater playbill."

She handed him the first painting. He read the inscription on the overlay: *1913 One November day, Charlotte Knarre left her parents' home and threw herself into the water.*

"She was my Aunt Charlotte Gruenstein. I've changed the names."

Stricken by this tragic start, he stared at her.

"Yes. In a suburban lake. Kilometers from where she lived."

"I feel her aloneness. And I can't help asking why. A young woman fleeing her home? How she must have suffered. I thought this was going to be a story of your life."

"No, not in any sense an autobiography. It's a way to remember the suicides, so long a closely guarded family secret."

With his chin in one hand, he studied the picture. "I like the repetition of the figure. It draws the eye to walk along with her. Her last walk."

Charlotte showed him a few of the childhood paintings. Nostalgia overwhelmed her for those happy times, combined with the pang of so much that was irretrievable. She flipped to a page of a young woman—herself—standing before the four-story Berlin Art Academy building. It read: *Only he who dares can win. Only he who dares can begin.*

How optimistic and determined she had been. She turned to portraits of Katharina in her full-throated glory.

Next came a page of Wolf expounding his philosophy: *Art exists not for its own sake. It must flow from life.* She longed for him to know her as she was today. The separation from him—everyone—and the impossibility of regaining the past made her body heavy with sadness.

There were hundreds of pages related to Wolf: him alone, her waiting for him, and the two of them together at cafés and Wannsee.

"But for him I wouldn't be sitting here, alive. But for him I would not have made this."

He didn't say a word, only nodded.

Then brown shirts marching through the streets. Charlotte smiled at the swastikas on the flags, each one inverted. Dr. Mercier did too.

She placed the second stack in his lap. He admired paintings of the Mediterranean coast, the gardens at l'Ermitage, and the sea. These pages made the times depicted in her first years in France a distant, naive past, when terrible happenings—roundups, deportations to who knows where—had been rumors from afar.

He slowed at the many pages covered with disembodied faces of Luitger—blue eyes and white beard floating against a neutral background. Charlotte had recorded Luitger's litany of the family suicides verbatim.

"Good God! You told me about these when you returned from Gurs, but to see them here—"

His horror reminded her how much she'd put behind her. She was now capable of comment without veering in the direction of madness.

"I myself survived the call of suicide."

He looked at her, only half stunned. "I'm so glad you did, Charlotte. The baby will be here before you know it. A new being. A new family." He smiled the smile of faith and trust in the future. "And you got here by recounting profound trauma."

"Yes, of what actually happened. After years of secrets and play-acting as though nothing happened."

"Ah! A document of resistance." He added, "And the perpetrator exposed."

He came to the last page. Charlotte the artist sat on her heels in the sand, back to the viewer, facing the water, with brush in her hand and board on her lap. A few black strokes outlined her form, barely separating her from the seascape. Her wholly transparent easel was like a window. Through it, the blue sea shone.

He returned to the first painting of Aunt Charlotte's suicide. Then back to the last. He said, "The story of survival. Of becoming an artist."

Dr. Mercier opened his mouth to say something more, but nothing came out. Charlotte could hear his breathing. She was drowning in a river of sorrow. He sat straight up.

"This is very daring, Charlotte, I suppose you know. And, yes, I'm honored to keep it until—" His eyes took on a pained expression. To Charlotte, they were portentous. He recomposed himself. "Until you can retrieve it."

Her chest expanded. She floated on her own accomplishment and maturation while slowly rewrapping both bundles. Here it was. She was flooded with love for it.

He held out his hands. She was unable to relinquish it. They sat side by side. She reminded herself: *Its chances of survival are better than mine.*

When she'd finally turned the bundles over to him, he set them on the table. She could not take her eyes off them.

Dr. Mercier asked her how she was doing, and she remembered to ask him about a midwife. He assured her she could get by without one for now. He had a small room for checkups. Matilde held her hand while he examined her.

"All good. Four months, for sure. Maybe a little more."

When they were seated again in the front parlor, she told him they had been in for the Donati escape plan botched by the Americans, and asked what he knew of the goings-on in Nice.

"Where the French colors flew above the railway station, now the swastika. Huge."

Charlotte shuddered with a familiar fear at the image in her mind of the Nazi flags on display everywhere in Munich and in Berlin and carried by the thousands in parades. Dr. Mercier seemed to feel that this new prefecture was a good one.

"Monsieur Chaigneau. He destroyed his list of Jews."

If only her marriage record identifying her and Henri as Jews living at l'Ermitage on Rue Cauvin might be destroyed too.

She had to assume no, it had not been destroyed.

"Even so—"

His voice was low and controlled, but the look on his face was like someone who'd seen what no one should see and felt morally bound to warn. He started slowly. She felt he was giving her time to prepare herself.

"A manhunt of monstrous proportion is going on right now."

He stopped, gauging her response. Charlotte went into high alert. It was as they had feared. Jews in Nice were being forcibly removed from their homes and corralled in droves off the streets, plucked out of cafés and restaurants. The Gestapo were trolling the beaches, making the men drop their pants. The Nazis were determined to capture every last Jew. All were being herded into the Excelsior Hotel, commandeered by one of the most brutal Nazis, Alois Brunner, who brought with him around a dozen torturers from Drancy.

"Cruel beyond comprehension," he said, shaking his head. "Brunner strides about with a Singapore cane, which he soaks in water so that his violent blows won't break it."

Charlotte's belly contracted, rock-hard. She felt frantic.

"Wounds from that rattan stick will never heal. I've volunteered to tend the victims."

Her limbs shook, and she thought she might cry out. But she swallowed hard and didn't flinch from the rest. People were being pushed into rooms without beds, heaved upon each other like potato sacks, emerging bloodied and half dead, or carried out in a coma. Then they were being sent off to Drancy. From there, who knew? Rumor had it, to the unknown east. Meanwhile, the leaders of the Comité Dubouchage were being hunted down and had had to leave Nice. The doors to all the organizations supporting Jewish refugees had closed, including the Federation of Jewish Societies of France, which had created underground committees and forged identity papers, and the local UGIF and the child-rescue organization.

"The leaders have all fled."

And Angelo Donati? He was still in Italy. Hopefully he would not return. The Gestapo had already ransacked his house at 37 Promenade des Anglais.

Fright flashed up her spine. Her bladder loosened. She couldn't hold it any longer. He pointed the way to the bathroom. After washing up, she looked in the mirror and pressed her hands to her stricken face, where the rosy bloom of gestating life had drained away. She emitted an uncontrollable whimper. When she returned to the front room, Dr. Mercier took her hands in his.

"Now, listen to me, Charlotte. There must be no activity at l'Ermitage. It should appear as though no one lives there anymore. Do you have a hiding place?"

She mentioned Henri's secret loft.

"Don't waste a moment moving there. Neither of you is fit to flee. And you mustn't step off the property. Lock and chain the front gate. Make your presence undetectable. No lights. No doors opening and closing. No obvious movement. Hunker down and hold on. Promise me."

She licked her lips and tried to swallow. "Yes. I promise."

He would contact Delmira and have her leave cooked eggs and what-else toward dusk, in the guise of looking after the villa. They were not to retrieve these provisions until dark, lest neighbors or passersby see them. If some need arose, they could send a note via Delmira. It was the best that could be done.

"Don't forget the milk," he said. He handed her the quart jar Matilde had brought.

Charlotte gazed at her work, the two great volumes. The agony of separation might have made her renege.

"Don't worry. I'll take good care."

Hope landed and made her breath release into a sigh, which floated her free, relieved of a great burden.

"Thank you, Dr. Mercier." She pointed to her work. "This is my whole life."

Even as she said her goodbyes, she couldn't help glancing back at her monumental work wrapped in humble brown paper.

"Wait," he said. "You risked everything to come here. You could be picked off the street on your way back. Allow me to walk you home."

CHAPTER 35

VILLEFRANCHE-SUR-MER

After Charlotte had relayed Dr. Mercier's description of the roundups and brutality that was unfolding in Nice, she and Henri had decided that since the hideout was not furnished with provisions, they would have to stay in the chateau until that task was complete, a day or three at the most. It took Charlotte three full days to pack clothing, bundle blankets, create bins of tinned foods, others of dishware, cups, and cutlery, also books and flashlights. She filled empty bottles with water and left everything in the kitchen for Henri to take to the loft. She was waiting for more food from Delmira that night, hopefully a generous supply of pickles. Tomorrow they were scheduled to climb up.

Charlotte had not been to the outbuilding for quite some time because the dust caused by sawing and hammering bothered her. But on this third day after her visit with Dr. Mercier, she decided to take a stroll outside and see the progress for herself.

The outbuilding had once been a small barn and in recent years had been converted into a workshop. It smelled of oils, sawdust, and metal shavings. Long, beat-up wooden tables, a multitude of tools, and several small machines stood neatly organized. At the far end, on the false wall rigged to slide open, several bicycle wheels hung on hooks, along with tires, pedals, and handlebars.

She approached the table where Henri was hammering two pieces of wood together. A large piece of plywood the length and height of the table rested against it, creating a half-wall between them.

Charlotte said, "You gave Max the impression this was done." Her attitude was unfriendly. Her voice carried an undertone of alarm.

"Yes. I'm sorry. I didn't want him to be concerned for our safety here."

"But then…we're not actually safe. We have nowhere to hide."

"We *were* safe. At least, I thought so. Turned out the rope ladder was too flimsy. There was no way to get our supplies up there."

"You're saying our supplies are not in the loft?"

"I managed the clothing."

"And the rest of it?"

Henri came around to her side of the table and pulled away the plywood. Everything she had so carefully gathered was stacked under the table.

"Henri! We're supposed to go up tomorrow. And you're in here casually hammering away." She felt slightly hysterical, like she was going to cry, but she wouldn't let herself give way to a display.

"I'm not 'casually hammering away.' I'm building a wooden ladder. It will be sturdy enough to get our provisions up there."

"But if they find the sliding wall and then see a ladder, we're done for."

"We'll pull the ladder up. That's not the problem."

The problem? She cocked her head, actively listening for the obstacle to completing their hideout, the thing that might spell doom. Suppressing her anxiety, she spoke in a soothing, placating voice. "Which is what, may I ask?"

"I don't have enough wood."

"What about this?" She pointed to the plywood in front of them.

"Not enough." He paused and shook his head. "I need twice as much, at least."

Charlotte's leg muscles tightened. She had the urge to start running right out the door toward safety. Feeling dizzy, she grabbed onto the table for support.

Henri tried to take her in his arms. She resisted out of anger, then surrendered. He said, "I wish you hadn't come out here. It's only upsetting you, and that's not good for baby."

She pulled away so she could look him in the eye. "But I need to know. I don't like that you've kept this from me."

"I was trying to protect you."

"Not knowing makes me upset. Far more than knowing does."

"All right, I understand, and I'm sorry. But you're not to worry. I've figured it out. I'm going to tear down part of that old shed. It's practically fallen down as it is."

"But Olive stores her gardening tools there. We can't be destroying her property."

"We'll make it up to her. But we won't be able to do that unless we save ourselves."

"What about the noise? Dr. M said—"

"Yes, I know what he said. But this has to be done. And we need to stop talking so I can get to work."

A beam of sunlight coming through the slatted wall fell across Henri's face and illuminated his scar. Charlotte softened, kissed him, turned, and left.

That evening, while they were waiting for it to get dark enough to collect Delmira's drop-off, Henri said, "You want to know everything, right?" Then he told her how, while he was tearing down the shed, he spotted someone on the road who was looking in through the fence. He had stopped work and hidden out of sight while still being able to peer at the possible intruder.

"It was the chemist."

"The one from the pharmacy at the bottom of Rue Cauvin?"

Henri nodded. "I'm sure of it. But I'm not sure he saw me."

"Well, he must have heard you working. That's why he stopped to look. What was he doing walking up the road? In all these years we've never seen him do that."

"He's an antisemite, you know. Olive told me. When your grandparents first arrived, he took her to task for taking in Jewish refugees."

They fell into silence, lying on the chaise in the solarium, watching the daylight turn to dusk and dusk finally yield to darkness. With more care than ever not to betray their presence, they collected Delmira's delivery. Later, Henri broke the silence.

"So, where will we live when this is all over? Paris? Villefranche? We obviously can't be in both places."

Charlotte hadn't been thinking beyond the next right thing to do. Eat something. Walk around and around inside the chateau to get a little exercise. Take a nap. But hearing the words "when this is all over," she felt light and alert.

"I've been thinking," Henri said. "I have a proposal. We set ourselves up in Paris. I can take child education classes and start an orphanage there. The city has so many services."

"But I thought you wanted to do that with Olive here at l'Ermitage."

"I can't rely on Olive. I want a way to be assured I can do it on my own. And if she's amenable, we can make an arrangement. A city place and a country place. We could be joined."

Charlotte's mind immediately traveled back to Gurs, to Lou Albert-Lasard, the offer she had made to introduce her to artists in Paris. Lou, of the coal-black eyes, had been so sure of landing back there herself. Living in Paris with Henri—Charlotte could see it, feel it. She would also have a friend in Lili and meet the famous artists and study the new movements. She would have her baby. She imagined its face, a miniature of Henri's. They would raise their child together and support each other in reaching for their dreams in this life. They would be a family. There would be no theater erected for anyone to assume a role and keep secrets. Honesty, openness, and a willingness to be their own true best, for themselves and one another, would rule. From the well of her new life, new art would emerge. Whatever she created would not be a matter of survival like *Life? Or Theater?* had been. Life would be assured, so art would be something else. She could feel it distinctly—her imagination activated. She would work with baby in the studio, cover the walls up to waist height with paper, and scatter about the floor containers of crayons, paints, and small brushes.

There was so much possibility, she wanted to cry out in joyful anticipation. Her fears of the chemist, which had arisen in the afternoon, were soothed. The future came into high relief, more tangible than the present.

They had hung layers of sheets in the solarium to block out any light they needed at night. They'd gone outside to test it and decided they could get away with one small candle. Now they became relaxed enough to read. Henri was almost finished with Jean Piaget's *Judgement and Reasoning in the Child*. Charlotte was midway through an art history tome.

A sound of rustling reached them in their absorption, which was never complete, as they each had one ear out for any unusual sounds. Perhaps it was a small mammal.

Charlotte said, "There's been no car on the road." She whispered, "And the gate is locked?"

"Yes. But there are back ways onto the property where the fence needs repair."

Then, a tapping on the window.

Henri blew out the candle; they both went still.

The sound did not recur. They barely breathed, listening with their whole bodies. Another sound started up. Somewhere else. Far. On the other side of the chateau. Knocking.

"Where is that coming from?" Charlotte whispered. Her own heartbeat was almost as loud as the knocks.

They came again, sharply.

Henri said, "I'm going to see. Stay here."

"I'm coming too."

They padded quietly out of the solarium, Charlotte behind Henri, one finger hooked into his waistband. As they crossed the long library, through the drawing room, around the furniture covered in sheets shining white in the moonlight, and into the front foyer with its great staircase, the rapping became louder and continuous. It was coming from the kitchen.

Across the dining room they crept, around the table to the door that led into the kitchen. They stopped with their backs against the wall, listening to the thumping. Knuckles on wood, then on glass, then on wood.

Henri peered through the door.

"Can you see?"

"Oh, my God!" In an instant, he was gone from her side. She stepped forward and watched him open the door. In walked Anneliese and Max with Rui on his back.

CHARLOTTE RAN TO THEM. She took Anneliese in her arms. Henri closed the door and ushered them out of the kitchen. Together he and Charlotte shepherded them in the dark all the way back across the chateau to the safety of the solarium, where it took them a minute to drop their packs and lay sleeping Rui down.

As they settled, Henri relit the candle. Charlotte could see their faces. They were dirty, haggard, and thin. Immediately, she fetched water and some nourishment—hard-boiled eggs and grapes.

"We got lost," Max said. He told the story of their trek to high ground and into the peaks of the Mercantour, how he was sure he knew the way, from the directions he had been given, to the point of safe crossing, the pass of Fenestre, where they would be met by one of the guides who automatically showed up there every night. But they couldn't find the spot. The trails were narrow and tortuous. They were often just barely poised over high precipices. Anneliese described how on the sixth day she lost her footing and one of their food packs had fallen into a ravine. They saw too many Germans by day and so walked only at night. They had wandered around looking for the crossing for several nights. Spotting armed Germans patrolling the border, they decided they had no choice but to head back.

Max's head was bowed. Henri stood and retrieved a piece of paper and pencil and began writing. They all stared at him. He looked up.

"Dr. M. I'm writing a note to him. Delmira will pick it up tomorrow. Hopefully he'll have some advice."

Charlotte repeated all that Dr. Mercier had described to her about the goings-on in Nice and the need to hide out. Max wanted to know why they weren't in the loft. They had knocked at the outbuilding there first. Henri had to admit how he had misrepresented the readiness of the loft and reported on its present status. They drew up a plan for the following day. Max would help Henri finish the ladder and store the provisions.

"But first," Max said, "I'm taking this note directly to Delmira. I'll leave it where she'll see it first thing. Our presence here is jeopardizing you. We can't afford to lose a day."

"That's much too dangerous," Charlotte said. "You can't go skulking around at night."

"I won't go by the road."

"But you'd have to scale fences and walls."

"We just came through the mountains, so I think I can manage."

He took the note from Henri and the pencil and scribbled an addition. "I'm asking for someone who knows the crossover point, to take us to it, so that we don't get lost again, a guide."

THE NEXT DAY, while Henri and Max worked on the ladder, Charlotte and Anneliese sat in the solarium and sewed and patched the clothing that had become ripped during the attempted crossing. They had risen before dawn to wash the clothes and dry them in the Hamilton, which made a rumbling noise. It was in the underground cellar, and they determined it couldn't be heard from outside.

"You could stay with us," Charlotte said. "We could all cram into the loft."

"Max said the loft wouldn't sustain the weight of all of us. And even if it could, Rui could give us all away. No, we have to get out again."

After the last batch of clothes had been piled into the dryer, Charlotte and Anneliese made breakfast. As Charlotte broke the fresh farm eggs into a bowl, she was drawn back into that one moment when she could have emptied the full bottle of veronal into Luitger's omelet. She was glad she had not done that. But that moment was followed by another: her refusal to take him to Emmet's. It was more subtle, a failure to act rather than an action, but equally implicating. She hated these moments when they recurred.

How many suicides had he had a hand in? She didn't know, so she had painted them all, because all of them were secrets, all of them were persons without a voice. Had this been a form of atonement? She hadn't known what else to do. She had become rage-red inside out, trying with everything she had to resist that man. He had made her complicit in his death. She had been his slave. She had had the right to free herself. Still, she was ashamed. His eyes open and fixed on the sofa. She realized she could never get rid of the pen-and-ink death mask she'd made of him without getting rid of her "Death and the Maiden." She couldn't help feeling the meaning of her entire life lay between those two drawings, back-to-back on the same sheet of paper.

The cloying substance of guilt made her throat thick, constricted, a reminder of how close she still was to being strangled from the inside.

She had never told Anneliese, and now, more than anything, she wanted to spill out the whole story to her sister-in-law. She'd already told Henri; it shouldn't be hard to confess.

But the things Luitger had done to her or the history of his other violations—she had never told Henri any of that. Henri would have cursed Luitger, saying that if he were still alive, he'd kill him himself. But he wouldn't have been able to understand. He wasn't a woman. Perhaps it was Anneliese's bright smile, her cheery disposition—how she took everything in stride—that invited Charlotte out of her isolation as they sat sewing.

"I refused to help him up and down Rue Neuscheller, you know. To visit a friend. He collapsed on the way home."

Anneliese managed to shrug while pulling her needle through. "I wondered how."

"How he died? Or my part in it?"

"He was terrible."

Charlotte longed to tell her just how terrible. Her voice was a whisper.

"One night, after evening entertainment in the Great House, I returned to the cottage." She recounted how Luitger came into her bed.

Anneliese stuck her needle into the shirt sleeve, put it down, and stared straight at her. The usual resolve on her face, for efficiency and to get the next thing done, fell away. Her features softened, alert to Charlotte's testimony.

When Charlotte got to the part where she'd kicked Luitger, her voice was wavering. Anneliese gently took Charlotte's sewing from her and laid it aside. She stood her up and took her by the arm, told Rui he could come along if he was quiet, but he continued drawing. She walked Charlotte outside to the garden, where they sat down on the bench under the oak. The rising and falling whistle of the wall creeper, rarely heard, the whispering of the gentle wind in the leaves, the changing shadows on the wall of the chateau—nature's way of going about its business calmed Charlotte, and she continued through every last bit, ending finally with Luitger's dogged insistence that she kill herself, his assault on her at the window, and her staunch refusal to help him navigate the hill.

"To the very end, he denied the abuse he had inflicted on his own daughters. Tried to justify what he'd done as a form of sexual initiation."

Anneliese's lip curled in disgust, but she did not turn away.

"I could have taken him to Emmet's. I'd done it many times. Something happened to me. I don't understand it. I let him go."

With her head hung, her mind was twisted into fierce concentration on the past. When she looked up, she was surprised to be sitting so close to Anneliese.

"I don't blame you, Charlotte." Her tone was gentle.

"Oh, but you must. I killed a person. However despicable, he was a human being."

"These are terrible times. People are being killed in battle. Others taken to camps and killed by hunger or disease. Desperate people kill strangers in the streets to survive."

"This wasn't like that. Luitger was my grandfather, not some stranger on the street."

"But if it weren't for these times, you wouldn't have been living with him. Given the setup. Your confinement with him after Marina's suicide. Your escape when you risked everything to live at La Belle Aurore. Think of it this way—that risk *you* took, it extended *his* life. When you were hauled back to Nice, it was inevitable that the battle between you two would spiral out of control. He might actually have succeeded in heaving you out the window. You were angry. You didn't want to cater to him at that moment. It's understandable. He chose to go on his own. He refused help getting home. So he died. You mustn't judge yourself."

Her logic didn't alter Charlotte's feelings. Her shoulders quaked with repressed sobs. Her voice broke. "But I do."

He was a person who had once been an innocent child. He grew up with great losses, including a father who'd committed suicide. Somewhere along the way, he'd become twisted. He had been a wounded man. Maybe the story she had been telling herself was all wrong. Maybe she could have gotten him through the war, brought him back to l'Ermitage to wait it out, and afterward returned him to Berlin, where he could have lived out his life with his Schiller and walks in the Tiergarten.

Anneliese seemed to sense that Charlotte's remorse was almost as unbearable as her guilt.

"He might've succeeded at another time in pushing you out the window, and no one could say you hadn't jumped. He gambled on you taking the veronal because it would have saved him the trouble. One way or another, he was bent on your death. No doubt about it."

"But why? Why would he want to get rid of me?"

"Isn't it obvious? You threatened him. You were too independent for a woman, unwilling to surrender your will to his. And an artist? That undermined his domination. In his mind, it was no different than being a prostitute, shameful to him and his reputation. A woman like you was easily dispensable. Plus he'd have had more ration cards, a surer chance at survival. Who knows? Maybe he'd gone insane."

Charlotte was able to follow the various threads, arguments, and ways to reason it, but unable to hang onto one, and when she let go, it was she, not the argument, that started to unravel. Her mind loosened in a way that was all too familiar, drawing her toward madness.

Anneliese looked at her with the same fierce intent she'd riveted on Rosemarie during her childbirth in Gurs. Her big, dark eyes directed Charlotte to comprehend, and Charlotte strained to do so.

"You feel shame. You think it's because you failed to prevent his collapse. But it's not." All the while her voice remained soothing, a silky caress mobilizing Charlotte's attention.

"It's what he planted in you, the abominable part of him, when he dared to take possession of you." Anneliese took her hand in hers. "It's a sticky thing. You'll have to work to discard it."

Charlotte's next breath startled her, the way an insight brings one up short. It took her a minute to digest what Anneliese had said.

"The shame I feel is actually his?"

Anneliese nodded. The leaves of the oak above them rustled in the breeze, which passed over her face, cooling it. Charlotte's gaze turned inward.

Her sister-in-law had rotated the telescope so that what was so far away, it couldn't be discerned was now close and in clear focus. A long sigh started to release what was not her, and she felt a speck lighter. She was now able, just, to bear this burden—the horror of what she had found herself capable of.

CHAPTER 36

———

VILLEFRANCHE-SUR-MER

SEPTEMBER 1943

B y nightfall, the hideout was complete. The ladder, though crude, served its purpose. All supplies had been hoisted up into the loft. Henri brought in Delmira's food basket, which had a note tucked into the bottom. She had a nephew, Gabrielle's cousin, who was a scout and would guide Max and Anneliese to a safe crossing. They were to be at Delmira's at midnight.

Max urged Charlotte and Henri to take to the loft right away, but they insisted on waiting up with them until they had to leave. Charlotte fell asleep, and when she woke up, it was still dark, but Max, Anneliese, and Rui were gone. Gone, too, their neatly repacked rucksacks. Perhaps it was better this way, without another wrenching goodbye, but she felt sad and couldn't fall back to sleep.

She wandered the main floor, then went up the staircase and down the hall to Olive's room. Moonbeams streamed across the satin bedcover. Olive's dressing gown with the cabbage roses lay draped there, as though that bright, stalwart American woman with endless good cheer might walk in from the bath and put it on. Recalling the early days with Olive, eating pastries and drinking real coffee, Charlotte sat on the end of the bed and stroked the dressing gown. Then she slipped it on. Padding down to the kitchen, she felt protected the same way she had in Olive's presence. She made some tea with the garden mint Delmira had pinched and took a tray with the pot and cups back to the solarium. The candle was burning, and Henri was awake.

"Where were you? We should go up."

"A little while more, please. It's still the dead of night. Last tea."

She poured the tea and talked about Olive, sharing memories of their mornings together and how Anneliese had been like a sister, mother, and friend all rolled into one. Henri lit a cigarette, surrendering to a longer stay. He talked about how Max had always been his hero and guardian. When he exhaled, his eyes had a faraway look. His scar came in and out of relief with the flickering of the candle.

A small darkness in Henri underneath his skillful, clever, optimistic personality had always eluded her. Why dig for the dark, she had thought, and had left it alone. But now she touched it.

"Tell me," she said. "It wasn't on the crossing into France, was it?"

He shook his head, crushed out his cigarette, and folded his hands in his lap.

"When our parents were captured, I was the one who thoroughly fell apart while Max stayed strong. And the stronger he became—conferring with Anneliese, evaluating our situation, considering our possibilities, choosing the mountain trek—well, the more I unraveled. I was frozen hard. Like a rock. I couldn't think. I couldn't participate."

Henri covered his face with his hands. After a few moments, he looked straight at Charlotte.

"There came this one moment. I was in a deluded state. Rage. Grief. I don't know. I attacked him. Max. My brother. With a knife."

Word by word, Charlotte had grown still.

"He managed to get it away from me, but not without inadvertently cutting my face."

She heard a sob trapped in his throat. Or perhaps a howl.

"By then, no Jew could go to the doctor or show up at the clinic. Anneliese sewed it up. But I swore her to secrecy about how it happened. And she never betrayed me."

"No."

Some part of Charlotte's heart, which she did not even know was closed, opened fully to Henri, to what it must have been to be the smaller and more sensitive of the two, to have lost control of his mind and assaulted his own brother. A knife. It could have been deadly. She thought she understood something of what that was like. She saw more deeply who he was. He was human. He was wounded by loss. He had inhabited mental extremity. Like her.

She reached out, took him in her arms, and said, "He's clearly forgiven you. You need to forgive yourself."

She guided him to lie down and held him while he shook and sobbed. After he'd released it all, they were silent for a long time. The candle snuffed out. Henri drifted off.

Charlotte remained awake, feeling closer to him than ever, feeling blessed beyond belief for love. At the same time, something nagged at her, something undone. She had felt it when they married and again when she took *Life? Or Theater?* to Dr. Mercier. She could not fall asleep. After sliding away from Henri, she ventured outside the solarium into the night.

There was a chill, and she tied the sash of Olive's dressing gown around her. Taking a seat on the bench under the oak where she had made her confession to Anneliese, she looked at the sky. It was clear, and the stars were numerous. Tears rolled down her cheeks, partly because it felt as though some kind of ending was near. Partly for having begun and finished her work—she'd claimed her destiny—and having saved it. By the time the stars winked out and the sky grew violet, softly announcing the dawn to come, Charlotte knew what she had to do.

It felt important, an urgent matter.

She went in search of paper, paint, and brush, and brought her supplies and lap easel back out to the bench. What she had in mind wasn't a painting, but a letter. She wrote:

Dearest Friend,

It took me years to understand all you tried to teach me. But the vitality of your spirit and your unique and wise way of thinking did take hold. And I woke up, yes, to my life!

She wrote page after page to Wolf, using her brush and paints, letting him know how she had learned to live within the knowledge of dying.

Now the violet in the sky had disappeared into the palest yellow. Chill had dissolved, but the day was not yet warm.

She tried to reconcile her love for Wolf with her marriage. Two loves having nothing to do with each other. Perhaps one really was a soul connection resonating in the spheres, the other an earthly, embodied devotion. She saw, in these trying years of loneliness, that Olive Miller had left behind for her a man, a fellow refugee and protector—affectionate, sincere, and loyal.

She came back to the brush, writing on, many of the important events that had transpired in this spot in the South of France. She wrote about Olive Miller and what she had found at l'Ermitage, the falling-out with her grandparents and their move to Nice. Her grandmother's suicide, of course. Especially, she let him know about the huge revelation of all the suicides in her family and wondered whether he might have known as much from Katharina. She wrote him that with the war in full throttle,

> *I returned to the sea to sit by it and contemplate the state of the world. I penetrated the core of those women in my family. I inhabited their lives, wore the mantle of their souls, trod their way, and so understood the essence of the work I had to create. Having portrayed them, I was able to resist suicide.*

She detailed how she had had to go further into solitude, completely away from humanity, wander afar, like Ulysses, to find her way home.

> *And to do so I had to withdraw from the world, like a monk, and let go of every connection.*

What motivated her to wrestle and distill her thirteen hundred paintings into something of value was the revelation within them of a story told to someone, as the mother pulls the child into her lap.

> *And when I began to make the paintings a story with words, I had to ask, to whom is my story told? And the answer came. It was something like the moment when Ulysses in Polyphemus's court hears the bard tell a story that reveals his identity. Only then could Ulysses tell it in his own words. And that carried me through. I could say a Presence became manifest, the*

unembodied You to whom the story is told, though immediately the experience eludes capture in words. But I trust you, Dearest Friend, and I know you will understand completely.

She gave the best description she was able of Luitger and how he'd tormented her.

I believed I needed his protection as provided by the Gurs certificate. The way all the women before me believed the myth that life required a man's protection. And I couldn't endure it.

Then she described to Wolf exactly how she had allowed Luitger, as an old man in his eighties, frail and malnourished, unsteady on his feet, to traverse the steep hill in front of their apartment without her aid. How she'd simply sat in her room and let it happen.

He wasn't worthy of my care.

At last, she wrote how she found someone who loved her, even about the baby they were expecting. Hopefully by then, the war would be over.

Then, Dearest Friend, perhaps theater games will be abandoned, and humanity will turn toward a truer life.

She folded the pages, then made her way, room by room, into the kitchen and put them in Delmira's basket with a note to Dr. Mercier, asking him to place these pages at the end of *Life? Or Theater?* As she did so, the darkness that had haunted her from childhood, that her grandfather had flung in her face, finally seeped away, all at once and forever.

WHEN CHARLOTTE RETURNED to the solarium with a fresh pot of tea, barley bread, and l'Ermitage's plum jam from the cellar, the sky through the skylight windows was daytime blue, and Henri was sitting up in the chaise in thoughtful contemplation. The copper-disk heater was emitting a cozy glow. It promised to be a perfect late-September day, sunny and a little cool. But there was something about the moment that made Charlotte recall the bitter cold of that January morning almost five years ago, when she had been hurriedly bustled onto a train departing Berlin.

"We should go up," she said.

"We can't afford to do that during the day. We'll have to wait until tonight."

The sweet-tart jam was so delicious. She was pleasantly empty after their talk last night and writing her letter to Wolf. She wanted to enjoy their morning meal. Yet she felt tense. It was already four days since she'd seen Dr. Mercier, and she remembered his warning.

The sound of a car engine came to them from the road. It braked and idled at their locked gate. The color went out of Henri's face, which sent her into a fright.

"A Citroën," he said. In one swift motion, he stood, grabbed her hand, and pulled the heater's plug from the wall.

"Come on."

"Our plates. Evidence."

"We have to leave them."

They went out the solarium's door as fast as he could move and around the back of the chateau. The air bristled with a foreign electricity. Henri hung onto her hand as they slowed down, staying close to the wall or in the thick of the bushes and trees. Charlotte's attention was riveted to his face. The sound of the Citroën's engine came to them as uphill acceleration, and then was gone. Henri's color returned.

He moved quietly, catlike. The sound of another motor on Rue Cauvin brought him to a full stop. They squeezed into a space between a large hydrangea bush and the outside wall. Charlotte went completely still so as not to rustle the foliage.

"A Peugeot," Henri said. The car drove past l'Ermitage's gate.

He rotated his leg in his hip socket once or twice, shook it out, and they continued along the stone wall to its end. The outbuilding was in sight, but they would have to come into the open. There would be the benefit of tall, overgrown grasses, but nothing more.

"I'll go first. Wait for my signal. Crouch and move swiftly."

Charlotte had faith in Henri's skilled stealth. She had confidence in his ability to protect them, but the moment he was gone from her side, her pulse raced. Suddenly she was breathing in more air than she could breathe out, and she couldn't control it. Her legs trembled. Henri became smaller and smaller in the distance. Was he waving at her? She wasn't sure. He was a blur. She became dizzy. Blackness closed in. She put her head down to get some blood to it, placed her hand on her belly, and urged herself to hang on.

She looked up. He was waving. She saw it clearly now, his raised hand. She stepped out, her heart in her throat. Another car roared uphill. Casting his eyes frantically about, Henri made a downward hand motion. Charlotte crouched low into the grass, breathing heavily. Strength returned to her legs. She toddled in a squat across the open space. Henri was getting bigger. He was waving her in. She had only a little way to go. She stood and ran until she grabbed his outstretched hand, and together they orbited the outbuilding to the door side. He opened it, and they were in.

The door closed with a jarring clang. They took no time to catch their breath but made for the false wall. Henri slid it open. Behind was the wood ladder leading to the loft.

Charlotte went first. Henri slid the wall closed, followed, and pulled up the ladder.

They both let out a stifled sigh of relief. They hung onto each other, gulping air, breathing together, listening together, more one than two.

When they'd grown calm, Charlotte was astounded to see the little efficient living space: shelves full of their bottled water and tinned foods; a bin of dishware, cups, and cutlery; cubbyholes with folded sweaters, trousers, and socks; built-in recesses for books and flashlights; a clock; and a radio. All the things she'd collected. And pickles.

"What's that?" she asked about a bucket with a lid.

"For nature's call."

"Oh, how could I have forgotten about that?"

He lifted the sash on the one window. The charming song of a calandra lark was nearby. The bird alighted on the outside sill, peered in as though it might enter, and flew off.

That night, Henri went out the window and down the rope ladder to lock the door and retrieve Delmira's drop. When he was safely back inside, they had a bite to eat, figuring out how to maneuver a meal in their tiny space. Afterward they stretched out on the bedding covered with layers of blankets and quilts and a prop of pillows. She rested her head on his chest. His heartbeat was steady. She was startled by a sweet, delicate sensation.

"Oh! I just felt it."

"You did?" Henri's voice popped with excitement matching her own. "Tell me. What did it feel like?" His eyes were big.

"As though a butterfly made a somersault inside me."

He put one hand on her belly, which was profoundly comforting, like the arrival of some unexpected mercy, a sheltering presence. Charlotte nestled under it and covered it with her own. Her gratitude was immense—like the sea, like the sky, like the unknowability of life itself and its persistent vitality. Now she couldn't help but go dreamy. Behind her eyelids, she painted visions of the future. There was just this, their survival. *We three.* Their reunion with everyone they loved...and then everything new...Paris...as they dared together to claim their shared destiny, dared to begin.

And if not?

She wanted to believe that someone would discover her work. Dr. Mercier would give it to Olive, and then—she couldn't see the pathway, but somehow it would reach a public. She formed images of it: a staged musical attended by audiences, a ballet, a book to be paged through as Dr. Mercier had done, a showing in a museum winding around the walls of gallery after gallery—who was that future woman, so keen to discover her? A story people could walk through and know that she, Charlotte Salomon, had not been a nonbeing. She had lived.

EPILOGUE

AMSTERDAM

2017

Fingering the brand-new, soft-hair sable brush in her pocket, stroking the tip, she waits among the crush of gallery-goers to move along the wall. A grant supports her own art-making, but she doesn't feel like an artist, not having been in her studio for several months. She left Berlin yesterday to make this show in Amsterdam at the Jewish Historical Museum. In honor of the one-hundredth anniversary of the artist's birth, the entire work is on display for the first time.

Her interest veers toward women artists, not the woman behind the great man or the one posing for him, but the great artist who happens to be a woman, buried or half-buried by history, now resurrected from the past. In this case, a woman of twenty-four, twenty-five.

She stands still before the first painting, narrating it to herself.

A female figure moves through city streets just before dawn when lamps still pierce the dark. Her brown dress is drawn in the barest lines. Swinging her arms in flight, the figure enters a park and turns toward a bridge. The bridge is red. She assumes a reclining posture and slips into the water.

The technique strikes her: repeating the figure across and down the page creates a story within one frame. But the feeling, more than the technique—or the feeling that the technique evokes—impacts her even more strongly. The darkness, a woman fleeing her home. So sad. Why would she? What is going on in that home that would make her run out in the night in just a dress, no coat or shawl?

The date is inscribed on the painting: *1913*. The suicide was before the Great War. The artist painted it during the second.

She breathes a sigh of relief that she herself is not living in a time of war. Germany at peace. Europe at peace. But she is not internally at peace. She is here with discomfort, sometimes roiling, always nagging, if only in a nasty whisper, even though the family story is emphatic—her grandfather was not a Nazi.

How does she know if that's true? Not one of her contemporaries claims differently. No one's family has owned up to their role, for instance, in refusing to hide prisoners of war, in refusing to hide Jews. If what everyone says about their family is true, then there were no Nazis in Germany.

The word *guilt* hangs. She tugs at her collar. She doesn't think she should feel this way. The intrusion of this cloying thought is practically a belief. Is she a caricature of the still-guilty German two generations later? She hesitates to accept the word, as if to do so would trap her. Her freedom might take flight.

The Nazis cannot have poisoned the people for all time. She cares about art, becoming an artist, and for that she admires this woman, who is her age in a different time. She thinks that her courage is inspiring. But she doesn't know how to embody that inspiration, and doubts she has courage.

Her attention shifts back to the suicide before her, obviously a seminal event shaping the artist's life. She moves on slowly because the one room is crowded with viewers inching their way along the wall, looking at the row of paintings at eye level and then at the row above, making a right turn when they reach the wall, coming back down the aisle along displays of more paintings set out in rows within waist-high vitrines.

She's not in a hurry. Each painting is complicated and endlessly interesting, accompanied by writing, which is a narration of sorts, including dialogue. It takes time to absorb it all.

In the first section, there are many paintings that have multiple small pictures within one frame, which makes them like miniature storyboards. A wedding, for instance: the dressmaker fitting the bride, the ceremony with the ring, the wedding march—all in one panel. As she goes further, the style becomes bold, both in the primary colors and the brushstrokes, which are economized yet immensely expressive, and there are many portraits of women. There are literally hundreds of paintings of a somewhat older man with dark curly hair and spectacles who influenced her and supported her as an artist. Later, many paintings of her demonic grandfather's ghostly head, disembodied, floating on the page, with white beard and ice-blue eyes.

By the time she reaches the end of the exhibit, she has traversed the entire room, painting by painting. She pauses to let her eyes sweep over the whole. Then she moves into an area dedicated to education.

A tack board lists the characters and the corresponding real people. A biographical display recounts the events of her life. The artist lived in horrific times. The highest rates of suicide in the western world were among upper-middle-class Jewish women in Germany. Never report. Remain silent. Don't give them a reason to decry the Jews. Sexual abuse also shushed, denied, not like today's exposures, like Harvey Weinstein and Kevin Spacey.

A letter is displayed, which had been withheld for decades. In it, the artist confesses to having poisoned her grandfather with veronal, which she claims to have laced into his omelet. The commentary sheds doubt because the letter was found as an addendum to the work. Since the work is considered a fiction, so must be the confession, the scholars assert. No one knows.

Everything must have felt urgent for the artist. She herself does not feel urgent. Though now that she thinks about it, there are plenty of reasons to be. Donald Trump is on a campaign to ruin America and that will rock the world order. This is the year climate change is hitting: heat waves already causing tens of thousands of premature deaths in Europe, hurricanes, high water, flooding, droughts, and infernos of wildfires. Military conflicts started years ago, some decades ago, still raging: Afghanistan, Syria, Iraq civil war, Mexican drug war—death tolls mounting in the five figures.

The Bramble Cay melomys, a small Australian rodent, is likely to be confirmed extinct. The first known mammal to die out because of human-caused climate change.

Birds in Brazil are disappearing as a cause of simply having been discovered.

Only three northern white rhinos left. Elephants going; giraffes, large cats, honeybees.

She wonders: Do we really think we can live all alone on this planet?

On the other hand, Germany, working with NATO and the UN, is training civilians and sending them on peacekeeping missions: Afghanistan, Iraq, Mali, the Mediterranean. She tries to keep herself informed.

THE ARTIST, TWENTY-SIX YEARS OLD and five months pregnant, was murdered in Auschwitz. The husband too. She already knew this, but seeing it in black and white, her heart constricts sharply.

She tells herself that she doesn't need to feel this thickness in the back of her throat. Angela Merkel is upholding liberal democracy now. Yet the German Palestinians who tried to burn down a synagogue on the anniversary of Kristallnacht were found not guilty because they claimed to only want to draw attention to the conflict in Gaza. The court declared it anti-Israelism. Not antisemitism.

She returns to the end of the artist's story. She stops there. She takes a hard look at the final painting. The artist herself sits by the sea, which shines through her transparent body. She asks herself: What does the whole thing mean? Pondering the question seems more to the point than coming up with a single answer.

She is gratified and suddenly feels saturated, tired. Perhaps a rest.

THE CAFÉ IS STILL OPEN. She orders a dark coffee and asks the person behind the counter which pastry she recommends. Boterkoek, very nice with coffee. She takes her tray to one of the sleek white tables by the windows, realizing she's come up from below ground level where the exhibit was, making her think of bunkers and hideouts and bomb shelters.

She's surprised how few people are seated in the café. It's quiet, and she allows herself to feel enveloped by her solitude. The dense butter cake flavored with vanilla is delicious, and eating it is soothing. The coffee is the perfect accompaniment. She realizes her nerves have gotten up, and it was right for her to take this break.

Someone has left a newspaper on the adjacent table. From where she sits, she can read the headline: *Man waving Palestinian flag smashes Amsterdam kosher restaurant window.*

She reaches over to the table and turns the paper over, so the headline is face down. Then she finishes her cake and coffee while pondering the fullness of her experience of the artist's work and the emptiness inside her where her own should be. Intense aesthetic satisfaction and equally intense longing rub up against each other.

She buses her tray, returns to the table for her coat and purse. In the museum's gift shop she lingers, eventually buying two books, a biography of the artist, and a newly published book analyzing the artist's work. Perhaps they will unlock the mystery of who the artist was and how she came to create a magnum opus, a unique masterpiece.

As she readies to leave, she wants to see all seven hundred sixty-nine paintings, the whole show, all over again. Maybe she'll come back tomorrow.

Half reluctant, she steps out into the day. Though overcast, it's bright compared to the inside of the stone building. She crosses the street, thinking how the artist risked her life to save her work.

She pauses and looks back. A huge banner hangs across the front of the building.

She is not yet ready to flag a ride. She stands and stares.

It's acutely painful, incomprehensible, and wonderous that the artist was murdered and yet she is here, alive.

Then it strikes her, the terrible times she herself lives in—the global wars, climate change, rising antisemitism and other forms of far-right extremism. She wonders what would happen if she really let it all in. And why, impossible as that is, does it seem ultimately easier than unearthing the story of her grandfather? She wonders whether there's a reason for the discomfort she will not name but knows. She fingers the new paintbrush in her pocket. She thinks maybe, when she gets back to Berlin, she should find out, push beyond the story she's been told, dissolve the theater. Maybe she should do the one thing she can do something about. She thinks brushstrokes on a blank canvas, expressing curiosity, openness, whatever the truth may be.

Before she turns away to hail a taxi, she takes a last look at the museum's banner, red and blue letters on a white background:

CHARLOTTE SALOMON EXHIBIT –
LIFE? OR THEATER?

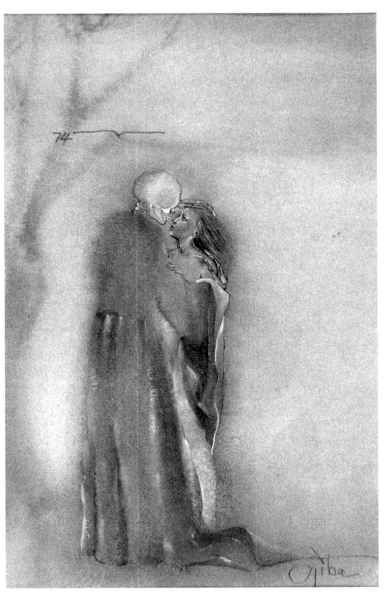

Death and the Maiden

AUTHOR'S NOTE

Charlotte Salomon Nagler and her husband, Alexander Nagler, were captured by the Nazis in late September 1943 and held by Alois Brunner in the commandeered Excelsior Hotel in Nice. They were put on a rail train to Drancy camp outside Paris, and from there they were sent to Auschwitz. In the transport document, Charlotte identified herself as a graphic artist. Upon arrival at Auschwitz on October 13, Charlotte, twenty-six years old and five months pregnant, was murdered in a gas chamber. Alexander was selected for labor. He died in Auschwitz in 1944.

Having survived the war in hiding, Charlotte's father, Albert Salomon, and stepmother, Paula Salomon-Lindberg, went to Villefranche in search of Charlotte and discovered *Life? Or Theater?* Eventually it found a home in the Jewish Historical Museum of Amsterdam. It has been exhibited around the world and made into a theater piece, a ballet, a film, a coffee-table book, and an opera.

THE END

Enjoy more about
*Charlotte Salomon Paints
Her Life: A Novel*
Meet the Author
Check out author appearances
Explore special features

ABOUT THE AUTHOR

PAMELA REITMAN is an award-winning writer with numerous publications in literary journals, news outlets, and magazines. She has a B.A cum laude in English from Columbia and an MPH from the University of California Berkeley. She is retired from a career in public health and community service aimed at reducing the stigma of mental illness. Ms. Reitman was a past Director of Makor Or: A Jewish Meditation Center in San Francisco. She is lay ordained in the Soto Zen Buddhist tradition. She lives in Northern California with her husband.

ACKNOWLEDGMENTS

I am not a Holocaust survivor nor a child of a Holocaust survivor. I am a member of the post-World War II generation, an American Jew of Eastern European descent whose ancestors perished in the Russian pogroms of the early twentieth century. My study of the Holocaust generally, and of Charlotte Salomon in particular, inspired me to write this story.

This novel honors the life that was unjustly taken from the artist. It is intended as a literary creation that aims at truth while maintaining that its story is not the life story of the real Charlotte Salomon, nor does it call into being the real subjectivity of the artist. Her life and experiences are unknowable. The writing has been an act of transformation of facts, materials, and partial understandings, also a projection of my empathy and my subjectivity upon these. The novel is not a historical text in any sense; it is a tribute to the artist and reflects my own musings and intuition, my attempt to create a psychologically believable character that one might imagine having grappled with the loneliness of exile, the legacy of suicides in her family, the force of her grandfather's abuse, and the terror of the Third Reich in order to become an artist and produce a great work. Moreover, this novel does not aspire to translate her work—*Life? Or Theater?*—into a life story. It attempts to imagine the life that produced it. I've sought to rescue the themes of the artist's life, especially the power of artmaking to transform suffering and trauma.

This novel is heavily dependent on the work of others. I would like to express my deep gratitude here to a number of those historians and scholars who made it the labor of their lives to produce works that introduced me to this subject and from which I learned so much. I've done my best to digest, integrate, interpret, and apply my own thought to the researched material to make my work my own. Any violation of fair use of others' material is entirely inadvertent. All factual errors and all changes needed to turn fact into fiction are my sole responsibility. Despite the many omissions and inventions, I hope that my rendering has rung true.

I first heard of Charlotte Salomon during a presentation of her life and work by her excellent biographer Mary Lowenthal Felstiner at an event commemorating The Shoah held at the Jewish Community Center of San Francisco in 2000. I bought and read Felstiner's *To Paint Her Life: Charlotte Salomon in the Nazi Era* not knowing how important this book would become to me as a resource for understanding Charlotte's life.

I am indebted to the artist's own work, which was first published in its entirety in *Charlotte: Life or Theater?: An Autobiographical Play by Charlotte Salomon* (Viking Press, 1981). My thanks to all those involved in the production: editor Gary Schwartz; translator Leila Vennewitz; author of the preface, Judith C.E. Belinfante; and author of the introduction, Judith Herzberg. The novel takes numerous cues from Salomon's work in this volume. The paintings suggested many scenes in the novel, incidences, turns in the story line, characterizations, conflicts, dialogues, conversations, moods, and tones. Many pronouncements made by Wolf Abrams in my novel are derived from *Life? Or Theater?*, spoken by Salomon's fictional character Amadeus Daberlohn. The real-life voice teacher was Alfred Wolfsohn. I drew on Sheila Braggins' *The Mystery Behind the Voice: A Biography of Alfred Wolfsohn* for an understanding of his life, theories, and relationship with Charlotte Salomon.

For a picture of Europe overall and Germany in particular, I owe a great deal of my understanding to Ian Kershaw's *To Hell and Back: Europe 1914–1949*; William L. Shirer's *The Rise and Fall of the Third Reich* and his *Berlin Diary: The Journal of a Foreign Correspondent 1934–1941*; Victor Klemperer's *I Will Bear Witness: A Diary of the Nazi Years, 1933–1941*; Raul Hilberg's *The Destruction of the European Jews*; Marion A. Kaplan's *The Making of the Jewish Middle Class: Women, Family, and Identity in Imperial Germany*; and *The Holocaust Chronicle*, edited by David J. Hogan.

Scenes of Kristallnacht found their source in *The Night of Broken Glass: Eyewitness Accounts of Kristallnacht*, edited by Uta Gerhardt and Thomas Karlauf and translated by Robert Simmons and Nick Somers, and in Martin Gilbert's *Kristallnacht: Prelude to Destruction*.

For passages that take place in Munich's *Degenerate Art* exhibit, I relied on *"Degenerate Art": The Fate of the Avant-Garde in Nazi Germany* by Stephanie Barron and *Hitler's Degenerate Art: The Exhibition Catalog* (series editor Joachim von Halasz). I also consulted *Degenerate "Art": Exhibition Guide*, translated by William C. Bunce. Together these sources provided a wealth of information on the layout of the rooms, what was on exhibit, how the works and slogans were hung, and the experience of exhibit attendees. For background on German art, I turned to *The Visual Arts in Germany 1890–1937: Utopia and Despair* by Shearer West.

To understand the Vichy regime, I studied Michael R. Marrus's and Robert O Paxton's *Vichy France and the Jews*; Renée Poznanski's *Jews in France during World War II*; Vicki Caron's *Uneasy Asylum: France and the Jewish Refugee Crisis, 1933–1942*; Richard I. Cohen's *The Burden of Conscience:*

French Jewish Leadership during the Holocaust; Michael Curtis's *Verdict on Vichy: Power and Prejudice in the Vichy France Regime;* Shannon L. Fogg's *The Politics of Everyday Life in Vichy France: Foreigners, Undesirables, Strangers;* Varian Fry's *Surrender on Demand;* and Susan Zuccotti's *The Holocaust, the French, and the Jews,* as well as her *The Italians and the Holocaust: Persecution, Rescue, and Survival.*

Werner L. Frank's *The Curse of Gurs: Way Station to Auschwitz* and *Art of the Holocaust,* edited by Janet Blatter and Sybil Milton, shed light on camp conditions and the making of art in Gurs. *Spiritual Resistance: Art from Concentration Camps 1940—1945, A selection of paintings from the collection of Kibbutz Lohamei Haghetaot, Israel* by Union of American Hebrew Congregations provided visual sources. I came first to know of Lou Albert-Lasard and Lili Rilik-Andrieux in Monica Bohm-Duchen's essay "A Life before Auschwitz" in *Reading Charlotte Salomon,* edited by Bohm-Duchen and Michael Steinberg. That essay led me to the actual images (including Rilik-Andrieux's "Three Women Toasting Bread") in the Israeli publication *Images and Reflections: Women in the Art of the Holocaust, Works of Art from the Art Collection of the Ghetto Fighters' House Museum.*

Helpful to me in understanding what life was like in the South of France included Robert Kanigel's *High Season: How One French Riviera Town Has Seduced Travelers for Two Thousand Years,* as was Tobias Smollett's charming *Travels through France and Italy* and the contemporary memoir, *A Year in Provence* by Peter Mayle. For life on the Côte d'Azur in the 1940's, I read *The Inside Story of an Outsider,* published in 1949 by Franz Schoenberner, exiled editor of the satirical German weekly *Simplicissimus.* Finally, more recently published, *The Riviera at War: World War II on the Côte D'Azur* by George G. Kundahl provided many particularities.

To learn something of the making of watercolor and gouache paintings in the time of the novel, the closest I managed to get was Arnold Blanch's 1946 *Methods and Techniques for Gouache Painting*. I also drew from *Wash and Gouache: A Study of the Materials of Watercolor* by Marjorie B. Cohn, which was the catalog for an exhibit by Rachel Rosenfield at the Fogg Museum. Mostly I learned from Stephen Quiller's *WaterMedia Painting: The Complete Guide to Working with Watercolor, Acrylic, Gouache, and Casein*. Many paintings the protagonist creates in the novel can be found in *Life? Or Theater?*

Darcy C. Buerkle's fascinating book, *Nothing Happened: Charlotte Salomon and an Archive of Suicide*, was influential in how I came to shape the conflict between Charlotte and her grandfather. Buerkle sets Salomon's work in the context of early twentieth-century Germany while making a carefully documented case for the erasure of female suicide as integral to that country's social history and providing insight into Charlotte's refusal to submit, in the end, to her grandfather. I am grateful to Ms. Buerkle for gifting me a copy of her book when I could not obtain it through the normally extensive reach of the San Francisco Public Library system, and for our email exchanges.

I am grateful to the Internet. I can't possibly enumerate all the websites that aided in my retrieval of information necessary to the novel. A few important ones are Yadvashem. org, Jewishvirtuallibrary.org, Ushmm.org (United States Holocaust Memorial Museum), Yivoencyclopedia.org (The YIVO Encyclopedia of Jews in Eastern Europe)-YIVO Institute for Jewish Research, and Jewish Review.org.

I was fortunate to travel to Amsterdam for the centennial celebration of Salomon's birth, commemorated in 2017–2018 by the Jewish Historical Museum with the first-ever exhibit of *Life? Or Theater?* in its entirety. This trip inspired the epilogue of my novel. There I discovered Griselda Pollock's definitive study of Salomon's work, *Charlotte Salomon and the Theater of Memory*. Back home, as I surveyed every one of Charlotte's paintings once again, this time in the (then) newly released *Charlotte Salomon Life? Or Theater?* (Overlook Duckworth, 2017), Pollock's book was a trusty companion, adding immeasurably to my understanding of the art-historical significance of Salomon's project and Salomon's place in the history of art. That study also became critical in my decision to portray the grandfather as an abuser. Here, too, in the Duckworth edition, for the first time, was an English translation of the complete postscript letter of Salomon's confession, which explores the full depth of the artist's despair.

While entirely fictional, many characters in this novel were inspired by real persons, and many of the incidences did happen in real life in some form. I have changed almost all the names for two reasons: 1) to keep in the mind of the reader that this is a work of fiction; and 2) in a nod to the artist, who changed the names of the characters in her own work.

There is no evidence that Salomon attended the *Degenerate Art* exhibit in Munich, though she may very well have attended it when it came to Berlin. I wanted to show Charlotte willing to take risks, confronting Fascism without the mediation of her parents, and seeing her place as a Jew and an artist under the Third Reich. Salomon is not known for having experimented with the development of iridescence in paint.

My reading of *Life? Or Theater?*, Buerkle, and Pollock together led me to point to sexual abuse as the cause of many of the female suicides in Charlotte's matrilineal line. I chose to dramatize this through Eugenia Mahlick, a fictional character who plays a pivotal role offstage of the novel by putting the grandfather's past behavior on grounds that are more verifiable (and therefore more convincing) than the grandmother's ravings alone.

Angelo Donati did enact a grand plan to rescue the Jews from the South of France that was terminated by the Armistice, but there is no evidence that Charlotte's family was included in his escape plan.

Raymond-Raoul Lambert was a leader in the Jewish community and editor of *L'Univers israélite,* but there's no evidence that he and Charlotte ever met.

My hopes are that this novel has brought to life a remarkable woman and artist who deserves more attention, and that the reader will want to examine her work, which—in its totality of image, narrative, dialogue, and musical prompt—is accessible not only in the Overlook Duckworth edition but also on the website of the Jewish Historical Museum of Amsterdam. The reader will be happy to know that among its many representations in the world, *Life? Or Theater?* has been exhibited in at least 12 countries, performed as a theater piece and a ballet, and made into an opera.

I give thanks to important teachers/shepherds/angels who helped me along the path, some in big ways, others in short but emboldening conversations, a few with a kind word dropped my way: Pat Schneider, Sherril Jaffe, Jacqueline Shelton, Katherine Neville, Sarah Smith, Nancy Binns, Susanna Porter,

Roger Grunwald, Rita Goldberg, Elizabeth Rosner, Louis Bayard, and J.J. Wilson and Karen Fitzgerald of The Sitting Room. Special thanks to Barbara Lesch McCaffry.

I'm grateful to people at the Jewish Historical Museum of Amsterdam: Bernadette van Woerkom for welcoming me to the commemorative exhibition of *Life? Or Theater?* and Anton Kras who has kindly assisted in my use of Charlotte's paintings. Thanks to the Charlotte Salomon Foundation for granting rights.

Also, gratitude extended to the folks at Indigo: owner Ali Shaw, and Kristen Hall-Geisler, who edited my manuscript at an early stage. And to Karen Bjorneby, who oversaw my early work of revision.

Unfortunately, I was stricken with breast cancer in 2020 and but for Breast Cancer Over Time, led by the inimitable Polly Marshall, I would not have had the courage to go on with my work or have a place to talk about survivorship with the wonderful women I met there. I am also grateful to Amherst Writers & Artists for helping me start writing again when I was stuck.

I could have not done this without the support of other writers: my first writing group including Mary Hower, Giana Miniace, and Laurie Barkin. Also, thanks to Birgitta Hjalmarson, Jane Anne Staw, Joan Gelfand, Valerie Ohanian, Robin Gabbard of Redwood Writers, and my Yale Summer Writing Program friends, Parul Kapur and Heather Adams—we emailed each other at least once a week for the last ten years.

For spiritual support, my gratitude extends to my dearest of dear teachers Norman Fischer and the whole of Everyday Zen. I'd like to make special mention of the Everyday Zen San Francisco Dharma Friends group, with whom I study

and share deeply from the heart, led by Andrea Jacoby: Allen
Frazier, Anthony Bernheim, Sara Tung, Jane Swigart, Laura
Meltsner, Nancy Sheldon, and Michael Gelfond. Thanks to
Heart of Compassion Zen Sangha led by Jaune Evans, to
Steve Costa, Nora Burnett, longtime friend and now sangha
sister, and especially to all my *jukai* sisters and dear study
partners, Dahlia Kamesar and Mary Christy-Cirillo.

Thanks to my Barnard Book Club (Peninsula Chapter) for
years spent reading together, led by Preeva Tramiel.

Many friends have jumped in with a good word and loving
support: Annie McGeady, Jennifer Kaufman, Katie Mazda,
Sue Saperstein, Irene Borger, and Pam Laird.

I must separately thank my oldest and dearest friends who
have truly understood my mission from the beginning and
patiently supported me during the many stretches of time
when I was not available: Delia Dempsey, Ellen Ingraham,
Ellen Shireman, and Joan Sprinson.

Helen McKenna, Erin Sheehan, Dierdre O'Bryan, and Jessica
Boyer have shored up the more fragile parts of me during this
long journey.

Full-hearted thanks to the Golob-Paluch Family (Larry, Jen,
Benjamin, and Naomi) for taking care of me and my husband
all through the Covid epidemic and beyond. David Malman
and Ellen Shireman vacated their house in San Francisco for
our exclusive use during our recent transition out of San
Francisco. Nancy Rabkin and Rob Gorlin, our good neighbors, also opened their house to us for frequent forays back
to the city.

I can never thank Sibylline Press enough for choosing my
manuscript and for the unimagined support I received from

everyone there all the way along the line. Special thanks to those who guided me in this truly collaborative effort: the publisher Vicki DeArmon, the editor Julia Park Tracey, Suzy Vitello, Alicia Feltman for the striking cover design, Anna Termine, and Sang Kim for finally making me learn how to use a spreadsheet and keeping everything on track. I appreciated the support of the other Spring 2025 Sibylline authors: Jennifer Safrey, Diane Schaffer, and Kate Woodworth. It was a remarkable experience to have a supportive cohort of fabulous women.

Family members have rallied round. Special thanks to my sister-in-law JoAnn Forman, an early and enthusiastic reader. Her belief in this project and unflagging support has meant so much to me. Thanks, too, to my brother Barry Forman, who sadly passed before he could see my novel come to light. I'm also grateful to my nieces and nephews, Ben and Brittany Forman and Rosalie and Noah Samuels. And to Rosalyn Menashe, Elise Menashe and Jay Miller, Marlinda Menashe, Lisa Kotzen, and the Carlsons (Carla, Steve, and Will).

Loving thanks to my son, Jonah, my most ardent supporter. Most important of all, gratitude and love forever to my dear husband and life companion, Moe, who gave me the precious and unparalleled gift of time to withdraw from the world and without whom this book could never have come into being.

BOOK CLUB QUESTIONS

1. Did Charlotte's father and stepmother do the right thing by sending her into exile? Why do you think her parents didn't go with her? How would her life have been different if she had stayed in Berlin? What would cause you to flee your country?

2. Hitler's actions against the Jews were unthinkable. How would you react to something unthinkable happening today against the Jews or any other marginalized group in your country? What should American Jews do today to protect themselves from the unthinkable recurring here? What should Jews do in countries in which antisemitism is on the rise?

3. When Marina shows Charlotte the letter from her friend Gertrude Mahlick, she tells her that "something happened" in their own family. Why did Marina not reveal the family secret? Why did she leave it to Luitger? Contrast "something happened" with Charlotte's words, "nothing happened," a phrase she uses later as she recalls Marina's suicide. How do these vague phrases reflect a culture of erasure when it comes to suicide?

4. Charlotte spent several weeks in Gurs camp in the Pyrenées where circumstances were brutal; people were starved and stripped of their identity. Despite that, how was Gurs a positive experience for Charlotte?

5. Charlotte and Luitger strongly disagreed about her purpose in life. Was their conflict resolvable? Do you think she did the right thing by abandoning him for a room at La Belle Aurore? If so, why? If not, why?

6. The central theme of this novel is the power of art to transform trauma. What is (are) the trauma(s), both external and internal, with which Charlotte wrestles in her artmaking? What is your own experience, or those of people you know, with art and trauma?

7. Charlotte's paintings are largely of people, among them: her mother and father, grandmother and grandfather, ancestors who committed suicide, and Wolf Abrams. What is the connection between her focus on these individuals and the novel's title?

8. There are many non-Jews, righteous gentiles, such as Olive Miller, Dr. Mercier, the Pichés, and even the gendarme on the deportation bus. How do each affect the story and Charlotte's destiny?

9. Charlotte took many risks, for instance, leaving Luitger to live without identity papers and in violation of her Condition of Release from Gurs, going to Nice to register with the census, later getting married, and finally taking her work to Dr. Mercier. What do you think about each of those decisions? Was she foolish or courageous?

10. Charlotte blames herself for Luitger's death. Do you blame her? Why or why not?

11. How did the Epilogue influence your experience of this book?

Sibylline Press is proud to publish the brilliant work of women authors over 50. We are a woman-owned publishing company and, like our authors, represent women of a certain age.

Mortal Zin: A Mortal Zin Mystery
BY DIANE SCHAFFER

MYSTERY
Trade Paper, 412 pages (5.315 x 8.465) | $22
ISBN: 9781960573933
Also available as an ebook and audiobook

A crusading attorney's death. Sabotage at a family winery...As threats mount and the winery teeters on the brink of ruin, Noli and Luz must navigate a treacherous landscape of greed, revenge, and long-buried secrets. Can two fearless women from different worlds unravel the truth before it's too late?

After Happily Ever: An Epic Novel of Midlife Rebellion
BY JENNIFER SAFREY

FICTION, FANTASY
Trade Paper, 388 pages (5.315 x 8.465) | $22
ISBN: 9781960573179
Also available as an ebook and audiobook

Princesses Neve, Della, and Bry are sisters-in-law, having married into the royal Charming family, and for the last thirty-plus years, they've been living a coveted happily-ever-after life in the idyllic kingdom of Foreverness. As they each turn 50 however, they begin to question the kingdom's "perfection." Can each of the women create a new happily-ever-after and will the kingdom of Foreverness survive it?

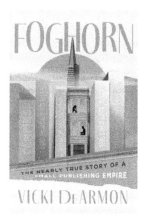

Foghorn: The Nearly True Story of a Small Publishing Empire
BY VICKI DEARMON

MEMOIR
Trade Paper, 320 pages (5.315 x 8.465) | $20
ISBN: 9781960573926
Also available as an ebook and audiobook

The heyday of small press publishing in the San Francisco Bay Area in the 1980s and 1990s lives again in this never-before-told story of how small presses—armed with arrogance and personal computers—took the publishing field. Vicki Morgan was an ambitious young woman publisher, coming-of-age while quixotically building Foghorn Press from scratch with her eccentric brother to help.

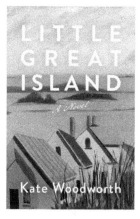

Little Great Island: A Novel
BY KATE WOODWORTH

FICTION
Trade Paper, 356 pages (5.315 x 8.465) | $21
ISBN: 9781960573902
Also available as an ebook and audiobook

When Mari McGavin flees with her son back to the tiny Maine island where she grew up—she runs into her lifelong friend Harry, one of the island's summer residents, setting off a chain of events as unexpected and life altering as the shifts in climate affecting the whole ecosystem of the island…from generations of fishing families to the lobsters and the butterflies.

For more books from **Sibylline Press**, please visit our website at sibyllinepress.com